Peter May was born and raised in Scotland. He was an award-winning journalist at the age of twenty-one and a published novelist at twenty-six. When his first book was adapted as a major drama series for the BBC, he quit journalism and, during the high-octane fifteen years that followed, became one of Scotland's most successful television dramatists. He created three prime-time drama series, presided over two of the highest-rated serials in his homeland as script editor and producer, and worked on more than 1,000 episodes of ratings-topping drama before deciding to leave television to return to his first love, writing novels.

He has won several literature awards in France, received the USA's Barry Award for *The Blackhouse* – the first in his internationally bestselling Lewis Trilogy; and in 2014 *Entry Island* was awarded the ITV Specsavers Crime Thriller Book Club Best Read of the Year, as well as the Deanston Scottish Crime Book of the Year. May now lives in south-west France with his wife, writer Janice Hally.

Praise for Peter May

'He is a terrific writer doing something different'
Mark Billingham

'From the first page I knew I was in safe hands.
I knew I could trust this writer'
Sophie Hannah

'Wonderfully compelling' Kate Mosse

'A true pleasure to read' *Guardian*

'Lyrical, empathetic and moving' Alex Gray

'Peter May is a writer I'd follow to the ends of the earth'
New York Times

Also by Peter May

FICTION

The Lewis Trilogy

The Blackhouse
The Lewis Man
The Chessmen

The China Thrillers

The Firemaker
The Fourth Sacrifice
The Killing Room
Snakehead
The Runner
Chinese Whispers
The Ghost Marriage: A China Novella

The Enzo Files

Extraordinary People
The Critic
Blacklight Blue
Freeze Frame
Blowback
Cast Iron

Stand-alone Novels

Entry Island
Runaway
Coffin Road

NON-FICTION

Hebrides (with David Wilson)

PETER MAY
I'LL KEEP YOU SAFE

riverrun

First published in Great Britain in 2018 by riverrun
This paperback edition published in 2018 by

riverrun

an imprint of

Quercus Editions Ltd
Carmelite House
50 Victoria Embankment
London EC4Y 0DZ

An Hachette UK company

ISBN 978 1 78429 497 7
EBOOK ISBN 978 1 78429 495 3

10 9 8 7 6 5 4 3 2 1

Typeset by CC Book Production

Printed and bound in Great Britain by Clays Ltd, Elcograf S.p.A.

For Danielle Dastugue

Harris Tweed is the only cloth in the world to be defined by an Act of Parliament and is described in the 1993 Act as follows: *'Handwoven by the islanders at their homes in the Outer Hebrides, finished in the Outer Hebrides, and made from pure virgin wool dyed and spun in the Outer Hebrides.'*

PRONUNCIATIONS

('ch' as in 'loch')

GAELIC

Amhuinnsuidhe	Av-an-sooey
Anndra	Aoundra
Bilascleiter	Bill-is-clay-churr
Bodach	Bottach
Bothag	Baw-hag
Breasclete	Bree-as-clitch
Cianalas	Key-an-alas
Cuishader	Coo-e-shaadur
Eachan	Yachan
Linshader	Leen-u-shaadur
Niamh	Neave
Ranish	Rannish
Róisín	Rosheen
Ruairidh	Roo-are-ee
Seonag	Shonnak

| Taigh 'an Fiosaich | Tie-an-fisseech |
| Uilleam | William |

FRENCH

Braque	Brack
Faubert	Foe-berr
Gilles	Zheel

PROLOGUE

All she can hear is the ringing in her ears. A high-pitched tinnitus drowning out all other sounds. The chaos around her has no real form. Flaming fragments from the blast still falling from the night sky, bodies lying on the concrete. The shadows of figures fleeing the flames extend towards her across the square, flickering like monochrome images on a screen.

She can make out the skeleton of the car beyond the blaze, imagining that she sees the silhouettes of the driver and passenger still strapped in their seats. But how could anyone have survived such an explosion intact?

Bizarrely, traffic continues to move along the Boulevard de Magenta, but slowly, like a river of coagulating blood. Neon lights still glow in the dark, the final moments of normality frozen in time. But the hope that she might save her marriage is gone. Because she knows, with a deep, hollowing sadness, and beyond any shadow of a doubt, that he is dead.

CHAPTER ONE

The last hours of their life together replayed themselves through a thick fog of painful recollection. Did people really change, or was it just your perception of them? And if that was true, had you ever really known them in the first place?

The change in a relationship happens slowly, without you really noticing at first. Like the transition between spring and summer, or summer and autumn. And suddenly it's winter, and you wonder how that dead time managed to creep up on you so quickly.

It wasn't winter yet. Relations between them hadn't got quite that cold. But there was a chill in the air which seemed to presage the plunge of Arctic air to come, and as they moved with the flow of the crowds leaving the Parc des Expositions, Niamh shivered, even though the air of this September evening was still soft and warm. Only the fading light betrayed the changing season.

It was standing room only on the RER, and the train rattled and clattered its way through the north-eastern *banlieues* of Paris. Villepinte, Sevran Beaudottes, Aulnay-sous-Bois, where

PETER MAY

no one got on or off. She was uncomfortable, bodies pressing in all around her, male and female. The smell of garlic on sour breath, of sweat on man-made fabric, faded perfume, hair gel. Her knuckles glowed white, fingers clutching the chrome upright to keep her from falling as the train decelerated and accelerated, in and out of stations, and she tried to hold her breath.

Ruairidh was sandwiched between a tall man with an orange face who painted his eyebrows and wore lipstick, and a girl with tattoos engraved on every visible area of skin. Her dyed black hair and facial piercings seemed dated. Goth. Retro. Niamh saw Ruairidh force a hand into his pocket to retrieve his iPhone. The glow of its screen reflected briefly in his face and drew a frown that gathered between his eyes. He stared at it for a very long time before glancing, suddenly self-conscious, towards Niamh and thrusting the phone back in his pocket.

There was an exodus of passengers at the Gare du Nord, but a fresh influx of bodies from a crowded platform, and it was not until they got off at Châtelet les Halles that she was able to ask him about it. 'Bad news?'

He glanced at her as they climbed the steps to the street, and the same frown regrouped around the bridge of his nose. 'Bad news?'

'Your email. Or was it a text?'

'Oh. That. No. Nothing.' He shrugged an uncomfortable indifference. 'Shall we get a taxi?'

*

3

The Whisky Shop Paris threw light out across the Place de la Madeleine, casting shadows among the trees in the gathering gloom. Inside it seemed unnaturally bright, hanging globes reflecting light from white walls, whisky bottles glowing amber on lines of glass shelves. The sweet smell of it permeated the air like perfume. A girl took their coats at the foot of the stairs, and they climbed to the reception room on the first floor.

Harris Tweed Hebrides had imported two young island lads to provide the Celtic entertainment, and they stood in a corner, accordion and violin infusing the atmosphere, like the whisky, with a sense of home. Incongruous here in the heart of the French capital.

Ruairidh accepted his whisky cocktail, but Niamh was not in the mood for alcohol and they stood self-consciously amidst the buyers and designers and agents, feeling oddly alien. Their hosts, after all, were really the competition, though they clearly didn't see themselves as such, and were happy to share a stand with Ranish Tweed at Première Vision. They were all Scots, weren't they? Islanders. Selling the Hebrides as much as their cloth.

Different markets anyway.

Ruairidh was examining his phone again. 'I'm going to have to go to the offices of YSL after we get back to the hotel.'

'Why?' Niamh felt a cold mist close around her heart.

'Forgot to initial the contracts,' he said. 'Head office won't process them until we do. And there's no time tomorrow.

4

We've got an early flight.' As if she didn't know. In any case, she didn't believe a word of it. Ruairidh had lunched with the buyer from Yves Saint Laurent earlier that day, or so he said, while she manned the stand. It was an important order. One of several they had secured at this year's Paris textile fair. Forgot to initial the contracts? She decided to test him.

'Want me to come with you?'

'No.' His response came just a little too fast. He tried to take the curse off it. 'Won't take long. I'll be back in no time.'

They were on the stairs to go, having stayed for what they deemed a respectable period of time, when the PR man called them back. 'You can't go yet, folks,' he said. 'We're just about to draw the raffle.' They had been given tickets when they arrived. The winning number, drawn from a hat, would secure Ian Lawson's extraordinary photo book, *From the Land Comes the Cloth*, a visual evocation of how the colours and patterns of Harris Tweed have drawn their inspiration from the landscape since the time islanders first began weaving it. A huge and weighty tome, it sold in special editions for around two hundred euros. Harris Tweed Hebrides were clearly keen that it should end up in the hands of a favoured customer, but politeness had demanded that all their guests be included.

And so smiles were fixed when it was Ruairidh's number that was drawn from the hat. Niamh masked her embarrassment by suggesting they forgo their good fortune and offer the book back for another draw. But no one would hear of it, and now they sat either side of it in the taxi, where it had morphed into a physical manifestation of the barrier that seemed to have materialized between them. Ruairidh said, 'I'm glad they wouldn't take it back. I've always wanted that book.' He could have bought it a hundred times over, but somehow had never got around to it. In the end it was luck that had delivered it into his hands. The same luck that would desert him in less than an hour.

When their taxi dropped them outside the Crowne Plaza in the Place de la République, darkness had fallen, and the nightly gathering of police trucks and vans was already lining itself up along the pavement. Armed officers in flak jackets stood around in groups cradling automatic weapons and drawing on cigarettes. You could smell the smoke in the cool of the night, and sense the conflicting emotions of boredom and fear that stalked them, like the ghosts of both the terrorists and their victims whose blood had stained the streets all around this *quartier*. You just never knew when something might happen. The reality, these days, of life in the City of Light.

They took the lift to the second floor in silence. Niamh stole a glance at her man, but he was somewhere else. Somewhere, it seemed, that she was no longer welcome. He appeared older, suddenly, than his forty-two years. Short dark curls greying around the temples, shadows beneath blue eyes that had spent much of their time avoiding hers these last weeks. And she ached with a sense of loss. What had happened to them? A lifetime of love, ten years of marriage, evaporating before her eyes like rain on hot tarmac. It didn't seem possible. Any of it. And it made her all the more determined to guard the secret she had been keeping from him.

As he held the door of their club room open for her she saw the slim package in its brown paper wrapping lying on the dressing table where she had left it. She hurried across the room and slipped it into her bag before he could see it and ask what it was. 'I'm going to take a shower,' he said, and he threw his jacket on the bed and went straight into the bathroom.

She heard the water running, and it only emphasized the silence in the room and her sense of loneliness. So she turned on the TV, just to create the illusion of life. Of normality. And walked to the window to gaze down into the courtyard below. Guests sat around tables beneath large, square parasols, eating and drinking, their chatter animated, laughter reaching her on the gentle night air, as if in rebuke for her unhappiness.

She didn't turn when Ruairidh came out, wrapped in a towelling robe, and she heard him rummaging in his case for a clean top and underwear. Then he was in the bathroom again, and she heard the spray of his deodorant and the slap of palms on cheeks applying aftershave. This time, when he emerged, she smelled him. When finally she turned, he was pulling on a black polo shirt and running his fingers back through still damp hair. 'Making yourself beautiful for your girlfriend?' She couldn't help herself.

He stopped, with his hands still raised. The frown again. 'What are you talking about?'

'Irina.'

'What?' His incredulity was almost convincing.

'Oh, come on, Ruairidh. Irina Vetrov. You've been having an affair with her ever since you came to Paris last spring to seal that deal to provide Ranish for her next collection.'

He almost laughed. But there was something not wholly convincing about it. 'Irina Vetrov? You think I'm having an affair with her?'

Niamh knew that people often repeated an accusation to play for time, to compose a response. But she didn't want to hear it. Instead, she walked briskly across the room to the wardrobe, throwing open the door and crouching to unlock the safe. She really hadn't meant to confront him, but somehow there was no avoiding it any longer. She took out her iPad and flicked open the cover. A four-digit code brought up the welcome screen, and a couple of swipes opened her mailer. She stabbed a finger at the screen and held it out towards him.

He took a step towards her, consternation now in his eyes, and took the iPad, glancing down at the screen. She knew what he was reading. Words engraved in her memory. Read, and reread, and read again. *Your husband is having an affair with Irina Vetrov. Ask him about it.* She watched closely for his reaction. He looked up. His frown had become a scowl.

'Jesus Christ, what the hell's this?'

'Self-explanatory, I think.' Her certainty already wavering.

He lowered his eyes to the screen again, and read,

'a.well.wisher.xx@gmail.com?' Then raised them to meet hers. 'Who the fuck is that?'

'You tell me.' Which immediately struck her as a stupid thing to say, since he clearly didn't know. He threw her iPad dismissively on to the bed.

'It's crap, Niamh. Just not true. I can't believe you think it is.'

'Well, what am I supposed to think? You've been so secretive recently. Meetings and rendezvous without me. The little wife left to keep shop.'

'Oh, for God's sake!'

'Do you deny it?' She could hear herself getting shrill.

'That I'm having an affair with Irina?'

'Yes!'

'I think I just did.'

'So why would someone write and tell me you were?'

'I think you'd have to ask them that, but I haven't got the first idea.' He seemed genuinely hurt. A glance at his watch and he said, 'I have to go.'

'Where?' She turned, catching his arm as he walked past her. He pulled it free.

'I told you.'

'YSL?'

'Yes.'

'I don't believe you.'

He stared at her long and hard. 'They say that when trust is gone, love is dead. Don't wait up.'

He slammed the door behind him and she stood, a cauldron

of mixed emotions bubbling inside her. Now she felt guilty. As if it were her fault. As if the lack of trust she had just so clearly demonstrated was without cause. But it *was* justified, wasn't it? The way things had changed between them recently. His strange, guilty behaviour.

The email.

She perched on the edge of the bed resisting the urge to weep. She wouldn't give him that satisfaction. Then realized he would never know if she did. But *she* would. And she was determined not to.

To her left the screen of her iPad, still lying on the bed, had dimmed a little, but the words of the email remained clear and legible. *Your husband is having an affair with Irina Vetrov. Ask him about it.* Well, she just had, and all it had brought was pain and confusion. *Don't wait up*, he had said. But how could he even imagine she could go to bed with everything that had just happened between them left unresolved?

She sat for what felt like hours, but was probably only minutes, before she got up and wandered to the window. People were still eating and drinking and laughing down there. How she wished she were one of them. That things could just be back to how they were before. They had been through so much together, she and Ruairidh, and always come out the other side of it stronger. Or so she had thought.

She stiffened and felt the skin stinging across her scalp. Ruairidh had just emerged from the bar into the courtyard below, a glass of beer in his hand. He sat at an empty table and placed his beer on it, untouched. She watched as he leaned forward, elbows on his knees, before dropping his head briefly into his hands. When he raised it again, he sat back folding his arms and stretched his legs out, gazing at the fizzing amber liquid in his glass. But he made no attempt to drink it.

Niamh watched for a long time, aching inside. So many moments of magic, and madness, between them. So many memories. She was tempted to go down and join him. To say sorry for doubting him. To ask him what it was that had gone wrong and how they could put it right.

And then Irina stepped from the bar. Niamh saw her look around before spotting Ruairidh and walking towards him. She was shorter than Niamh, willow-thin, with long chestnut hair cut in a straight fringe that hung in a curtain over her eyes. Almond eyes, almost slanted. So dark they seemed to soak up all the light. Everything about her was feminine. The way she walked, the way she held her hands, so elegant with their long, slim fingers. The seductive, slightly hoarse quality of her voice. Niamh had only met her once, but she had made Niamh feel big and clumsy, which by any normal standards she was not. Tall, yes. Nearly five-eight, but certainly not overweight. Her long, slender legs had been the envy of all her friends at the Nicolson. And her thick-cut, shoulder-length wavy blonde hair gave her the air of a thirty-year-old, rather than the forty she had just turned this year. Still, she had felt oversized next to the petite Irina, and watched her now with a growing jealousy.

Ruairidh stood up when he saw her coming and kissed her

on both cheeks. They exchanged a few earnest words and Niamh wished she could lip-read. Then they turned and walked out together into the bar, leaving his beer undrunk.

Niamh felt a sense of hopelessness wash over her. And then desperation. If she let him go now, let him walk out of the hotel with Irina Vetrov, she feared she would be letting him walk out of her life. For ever.

An impulse led her to snatch her Ranish Tweed jacket from the back of a chair, and her bag, and almost run across the room to the door. She was still pulling on the jacket as she hurried down the hall, turning right past tall arched windows that looked down on to the courtyard. She pressed the call button for the lift several times and was considering running down the stairs when suddenly it arrived. By the time she got to the lobby, Ruairidh and Irina had left the hotel. Through glass doors that gave on to the square, Niamh saw them getting into Irina's car, a white A-Class Mercedes, its hazard lights flashing.

Niamh sprinted through the lobby, pausing breathlessly to let two sets of sliding doors open, before running out on to the pavement, assailed by a thousand city smells and sounds carried on cooling night breezes. The Mercedes was already accelerating away, past the lines of police vehicles, towards the traffic lights at the far end of the Place.

A classical-looking building on the block beyond the Crowne Plaza was clad in scaffolding, and simmered darkly behind mesh screening. Workmen's trucks and a couple of skips lined up along the pavement in front of it, abandoned for the night.

Niamh ran out into the middle of the street, past a classic revolving Morris column, with its domed top, advertising a rerun of *Le Fusible* at the Théâtre des Bouffes Parisiens. Several armed police officers turned to look at her, suddenly alert. But she didn't even see them. The brake lights of the Mercedes glowed red as it stopped at the lights beyond the workmen's trucks, and the left indicator began to flash. Niamh glanced across the square, beyond the thirty-foot statue of Marianne picked out by symbolic red, white and blue spots, and thought that if she ran a diagonal across the slabs, she could reach the far end of the square in time to cut the car off before it was gone for good. If only the lights would stay red long enough.

She ran past the graffiti-covered red containers that lined the nearside of the pavement, sprinting beyond Marianne and the steps that led down to the Métro République. Off to her left she was only vaguely aware of the diners who sat out at green metal tables at the Café Fluctuat Nec Mergitur. Destroyed by fire early in 2015, it had been reopened, and renamed with the motto of Paris following the terrorist attacks later that same year. *Tossed by the waves but never sunk.* It was about to be tossed once more.

Niamh saw the lights change to green and the Mercedes start to turn left across the flow of traffic. And then she was blinded. A searing, burning light that obliterated all else, just a fraction of a second before the shockwave from the blast knocked her off her feet. As she hit the ground, sight returned. She saw glass flying from the broken windows of the Fluctuat Nec Mergitur, tables and chairs spinning away across the square. As she rolled over, the Mercedes was still in the air. Later she would remember it as being ten feet or more off the ground. But in fact it was probably no more than eighteen or twenty inches. Flaming debris showered down across the Place de la République as the car slammed back on to the road, a ball of flame.

While her sight had returned, her hearing had not. The tinnitus was deafening. Then somewhere beyond it she heard a voice screaming. It was some moments before she realized it was her own. She pulled herself to her knees but did not have the strength to stand up, supporting herself on her arms and transfixed by the blazing vehicle on the road. Somewhere in her peripheral vision, beyond awareness, she saw dark figures running in the night. Long, flickering shadows cast by the light of the burning car.

Screams still tore themselves from her throat. Repeated, hysterical bursts of them. Before she understood that it was his name she was shrieking at the night. She felt hands grasp her arms on either side, men in uniform and dark body armour lifting her to her feet. One of them was shouting at her. His lips were moving, but she couldn't hear him. And then a woman moved into her field of vision. A woman with long dark hair cascading over shoulders draped in silk, a shawl wrapped around her above a pencil skirt and high heels. She flashed a wallet from her bag at the men who held Niamh. With the blaze behind her, Niamh couldn't see the woman's face. And yet somehow her voice cut through everything else. A commanding voice edged with concern.

Niamh felt tears burning tracks down her cheeks and stopped screaming to draw breath. Although she could now hear the words, she couldn't understand them. She shook her head hopelessly. Then suddenly there was clarity. The woman was speaking English.

'You are English?'

She almost certainly only wanted to know that Niamh understood her. But Niamh had never been able to think of herself that way. 'Scottish,' she said, her voice was hoarse already. Then she thought what an absurd distinction it was in a moment like this.

'You were running towards the car.'

'Yes.'

'Why?'

'Ruairidh . . .' Just saying his name caused her throat to close and fresh tears to scald her face. She took a moment to find her breath again. 'My husband.'

'Your husband was in the car?'

Niamh nodded vigorously. 'And Irina.'

'Irina?'

'Vetrov. The fashion designer.' She found light now in the woman's eyes. 'They're dead, aren't they?'

The woman nodded.

Niamh broke down again. Sobs contracting in her chest, almost completely blocking the flow of air to her lungs. The woman put a reassuring hand on her shoulder. 'Why were you running towards the car?' It was a refrain that would repeat itself often in the hours to come.

'They were . . .' In her shock and confusion she searched hopelessly for the right word. 'Lovers.' She sucked in air between sobs. 'All this time and I never knew it.' She searched the light in the eyes that gazed at her, looking for . . . what? Sympathy? Reason? 'Now I'll never be able to ask him why.'

CHAPTER TWO

It seemed she had been sitting here for hours. And yet time itself had become somehow timeless. It might have been only minutes. But her memory of the time which had passed stretched back further than that.

The room was entirely naked. The floor was tiled, a dirty beige. The walls had been painted a pale yellow at some indeterminate point in the past, but had lost almost all colour now, scored and scratched and scrawled on by the endless procession of cops and criminals who had conducted their business here. A wooden-topped table was supported on tubular legs, scarred and stained by the years. Her folding wooden chair was hard and unforgiving. Two empty chairs stood opposite.

High up on the wall facing the door, a barred slit of a window opened on to the night lights of the city, almost lost in the fluorescent glare of the strip light on the ceiling. On the wall beyond the empty chairs, a wooden-framed window was blacked out, offering her only a mocking reflection of herself in its darkness. Someone, she was sure, was watching her from the other side of it.

17

Strangely she felt nothing, as if some narcotic drug had numbed her body and robbed her of her senses. She had expected to cry. But the tears wouldn't come.

She gazed at her hands folded on the table in front of her. Hands that had touched him, stroked him, loved him. Hands he had held in his. And now they seemed lost, useless, dissociated.

She was almost startled when the door opened. A man of around fifty, with dyed black hair and a grey weary face, walked briskly into the room carrying a brown briefcase. He wore jeans that were a little too tight for him. His white shirt, tucked in at the waist, stretched across an oddly protuberant belly on an otherwise skinny body. The woman from the square followed him in. She had dispensed with the shawl, and her open-necked blouse revealed a hint of modest cleavage. Her pearl necklace, pencil skirt and high heels seemed distinctly inappropriate, as if she were on a romantic night out with a lover, instead of entering a police interview room. Niamh saw now that she was probably only a year or two younger than herself, soft shiny hair tumbling around a face that was unlikely to turn heads, but was not unattractive.

They sat in the two seats opposite Niamh, and the man dropped a modest folder on to the table in front of him. But he didn't open it. He reached down and from his briefcase took out a small digital recorder which he placed beside it. A red light began winking when he pressed a button on one side.

Niamh smelled cigarettes off his clothes, and on the stale air that he drew from his lungs and breathed across the table at her. She jumped focus to the faded *Défense de Fumer* sticker on the wall behind him, then back to the orange nicotine stains on his fingers. As some kind of deflection from dwelling even for one moment on the events of earlier that night, she wondered if they made him stand and smoke outside in the cold and the rain these days. Long gone, the smoke-filled interview rooms of old.

Then awareness that he was speaking invaded her consciousness. 'This is Lieutenant Sylvie Braque,' he said. 'Of the Police Judiciaire. Brigade Criminelle.' His English was heavily accented. Niamh's eyes strayed momentarily towards Braque then back again to the smoker. 'I am Commandant Frédéric Martinez, of the SDAT.' He paused. 'You know what that is?'

She shook her head.

'*Sous-direction anti-terroriste*. The Anti-Terrorism Sub-Directorate. Also of the Police Judiciaire.'

For the first time, Niamh was shaken out of her torpor. 'Terrorism? You think this was a terrorist attack?'

'France is still on high alert, Madame, after recent events. Any such incident is regarded as a possible *attentat*.' He paused to draw breath, and Niamh wondered if he wished it were smoke he was sucking into his lungs. 'However, there are several reasons why we are looking at other causes. Not least because the bomb blast was directed upwards, deliberately aimed at inflicting maximum damage to the occupants of the car.'

Niamh clenched her teeth to stop her jaw from trembling. Did he not understand that he was talking about her Ruairidh?

He appeared oblivious. 'A terrorist bomb would have been designed for maximum carnage, sending shrapnel in every direction. In which case you would not have been sitting here tonight. Miraculously collateral damage has been minimal. No one else was killed.' He opened his folder now, and scanned the few pages it contained. 'We have established that the vehicle did indeed belong to Irina Vetrov, and we have several witnesses who saw both her and your husband getting into it and driving off. What we don't know is why someone put a bomb under it.' He raised his eyes towards Niamh, and the question was there in their opaque milky brown.

Niamh found her voice with difficulty. 'I have no idea.'

He nodded and took out a pen. 'Let's get one or two details for the record, shall we? Your husband's name was . . .' He hesitated. 'Roo . . . Roooai . . .'

'It would be easier for you just to say Rory,' Niamh said. 'It's a Scots Gaelic name. That's the English pronunciation.' How often had they been forced to trot out the same explanation over the years. For them both. 'And in case you're wondering, my name is pronounced *Neave*.' She spelled out both names.

Martinez gave up trying to follow her and scribbled down their phonetic representations. Then, 'Macfarlane,' he said carefully. She nodded. 'And what were you and . . . Rory . . . doing here in Paris?'

'We were attending Première Vision at the Parc des Expositions.'

He frowned. 'Which is what?'

20

'It's the world's biggest international fabric fair, Commandant,' she said wearily. This all seemed so prosaic. Irrelevant. Ruairidh was dead. 'Top fashion designers and clothing manufacturers from around the world come to Paris twice a year to buy the fabrics that will appear on the catwalks and in the stores the following season.'

'And why were you there?'

Niamh closed her eyes and tried to summon the will to find answers to the smoker's questions. It was hard to think beyond the grief. 'Ruairidh and I were not just life partners. We were business partners. A small weaving enterprise in the Outer Hebrides of Scotland called Ranish Tweed.'

'Like Harris Tweed?'

Niamh never ceased to be amazed by how many people had heard of Harris Tweed around the world. A fabric created by a handful of weavers in their own homes on a tiny archipelago off the extreme north-west of Europe. From somewhere she found the palest of smiles. '*Like* Harris Tweed. But different.'

CHAPTER THREE

The first time that Ruairidh spoke to me about Ranish it came completely out of the blue.

By then I had already succumbed to what seemed like the inevitable, although I had been resisting it for long enough. And I still don't really know why I gave up my career in favour of home-making and motherhood. Except that somehow it was what had been expected of me all my life.

After university, I worked in Glasgow and London, then at Johnstons of Elgin. The Johnstons mill was based in Moray in the north-east of Scotland. It produced the most wonderful fabric, rich in cashmere, and it was there I found the job in sales and marketing that my entire education had been preparing me for. A job that allowed me to spread my wings for the first time – a lassie born and raised in the tiny village of Balanish on the west side of the Isle of Lewis chasing orders in places like Paris and Frankfurt and Milan.

I loved it.

But, then, I loved Ruairidh, too. And when he asked me to marry him I had no hesitation in giving up my precious job at Johnstons to return to the island of our birth and build the nest in which we would raise our children. It just seemed like the natural thing to do.

It would have been a different story had I known then that he would be unable to find work back on the island, and that I would spend weeks and months on my own restoring the old whitehouse on his parents' croft. Like most Lewis boys, he never wanted to move far from his *mamaidh*. His parents still lived in the new house at the top of the croft, a spit away from the whitehouse his paternal grandparents had built when finally they had abandoned their old blackhouse just before the war. It didn't help that the Macfarlanes and I saw eye to eye over almost nothing. On the islands, history stays long in the memory. So I was spending much of my time at my parents' house at the other end of the village.

They were pleased to have me back on the island, but Ruairidh was a taboo subject at home, as it had been for years. And so we never talked about him. When I first told them that we were getting married, there had been fights and tears and accusations of betrayal, before finally they announced that they would not be going to the wedding. I had feared as much, and rather than cause embarrassment, Ruairidh and I married in a registry office in Aberdeen with a couple of witnesses off the street.

I don't think his parents ever forgave me.

Ruairidh was due home that week. Just for a few days, he had said. But I had been counting off the hours, and then the minutes. I missed him. I was hungry for him. We had spent so little time together since the wedding, and not unsurprisingly there was still no sign of a baby. But the news he brought with him caught me completely off guard.

I suppose that the tweed had always been in my blood. There was an old Hattersley loom lying gathering dust in the blackhouse behind our croft. My father had put a new tin roof on the building, rust-red now, and used it as a storehouse. His father had been a weaver most of his days, working for a pittance for the mills in Stornoway, spending hours in that dark, draughty old building weaving his cloth. When I played there as a child, sometimes I imagined I could hear the distant echo of his shuttles flying back and forth across the warp. In those days you could hardly walk through any village on the island without hearing the clack, clack of the shuttles coming from sheds and garages.

No one touched that old loom after he died. Not until my father retired from his job with the council and took up the weaving himself. He spent weeks restoring it, and it warmed my heart to see and hear the ancient Hattersley brought back to life.

My mother's brothers were both weavers. They shared a shed at Bragar, just a few miles up the road. When we used to visit, me and my cousins would run in and out of that shed, round and round the looms, until one or other of my uncles would lose patience and shout at us to get out.

My mother was a great knitter. When the weather was bad, which was often, she would spend hours in an armchair loading peats on the fire and knitting me and my brothers scarves and jumpers and gloves, and goodness knows what else. One thing's certain, we were never short of something warm to wear.

Knitting never much appealed to me, although of course I learned how to do it at an early age – knit one, purl one. But I preferred to sit at the table with a yard or two of fabric and fashion clothes for my dollies. When I started making clothes for myself, my mother would take me into Stornoway to search for fabric at Knit & Sew, or at the occasional fabric fairs that visiting salesmen would organize in the Seaforth Hotel. So it seemed only natural, somehow, that I would excel at Home Economics at the Nicolson Institute, and then go on to textile college on the mainland.

It was blowing a hooley the day Ruairidh got back. It must have been March or early April. And the rain was driving in from the south-west on the edge of an equinoctial gale. The Macfarlane croft was west-facing, a narrow strip of land that sloped right down to the shore, and I watched the rain coming in across the bay. Beyond the headland the sea was rising in great white horses that crashed over black and pink seams of gneiss, teetering atop waves of deep green that rolled in off the Atlantic in slow motion.

When I heard the car I ran out into the rain, and we kissed and held each other, battered by the elements, not giving a damn about the wet, or the cold, or getting blown off our feet. We were laughing when we got inside, soaked to the skin, and I suggested pouring a couple of drams. But his smile faded, and I knew straight off that there was something wrong.

He turned away, avoiding my eye. 'I've been made redundant, Niamh.' And it felt like the bottom had fallen out of our world. I knew I would have to go back to work. Still, I was perplexed.

'Why, Ruairidh? The oil price has been booming since the financial crisis.' It made no sense.

He shrugged. 'Sometimes when business is good companies think they can dispense with people. A rationalization, they're calling it. It's not the firm in Aberdeen, it's the mother company in America.'

'Could Donald not have spoken up for you?' Donald was Ruairidh's older brother by some years, and high up in management. It was Donald who had got Ruairidh the job in the first place.

Ruairidh made a face. 'He did. Or at least he said he did. But I think everyone's frightened to speak up, or speak out, in case they're next.'

I remember sitting down heavily on a kitchen chair and looking around me. This miserable place where I had spent the last few months trying to build our future. Coordinating tradesmen, cleaning and cleaning. Endless cleaning. And painting. It all seemed like such a waste of time now. 'What are we going to do?'

But I should have known that Ruairidh had a plan. Ruairidh

always had a plan. And when I looked up there was a funny, mischievous smile on his face. 'Every cloud, Niamh . . .' He flicked his head towards the window, grinning now. 'And who should know that better than us, growing up here?' I knew what he meant. No matter how cloudy the sky, the wind was always shredding it, and the sun was always there, somewhere, ready to splash its gold or silver on the sea, and line every torn edge with gilt. He said, 'They've offered me a very generous redundancy package.'

Which did little to lift my spirits. Money, no matter how much of it you have, runs out very quickly if there's not more coming in. He saw my despondency and took me by the shoulders, raising me to my feet. His eyes gazed into mine, dark expressive eyes that I had always found so compelling.

'I want to invest it in our future.'

I felt consternation crinkle around my eyes. 'How?'

'A wee idea I've had for a while now.'

'Oh? A wee idea that you've never discussed with me?' I cocked an eyebrow at him and he laughed.

'It was just a dream,' he said. 'Never ever thought I could make it happen. Until now.'

I felt a stab of disappointment. 'Dreams are for sharing, Ruairidh.'

'Well, I'm sharing it with you now, amn't I?' He grinned again. 'Put on a face and get yourself ready to go out. We want to make a good impression.'

*

All down the coast to Garynahine the wind battered our car from the west, and then blew us east across the Leurbost road, the great, dark plain on our right fading off to the south, littered with scraps of lochs catching what little light there was, before rising up into the black mountains of Uig, which were almost lost in cloud. The village of Achmore huddled itself along the roadside, lifting towards the television mast, the only settlement on the island that wasn't on the sea. And all that way Ruairidh remained resolutely silent. When I asked, with growing exasperation, where we were going, he just smiled that enigmatic smile of his and said, 'You'll see.'

Beyond Leurbost and Crossbost the land dropped towards the sea at Ranish and the wind shaded off, the bog punctuated by rock that rose silvery grey out of its burned red winter grasses. It was sheltered here from the fierce Atlantic gales, and the road fell in undulations to a jagged shoreline, the sea breaking white on black rock.

Croft houses sat in sheltered hollows with faces turned towards the Minch and a view on clear days, beyond myriad islands, to the dark shadow laid along the horizon by the Isle of Skye. Ruairidh drew the car into a passing place on a promontory and we stepped out into the blustery afternoon. The rain had stopped, but I felt my hair whipping about my face. 'Down there,' he said, pointing, and I followed his finger to a whitewashed cottage that squatted between rocky outcrops. A kelp-covered shoreline dipped steeply away below it, a broken old concrete slipway vanishing into black water that would be

28

a luminous blue in better weather. A flaking pale grey fishing dinghy which had seen better days was pulled up high on the slipway and secured by stout rope to a rusted metal ring. Behind the house, a long, narrow outbuilding was a tashed white, with a green-painted corrugated roof.

I turned and looked at Ruairidh across the roof of the car, patience exhausted. 'Okay, now you're going to tell me what we're doing here.'

His face was flushed pink by the wind, and there was a light in his eyes. 'A man called Richard Faulkner lives down there. That's who we're going to see.'

'Why?'

He ignored my exasperation. 'He retired here nearly twenty years ago, from what by all accounts was a very successful business in the south of England. He taught himself to weave and established a one-man business that he called Ranish Tweed. It's not Harris Tweed. It's lighter, and softer. He uses lamb's wool, and cashmere, and other gentler yarns. But it looks like Harris Tweed, and feeds off its reputation.'

I shrugged and had no idea where this was going. 'Never heard of it.'

Ruairidh smiled. 'Most people haven't. At least, not on the island. But it's achieved a considerable cachet among some of the top tailors in Savile Row. Apparently there is a constant stream of them coming up from London to talk patterns and design with Faulkner, and to place orders in person. And Ranish jackets, it seems, have found favour with the Royals.

29

Which in turn has made them popular with their hangers-on. Who, as you know, are only too keen to ape their superiors.' A sardonic smile reflected his well-worn republican sentiments. 'Not,' he added quickly, 'that I would hold that against them if it meant I could sell them a few.'

I frowned. 'Why would you be selling jackets to the Royals, or anyone else for that matter?'

'Well, if I were the proprietor of Ranish Tweed, I'd want to sell as much of it as I possibly could.'

I wish I could have seen my own face, because it certainly made him laugh. He rounded the car and took me in his arms, brushing the hair from my eyes.

'Oh, Niamh. Ranish could be ours. Faulkner's selling. The business and the brand. He's in his seventies now, and arthritis means he's not going to be able to work the loom for much longer. But he won't sell to just anyone.'

'But Ruairidh . . .' I shook my head. 'Neither of us weaves.'

'No, but I could learn. And my dad weaves. And yours. My mum used to work as an assistant to the designer at the Carloway Mill.' He grinned. 'And, Niamh, you were the best sales and marketing person Johnstons of Elgin ever had.'

Which made me laugh. 'I think Johnstons might take issue with that.' But his enthusiasm was infectious, and I felt the first stirrings of excitement. It would be a dream, Ruairidh and I working together. Owning our own company. Weaving our own fabric, a cloth worn by kings and courtesans. 'Could we afford it?'

'My redundancy'll be enough to buy the business. But we'll have to persuade him that we're the ones to sell it to.' He paused to kiss me, holding my face between his palms. Then he looked at me, exultant I thought, and said, 'And you might just be our secret weapon.'

We heard the loom at work as we climbed down uneven steps to the shed at the back of the house. I knew it was a Hattersley straight away. I had grown up with its distinctive music ringing in my ears. It was the soundtrack of my childhood, and for a time it had all but disappeared as the bottom fell out of the Harris Tweed market, and the famous cloth became almost extinct. On the other side of the island there was new investment now in old mills, and the tweed was about to be reborn. But the old Hattersley looms, which had been weaving cloth on the islands for more than a century, were being replaced by the new, improved, double-width Griffiths machines. Though to me their music was second-rate rap compared with the new romantics of my youth, and I was pleased to know that Ranish was still being woven on a Hattersley.

Old man Faulkner looked up from his machine as we walked in. His collie dog, curled up in a basket by the door, was on his feet in an instant barking at the strange smells the newcomers had brought with them.

'Wheesht, Tam,' the old man admonished, and Tam immediately averted his eyes and reluctantly settled back on to his blanket.

Faulkner's feet slowed to a halt on the treadles and the wooden shuttle ceased its endless passage back and forth. In the silence that followed you could hear the wind whistling among the rafters. Rafters hung with rope and yarn and lengths of cloth, the wall behind him draped with yet more yarn in multifarious colours. An old bicycle was suspended from metal pegs hammered between the stones, and tools and oil cans and tins of cleaning fluid lay scattered across a wooden workbench among piles of pattern sheets coded in a clumsy scrawl that no one but Faulkner himself would ever be able to read. The floor was laid with flagstones, and I could feel the cold seeping up through it into my bones. It was not a place I would have cared to work. He cast Ruairidh a cautious look.

'So you're back.'

I glanced at Ruairidh, but he assiduously avoided my eye. 'I have the money now, Mr Faulkner,' he said. 'And I thought you might like to meet my wife, and hopefully future partner in Ranish.'

I stepped forward to shake his hand, and his big, callused paw very nearly crushed it. 'Pretty girl,' he said. 'But what do you know about tweed?'

'I have an MSc with Distinction in Clothing Management, and wrote my dissertation on the marketing of Harris Tweed.'

He raised an eyebrow. 'Did you now?'

'I did.'

'There's a big difference between the theory and the practice, you know, young lady.'

32

'Oh, I do,' I said and smiled. 'I have also sold Johnstons Cashmere in England, Italy and France.'

A smile creased skin the colour of leather beneath a disarray of tousled white hair, and he dragged long thin fingers through a thatch of beard that was like horsehair bursting through a mattress. The palest of grey eyes scrutinized me with amusement before he turned them towards Ruairidh. 'Let's go into the house and have a wee cup of tea.'

The house was as shambolic as his loom shed. A battered old Land Rover sat out front, and Tam followed us inside. The place was cold and smelled of damp, and something else unpleasant that I couldn't quite identify. The fire was long dead in the hearth, and the worn square of carpet in front of it was thick with dog hair.

Clothes and towels and lengths of fabric were draped over the chairs and sofa of a very old three-piece suite. It seemed more like a squatter's hovel than the home of a retired successful businessman. Except for the paintings that crowded the walls. Wonderful, colourful evocations of the islands. At sunset and sunrise. In storms, and sunny spring days, the machair alive with flowers. Of boats in storm-battered bays beneath dramatic skies, or tethered to quays and bobbing on turquoise waters. Originals, signed by the artist. Thick paint standing out like veins. Paintings, I was sure, that would fetch big money in mainland galleries.

Faulkner had gone into a kitchen at the back to put on the kettle. 'I love your paintings,' I called through to him.

'So do I,' he called back. 'The landscape of these islands inspires so much.'

'Even the tweed,' I said as he reappeared at the kitchen door. I lifted some cloth from the back of a chair. 'Is this Ranish?' He nodded. It was soft and luxurious and felt almost sensual when I ran it through my fingers. But it was the colours in it that attracted me. 'This is beautiful. It makes me think of peat-cutting up on the Pentland Road on a sunny day. All those different hues. The first new growth through winter grasses. Green and red. And the brown of the heather roots, and the blue of the sky reflecting in all those tiny scraps of water.'

When I raised my head to look at him there was a fondness in his grey gaze. 'You sound like my wife.' And he nodded his head towards the paintings that covered every spare inch of wall. 'She did those.' A moment's reflection. 'She absolutely loved the islands. Accused me of keeping them from her all these years.'

From his use of the past tense, to the sadness that coloured his tone, I knew that she was gone. 'What happened?'

'Oh.' He sighed. 'The usual. Cancer. We live all these years, we fight to survive, to be successful, to be happy. And it all ends in shit. Like a bad punchline to a long joke.'

The kettle boiled and he went back into the kitchen. Ruairidh and I exchanged glances.

His voice came back through to us in the sitting room. 'Isabella died six months ago. Which is what decided me to put Ranish on the market.' We could hear the chink of china,

34

the sound of water pouring into cups. Then he reappeared at the door. 'I tell folk it's the arthritis in my knees. That I have no choice but to sell. But it's not that at all. I have no will to carry on since Isabella passed. Married just over fifty years, you see. We were one person, really. I am not motivated to keep it going without her.'

CHAPTER FOUR

Niamh wondered where she would find the strength to carry on without Ruairidh. *We were one person really*, old man Faulkner had said of himself and his beloved Isabella. And in so many ways that had also been true of Niamh and Ruairidh.

Lieutenant Braque spoke for the first time, softly, without accusation or insinuation. But she was watching her, Niamh thought, very carefully. 'In the Place de la République you said that Irina Vetrov and your husband were lovers.' Niamh did not feel this merited a response. It was a statement, not a question. That came next. 'How did you know that?'

Niamh dropped her eyes to gaze again at her hands, fingers twisting and interlocking now, an outward expression of her inner turmoil. 'He ... we ...' she began, not really knowing how to say this. 'Things had not been right between us recently.'

'In what way?' Braque again.

Niamh lifted one shoulder a little and shook her head. 'It's hard to explain. You are the way you are with someone, then something changes. I can't give you specifics. Except that to

36

me, he was behaving oddly. He'd started making excuses, leaving me behind when he went to meetings. At first I didn't think anything of it, then . . .' Her voice tailed away and there was a long silence.

'And?' Braque prompted her.

'There was the email.' She was still looking at her hands and felt rather than saw her inquisitors exchange glances.

'What email?' Martinez this time.

'I got an email from . . . I don't know who from. A *well wisher.*' And she thought how ironic that was. No one who sent you an email like that wished you anything but harm. 'It said Ruairidh and Irina were having an affair.' She raised her head to meet their eyes. 'And that I should ask him about it.'

'And did you?' Braque's gaze was unwavering.

'Yes.'

'When?'

'Tonight. Just before he left for a meeting at YSL.'

'YSL?' Martinez frowned.

'Yves Saint Laurent. But he didn't have a meeting there. He had a rendezvous with Irina Vetrov. I saw them together in the courtyard from my hotel room. When I went down to the lobby her car was just pulling away from the door of the hotel.'

Martinez said, 'And you chased them across the square.'

'Yes.'

'Why?'

Niamh wondered how she could tell them what she could

hardly even explain to herself. 'I don't know, I . . . I thought that if I let them go, it would be an end to my marriage. No going back, I thought . . . I don't know what I thought.' She looked at them as if they might provide her with illumination. 'That maybe if I could intercept the car, somehow I could stop that from happening.' She shook her head hopelessly. 'Stupid.' And she saw scepticism in their eyes. How could you make sense of the irrational?

Martinez reached an open palm across the table towards her. 'Do you have your phone there?'

Niamh looked at the open hand, then at the opaqueness of the man's eyes. For some reason she felt defensive. 'What do you want my phone for?'

'I'm assuming the email will be in it?'

'Yes,' Niamh conceded reluctantly.

'Then I'd like to see it.'

She reached down to lift her bag from the floor, rummaging through it until she found her iPhone and slid it across the table.

'I'll need your pin to unlock it.'

Now this felt invasive. Bruised and hurting, physically and mentally, it was just one more violation. But she was in no position to refuse. 'Four-five-nine-five.'

He lifted the phone and tapped in her code, then went straight to her mailer. 'How is it titled, the email?'

'*Something you should know.*' And Niamh wished she could simply erase that something from her mind, as if she thought that could bring Ruairidh back. She watched as Martinez found the email and read it. He was impassive as he handed it to Braque. She read it, too, then her eyes flickered briefly towards Niamh before glancing at Martinez.

He took the phone from her and turned it off, slipping it into his pocket. He made a note of the pin. Niamh wanted to object. But the objection never got past her lips. He said, 'We have people who will want to take a look at this. You'll get it back when they're finished.' He hesitated. 'Unless we retain it for evidence.'

'Evidence of what?'

'Against you.' His voice was level, and his eyes watched her through clouds of obfuscation.

For the first time two further emotions squeezed their way past her grief.

Fear. And confusion.

'Me?' she said. She looked at Braque, as if in the policewoman who had taken her from the hands of armed officers in the Place de la République and brought her here, she might find a friend.

But Braque was implacable. She said, 'If this is not an act of terrorism, Madame Macfarlane, which seems less and less likely . . .' She glanced at Martinez. Then back to Niamh. 'It will become a murder investigation. Given that the occupants of the vehicle were Irina Vetrov and your husband, whom you believed to be having an affair, given that it was almost a week since you received the email alerting you to that fact, and given that you fought with him just before he left . . .' She paused. 'We would have to regard you as a prime suspect.'

The corridor stretched into darkness. A fire door at the far end was barely visible. The strip light on the ceiling, above the half-dozen chairs pushed against the wall where Niamh sat, flickered and hummed intermittently. At the near end stood a door with a window in it, barred on the far side, and Niamh could see the shadow of someone standing guard beyond it.

It was cold, and she was glad of her tweed jacket. Still, she folded her arms for warmth. It was over two hours since they had left her sitting here. At first she had glanced at her watch with a manic frequency, before finally giving up. Time never passed more slowly than when it was being watched. And now her whole focus was on keeping her mind free of all thought and emotion. How could anyone possibly think she had killed Ruairidh?

She concentrated on listening to the sounds that gradually invaded her consciousness, seeping from the walls, through doors and ceilings. Distant voices. The warble of a telephone. The chatter of a printer. All punctuated by long periods of total silence broken only by the hum of the strip light.

When the near door swung open, its hinges sounded inordinately loud and Niamh was startled. A uniformed officer in shirtsleeves approached and held out her phone. She glanced up at him before taking it. And as he turned away she said, 'Does this mean I am no longer a suspect?' But either he didn't know, or wasn't saying, or didn't speak English. Without a word he pushed open the door and was swallowed by the building beyond it.

Niamh examined her phone, switching it on and checking her mailer. '*Something you should know*' was still there in her in-box. She noticed that the battery was almost exhausted, and was sure that it had been around 80 per cent when Martinez took it. She had recharged it on the stand at Première Vision late that afternoon. What, she wondered, had they been doing with it? The home screen looked exactly the same as it always did. But she noticed with something of a shock that the time was now 2.17 am. Had she really been here all these hours? She double-checked with her watch. Ruairidh had been dead for more than five hours. Forty-two years snuffed out in a moment. And time, the healer, just kept moving on, until one day he would be just a distant recollection, residing only in the memories of those who had known him. And when they were gone, too, what traces would any of them have left on this earth? What point would there have been to these lives they deemed so precious? She closed her eyes to let the moment pass, then slipped the phone back into her bag.

Yet more time drifted by. How much of it she didn't even want to know. There was a comfort to be found in this state of limbo, requiring no thought, no decision, no action. She would have liked, there and then, simply to close her eyes and never need to open them again.

Then the sound of the hinges on the door once more brought

her head around. Another uniformed officer held it wide for a tall man wearing a dark suit and white shirt open at the collar. A man somewhere in his forties, Niamh thought. Black hair thinning a little, unshaven, sallow skin pale from lack of sun. And yet he had a certain style about him. In the cut of his suit, and in his carefully plucked eyebrows and manicured nails. The police officer nodded towards the row of seats where Niamh sat and retreated once more, closing the door behind him. The man glanced at Niamh, unsure whether to acknowledge her or not, then sat down in a seat at the end of the row. He clasped his hands between his thighs and leaned forward on his forearms.

They sat in silence for a long time then, Niamh listening to his breathing. A distraction from the hum of the light overhead. She felt his discomfort, and although she stared straight ahead at the wall, was aware of his head turning several times in her direction. Finally he cleared his throat and said something in French that she didn't catch. She turned awkwardly and said, 'I'm sorry, my French isn't very good.'

He looked at her a little more closely and nodded. This time he spoke in a softly accented English that Niamh took to be Russian, or at least Eastern European. 'Are you here in connection with the explosion in the square?'

'Yes.'

A long pause. 'You are a witness?'

'My husband was killed in the blast.'

He seemed startled and sat upright. 'He was in the car?'

'Yes.'

Another long pause. 'Did you know Irina?'

Her mouth seemed very dry then, and bitter words came with a bad taste. 'My husband did.'

He appeared oblivious to the implication implicit in her tone. He said, 'Irina is my sister.' Then corrected himself. '*Was* my sister.'

Niamh looked at him afresh, and this time saw him very differently. The whites of very black eyes were bloodshot, and he might well have been crying. Whatever Irina's sins, they were not his. Like her he had lost someone close and was probably still in shock. For the first time she felt pity for someone other than herself and gave voice to it. 'I'm sorry.'

He nodded again and returned to his previous position, leaning forward on his thighs, hands clasped between them as if in prayer. Suddenly he said, still staring at the floor, 'You never imagine your little sister will go before you. You always think you will be there to protect her.' There was a crack in his voice as he added, 'I *should* have been there to protect her.'

And Niamh wondered if it should have been her job to protect Ruairidh. Death, it seemed, was always accompanied by guilt. Irina's brother turned to stretch an arm across the space between them, a hand offered in empathy. 'Dimitri,' he said.

Niamh took it and felt how cold it was. 'Niamh.'

Then they returned to their respective positions, several seats apart, and silence fell between them again. But it only lasted a few moments. And it was Dimitri who broke it. 'Apparently they think it was Georgy who did it.'

Niamh sat bolt upright. 'Georgy? Who's Georgy?'

'Irina's husband. He is from the Caucasus.' As if that explained everything.

'Why would he kill his own wife?'

Dimitri turned to look at her, and she saw in his eyes the hatred he harboured for his brother-in-law. 'Georgy is a brute of a man. I never knew what she saw in him. But he was like an addiction. The more he was bad for her the more she wanted him. And to him? Irina was his possession. He owned her. I have never known a man so jealous. God help her if she ever tried to leave him, or anyone tried to take her from him.' He hesitated before adding awkwardly, 'It seems he might have thought she was having an affair with the man in the car.'

Niamh's carefully contrived calm was suddenly flooded with emotions that very nearly overpowered her. Anger, hate, sorrow, revenge. 'Is he in custody? Do they have him?'

Dimitri shook his head. 'He's gone missing since the explosion. The police are very anxious to find him.'

CHAPTER FIVE

Irina and Georgy's apartment was in the Rue Houdon, above her workshop and the boutique on the corner below it. This was a narrow cobbled street near the top of the hill in Montmartre. It fell steeply away from the Rue des Abbesses and the little Jehan Rictus garden square just above that, famous for its Wall of Love. Forty square metres of blue tile on which the words *I love you* are written 311 times in 250 languages. Words that Georgy Vetrov had perhaps taken just a little too seriously.

It was still pitch dark when Sylvie Braque arrived to meet up with a van full of officers from the *police scientifique*, two uniformed policemen and a colleague from the *brigade criminelle*. The streets were deserted, too early yet for the municipal water wagons that would sluice down the gutters and spray the sidewalks. But lights shone from the odd *boulangerie*, and the occasional delivery truck climbed its weary way up the hill.

Vehicles lined one side of the Rue Houdon, vans and private cars, and a tall square trailer covered in graffiti and old torn posters that looked like it might have been abandoned. So

45

they all had to park around the corner in front of the Café L'Aristide and walk down.

Philippe Cabrel was younger than Braque, but held the same rank. He was short and cocky and losing his hair, but for some reason that Braque could never fathom was popular with the ladies. Dishevelled and bleary, he looked as if he might have been dragged from the bed of one of them within the last hour. He cast an incredulous eye over Braque. 'What the hell, Sylvie? You didn't get all dressed up like that just to search an apartment.'

'No, I didn't.'

'So where were you?'

'I wasn't anywhere.'

'Oh come on. Sexy skirt, high heels, low-cut blouse. You must have been somewhere. Got a secret lover you haven't been telling us about?'

To Braque's annoyance her heels clicked loudly on the pavement, echoing off the buildings that rose all around them. 'If you must know I had a date.'

'Ohhh.' Cabrel grinned. 'Anyone we know?'

'No.'

The *police scientifique* and the uniformed officers were waiting for them by the door to the stairs of the Vetrov apartment. 'No reply,' said one of the uniforms. Braque had already tried calling several times.

She waved a warrant. 'Better break it down, then.' The officer smiled. A chance to do some damage.

'Hang on,' Cabrel said. 'No need for that.' He knelt down and took a keyring full of slender steel instruments from his wallet, and choosing the right one expertly picked the lock. The door swung open. 'There we are. No need to wake the neighbours.'

The uniform looked disappointed.

As they climbed the stairs to the apartment itself Braque said, 'Where did you learn that little trick?'

He grinned. 'When you've spent as much time undercover as I have, Sylvie, you pick up a thing or two.'

At the door of the apartment he repeated the process then pushed it open into a narrow hallway, reaching in to switch on a light before stepping aside to let the forensics team in their Tyvec suits and bootees go in first. He picked up on his earlier theme.

'So, are you going to tell me about this date or not?'

'No.'

He tutted and raised his eyes towards the ceiling. 'Why not?'

'Because it never happened.'

He looked surprised. 'How's that?'

She sighed and realized she was going to have to come clean. 'It was a blind date.' Then qualified herself. 'Well, not exactly blind. I'd seen photographs of him.'

'A dating website?'

'Yes.' She was glad that there was so little light spilling from the apartment on to the landing and he couldn't see her embarrassment. 'I was supposed to meet him in a Korean

47

restaurant in the Rue Amelot. But the bomb went off in the square before I got there and, well . . . I never did get there.'

'He's going to think you stood him up. Could you not have phoned?'

'I didn't have a number. And anyway . . .' She gave him a look. 'I was *busy*.'

'Yeah, me too.' He grinned. Then, 'I don't suppose that'll do your standing on the website much good.'

'No it won't.' She pursed her lips in annoyance. Another dead end in her search for a relationship to replace her marriage. It was a constant source of irritation to her how quickly her ex had been able to replace *her*.

'Who's looking after the kids?'

'They've been with their dad this week.'

She saw the mischievous twinkle in Cabrel's eye when he said, 'He still with that new girl?'

'Yes.' She almost spat it at him.

The senior forensics officer called from the other end of the hall. 'Okay guys, you can come in now. Gloves on.'

They each pulled on latex gloves and walked into the apartment. It was bigger than it seemed from the outside. Three bedrooms, a large open-plan lounge and kitchen with views from windows on two walls that looked out over the city. Lights twinkled below them into a misted distance. The furniture was Scandinavian. White walls were hung with original artwork. Cabrel examined the *tableaux* briefly, reeling off the names of the artists. Martin Barré, Turner Prize winner Laure

Prouvost, Mickalene Thomas, Enoc Perez. Art theft was one of his specialities. 'Expensive,' he said.

A laptop computer sat open on the dining table, amidst a scatter of papers and books. A MacBook Pro. Braque sat down at it and tapped the space key. The screen lit up. She went straight to system preferences and brought up Users and Groups. Current user and administrator was Georgy Vetrov. This would have to go back to HQ for forensic examination by a computer expert. But before she closed and bagged it she checked his mailer to see if he, too, had received an email from 'a.well.wisher.xx@gmail.com'. Nothing.

'Hey Sylvie,' Cabrel called from down the hall. 'We got a staircase here leading down to what looks like her workshop. Want to take a look?'

Irina's workshop was spread across a mezzanine level above her boutique. There was a draftsman's desk, a workbench strewn with scissors and clips and needles and dozens of off-cuts, several tailor's dummies, and racks and racks of hanging clothes. Jackets and trousers and capes and skirts, and any number of tops in a range of colours and styles. The place smelled faintly of incense. Musky, like sandalwood.

A laptop on a stand beside the draftsman's desk woke from sleep at Braque's touch, its screen filled with diagrams and patterns in a complex piece of dressmaker's software. Braque supposed that it, too, should go back for examination.

She looked around. Here was Irina Vetrov's creative soul. Everything had come out of her imagination. A reflection of who she was, or rather who she had been. There was a dress under construction on one of the tailor's dummies. Eighties retro, with subtly padded shoulders and short sleeves. A dress designed for a slender figure, with a daring slash at the cleavage, and another at one thigh. It was cut from a soft, textured fabric whose weave of a dozen or more coloured threads created the illusion of pale mauve verging on blue. Braque wondered how much a dress like that might cost. Thousands probably. Well beyond her pay scale. But she fancied that it might well fit her, and that if it did she would look like a million euros in it.

The chief forensics officer came down the stairs. 'We'll get DNA from his razor, and hers from the hair in her hairbrush. Looks like he might have left in a hurry. If he's packed anything at all it must have been in an overnight bag.' And Braque knew that she was unlikely to get any sleep tonight.

CHAPTER SIX

It was now a little after 4 a.m. Niamh only knew because Dimitri kept looking at his watch, delivering a running commentary on the passage of time as his frustration grew. She was still endeavouring to keep her mind a blank.

Then the near door pushed open, crashing into their separate worlds of pain and silence, and Martinez stood holding it wide with one arm. Under the other, he grasped an untidy folder bulging with papers. If it was the same one he had brought with him into the interview room earlier, Niamh thought, then it had grown considerably fatter. There were shadows beneath his eyes, and his skin was a putty grey. 'You can go now,' he said curtly. And as Dimitri stood up he said to him, 'Come tomorrow at eleven. We'll take a full statement.' He turned to Niamh, wedging the door open with his foot, and held out his free hand. 'Your passport, please, Madame. You are not free to leave Paris until I say so. Everything will be returned to you then.'

'Am I still a suspect?'

'You are a material witness. And, anyway, I am assuming you will not want to leave without your husband's remains.'

Niamh had often heard bodies referred to as *remains*. But in this very personal context, in the aftermath of a car bomb, the word took on sickeningly macabre connotations. She felt a wave of nausea rise through her body, and a sudden weakness in her legs caused her to stagger slightly. Dimitri caught her arm and glared at Martinez. 'Not a very clever choice of words, Commandant. Perhaps you were absent the day they taught tact at the police academy.'

Martinez looked fleetingly uncomfortable. He was still holding out his hand. 'Madame?' Niamh took her passport from her bag and placed it in his hand. He jerked his head towards the corridor behind him. 'Along the hall and down the stairs.' And she was glad of Dimitri's support as he led her towards the staircase.

Outside, the early morning had leached all warmth from the preceding day and there was a penetrating chill in the air. The lights of the city reflected on the dark flow of the Seine, and at the far end of the Île de la Cité the floodlit Notre-Dame infused the night sky with light, obliterating the stars. Police vehicles were lined up all along the Quai des Orfèvres. Traffic still criss-crossed the Pont Saint-Michel. Niamh found something painful in the prosaic sense of life continuing as usual. Other people's lives. Not hers. Not Ruairidh's. And she was overwhelmed by a sense of desolation. What on earth to do now? About anything. Nothing mattered any more. Without Ruairidh, what point was there in even putting one foot in front of the other? And yet here she was, tipped out by into the city in the middle of the night. Thoughts to be gathered, decisions to be made. Dimitri saved her from having to address either for the moment. 'I need a drink,' he said. He buttoned his shirt at the neck and turned up the collar of his jacket. 'What about you?'

She nodded, unable to find her voice, and became aware that she was shivering.

'You're cold,' he said. 'It's not too far to the Rue Coquillière. The bars there are open all night. The walk will warm us up.' He crooked an arm through hers, and she drew in against him as they set off north across the Île de la Cité to the Pont Neuf. She was grateful for the comfort of his warmth, and the closeness of another human being. Grief was such a solitary affliction.

It took them fifteen minutes, walking briskly and in silence, to get there. Self-consciousness had caused her finally to slip her arm from his. After all, he was a man she barely knew. But she was still cold, wearing only a thin white T-shirt beneath her jacket, white sneakers without socks below her jeans.

Amazingly, the Rue Coquillière was alight with restaurants, bars and tables filled with all-night revellers. The Au Pied de Cochon was crowded. The only seats available were on the cold of the *terrasse* among the smokers. So they continued, past a domed and floodlit building away to their left, to the Taverne Kalisbrau on the corner. Inside, stained-glass ceilings threw coloured light on to tiled oak tables, and a hand-painted bar pumped Alsatian beers on draft. Voices raised in laughter seemed obscenely inappropriate, people whose lives had not been touched by death that night.

They found a quiet corner and Dimitri ordered two beers. But Niamh shook her head. 'Coffee. Black.' At least it was warm in here, and although a beer fizzing cold around her lips might have offered the possibility of escape she was not ready to lose her pain. He watched her as she sipped on her espresso. Then without preamble said, 'They told you that you were a suspect?'

She replaced her cup in its saucer and nodded.

'Why?'

'Because I knew that Ruairidh and Irina were having an affair.'

'He told you?'

Niamh shook her head. 'I received an anonymous email.'

He raised an eyebrow in surprise. 'You confronted him with it?'

'Yes. Just before he left the hotel.'

'And?'

'He denied it.'

'You believed him?'

She shrugged, unwilling still to fully accept that it was true. 'He told me he had a meeting at Yves Saint Laurent. But actually he was meeting Irina.'

Dimitri appeared to digest this. Then, 'They told me that the bomb was almost certainly triggered by someone using a remote control. Probably a phone. Someone who was in the square and who picked his, or her, moment.'

Niamh remembered how they had made her empty her pockets when she first arrived at police headquarters, and searched her bag. And then later taken her phone away for several hours. Was that why they'd let her go? Because she was carrying nothing that could have remotely detonated the bomb? Even had she wanted to, how could she ever have contrived such a thing?

As if he were able to read her thoughts, Dimitri said, 'Georgy spent five years in the Russian army. He fought in Chechnya. I guess he would know how to do something like that.'

Niamh looked at him, pricked by curiosity for the first time. 'What brought you here? To Paris, I mean. You and Irina.'

He shrugged listlessly. 'We've been here for years. Irina was ten, I think. I was thirteen. Our parents were dissidents in the old Soviet Union. It became too dangerous for them to stay. How were they to know that the USSR would collapse just a few years later? Irina wanted to go back after they died. It was me who persuaded her to stay. The future was here in the West, I told her.' A tiny puff of self-contempt exploded around his lips. 'What future? If she had gone back when she wanted to she would still be alive today.' She saw him bite on his lip, hard enough to draw blood. He lowered his head to gaze at his hands cradling his beer glass in front of him. Niamh saw him blinking furiously and knew he was fighting back tears he did not want to shed in front of her.

She said, 'If you could go back and change one thing in your life, it might change everything else in your future, but not necessarily the thing you would want to change. All you can ever regret are the decisions you make in the full awareness of their consequences. And, God knows, there are enough of them.'

He raised his eyes to look at her thoughtfully. 'I wish . . .' He smiled wanly. 'I wish I could have met you in other circumstances.'

She examined his dark liquid eyes for a moment then drained her cup. 'I should go.' She stood up. 'Thank you for the coffee, Dimitri.' She glanced through the window towards the world outside. 'Will there be taxis at this hour?'

He nodded. 'Of course.' He took out his phone. 'I can call you one.'

'No. I'd rather walk, at least part of the way. I need some air. And some time.'

He shrugged. 'Just keep heading north. You're bound to find a rank on one of the boulevards when you want one.'

The combination of the grief, her fatigue and the cold night air made her feel a little heady when she stepped outside. Through the glass she saw Dimitri catch a waiter's eye to indicate that he wanted another beer. She wondered how long he would be sitting there, and how many beers it would take to wash away his guilt.

The Rue du Louvre was dark and deserted, a slight breeze

rustling already brittle leaves in trees that would, in a week or two, succumb to the onset of autumn. She walked for a long time, breathing deeply, trying not to cry. An urge that came in waves, with a moment recalled, or an unexpected memory. Things she seemed unable to prevent from seeping into conscious recollection. All she wanted was Ruairidh back. She would, right now, have forgiven him anything, if only she could feel his arms around her. It was still impossible to believe that he was gone. From childhood you know that life will end in death. But nothing prepares you for its finality. The irrevocable, irreversible nature of it.

From somewhere not far behind, she heard what sounded like a cough. She turned to look. But the street was empty. Not a soul, not a vehicle in sight. She glanced up. Above the shops, apartments lined the street. A window left open, perhaps. Someone coughing in their sleep. But it made her feel suddenly vulnerable, and she hurried to cross the road, quickening her pace. Now she imagined she heard footsteps, and turned quickly to catch sight of whoever might be following her, but again there was no one. Nothing. She strained to see in the dark and wondered if she saw a movement in the shadows of a doorway some way further back.

She decided not to hang around to find out, turning into the narrow Rue d'Argout, and regretting it at once, as tall buildings closed in around her. Shops and restaurants shuttered and simmering in silent obscurity. Too late to go back. She started to run. Past a clothes shop, a furniture store, a crêperie, the gaudily painted frontage of an African bar. The lights of the Rue Montmartre ahead were still frustratingly far off.

She glanced over her shoulder and fear stabbed her chest like a tiny, well-honed blade. There was a figure silhouetted against the lights of the street she had just left behind. She turned and sprinted now to the end of the street, and out into the Rue Montmartre. Up ahead lights shone along the Rue d'Aboukir, cars and the occasional bus drifting by. She forced herself to stop running and walked quickly towards them. To her relief a line of taxis stood on the corner, green lights on roofs. She slipped into the car at the head of the line and woke up a startled driver.

'Crowne Plaza,' she said breathlessly. 'Place de la République.' And she turned to look out of the rear windscreen, back along the street from which she had just come. It was quite empty. She could see the darker junction with the Rue d'Argout, but there was no one there, no movement among the shadows. She turned to breathe a sigh of relief, sinking into the seat as the taxi pulled away, and cursed her overactive imagination.

Staff at the hotel were extremely agitated when she got back. A manager was called from an office somewhere behind reception, and with a Heepian ringing of hands and profuse apologies explained that the police had searched her room. The hotel had been obliged to grant them access, since they had arrived with a warrant issued by a *juge d'instruction*. If Niamh wished a change of room, they would be only too happy to upgrade her. But all that Niamh wanted was for them all to go away, to leave her alone to retreat to the final space she had shared with Ruairidh. To have his things around her, to touch them and smell them and believe, if only for a moment, that he was still there, a presence among all the traces he had left behind him.

Whoever searched the room had left a mess behind, the contents of both suitcases tipped out on the bed, drawers and wardrobe emptied. They had even rifled through the laundry. The hotel must have provided a master key to let them into the safe, and they had left it lying open. For a moment Niamh thought they had taken her iPad, then remembered she had left it on the bed after showing Ruairidh the email. She looked around the room and spotted it lying now on the dressing table.

She crossed to the window and looked down into the court-yard where she had last seen him sitting on his own at a table. Before Irina arrived. The beer he had left there was long gone.

Wearily she began repacking both their suitcases, trying not to think. She was meticulous in folding and refolding everything, like someone suffering OCD. Anything to fill the emptiness of the room, the meaningless nature of time that she no longer knew how to spend.

It was only as she closed the lid of her suitcase that she spotted Ruairidh's briefcase leaning against the bedside table at his side of the bed. When she picked it up she saw that both straps had been unclasped. So they had been through that as well.

She sat on the bed and opened it, sifting through papers and folders, until she came across his diary tucked into one of the sleeves. For some reason he always preferred to mark up his appointments in an old-fashioned hardback diary, while she had long since gone electronic, entering everything on her iPad or phone.

She flipped through the pages until she came across his entries for the four days they were spending in Paris. There were three 'RDV with I.V.'s on days and at times he had told her he had meetings with buyers or agents. I.V. – Irina Vetrov. She felt an enormous weight of anger and disappointment press down on her. Somewhere deep inside, she had still been harbouring the hope that somehow she had got it all wrong. That *well wisher* was just some malicious friend or colleague or customer who for some reason wished her ill. But here was the proof. And, anyway, hadn't he met Irina downstairs, and got into the car with her last night, when he'd told Niamh he was going to YSL?

Which is when she noticed an entry for the following Thursday. September 28th. Their tenth wedding anniversary. It was a reservation for two at Alain Passard's three-star Michelin restaurant, Arpège, opposite the Musée Rodin in Paris's 7th arrondissement. Niamh remembered their Italian agent telling them he had eaten there, and insisting that they must try it. But you had to book weeks, sometimes months, in advance. Had Ruairidh been planning to take Irina there? But why would he choose their wedding anniversary to do it?

PETER MAY

She flipped to the back of the diary, where a couple of pieces of flimsy white card stuck out from the top of it. They were air tickets. One in Ruairidh's name, one in Niamh's. Flights with Flybe from Stornoway, via Inverness and Manchester, to Paris. The outward flight was on the 27th, the return on the 29th. With trembling fingers Niamh unfolded a sheet of paper wrapped around them. It was a printout of an email from the Crowne Plaza confirming reservations for Ruairidh and Niamh on the 27th and 28th.

It wasn't Irina he had been planning to take to Arpège, it was Niamh. She let the diary and the tickets and the printout fall on to the bed. Why would he bother with such an elaborate surprise for their tenth wedding anniversary if he was having an affair with Irina Vetrov? None of it made sense. She buried her face in her hands and felt her head ache. A deep, hollowing ache born of grief and confusion.

Then she threw her head back and shouted at the ceiling, 'For God's sake, Ruairidh, what were you doing!?' The silence that followed said more eloquently than any words, that he would never be able to tell her.

She turned and lifted the shirt he had worn during the day yesterday. A soft cotton in his favourite pale green. And she held it to her face, breathing deeply. It smelled of him. Of his deodorant, and aftershave. But more than that, of the subtle, distinctive essence of the man himself, secreted through his skin in the oils that were unique to him.

It felt like she was inhaling him. And as she lowered the

61

shirt from her face, she cried for the first time. Tears torn from her reluctance to accept that he really was gone, and the knowledge that nothing could bring him back.

Sobs ripped themselves from her throat and chest, until both they and her tears had exhausted themselves. She sat for a long time then, coming only very slowly to the realization that she had to think ahead. That there were things to be done. People to be told. Her parents. She closed her eyes and breathed out deeply. Ruairidh's parents. But she knew she couldn't bring herself to speak to them right now. She took her phone from her bag and opened her Contacts app. She needed someone to share this with. Ruairidh's brother, Donald. She looked at the time. Nearly 6 a.m. An hour earlier in Aberdeen. But it didn't matter. He needed to know.

CHAPTER SEVEN

The alarm crashed into her dreams like the cacophonous chorus of a Peking Opera. Sylvie Braque opened her eyes only to shut them again, immediately blinded. Early-morning sunlight poured through her bedroom window, splashing gold all across her tortured duvet, illuminating the layers of dust long settled on almost every surface.

She fumbled for her phone on the bedside table to silence the noise, then lay on her back breathing rapidly. In her dream someone was chasing her in the dark. Someone she couldn't see. Someone so close she could feel their breath on her neck.

She squinted to her right and lifted the phone to check the time. It was just after 10 a.m. Little more than two hours since she had finally got to bed. But she had very little time. She forced herself to swing her legs over the side of the bed, and brushed the hair and the sleep from her eyes. As she rose to make her way into the hall she caught sight of herself in the mirror and shuddered. A favourite baggy cotton nightgown hung to below her knees. She had several of them. Passion-killers, her ex had called them. Most of the lacy lingerie he had insisted on buying her for birthdays and anniversaries still languishing in the bottom drawer of the dresser. She had never felt comfortable dressing up for sex.

Her hair was a tangle, and the make-up she had so carefully applied to her eyes the previous evening was smudged black around the shadows beneath them. Only a thin, broken line of lipstick remained, clinging stubbornly to her lower lip.

In the hall she passed the open door to the twins' room. They still shared a bed, and Braque posted a mental note to make it up before she left to collect them. She had been ignoring it for six days now. Toys and drawing books, and crayons and dollies lay about the floor where the girls had left them, taking only their favourite soft toys to their father's apartment. Sunlight fell in strips between the blinds, tracing distorted lines of yellow across the chaos.

She showered quickly, hoping to wash away the fatigue, stepping out to stand on a towel and briskly rubbing herself dry. Another glance in the mirror. Her face pale and unremarkable, the first signs of crow's feet around her eyes. No time to do anything with her hair. She grabbed the drier and gave it a quick blow-dry then tied it, still damp, in a plain ponytail behind her head. One more glance. The face that looked back at her was severe and unflattering. No time for make-up.

In the bedroom she hauled on the worn brown leather boots that tucked beneath her jeans and dragged on a fresh *pull*, flicking her ponytail out from the neck at the back. The phone rang as she was slipping into her faithful old leather bomber. She swore softly and grabbed it from the bed. '*Oui*?'

'Hope I didn't wake you.' The sarcasm was evident in his tone.

'No, boss. I'm just on my way out to pick up the girls.'

'Do it later.'

'I can't. My ex has had them all week. I have to get them this morning.'

'I need you to go down to the Quai de l'Horloge. The guys at the *police scientifique* have recovered important evidence from bits of the bomb.'

Braque sighed. 'It's my day off.'

'If you want days off, and holidays, and a thirty-five-hour week, then get yourself another job, Braque. You want to be a detective, or a mother? Make a choice.' His impatience reverberated in her ear. 'I need a report on my desk this afternoon. The Ministry want this publicly ruled out as terrorism asap.' He didn't wait for a response.

Braque closed her eyes. '*Putain*!' she breathed into the phone, knowing he was gone. Much as she would have liked to say it to his face, she needed the job and the money. How else could she keep the children?

She speed-dialled her ex, listening to the long, single rings punctuating the rapid beat of her heart.

His voice came, laden with resignation. 'Tell me.'

'I'm going to be late, Gilles.'

'Well, there's a surprise.'

'The bomb that went off in the Place de la République last night . . . you must have heard about it?'

'And?'

'I was there.'

Which clearly took him by surprise. A pause. 'You okay?'

'Yes. The thing is, I'm on the investigation.'

'I thought SDAT handled terrorism.'

'It's not terrorism. It's murder. We think.' She drew in a slow, controlled breath. 'I'm going to have to pick up the kids tonight.'

His anger was muted, and she guessed that the girls must be within hearing. 'And if that doesn't suit me?'

Sylvie had no answer for him. She was entirely at his mercy.

He lowered his voice even further. 'It's always at your convenience, isn't it? Everyone else organizing themselves around you, and your schedule. Do you have any idea how disappointed the girls are going to be?' She heard the irritation in his breathing. 'And what if I have to be somewhere else?'

'Do you?'

Another pause. 'Some day I will. Then what are you going to do?'

André Duran had been head of the forensics lab ever since Braque could remember. She had thought him old when she first met him nearly fifteen years ago, but he didn't seem to have aged. Still bald, still grey. His dark, rabbit eyes flickered behind thick-lensed glasses, and he always wore heavy tweed suits beneath his lab coat, whatever the weather.

They had driven out together to the warehouse on the north side of the city where the remains of Irina Vetrov's car, carefully collected beneath the unforgiving glare of arc lights all through the hours of darkness, were laid out on the concrete floor like an exploded jigsaw puzzle. Tables around brick walls were covered with white paper and littered with large and small fragments of the debris. Forensic scientists in white coats were examining and labelling every piece.

In the car, Duran told her they had lifted a fingerprint from the remains of the bomb casing. 'Normally, heat will obliterate any fingerprints,' he said. 'At least, those that we can identify by conventional means.' He grinned mischievously. 'That's what the bomb-makers believe, too. So they are careless. They don't bother about leaving prints on their handiwork. What they don't know – yet – is that we have new ways of retrieving them.'

Now, in the cold bright light of the warehouse, he gave her latex gloves and took her to the table where all the pieces of the bomb had been gathered. Braque was amazed that so much of it had remained intact, although none of the pieces of charred and mangled metal, lengths of wire and melted plastic strewn across the white paper would have identified themselves to her untrained eye as bits of a bomb.

'It's a professional job,' Duran said. 'It doesn't take too much explosive to make a bit of a mess, especially when you have a tank full of petrol to accelerate it.' He handed Braque a blackened piece of curved metal. 'All packed into a steel holder with the upper half cut away to encourage the blast upwards.

Simple but effective. Attached with magnets to the underside of the vehicle. Probably took less than thirty seconds to place it. Very often a tilt fuse, or mercury switch, is used. Mercury at one end of a glass or plastic tube, the other wired with the ends of an open circuit to an electrical firing system. The movement of a car as it accelerates would send the mercury down the tube to complete the circuit, and boom! But that's a very inexact science if you are wanting to choose the exact moment of detonation. If a tilt fuse had been fitted to this one it would have gone off long before Vetrov reached the hotel.'

'So it was detonated by remote control.'

'Exactly. Whoever placed the bomb wanted to be sure that both of the intended victims were in the car when it went off.'

'Which means he was in the square.'

'Had to have been.'

'And he used a phone.'

'That was our original assessment. Confirmed now by the pieces of mobile phone that have been recovered from the site.' He nodded towards a table further along the wall. 'Actually, the remains of the sim card itself. Untraceable, I'm afraid.'

'And the fingerprint?'

Duran lifted a shard of metal which had been polished clean. The tattoo of a very fine fingerprint clearly visible on it. 'This is just one piece. One print. I'm sure we are going to recover many more.'

'How?' Braque was curious.

Duran peeled off a glove and took the tip of one of his fingers between the thumb and forefinger of his other hand. 'The sweat on our fingertips,' he said, 'comprises a mix of water, sodium chloride and various other oily substances. It has an almost imperceptible corrosive effect on metal. While the heat of a bomb blast would normally destroy surface fingerprints, it actually increases the corrosive effect of the sweat residue, effectively engraving the print invisibly into the metal.' He chuckled. 'All these years we believed that bullets and bomb fragments were fingerprint-free, when they were there, right under our noses, the whole time.'

'So how do you know when there's a fingerprint there?'

Duran shrugged. 'It's a very simple process, Lieutenant, and amazing it took us so long to discover it. You apply a powerful electrostatic charge to the piece you are examining, and dust it with a fine carbon powder. The carbon particles cling to the areas of metal corroded by the sweat of a finger, *et voilà*, you have a perfectly readable print.'

Braque picked up and examined the print on the piece of metal. 'And do we know whose it is?'

Duran pulled a face. 'Afraid not.' He paused. 'But it's not unknown to us. We, and others in Europe and the Middle East, have pulled this one's prints off multiple explosive devices over the last couple of years. What do we know about him? Nothing. Except that he's a pro. Effectively a gun for hire. Terrorists, criminals, anyone who wants a professional, reliable bomb-maker would go to him, or someone like him.'

Braque laid the metal shard back on the table and blinked

the grit from stinging eyes. Her interest was piqued, despite her fatigue.

Duran was watching her carefully. 'Been up all night?'

She nodded.

'Me too.'

She looked at him very directly. 'So if you wanted to hire this guy to build a bomb for you, how would you contact him?'

Duran shrugged. 'On the Dark Web, I suppose. But I'm no expert on that.' He paused. Then, 'One other thing.' He led her across to another table and lifted a blackened object that was still clearly identifiable as a handgun. 'We also recovered this from the vehicle. An illegal weapon, serial number erased. But it is a Makarov 9×18 millimetre pistol, widely used by Russian police, military and security forces.' He turned it over to reveal areas which had been cleaned off and tested for prints. 'We have no idea who owned it, but it has Georgy Vetrov's finger-prints all over it.'

Marc Bouquand's workspace simmered in permanent dark-ness, illuminated only by the screens lined up along his desk. He ushered Braque in from a brightly lit corridor and it took some seconds for her eyes to adapt to the change. The wall above the desk was lined with shelves groaning with electronic equipment that winked green and red lights in the dark, and spewed cables in snaking sheaths the thickness of her forearm to junction boxes fixed to the wall below his worktop.

Bouquand was on attachment to the Police Judiciaire from

ANSSI, the Agence Nationale de la Sécurité des Systèmes d'Information, the French network and information security agency. He wore jeans torn at the knees, a T-shirt with the logo *A little radiation brightens my day*, and looked about twelve years old. But he was, Braque noticed, older than he seemed, the beginnings of grey creeping in at the temples around his shock of self-consciously permed and probably dyed auburn air.

'The Dark Web is not really dark at all, Lieutenant,' he was saying. 'It's not even that secret.' He pulled out a seat on castors for her, and slumped into his own state-of-the-art computer chair, swivelling to face her, and swinging one leg up over the other as he leaned back. 'It's just a collection of websites that are publicly visible, but hide the IP addresses of the servers that run them.'

'Which means what?' Braque was only barely competent when it came to actually using computers, and so this kind of thing was well beyond her.

'That anyone can visit a Dark Web site, but would find it impossible to figure out where it was hosted, or by whom.'

He swivelled towards his desk to pull a keyboard towards him, and his fingers rattled quickly across the keys. A screenshot of a website called *Silk Road* filled one of his screens.

'This, for example, is a dead site. It used to be one of the biggest Darknet markets for trading in illegal drugs, until the guy who founded it, Ross William Ulbricht, also known as Dread Pirate Roberts, got himself arrested and sentenced to life in prison without the possibility of parole. It had a kind of weird morality, though, banning stuff like child pornography, assassinations, weapons, that sort of thing. So other sites, like Black Market Reloaded, sprang up to fill the gap.' His fingers did more spidering across the keys to bring up a black page titled *Killer Network* in red, above a photograph of a man's face with a gun held against his cheek. Services offered included killing a target in the USA or Canada for 10,000USD, or one in Europe for 12,000USD. The young man grinned. 'Of course, who knows if it is genuine or not?'

Braque was shocked. 'How can you just access sites like these?'

Bouquand shrugged as if it were a stupid question. 'You could, too, Lieutenant. With the right browser. Most Dark Web sites use the anonymity software Tor. You can download it from your computer at home. Anyone can. Then you have free access to virtually any site on the Dark Web. Tor encrypts web traffic in layers and bounces it through randomly picked computers around the world. Each of those removes a single layer of encryption before passing the data on to its next jumping-off point on the network. In theory that stops anyone being able to match the origin of the traffic with its destination, even the people who control the computers in the encrypted chain. So you can conduct any kind of business you like in complete anonymity.'

Braque dragged her eyes away from the screen to focus on Bouquand. 'You said *in theory*.'

He laughed. 'Well, of course, theory and practice are two

different things. The FBI have cracked quite a few of those Tor hidden services, which is why Monsieur Ulbricht is now languishing in jail. And much of what we've been doing recently at ANSSI is hacking into sites being used by terrorists to buy and sell weapons and trade information. But it's not that easy.'

'And suppose I wanted to hire a hitman, or someone to build me a bomb, how easy would that be?'

'Well, there are people out there advertising their services. You could make contact easily enough, but they would be almost impossible to track down if you wanted to find them. In person, that is.'

'And how would I pay?'

Bouquand turned back to his computer and pulled up a website called *BitBear*. 'You'd go to a site like this and buy Bitcoins.'

Braque had heard of bitcoins, but had no idea what they were.

'It's a kind of virtual currency,' Bouquand explained. 'Again, anyone can buy them, and you can pay for services, from anyone who accepts them, in absolute secure anonymity. You really don't need to be a computer guru to buy and sell services anonymously on the Dark Web.'

Braque thought about it for a moment, then asked, 'What about the email we sent you?'

'What about it?'

'Are you able to say who sent it?'

Bouquand shook his head. 'No. The address is a simple

generic g-mail address. It could belong to anyone. The question to ask is where it was sent from.'

'Well, where was it sent from?'

He turned back to his keyboard, and brought up a document filled with tiny text, on yet another screen. Most of it seemed to Braque entirely incomprehensible. 'This is the raw source code of that email,' he said. 'But the IP address listed is not the address the email came from. The real address has been disguised, concealed by the sender. The email itself will have been rerouted many times over. A little like a Dark Web site. Bouncing around from server to server.'

Braque was disappointed. 'Untraceable then?'

Bouquand pulled a coy little smile. 'Well, not necessarily. No guarantees, but given a bit of time I might just be able to pin down a real location for you.'

CHAPTER EIGHT

Awareness came slowly. As if through a thick fog. The light seemed distant at first, then grew brighter, tinted red through the blood in her eyelids. Until they flickered open and sunlight falling through the window nearly blinded her. She screwed her eyes tight shut again and rolled on to her back, reaching across the bed to touch him as she always did first thing. But he wasn't there, and the memory of events that sleep had stolen from consciousness returned like the pain of a raw, open wound.

She sat bolt upright, sleep banished in a moment, and wondered how she could have slept at all. She was on the bed, not in it. Had lain down sometime not long before dawn, still fully dressed, just to close her eyes. And sleep had taken her. To a place where Ruairidh still lived. In her dream they had been walking hand in hand together along the shore, wind tugging at their hair and their clothes, and he had been telling her about some new pattern, something unique, a blend of colours never seen before. And she wished with all her heart that she could simply have stayed there, in her dream, and never woken up.

And then the phone rang. A series of single, penetrating trills that dragged her, reluctantly, back to reality. She checked the time, It was almost midday. Which day? For a moment she was lost in confusion about the passage of days and time. Donald was coming. Was that him already? She focused. No, Donald was coming tomorrow. She rolled over and swung her legs down to the floor, sweeping her hair back out of her eyes and lifting the receiver.

'Yes?'

'Bonjour Madame. This is Aurélie in reception. I'm sorry for disturbing you. There is someone here to see you.'

Niamh wondered who that could possibly be. The police? 'Who?'

'A Monsieur Blunt.'

Blunt's name struck Niamh like a slap in the face. Neither she nor Ruairidh had seen Lee since the falling-out. Cut out of his life as if they had never existed. While he had gone on from celebrity to superstardom. The great young guru of British fashion, who had both made and very nearly destroyed Ranish Tweed.

She stood up, her mind filled with confusion, and caught sight of herself in the mirror. She needed to get out of these clothes, to shower. She said, 'Tell him to give me fifteen minutes then send him up to the room.'

CHAPTER NINE

Our first meeting with Lee Blunt came early in our stewardship of Ranish Tweed, and it changed our lives.

We had hoped, when we first bought the company, that Richard Faulkner would continue to weave for us, at least until we managed to get ourselves on our feet.

Along with the business we had bought his order book, which would be enough to see us over the first few months while we sorted through the shambles that was his design archive, and got our two fathers up and running to weave Ranish on their own looms. Not to mention the training of Ruairidh to weave himself, which his father was going to do. Ruairidh had also signed himself up at Lews Castle College in Stornoway for day courses in business-management skills for people new to self-employment.

It was chaos in the beginning, and I was dispatched to go over to Ranish to sweet-talk old man Faulkner into seeing us through the transition.

He was very subdued when I phoned to ask if it was

convenient for me to call in and see him. 'Come tomorrow,' he said. 'About two.'

It was July, and we had just completed the complex business of drawing up and signing contracts, making sure there were no loopholes or tripwires before transferring the money from Ruairidh's redundancy account to make Ranish finally ours. After a miserable dull and damp June, bedevilled by midges and cleggs, the weather had finally turned, and it was a beautiful summer's afternoon when I drove over the moor to Ranish. A brisk breeze from the west sent what few clouds there were scudding on their way and kept the midges at bay. Unlike that first drive across the island with Ruairidh to see the old man, the moor to the south was green and lush. All those tiny scraps of loch reflected sunlight in shiny fragments, like so many pieces of silver paper strewn across the land. And the mountains of Uig and Harris stood in sharp outline against a crystal-clear sky.

Ranish itself was bathed in sunshine, shrubs and the odd rowan in leaf and flower in these more sheltered east-coast bays. The sea was impossibly blue, coruscating out into the Minch, and peppered by all those tiny basking islands in the mouth of Loch Erisort. The Barkin Isles, Tabhaidh Bheag, Tabhaidh Mhór. And it felt like you could almost reach out and touch the Isle of Skye.

I parked at the road end and made my way down the crooked steps Faulkner had set into the hillside in some distant past. There was no sound of flying shuttles emanating from his shed, and I was drawn towards the house by the barking of his dog. The Land Rover was parked out front where it usually stood, and Tam was tied on a long leash to a ring set in stone to one side of the front door.

He seemed inordinately pleased to see me, barking and leaping around my legs. We had got to know one another quite well during the months of negotiation and to-ing and fro-ing. I knelt down and clapped his head and ruffled his ears. 'Good boy! Where's your daddy? Is he in the house?' Which seemed to get him even more excited.

I knocked on the front door and went inside. Despite the warm summer's day on the outside, it was cold in here, and still smelled of damp and wet dog hair.

'Mr Faulkner?' I called out. 'Hello, are you there?' A resounding silence was the only response. I went into the kitchen. A mug of tea stood on the worktop by the sink. Barely touched and stone cold. I brushed my fingers against the kettle. It was cold, too. I went back out into the sitting room and called again. Still nothing. And all the while Tam was barking and barking outside.

I went out again, blinking into the sunshine, and followed the wall around to the back of the house and the long stone outbuilding with its green-painted tin roof where old man Faulkner did his weaving.

There was some sixth sense by now telling me that all was not well. And it was with considerable apprehension that I pushed open the old wooden door. I can remember the sound of it to this day. Wood and hinges groaning in the half-light that crept in through tiny windows along the back wall where the hillside blocked out the sunlight.

I didn't understand at first what it was that I was seeing. Something dark and heavy draped from the rafters along with all the loops of yarn and bolts of tweed that stood leaning up against them. But with the breeze that followed me in through the open door, the hanging shape revolved a half-turn, and I saw the light catch the old man's profile. His eyes were open, his mouth gaping, head tilted at an unnatural angle, resting against the rope that stretched under tension from the beam above him to the loop of it around his neck. An old wooden chair lay on its side on the floor where he had kicked it away to let his own weight squeeze the life out of him.

I suppose I might have screamed had my voice not deserted me. I could still hear Tam barking, and the sound of the sea breaking gently all along the ragged coast, like the sound of the breath that had long left old man Faulkner. And I was remarkably calm.

His lifeless form held my gaze for several long moments, before my eyes flickered down to the folded sheet of white paper lying on the warp threads of his loom. I moved carefully across the shed, not wanting to make a sound. Somehow death demanded your silence. As if by showing it respect you might one day avoid it yourself. Though only the deluded might believe that.

I lifted and unfolded the note he had left on the unfinished weave and recognized his big, untidy hand.

My dearest Niamh,

Please accept my apologies for inflicting this upon you. But I might not have been found for weeks, and poor Tam would have starved to death. I know you will find him a good home. I live on with you and Ruairidh in Ranish, and I wish you all success. But I could not bear to be parted from Isabella any longer.

Yours,

Richard

The weeks that followed were difficult. It was as if a part of Ranish Tweed had died with its creator, and it was all that we could do to breathe life back into it.

Ruairidh spent days and days with his father, learning the arcane skills of the weaver. There were courses in how to work a loom, but they were mostly now for the Bonas-Griffith double-width loom that nearly all Harris Tweed was being woven on. And we were determined to maintain the uniqueness of Ranish by sticking with the single-width.

Tam found his new home with me and Ruairidh in the half-restored old whitehouse on the Macfarlane croft, and there was something reassuring in his presence. Almost as if he were keeping a watching eye over us on behalf of his master. I'm sure he missed him, but I think he also took comfort from the sound of the Hattersley in Mr Macfarlane's loom shed. He found himself a spot there to curl up and sleep while Mr Macfarlane taught his son how to weave.

It was my job to replenish the diminishing order book. I persuaded my father, who was good with figures, to decipher the codes old man Faulkner had used for his cloth patterns, and he turned them into recipes that we could all make sense of. We cut samples from the bolts of cloth that we found in Faulkner's weaving shed, and produced a few ourselves from new designs that Mrs Macfarlane had been working on, and I was sent off to London to solicit fresh orders that would get the business up and running again.

The trip was a disaster.

I had a list of the names and addresses of all of Ranish Tweed's customers in Savile Row and elsewhere. Tailors, mostly, producing bespoke suits and jackets for exclusive clientele. I had decided not to phone or write to ask for appointments in advance. It is too easy for someone to turn you down at a distance. So I went cold-calling instead. But fashion is a fickle friend. It can change direction and colour and taste in the blink of an eye.

Since Isabella's death, old man Faulkner had let the business slide. Although there were still orders on his books, he had not gone chasing others to replace them. And this was at a time when Harris Tweed was rising from the ashes of its own demise. Old mills at Shawbost and Carloway, and in Stornoway, were being revived. Fresh capital invested. Suddenly Harris Tweed was in demand again. Which made Ranish a very hard sell for me.

Everyone in London was very kind. They spoke with great fondness of Richard Faulkner. Of their trips to the island to meet him, to discuss patterns and orders over copious amounts of whisky and wild salmon. But they had moved on. Customers were looking for something more traditional, and Harris Tweed had a history and reputation that we couldn't begin to match. I returned from the Big Smoke empty-handed, and the whole enterprise, along with most of Ruairidh's redundancy money, looked all but lost.

Then our hopes were raised, unexpectedly, when I managed to secure a place for Ranish on a Scottish Development International trade trip to Japan. I already knew that there was a huge textile market in Japan, culminating each year in the JITAC Tokyo Fair. Hitching a ride with SDI could give me the opportunity to introduce Ranish Tweed to a whole new marketplace. Ruairidh was dead jealous, but we couldn't afford for both of us to go.

Sadly, it failed to provide the breakthrough we were looking for. I returned from the trip having learned that selling to the Japanese was a long and complex process. If you are lucky enough to establish a relationship with a Japanese buyer, he will only ever kick-start it with the smallest of orders. A gesture. If things go well, eventually he will take you for a drink and the order will increase in size. The next step is karaoke, and at some point you have to get up on stage with a microphone in your hand and sing. Finally, if you are very lucky you might get invited to his home. Which is when you know you have really made it, and big orders will follow.

I returned with a contact book full of names, having sung not a single song, nor obtained a single order.

Ruairidh was waiting for me at the airport in Stornoway. I had rarely been so glad to see him, grabbing his face and smothering him with kisses, while people stood around the carousel waiting for their luggage and trying not to look. Japan had been an experience, but I was more than happy to be home. 'I never want to do a trip like that again without you,' I told him.

He grinned. 'Don't worry. I'm not ever letting you out of my sight again.'

But in the car as we drove down Oliver's Brae to the main road, his first flush of pleasure at seeing me wore off. A dark shadow fell over him and he glanced at me with an ominous gravity. 'We've got money problems, Niamh,' he said. 'We just don't have enough working capital to see us through to the point where Ranish is even going to start washing its face. And we have no idea how long that might be.'

The optimism I had tried to maintain through all the long hours of the flights home deserted me then. I stared grimly through the windscreen at the slate-grey Minch as our wipers smeared dead flies across the glass with the first of the rain. 'So what are we going to do?'

There was an anxiety now in what seemed like an almost furtive glance. 'My folks have got a proposition,' he said. 'They're waiting for us at home.'

My heart sank.

*

The sky was closed, a turmoil of dark clouds gathered low out over the water, sending showers in waves across the bay on the edge of a stiffening wind from the west. It somehow matched the mood of our little gathering in the front room of the Macfarlane croft house. Gloomy.

I listened in silence, gazing from the window and wishing I was anywhere else but here, as Mrs Macfarlane outlined their plan. They had an inherited property, she said, in Stornoway, which was currently a letting concern. But she and her husband were prepared to let it go to raise operating capital, since I had failed to bring in any substantial new orders from either London or Tokyo.

I didn't miss the barb, but clenched my teeth and let it go. I flicked her a look, and supposed that she might once have been a good-looking woman. But her face had fallen with the years, and her downturned mouth seemed a reflection of the bitter old biddy she had become. Hair dyed chestnut was more red than brown, and the silver it was meant to hide seemed always to show at the roots. Her husband was a tall thin whip of a man and said nothing, as usual. He had long ago given up any pretence of wearing the trousers in the Macfarlane household. And it had occurred to me more than once, that this was probably why he spent so much of his time out in the loom shed.

'We have a buyer interested. An offer on the table. All we have to do is accept. But, of course, we'll want our share of the company in return.'

My eyes wandered towards Ruairidh, but he was avoiding mine. I could see why he was prepared to go along with it. He had invested virtually all of his redundancy money in Ranish. If we let it go he'd have wasted the lot. Although the prospect of sharing the business with his parents filled me with dread, I didn't see how I could object. Then came the bombshell.

'One other thing we'd have to insist upon.'

When I swung my gaze back towards Ruairidh's mother, I could see in her eyes a glint of something almost malevolent.

'We can no longer employ your father as one of our weavers.'

I could feel anger burning colour on my cheeks. But she quickly pre-empted anything intemperate that might come involuntarily from my mouth.

'The mill tells us his work is substandard. The darners are spending all their time repairing the flaws in his weave. We can't afford passengers, Niamh. Not if we're to make a success of this.'

I noticed how Ranish was now being referred to in the collective ownership of *we*. As if it were all a done deal. I glanced at Ruairidh again and he shrugged. These were the terms under which his parents would bail us out. If I didn't go along with them, he and I would lose everything.

This was probably the most difficult moment I'd had with my parents since telling them that I was going to marry Ruairidh. We sat in silence in their little back room, which had seemed so big to me as a child, listening to the ponderous tick-tock of the old clock on the mantel. The smell of peat smoke from an early-season fire filled the room, bringing back mixed memories. Rain, like tears, ran down the window, and the pervasive gloom I had brought with me from the Macfarlanes' owed more, I think, to the darkness inside us than to the lack of light offered by the day.

They proffered no comment to the news that Dad would no longer be required to weave for Ranish, although I saw spots of red appear on his pale cheeks. I felt so sorry for him. He was at heart a good man, and he didn't deserve this.

They listened mutely to my explanation of Ranish's financial imperatives, and no matter how reasonable it all sounded, I knew that everything about it would seem unreasonable to them. When I had finished, my dad slapped his palms on his thighs and eased himself to his feet.

'Ah, well,' he said. 'Can't sit here chatting all day. Things to do.' His way of avoiding conflict or expressing emotion. I watched him walk stiffly to the door, and felt ashamed of myself. When I was young he had always seemed such a big, strong man. Now all I could see was the old man he had become. Diminished in so many ways.

When he had gone my mother looked at me very directly and spoke for the first time. 'As if it's not enough that we lose a son to that family, now we're losing our daughter to them as well.'

It was then, like a gift from the gods, that Lee Blunt came into our lives.

It was Ruairidh's idea that we weave what he called pattern blankets. A selection of samples in a single length, each blending one into the other every twenty centimetres. It would make for a unique presentation. Half a dozen pattern blankets, a rainbow of colours and choice. We would take them, he said, to the big international fabric fair in Paris. Première Vision.

I had been spending all morning on the phone, calling old contacts in Italy and Germany from my days at Johnstons, when he came in with the first of his pattern blankets. It looked stunning, and felt like silk to the touch.

'It's amazing,' I said. Then let reality in to cloud my enthusiasm. 'But, Ruairidh, we can't afford a stand at PV. Not even the share of a stand.'

'Doesn't matter.' He was grinning, and glowing with that enthusiasm he always seemed able to conjure out of even the darkest moments. 'I've been talking to some folk at the mill. Apparently there's a kind of side bar that takes place along one end of the sales hall at PV. Like a fringe fair, just off-piste. All sorts of private deals are done, without any need for a stand.'

'And the organizers are happy about that?' It seemed to me unlikely, since renting stands was how they made their money.

'Ah, well, not exactly.' There was mischief in his eyes now. 'We'll have to sneak our samples in.' And he grinned again. 'But what's life without a little risk?'

And so we ended up in Paris that September, the two of us, staying in the cheapest hotel we could find, and taking the

RER to the Parc des Expositions on the first morning of the fair, all of our samples crammed into a couple of rucksacks.

We were nervous as kittens as we followed the crowds from the station along the covered walkways, past the various exhibition halls. Design. Manufacturing. Accessories. Until finally we saw Fabrics, and followed the red path up to a wall of glass doors. We had bought our tickets online, and dressed scruffily, hoping to pass ourselves off as students so that our backpacks wouldn't raise any eyebrows.

We had passed the ticket check when to our dismay a large dark-suited security man drew us to one side and asked us to put our rucksacks on a table. It is hard not to look guilty when that's exactly what you are, and I was sure that my face would be a dead giveaway. To my amazement Ruairidh was smiling and seemed quite relaxed. He even managed a joke in his bad school French, and the security man cracked a smile for the first time.

Wearing white gloves, he went through both of our backpacks very carefully, laying our samples to one side on the table during his search, and then repacking them when he was finished. Which is when I realized that, of course, he was looking for explosives, not fabrics. He waved us through.

From a mezzanine level with coffee bars and restaurants we looked out over the hall itself. Hundreds, maybe thousands of stands, all closed off by opaque white plastic walls, shimmered away into a breathtaking distance. Each open-topped stand was illuminated by a rectangle of fluorescent light that hovered over it. A long way above that, rows of lights set into the roof illuminated the vastness of the hall itself. It seemed as if we were gazing down on to some small futuristic city, divided and subdivided by streets and alleyways crowded with people, like ants scurrying about an underground labyrinth. It was hard to believe that this was the breeding ground for the clothes that would adorn the models strutting their stuff on the catwalks of the coming winter collections. What we wanted to do was make sure that at least some of those models would be wearing Ranish Tweed.

Along one end of the hall there were coffee shops and restaurants set against the angle of the only windows in the entire building to let in natural light. Tables and chairs ran the length of the wall of stands that backed on to them, and it was here that people sat drinking coffees, making deals and phone calls, cementing friendships and swapping contracts.

Ruairidh installed me at a table with the rucksacks and a coffee to keep me going, while he went off to solicit trade. How he intended to do that I had no idea, and didn't want to know. I sat for a long time, watching the faces that drifted past, picking up snatches of conversations in English, French, Italian, Japanese. No one paid me the least attention. Eventually I put in my earbuds and turned on my iPod. An hour passed. An hour and a half. I'd gone through three coffees, and was beginning to think I was going to have to find a loo when Ruairidh reappeared, walking briskly through the tables towards me. Following him was a tall young man inclining to plumpness, who looked like a refugee from an art school diploma show. He was wearing a pair of Alexander McQueen bumsters, a torn T-shirt and scuffed sneakers.

I stood up as they arrived at the table. Ruairidh said, 'Niamh meet Lee. Lee this is Niamh.' Lee smiled shyly, revealing crooked teeth that were a little too prominent, and shook my hand. His face was unshaven, with the hint of a goatee clinging to his chin, while the sides of his head were cut to the wood and topped by a mess of tousled red hair like fusewire. It was only in that moment that I realized, quite suddenly, that this was the designer Lee Blunt, the new darling of British fashion. I had seen his photograph often enough, but he looked different in the flesh, and much taller than I had ever imagined. It was quite a bit later that Ruairidh confessed to me his certainty that the only reason he had managed to persuade Lee to come and see our samples that day was because Lee fancied him.

But it was Lee and I who hit it off when Ruairidh went to get coffees. Lee sat opposite me and cocked his head a little to one side, casting an appraising eye over me, head to toe.

'Take a photograph,' I said. 'It'll last longer.'

He laughed. 'I'm sorry, I'm just dressing you.'

My turn to laugh. 'Really? Most men want to undress me.'

'Well, I can understand that,' he said solemnly. 'Beauty should always be high visibility.'

'Flatterer!'

He grinned. 'I love your accent.' His was pure London East End.

'It's what comes from being a Gaelic-speaker.'

'Gaelic? Irish?'

'Scottish. We're both from the Isle of Lewis.'

His eyes lit up. 'Oh. My. God! My grandmother came from the Isle of Barra. She was a McNeil. We could be related.'

I shook my head, still laughing. 'I doubt it, Lee. There are about twenty-six thousand people in the Outer Hebrides. And anyway, Catholics on Barra, Protestants on Lewis. Oil and water.'

He waved a hand dismissively. 'Bloody religion!' He nodded towards my iPod lying on the table. 'What are you listening to?'

'Pink. *I'm Not Dead.*'

His face lit up. 'I loooove Pink. I listen to that album all the time. 'Stupid Girls'. And, oh, 'Fingers'! I mean, who else could write such a blatant song about masturbation and get away with it like that? It's sooo sexy. I'd almost turn straight to spend a night with Pink.'

I laughed. 'I love 'Mr President',' I said. 'Not many pop stars with the courage to go political these days.'

'Not like in the Sixties.' Lee clasped his hands. 'Me? I was born in the wrong era. I'd have loved to have dressed the Sixties.' His eyes sparkled and he sighed. 'And all that free love, without an AIDS virus in sight.'

Ruairidh returned with the coffees. 'What are you two laughing about?'

'Oh just sex,' I said.

'My eternal obsession.' Lee grinned. 'After fashion, of course.'

He glanced at his watch. 'Speaking of which, you have samples to show me, you said.'

'Yes.' I stood up, taking over, and lifted the rucksacks on to a couple of chairs. 'We call them pattern blankets. It was Ruairidh's idea. Basically to weave one sample into the next to give a sense, side by side, of the range of tones and colours and patterns available.'

I pulled them out and draped them over all the available chairs I could draw around our table, and literally watched Lee Blunt's jaw drop. He stood up and walked around the chairs, running the flat of his hands across the surface of the tweed, and then feeding it through his fingers. His eyes were burning with what I understood only later was raw inspiration.

'I want this,' he said very quietly.

'Which one?' Ruairidh said.

'Not one, mate. All of them. Just like this. All woven together. Yards and yards of it. Bolts of the bloody stuff.' He turned shining eyes on me. 'It's perfect. Just what I've been looking for. All my bloody life, I think. I'm going to make it the centrepiece of my next collection.' He grinned then, turning his big wide infectious smile on Ruairidh. 'And I'm going to build the whole show around the Highland Clearances. We Scots can all relate to that, right?' And I loved the way that suddenly he was Scottish.

The next few months passed in a blur. Lee flew up to the islands and spent long hours with Ruairidh's mother picking out the patterns and colours he wanted for the blankets. He and Ruairidh and I went off to the bar at the Doune Braes Hotel and got roaring drunk, laughing endlessly at his irreverent and often blood-curdlingly crude sense of humour. We really cemented our relationship with him that week.

And then it was down to work. Making those blankets was no easy task. It was a complex business managing the transition from one set of warp and weft yarns to another, as the weave bled from one pattern into the next. Single-width Harris Tweed would use just over 600 threads because of the thickness of the wool. Ranish, with its finer threads, used more than 800. So it was a labour-intensive and time-consuming job. We had to employ additional weavers so that we would make the deadline Lee had set for us. He needed the cloth in time to prepare for his show at London Fashion Week in February.

In January we got an invite from Lee to attend the show. Money was still tight. He hadn't paid us yet, and we had devoted all our time and energies to fulfilling his order, sub-sidized by money from the sale of the Macfarlanes' property in Stornoway. We got the bus down to London the following month, the day before the show. I had booked us into a student guest house in South Kensington for a little over £30 a night, and we intended to stay just the two nights.

The evening we arrived Lee picked us up in a big black Merc driven by a punkish girl with a face full of metal who took us to an apartment somewhere in St John's Wood. 'Pre-show party,' Lee said. He was sitting up front with the punk girl. 'In case the post-show party is more like a wake. You never know with these fucking fashion critics.' He turned his back on us then, and getting conversation out of him during the rest of the drive was like getting blood from a stone. He seemed nervous and distracted and not at all like the crude and outrageous character we had got to know during his stay on the island.

It was a rainy, miserable, dark winter's night and the street, when we arrived, was packed full of shiny wet Audis and BMWs and Porsches. Taxis were arriving, and a constant stream of strange-looking people under umbrellas were running into an elegant apartment block through a portico'd entrance.

'So,' I said, 'I suppose everything's all set for the show, then?'

'Christ, no!' Lee turned and growled at me. 'It's all a fucking mess. Nothing's finished. It's going to be a goddamn fucking disaster.' He got out of the car, slamming the door behind him, and walked briskly up the drive towards the front door.

The punk girl turned and grinned at us. 'Don't worry, he's always like this the night before a show. He'll pull it all together, he always does. Just go in,' she said. 'And enjoy.'

The apartment was on the second floor. We followed the noise up the stairs and wondered what the neighbours made of it. The door of the apartment stood wide, spilling light and music out into the landing. I followed Ruairidh in as he weaved his way through crowds of people who stood about on white carpets spilling red wine and cigarette ash. In amongst the smoke I smelled the distinctive musky reek of cannabis, with which I had become acquainted during my student days. But that was a long time ago. Ruairidh half-turned and pulled a face. This was definitely not our scene.

A large sitting room with open-plan kitchen and tall windows looked out over the road below. A congregation of mostly young people sprawled on sofas and chairs or stood in animated groups shouting conversations above deafening music. I had never seen such an array of outlandish clothes all in one place outside of a theatre dressing room. A maelstrom of mannequins, a thrum of thespians. Hats and boots, frock coats and dresses, flares and bumsters, skirts and tops that left little to the imagination. There were men kissing men, women kissing women and, incongruously, even the occasional man and woman exchanging kisses.

A group of people knelt around a glass-topped coffee table, cutting and accumulating lines of white powder that they took it in turns to snort through rolled-up fivers.

Someone thrust glasses of red wine into our hands, and we looked around for Lee. But there was no sign of him. We found seats instead, and sat together sipping our wine and watching as the circus unfolded around us. We made those drinks last, feeling distinctly out of place, although in truth no one seemed to notice our existence. I don't know how long we sat there. An hour, maybe more. But finally it was long enough for me. I pressed my lips to Ruairidh's ear. 'Let's go.'

He nodded. 'We'd better tell Lee, though.'

I thought he wouldn't even notice if we were gone, but Ruairidh was anxious not to offend him. We pushed through a group of dancers in the kitchen area and out into the hallway. There was no sign of him anywhere. A couple of doors led off the hall and Ruairidh opened one of them.

It revealed a bedroom awash with red light. A TV screen fixed to the ceiling above the bed was playing some kind of porn video that we couldn't see from where we stood. But the soundtrack was explicit enough. A naked man on the bed was hunched over on his knees, an equally naked woman with enormous breasts thrusting her hips towards his bare buttocks, flesh slapping on flesh. She turned and moved back a little as the door opened, and I was shocked to see her very large erection swinging towards us. She smiled, and in a strangely masculine cadence said, 'Hello, darlings. Join us.'

Ruairidh almost stood on my feet as he backed out of the room, and although I wasn't certain, I thought that the man bent over on the bed was Lee.

The punk girl was still sitting in the car outside listening to music. I rapped on the window and she wound it down. 'Can you take us back to South Kensington?'

'Sorry, sweetheart. No can do. I've got to wait for Lee and take him to the venue. He's going to be working on the show all night. But don't worry, you can get a taxi. And Lee's asked me to pick you up from your place at six tomorrow morning. So be ready.' She smiled and wound the window back up.

We picked up a taxi a couple of streets away, and I was shocked when the fare came to almost as much as a night at our hotel. So much for economizing.

We were still half asleep when the punk girl came calling, and took us off on what would be one of the most bizarre, unlikely and seminal days of our lives.

It was another miserable February morning, drizzle falling in the dark from a sky burned umber by the lights of the city. The chill of it seeped into our bones. We had no idea where we were going, but the punk girl sped us through the early-morning traffic heading east. Until we found ourselves cruising along shiny cobbled streets between crumbling brick warehouses.

Finally, she drew up alongside a phalanx of cars and battered white vans in a cul-de-sac surrounded by dark, derelict buildings. Light spilled out from vast open doors and was shot through by streaks of fast-moving white. It was sleeting.

The outside walls were slathered with posters advertising what it described as *The highlight and absolute culmination of British Fashion Week*. A billboard declared, *Fashion Sensation Lee Blunt Re-animates the Highland Clearances in Haute Couture*.

It seemed to us the most unlikely venue. British Fashion Week, in our imagination at least, projected an image of class and glamour. It was hard to imagine the great and the good of British fashion dragging themselves out to warehouseland in the East End of London from between their silk sheets in

Mayfair and Chelsea. But what did we know? This was the pulling power of Lee Blunt.

The vast interior beyond the open doors was filled with the roar of space heaters fighting to exorcize years of cold and damp. Electricians were constructing a complex lighting rig around a raised catwalk strewn with rocks and heather and seaweed carefully placed along its length by an army of assistants. Where they had acquired heather at this time of year we knew not, but the seaweed was fresh, and the salty smell of it filled the place like the smell of the sea.

The punk girl had told us in the car that many of the young people helping with the show were volunteers, fashion students hoping to learn something, or get themselves noticed. We noticed them now, setting out rows of folding tubular chairs along either side of the catwalk. Beyond the seating and the stage, as the lights came up, the rest of the warehouse receded into a darkness so profound that everything in the illuminated foreground seemed impossibly overlit, over-coloured and quite unreal.

A technician crouched at the end of the runway, fixing a scale model of a nineteenth-century sailing ship to a pedestal. He stood to position a spotlight behind it, casting its shadow large against the far wall and the opening through which the models would come, as if emerging from the hold of the ship itself. Beyond that, the backstage area was screened off by stretched canvas. Everything seemed so unexpectedly makeshift.

We followed the punk girl, picking our way through the debris that littered the concrete floor, and saw huge pools of black water reflecting light in the distance where the roof had let in rain. Up wooden steps and through hanging sheets on to an area of elevated staging beyond the canvas. And therein lay chaos.

This was one giant dressing room. Naked and semi-naked girls with pale and dark skin and bones more prominent than breasts ran around from make-up to fitting and back again. In chairs set around a long scarred table littered with jars and brushes, make-up artists daubed dirt and blood on alabaster and ebony skin, painting beautiful faces, and then defacing them with scars and bruises.

I turned to see Ruairidh gawping open-mouthed. I dug an elbow into his ribs. 'Watch it!'

He laughed and leaned in confidentially. 'I've never been attracted to stick insects. Ever since I read about the female praying mantis eating her lover after sex.'

I said, 'Sounds like a fine idea to me.'

A vast cutting table was strewn with Ranish Tweed. There were bolts of it unravelled and cut in short and long lengths. It hung down in folds on to a floor littered with offcuts. Rows of clothes racks hung with half-finished outfits. Jackets and tops and skirts and trousers. Lee, and a small group of trusted accomplices, were pinning them on the girls, cutting and sewing as they went, almost sculpting the clothes to their bodies.

Lee's cutting shears were like a wand in his hand as he shaped and cut with mesmeric speed, conjuring extraordinary outfits from virgin cloth, examining, re-cutting, re-pinning what his assistants had done

The models – I counted twenty of them – were blue with the cold, and stood around shivering but never complaining. This was a much-coveted gig, a stage on which only a select few would ever get to perform.

Lee spotted us, and abandoned his shears for a moment, opening his arms to hug and kiss us both, and announcing to the world, 'Everyone! These are the geniuses who made the cloth you are wearing.' And all the girls crowded around to fuss and kiss and hug and congratulate. Famous faces from the covers of *Vogue* and *Elle*, *Cosmopolitan* and *Harper's Bazaar*, naked and unabashed. And I wondered if the flush on Ruairidh's cheeks was from pleasure or embarrassment. I decided it was probably a mix of the two.

Lee's face glowed with excitement, shining with perspiration. His eyes on fire. It was the first time I had seen him so alive. An extraordinary talent wholly in its element. He turned towards racks of boots and shoes behind him. 'Look,' he said. 'Specially commissioned for the Clearances.' For that's what he was calling the show.

They were stunning. Amazing creations that blended leather and Ranish Tweed in startling designs. It made all the hairs on the back of my neck stand up. I found Lee watching me with wide, expectant eyes.

'Well?'

'Lee, they are fabulous,' I said. 'I've never seen anything like it.'

His grin was infectious. 'Wait till you see them in the shops.'

'So,' Ruairidh said, 'the show's still going to be a goddamn fucking disaster?'

Lee threw his head back and roared with laughter. 'Of course it is. I've built my whole reputation on disaster. I wouldn't want to let anyone down now.' He glanced at his watch. 'But go, go, go. I've reserved you seats at the front. We'll be starting soon.'

My turn to look at my watch. 'Lee, it's not even eight-thirty.'

He grinned wickedly. 'We start at nine. I like to get the bastards out of their beds. And they always do for a Lee Blunt show.' He crinkled his face with pleasure. 'Lets them know who's the one with power here.'

To our astonishment, when we stepped back out into the warehouse, the seats around the runway were very nearly full. The great and the good had, indeed, dragged themselves from their beds at an ungodly hour for Lee. A buzz of anticipation rose like smoke from amongst the baggy-eyed, powdered and painted faces crowded all around the stage. Seats at the front, in prime position, had our names on them, and we were aware of all the curious glances turning in our direction as we took our places. A flurry of flashes from the bank of photographers beyond the runway nearly blinded us, before we realized that *we* were the focus of their lenses.

Suddenly everything went black. Then the distant strains of bagpipes bled into the dramatic opening of a Capercaillie song, 'Waiting for the Wheel to Turn'. A song all about the Highland Clearances. Three models staggered on to the catwalk, linked by paper chains and driven on by a bare-chested man cracking a whip. The clothes they wore were fantastical creations of Ranish and leather and lace, torn trousers and baggy tops slashed open to reveal breasts and blood.

For thirty minutes the music swooped and soared, pipes and flutes and drums and haunting voices. Skinny, bloodied and dirty models tramped through the heather up and down the catwalk. Sometimes barefoot, other times in knee-high boots, bodies barely concealed beneath extravagant wraps and flowing capes.

While Lee had used a variety of other textures and textiles, leathers and laces, Ranish Tweed was centre stage. I was moved almost to tears by it, and when Lee emerged at the end of it all, to walk the length of the stage surrounded by his adoring models, I stood with the rest applauding until my hands hurt.

After the show everyone involved crowded into a pub in Shoreditch. The first reviews would appear in the later editions of the evening papers, and then tomorrow in the dailies, but everyone knew that it had been a triumph. It seemed that Ruairidh and I were as much the centre of attention as Lee, everyone plying us with champagne. Once or twice I caught Lee watching from afar and wondered if it was jealousy I saw in his eyes.

We were quite drunk, Ruairidh and I, when Lee took us out-side, where the punk girl was waiting in the Merc. He opened the door for us to get in. 'Just wanted to say my own special thank you,' he said.

We drove to one of his homes, which was an apartment in an end terrace, semi-detached brick and stone house some-where in Notting Hill.

He let us in by a stained-glass door at the front and led us upstairs to the apartment itself. 'To be honest, I don't spend much time here. It's a place I crash when I want to be on my own, or to bring special friends.'

He waved us into a white leather settee and opened another bottle of champagne. Ruairidh seemed to have an endless capacity for it, but I didn't know that I could drink any more. My head was already spinning. However, I had no desire to put a dampener on the occasion. It's not often that I can say I had to force champagne down my throat, but I did that day.

Lee, for all that he had consumed, seemed quite sober. He sat down at a shiny, glass-topped table, and started cutting lines of coke through the reflections. 'Join me,' he said.

I glanced at Ruairidh. This really was not something I wanted to do. But I could see from his eyes that he didn't want us to refuse.

Lee seemed oblivious. 'I love this shit,' he said. 'I don't think I could get through these shows without it.' He looked up, that infectious grin of his spread across his face. 'And I love you guys. I couldn't have done this without Ranish. It was just perfect.' He took out and rolled up a £20 note and hoovered a line of coke into his right nostril. Then he passed the note to Ruairidh. 'I'll let you into a little secret.' He leaned in, something intimate in his demeanour. 'I'm to be the new head designer at Givenchy. They're going to announce it next month.'

'Wow! Congratulations,' Ruairidh said, with less enthusiasm than perhaps Lee expected. I think he was distracted by the knowledge that he was expected to snort the next line of coke. I watched as he drew the white powder into his nostril, and nearly choked on it. As he handed me the £20 note I could see in his eyes that the elation had already kicked in.

I didn't want to do it. But I knew it was what Lee wanted. A celebration of the news he had just broken. An intimation that we were special to him. And for the first and last time in my life I snorted cocaine. I felt it choking and burning in my nasal passages and throat, before suddenly I was floating on a cloud of euphoric self-esteem, and wanted to hug and hold this funny, buck-toothed, talented gay man and never let him go. Even though right then, in that moment of cocaine clarity, I understood for the first time that Lee Blunt was entirely and only about power, control and ego.

The reviews were peerless. Lee's catwalk rendition of the Highland Clearances was the highlight of British Fashion Week. It received reams of coverage in the fashion pages of all the dailies, and photo features in the magazines and weekend supplements. Ranish Tweed went viral. Suddenly our phone never stopped ringing. Everyone wanted a piece of the cloth phenomenon that was Ranish.

Those Savile Row tailors who had been polite but lukewarm when I went cold-calling were now calling me, asking for appointments, flying up to the island to select their patterns and place their orders. Those contacts I had made in Japan were submitting orders, without a karaoke bar in sight.

It was more work than we could cope with. We were forced to take on half a dozen more weavers, and cut an exclusive deal with the mill at Shawbost to finish our product. And although I wasn't happy about it, Mrs Macfarlane employed my old childhood friend Seonag Morrison to keep the accounts and run the office, which at that time was still in the front room of our house.

Seonag had graduated from a course in business and computer studies in Manchester, before getting herself married, and then pregnant. And with her kids just recently started school, she was now back on the job market. Relations between us had cooled off in our late teens, and I would have preferred someone else, but I couldn't argue about her qualifications for the job.

In spite of the orders now rolling in, we continued to have a major cashflow problem, which wasn't going to sort itself out until we started completing and delivering. It was Seonag who alerted us to the fact that although it was now nearly three months since we had supplied our tweed to Lee, he had still not paid. She had noticed the unpaid invoice and thought it was probably an oversight, so had issued a reminder. Still no payment. Then she had tried phoning Lee's fledgling company in London, but nobody would take her call.

So Ruairidh called Lee on his mobile. He made no mention of the unpaid bill, but told him that we would be in London next week, and that maybe we could meet up for a drink. Lee suggested the pub in Shoreditch where we had all got drunk together after the show.

Ruairidh and I were both unaccountably nervous when we got the tube out east to keep our rendezvous with him. And before we went into the pub Ruairidh said to me, 'Don't you say anything about the money. Just keep him sweet. I'll do the talking.'

Lee was with a group of friends. A black guy who we had met before and went by the odd moniker of Cornell Charles Stamoran. Cornell wore bumsters and a pork pie hat and was chatting to a couple of strangely theatrical young men who looked as if they had stepped straight from the pages of an Evelyn Waugh novel. They had clearly been drinking for some time, and Lee greeted us with sloppy kisses, and over-enthusiastic hugs that nearly had all three of us on the floor. On the wave of a hand from Lee, Cornell ordered drinks for everyone.

Lee was loquacious, slurred words tumbling from his mouth so quickly they were tripping over each other on the way out, and I knew that he had been consuming much more than just alcohol.

'Day after tomorrow,' he said. 'The Givenchy announcement. Off to Paris to sign the contracts and then a press conference. Gonna be amazing!' He put his arms around me and very nearly crushed me. 'Hear things are going great for you up there, darling. You so deserve it, you guys, so deserve it.'

Ruairidh sipped on his beer and said, 'Yeah, lots of orders coming in. Which is great. But we're still a young company, Lee, no capital behind us and a real cashflow problem. It would seriously help us out if you could settle up for the cloth we supplied for the show.'

Like a fist beyond your peripheral vision that you never saw coming, Lee's mood changed. 'What the fuck? You want fucking money from me? You want money? You're kidding me, right? I put your fucking cloth in the limelight, I make it world-famous. And you want me to pay for it?' He stabbed a finger into Ruairidh's chest. 'Do you have any idea how much it costs to put on a runway show? Do you? Do you? No you fucking don't. I have to beg, borrow and steal every fucking penny for it. Cos no other fucker's going to pay.' He waved his hand in the air, spittle gathering on his lips. 'Not until I'm on the payroll at Givenchy. Every fucking farthing's coming out of my own pocket.'

I tried to be reasonable. 'Lee, come on. That order used up all our resources. Buying the yarn. Paying the weavers. Paying the mill.'

He turned on me. His face ugly now. 'And you're getting your reward for it now, bitch, aren't you?' I don't know what he was thinking, but his hand came up to my neck, closing around it as if he intended to choke me. In fact there was no pressure in his fingers. They were caressing more than choking. But it was enough to send Ruairidh off the deep end. He lunged at Lee, pushing him back against the bar. Drink and glasses went flying. But for a man so clearly under the influence of alcohol and drugs, Lee's reactions were swift and unexpected. A fist flew into Ruairidh's face and sent him crashing backwards over a table. I could hear my own voice screaming above others raised in anger and protest.

Ruairidh was on his feet quickly, blood pouring from his nose, and he hurled himself at Lee. Both men staggered backwards until they fell together to the floor, Ruairidh on top, each trying to punch the other, but too close to land blows of any account.

Cornell tried to pull Ruairidh off and his hat went flying. The Evelyn Waugh boys shrank back into the crowd of drinkers which had gathered quickly around the fight.

I was screaming over and over, 'Stop it, stop it, stop it!' It was like a playground scrap between two twelve-year-olds. As Lee got to his knees Ruairidh landed a blow full in his gut and vomit exploded from Lee's mouth all over the floor.

Then loud male voices cut above the uproar. Two large uniformed policemen dragged the brawlers apart and hauled them both to their feet. A huge, shaven-headed barman slammed a baseball bat on to the counter top and bellowed, 'You're barred!'

Everything had happened so quickly, blown up from nowhere to flat-out warfare, that there had been no time for thinking. For considered, rational responses.

Now, after hours to dwell on events in a featureless interview room in Shoreditch police station, Ruairidh was still seething, but silent. At first I had wept, but the time for tears was long past. All I felt now was anger and regret.

It turned out that the police station in Shepherdess Walk was just a stone's throw from the pub where we had been drinking, which is why police had arrived on the scene so quickly. We had been separated from Lee and the rest, and statements taken. After which we had been left to stew for what seemed an interminable length of time.

The light outside was starting to fade in the late afternoon when a shirtsleeved sergeant opened the door and nodded his head towards the exterior. 'Okay, you two, hop it.'

I rose uncertainly. 'You mean we can go?'

'Yes, go. As in depart. Leave.'

'But . . . what's happening? Are we being charged?'

'Nope.' The big sergeant looked less than happy about it. 'Mr Blunt has already made reparations to the landlord of the pub. No one's pressing any charges. Though I'd like to throw you all in a cell somewhere for wasting our bloody time.' He jerked his head again over his shoulder. 'Go on, go!' Money, it appeared, could fix almost anything.

Outside we walked down the steps straight into a crowd of reporters and photographers. Flashes popped in the gloom of the dying day. There was no sign of Lee or his friends. Only a clamour of voices punctuated by the flashing of the cameras.

'What happened, mate?'

'Who hit who?'

'Where's Blunt?'

'What started the fight?'

I wanted just to go, to push past them without a word and find a taxi at the road end. But Ruairidh was still eaten up by his anger, face bruised and bloody. He was determined to have his say. 'We're just a young company from the Scottish islands,' he said. 'Ranish Tweed. Trying to make a living. We very nearly bankrupted ourselves supplying Lee Blunt with the cloth he wanted for his Clearances runway show. And now he won't pay us for it. The man who's going to be the next head designer at Givenchy!'

I drew breath involuntarily. This hadn't even been announced yet. Pens scribbled in the dying light. But Ruairidh wasn't finished.

'A bloody millionaire. So tanked up on coke and vodka that when we ask him for our money, he attacks us. His hands round my wife's throat.'

One of the reporters said, 'When you say *coke* you mean cocaine?'

'Yes. And God knows what else.' Ruairidh snorted. 'The bastard's happy enough to pay for the damage done to the pub, but he still won't pay us.'

The tabloids were full of it the next day. Front-page headlines. About the fight in the pub, Ruairidh's rant outside the police station. One photograph of his bloodied face was captioned, *Lee Blunt's own version of the Highland Clearances*. Even the broadsheets carried the story, and the consequences of it all followed swiftly. Givenchy, the day after, announced a young Italian designer as their new in-house head of design. No mention was made of Lee. And it was clear that the couture giant wanted nothing to do with the *violent, drug-crazed British designer*, as one lurid headline had labelled him.

It was the end of a short, sweet relationship, and Lee Blunt's path and ours never crossed again.

Until now.

CHAPTER TEN

Niamh was looking at herself in the mirror, barely able to recognize the pale waif who stared back at her with bloodshot, shadowed eyes, when the knock came at the door. Her hair was still wet from the shower, and hanging in corkscrews around her face. It was not a face she wanted to present to the world, but the damage was done, and it would be a long time in repair.

She had no idea what to expect when she opened the door, heart hammering in a kind of dread anticipation. Lee stood there in the gloom of the hallway, and she was still surprised by how tall he was. He had put on weight. There was grey now in his hair, which to his credit he was not trying to hide. The suggestion of a goatee which had played around his jaw when they first met had developed into a full-grown beard, perhaps to disguise a burgeoning double chin. He was, for Lee, very conservatively dressed. A three-piece suit, white shirt, dark tie. Perhaps he had felt it more appropriate given the circumstances.

He stepped into the room without invitation and wrapped

his arms around her. 'Oh, my darling Niamh, I'm so sorry. I'm so sorry.' And to her embarrassment, unexpected tears bubbled up like water in a hot spring, and he held her even more tightly as she sobbed in his embrace.

He took her hand then and led her to the bed, where they sat together on the edge of it, side by side. She wiped away the tears with the flat of her hand. It was all so ironic somehow that Lee should be the first to offer his condolences.

He said, 'I read all about it in the papers when I flew in this morning. I saw a piece on the TV news last night about the explosion in the square, but I had no idea then that it was Ruairidh.' He squeezed her hand and put his other arm around her. 'I just had to come over. You know how I always felt about you, Niamh. You and me, we had something very special.'

They sat in silence for some moments. Niamh had no idea what to say.

'I . . . I just wanted to say how sorry I am for what happened back in the day,' Lee finally blurted. 'We were so young. And stupid.' He shook his head. 'I should have made it up to you a long time ago.' He paused. 'As it turned out, Ruairidh did me a favour. If I'd got that job with Givenchy it would have been like strapping myself into a straitjacket. As it was, I put all my energies into my own company, which I probably wouldn't have done. And the Blunt brand wouldn't have been what it is today. In a way, I've got Ruairidh to thank for all that.' She was staring into her lap, but aware of his head turning towards her. 'What happened?'

She shrugged listlessly. 'Someone wanted him dead. Probably both of them. The police think it's murder.'

There was shock in Lee's voice. 'But why?'

'Apparently they were having an affair.'

Now astonishment. 'Ruairidh and Irina?'

She nodded.

'I can't believe it. Why on earth would Ruairidh choose that little Russian mouse over you? It's not possible.'

'The police think that Irina's husband, Georgy, probably planted the bomb. An act of jealous revenge.'

'They've got him for it?'

She shook her head. 'No. He's gone missing.'

'Oh, my darling.' He put both arms around her again. 'My poor, poor darling. This is so horrible for you. And I still can't believe it. What was Ruairidh thinking? If you were mine I would never have let you go.'

From the depths of her wretchedness, Niamh somehow managed to find a smile. 'I think, Lee, if I were to be yours I'd need something a little more between my legs.'

Which elicited a roar of laughter. 'Oh. My. God. Niamh. you are . . .' He shook his head. 'Impossible. I'm lost for words.' He stood up, suddenly, still holding her hand. 'Let me take you home. I've got an executive rental jet at Orly. I can fly you back to the island.'

'I can't.'

'Why not?'

'I'm not allowed to leave Paris.'

Frown lines carved themselves deeply between his eyes. 'Why?'

She sighed. 'The investigation is ongoing. At first they thought I might have done it. And I might still be a suspect.'

'Well, that's just ridiculous. Anyone who knows you, knows you couldn't possibly have done such a thing.'

She looked up at him. 'Really? Who knows what anyone is capable of in the right, or wrong, circumstances?' Her eyes turned down again. 'And, anyway, I can't leave without Ruairidh.'

His frown deepened. 'Ruairidh?' Then it dawned on him, and his face dissolved into sympathy. 'Oh, yes. Of course.' He hesitated awkwardly. 'How long will they keep him?'

She shook her head, fighting the urge to weep again. 'God knows. I suppose there are things they have to do. A post-mortem. Lab testing. DNA.' She didn't even want to think about it.

'Well,' he said. And he took her other hand and pulled her to her feet. 'You might not be allowed to leave Paris, but you certainly don't have to be stuck here in some awful hotel room. I'm going to take you out on the town. Anywhere you want to go. Anywhere you'd like to eat.'

She breathed her despondency at him. 'I don't think I want to go anywhere or eat anything ever again, Lee.'

'Oh nonsense. Dwelling on it all is only going to make it worse. The first thing we need to do is take your mind off things. And I'm the very one to do that.'

She shook her head. 'No, I couldn't, Lee. I can't.'

'Nonsense! I've got a car waiting downstairs. Put a face on. I'm taking you out of here.'

It was early evening by the time Lee returned Niamh to her hotel. The square had reopened now, she noticed, windows in the Café Fluctuat Nec Mergitur had been replaced and the tables set out around it were full of young people sipping at pre-dinner aperitifs. A kind of defiant return to normality. It took no time, it seemed, for new skin to grow over fresh wounds, even if those wounds still ran deep beneath the surface. On the face of it, nothing had happened the night before. Parisian nightlife continued as it always does. Only the line of police vehicles and the armed officers who stood around in groups, still smoking, betrayed the nervousness of a city that had seen too many of its citizens violently murdered in these last few years.

The only thing that had changed from this same time the previous evening was that two people were dead. They would never play a part in the return to normalcy. Neither would Niamh. Her world could never be the same again.

Lee's driver dropped her off at the door of the Crowne Plaza. Lee kissed her and hugged her goodbye on the back seat and promised to call very soon. She slipped out into the warm evening air and made her way stiffly towards her own reflection. It divided in front of her to let her through and into the lobby.

He had taken her to lunch in a Michelin-starred restaurant where she had eaten very little, turning down all Lee's offers of champagne, only to watch him quaff a whole bottle himself and become more loquacious by the glass.

The rest of the afternoon had passed in a blur of Lee's drunkenness. A wine bar somewhere, all glass and steel, and disturbing reflections of Niamh everywhere she looked. Lee had ordered more wine, but Niamh could only bring herself to drink Badoit. Vincent Dancer, she remembered Lee saying as he raised his glass for the umpteenth time, but wasn't sure if that was the barman or the winemaker. It was as if he were drowning her sorrows for her.

He told her he wanted to use Ranish Tweed again for his next collection. Something different this time. Classier. An appeal to the country set. But she couldn't have cared less. Ranish meant only one thing to her. Ruairidh. And he was gone.

She slipped the electronic key in the door of her club room and was shocked as it swung open to reveal her bedroom filled with flowers. A profusion of roses, and colourful sprays of other seasonal blooms, in bouquets and arrangements set into hand-woven baskets. They were on the bed and the floor, on the settee and the dresser. Each had a card attached to it, every one of them signed by Lee. Which brought a tearful smile to her face. What on earth was she going to do with them?

She cleared a space on the bed and sat down, trying to think clearly. There were things she needed to do, that she had used the excuse of Lee simply to avoid. The immediate family knew about Ruairidh's death, and no doubt others were learning about it from the newspapers and the news bulletins which had been running all day on TV. But she knew it was her responsibility to let everyone else know. She would compose a standard, unemotional account of events and email it to her address list.

It took some minutes for her to summon the strength to stand up and retrieve her iPad from the safe.

It wasn't there. But she knew she'd put it safely away. Just before she had left with Lee. The safe seemed ominously dark in its emptiness at the bottom of the wardrobe. She stood up and looked around the room. Maybe she just wasn't thinking straight. Maybe she'd put it somewhere else after all. It was difficult to see with these flowers everywhere.

She called reception and asked for someone to come and take them away. Perhaps they could be donated to someone, or something. A hospital. An old folks home. The girl at reception said they would take care of it.

Then minutes later they were gone, and the room seemed very empty. But there was still no sign of the iPad. Now she noticed, too, that items of clothing and make-up that she had left on the dressing table had been moved. Perhaps by the people who had delivered the flowers. But she was starting to get spooked. The iPad was gone. Someone must have been in her room and taken it.

The phone rang and she shut her eyes in something close

to despair. She really didn't want to talk to anyone right now. But the insistent trill of it bored its way into her resolve and she eventually snatched the receiver. 'Yes?'

She waited. There was no response. Perhaps whoever was calling had already hung up. But, no. There was someone at the other end of the line. She could hear them breathing. Now she was alarmed.

'Hello? Who is this?' Still nothing. 'For God's sake!' And she slammed the receiver back in its cradle.

Now, for the very first time, it was fear that kicked in.

She locked and chained the door and went into the bathroom to grab a glass tooth mug. Then out again to the room, where she crouched to open the refrigerated minibar. The door pocket was jammed full of spirit miniatures. Whisky, gin, vodka . . . She tossed them all on to the bed, then sat down beside them. The temptation was strong to work her way through the lot until she lost consciousness. But she knew she would only regret it, and the only way she knew now to keep Ruairidh close was by feeling the pain of losing him.

With a wide arc of her arm she swept them all off the bed and on to the floor.

CHAPTER ELEVEN

Saturday morning and the twins were being particularly difficult. They were seven years old now, but Braque still found it hard to tell them apart. They knew it too, and took great delight in swapping clothes and pretending to be each other. Just to annoy her. And when finally she submitted to despair, they would own up and dissolve into fits of giggling laughter. Perhaps if she had spent more time with them they wouldn't find it so easy to make a fool of her.

Getting them ready for dance school was a nightmare. She had put their costumes through the washer earlier in the week, but forgotten to take them out of the drier. Now they were all crushed and the girls had been close to tears. Braque stood at the ironing board, still wearing her passion killer, spraying the skimpy little pink outfits with water and working the creases with a hot iron. But they remained stubbornly evident, and she could only hope that once they were on, the twins' body heat would do the rest.

Claire sat up on a high stool by the breakfast bar watching her with dismay. 'We can't wear those, *maman*!'

Braque looked up, harassed. She had stayed awake half the night going through the Vetrov–Macfarlane file. Interim reports back from forensics; a report from the first SDAT officers on the scene who had ruled out terrorism; background reports on Georgy Vetrov and Niamh Macfarlane; an initial autopsy report from the *médecin légiste* who had carried out a post-mortem examination of the human remains recovered from the vehicle – a short document.

'Go and brush your teeth,' she said.

'I already have.'

'No you haven't!'

'Have, too.'

'Claire . . .' The warning tone in her voice was clear.

The child laughed. '*Maman*, I'm Jacqui. Claire's in the bathroom brushing her teeth right now.'

'Well, get dressed, then.' She tossed a pink ballet outfit at the child. Jacqui examined it critically and pouted. 'Everyone'll laugh at us.'

'No they won't. Those creases will be gone by the time you get there.' Though she wasn't so sure. She raised her voice. 'Claire, get dressed! Madeleine will be here any minute.'

'Co-oming! But I'm Jacqui, *maman*!' the little voice chirruped from the other end of the apartment, and Braque glared at Claire.

Madeleine was Braque's best and oldest friend from school. Her daughter was six, born prematurely as the result of the condition called *placenta previa*, and Madeleine had been told that a second pregnancy would be unwise. She treated the twins like an extension of her own family and probably spent more time with them than Braque. She had offered to take the girls to dance class that morning, because the demands of the murder investigation meant that Braque had to work. Again.

It was all Braque could do to get the girls ready in time for Madeleine's arrival. Unlike Braque, Madeleine seemed always to be in total control of her life, and invariably arrived at the agreed hour.

Miraculously, Jacqui and Claire were dressed and ready, sitting at the table playing with their iPads when the doorbell sounded. They left the table in a clatter of excitement, and Braque's murder file went flying. Papers and notes all over the floor. Braque groaned inwardly. She would tidy up after they were gone.

The girls greeted Madeleine and little Patsy enthusiastically, and Madeleine kissed Braque on each cheek. She stood back and looked at her friend critically. 'Sylvie, you look terrible.'

Braque forced a smile. 'Thanks. That makes me feel so much better.'

Madeleine shook her head. 'You need to rethink your life, girl. You can't go on like this.'

Braque waved a dismissive hand. 'I know, I know, I know. I need to find a rich husband with a steady job and give up working altogether.' Which was not an inaccurate description of Madeleine's life. From which her friend recoiled as if slapped.

She masked her hurt. 'Life's all about choices, Sylvie. You're just making the wrong ones.' Then her smile returned as she looked down at the gaggle of girls running around her legs. 'Come on, girls. We don't want to be late.' A quick look flashed at Braque. 'See you later.'

And they were gone. Braque found herself breathing a deep sigh of relief.

One by one she retrieved all the spilled papers from the floor and reorganized them in her folder. Among them, the release documentation from the Procureur's office for the remains of the victims. Which seemed premature to Braque. But that wasn't her call.

She lingered instead over the report on Georgy Vetrov, and sat down to reread it. His military experience might, or might not, have equipped him for making the bomb himself – his role with Russian ground forces in Chechnya was unclear, and unlikely to be clarified by the Russians. He had worked, however, in IT for a French mobile phone company for several years, having acquired a computer science degree in Moscow before emigrating to France in 2003. What had brought him to France was also unclear, but there was little doubt that he would have been only too well equipped to access the Dark Web if he so chose, as well as possessing the skills to disguise the origin of an email.

His passport had not been recovered from the apartment he shared with Irina, but neither had it rung alarms at any international ports of departure. Although, assuming he had planned the car bomb well in advance, he would have had several hours to make good his escape by car. He could easily have crossed the border into Belgium before police had even placed his name on a suspect list. Within twenty-four hours he could have been back in Russia, where, in all likelihood, he would simply vanish below the radar never to reappear. Such were current relations with Moscow that cooperation from Russian law enforcement could not be relied upon.

He was gone.

The girl at reception in the Crowne Plaza glanced up at Braque, embarrassed, the phone still pressed to her ear. She looked down, then, at her computer screen as if something of great interest had caught her attention. Finally, she shrugged and hung up. 'I'm sorry there's no reply.'

Braque glanced towards the dining room, then at her watch. It was after eleven. 'I don't suppose she might be at breakfast?'

'Breakfast finished serving at ten.' She hesitated. 'The club room, perhaps.'

'Which is where?'

The girl indicated to her right. Just along the hall. 'But I'd need to let you in.'

Braque waited, but it was several long moments before the girl sighed and muttered to the young man at the club checkout desk that she would be right back. Braque followed her, then leaned into the club room as the girl held the door open for her. Several guests lifted heads from newspapers and coffees, but Niamh was not among them.

Back at the reception desk Braque said, 'And there's no way you can tell if she is in the hotel or not?'

'No.'

'Call the room again, then.'

The girl sighed theatrically and redialled Niamh's room. She was preparing to hang up and cock an insolent eyebrow in Braque's direction, when the phone was lifted at the other end. Her expression immediately changed. 'Madame Macfarlane, Lieutenant Braque is here to see you.'

There was something about the way she said Braque's name and rank that conveyed a hint of contempt. Braque rarely felt that her rank received the deference it merited. Although it had also occurred to her that it was perhaps not the rank but the gender behind it that failed to command respect.

The receptionist put her hand over the phone. 'She asks if you could give her a few minutes.'

'No. Tell her I'm on my way up now.'

Niamh looked dreadful when she opened the door to Lieutenant Braque. Her hair was a tangle of blonde curls, eye make-up smeared around her upper face, eyeliner clinging in coagulated clumps to her lashes. Tears and lack of sleep. The eyes themselves were bloodshot and gummy. Her skin was more grey than white, tinged green around the eyes.

She was fully dressed, but it was apparent from the

dishevelled nature of her clothes that she had not undressed since yesterday. A glance beyond her revealed to Braque a bed still made up, but rumpled as if slept on rather than in. Unopened bottles of spirit miniatures lay scattered about the floor. A pair of shoes kicked off and lying at odd angles at the foot of the bed.

'Come in.' Niamh held the door open and stood back listlessly.

Braque walked into the stale warmth of the room, and for the first time put herself in Niamh's shoes – the ones she had kicked off at some point during the night. How would she have reacted to the death of her own husband? Even if he was her ex. Or worse, if something had happened to one of the girls. That veneer of professional propriety that somehow got her through life would have dissolved into the mess that lay beneath it. She knew, without doubt, that she would simply have disintegrated. But none of that conveyed itself to Niamh. Braque unslung her leather satchel and placed it on the bed to open it. 'You are free to leave Paris, Madame.' She retrieved Niamh's passport and a handful of papers.

Niamh seemed startled by the news. 'What? Why? Have you caught the killer?'

'No.'

'But I'm no longer a suspect?'

Braque shrugged. 'You are free to leave Paris, that is all.'

Now Niamh was confused. 'You mean, I can go home, right? That's what you're saying?'

'Yes.'

Niamh walked unsteadily towards the window, absorbing the news. She swept the hair back from her face with both hands and turned to confront Braque. 'What about the email? Do you know who sent it?'

'No.'

Niamh sighed her exasperation. This monosyllabic French policewoman was infuriating. 'Someone came into my room and stole my iPad yesterday, did you know that?'

'No, I didn't.'

'I reported it to reception. And someone called me last night.' She nodded towards the bedside table. 'Phoned the room. And when I answered it there was nobody there. Well, there was, but they didn't speak. Wouldn't answer me when I asked who it was.'

Braque said, 'I'll speak to reception about the iPad.' She held out the papers she had taken from her satchel. 'The pathologist has finished with your husband's remains.' And she realized how cold she must sound. But how else to put it? 'As next of kin they will be released to you by a state-appointed undertaker in the Boulevard de Ménilmontant who will have prepared them for air transportation.' She hesitated. 'There are very strict rules that govern the shipment of bodies on commercial aircraft.'

Niamh felt sick. Reluctantly she took the sheaf of papers and glanced at the stamps and signatures on the half-dozen official documents which had been processed by a bureaucracy that would, no doubt, have applied the same degree of efficiency to ensuring the provenance of cheese.

'Under no circumstances,' said the lieutenant, 'are your husband's remains to be cremated. They are, and remain, evidence in a murder investigation.' Implicit in this was the warning that they could at any time in the future ask for Ruairidh, or what was left of him, to be disinterred.

Niamh said sullenly, 'You needn't worry about that. There is no crematorium on the islands.' And she recalled a decision that she and Ruairidh had made many years earlier which she had regretted ever since.

Braque saw a darkness cross her face, like the fleeting shadow cast by a cloud passing before the sun. A knock on the door broke the moment.

Niamh brushed past the policewoman to open it. A tall man in, perhaps, his late forties or early fifties stood awkwardly in the hall. Inclining to plumpness, his pale skin spattered with countless tiny freckles, his ginger hair going white at the temples and close-cropped across his skull.

'Oh my God, Donald!' Niamh threw her arms around him, and he stood holding her, emotional but embarrassed as she sobbed into his chest. 'I'm so glad you're here.'

His green eyes darted about in discomfort, and he offered a face to Braque that lay somewhere between acknowledgment and apology.

Niamh broke away and took his hand to lead him into the room, brushing away her tears. 'This is Ruairidh's big brother,

Donald.' She glanced at Braque. 'This is the police officer investigating the murder. I'm sorry, I've forgotten your name.'

'Lieutenant Braque.' Braque turned to Niamh. 'I have your contact details.' She laid a business card on top of the dressing table. 'If you need to contact me for any reason . . .'

Niamh nodded and said to Donald, 'They've just released the body. We can take him home now.'

CHAPTER TWELVE

The taxi had gone before Niamh realized that it had dropped them in the wrong street. They were in the Rue des Rondeaux instead of the Boulevard de Ménilmontant, which sounded very different to her. But perhaps the confusion had been with the name of the *pompes funèbres*. The Rue des Rondeaux was full of funeral parlours, but not the one they were looking for. All the streets around Père Lachaise, possibly the most famous cemetery in Paris, were full of shops offering funeral services. A map at the Porte Gambetta revealed that the Boulevard de Ménilmontant ran along the bottom end of the cemetery. The most direct route to it was through the cemetery itself.

This was where the rich, and the famous, came to rest their bones for eternity. Writers, musicians, singers, poets. Even the transient and relatively insignificant American pop star Jim Morrison of The Doors had found unexpected celebrity by being buried here.

Père Lachaise seemed shrouded in a silence incongruous in the heart of the city. Visitors walked its cobbled streets in hushed reverence, passing among the tombs and mausoleums as leaves fell prematurely from trees which had not yet surrendered their greenery to the colours of autumn. But it had been a long, hot summer, and the foliage was burned and bone-dry.

Niamh and Donald stopped briefly to look at a guide to the locations of all the famous names residing here in this city of the dead. Balzac and Maria Callas. Chopin and Edith Piaf. Marcel Proust, Gertrude Stein, Oscar Wilde. A roll-call of names celebrated across centuries of Western European culture. Ruairidh would not be joining them. He was just passing through.

From the main thoroughfare transecting the cemetery from east to west, they had a spectacular view out across the west side of Paris, towards the Seine and the Eiffel Tower. A view to die for.

Niamh and Donald had not spoken much since his arrival at the hotel. He had waited for her downstairs, booking their flights back to the island on his phone, while she showered and changed. And then in the taxi neither of them had felt inclined to talk. Her phone call to him in the middle of the night two days before had been traumatic enough. And Donald was typical of the post-war Scottish male. He would never show his emotions. Whatever he felt would be held inside him like a clenched fist, and prised free only with acute embarrassment.

Now he said, 'How are you holding up?'

She shrugged. 'As you see.'

He nodded. 'Mum and Dad are pretty devastated.' She turned to look at him. There was an odd anger, somehow, behind his words. Then he said, 'I'm so sorry, Niamh, that you're having to go through all this. It doesn't seem fair.'

'Nothing fair about death,' she said. 'Not much fair in life, either. We live it in the certainty that it will end. Just not how or where.' She paused. 'Ruairidh certainly never expected it to be here. Or now.'

They walked down the hill in silence for several minutes, before he said, 'I keep thinking about that poor girl in the car with him.'

Niamh turned, surprised. 'Really? Maybe it's bad of me. I haven't given her a single thought.'

Donald said, 'Do you really think he was having an affair with her?'

'I don't know what to think, Donald. I wouldn't have believed it of him. But the evidence is pretty damning. I'm just wondering if I'm ever going to be able to forgive him.'

He nodded gravely. 'I can understand that.' They were almost at the big stone-pillared gates when he said, 'For what it's worth, I don't believe it for a minute.'

As they passed from the place of the dead, back to the city of the living, Niamh glanced up at the inscription engraved on the stone pillar. She read it aloud, as she thought it pronounced. '*Spes illorum immortalitate plena est.*' And turned to Donald. 'You studied Latin, didn't you? What does it mean?'

'Their hope is full of immortality,' he said.

133

And Niamh thought how all her hopes had died along with Ruairidh. Immortality was an illusion.

Lacroux Frères, *Marbriers Funéraires*, stood opposite the walls of the cemetery, in the Boulevard de Ménilmontant. A classical stone façade with a modern glass frontage. Green neon lettering above the door read *Assistance Décès*, which Donald translated for Niamh as *Help with Death*.

'It's not death I need help with, it's life,' she said.

The funeral director was a small, wizened man whose bald pate was fringed with dyed black hair. His black moustache might well have been dyed, too. He wore a dark suit and an air of indifference. Death was his business. The currency of his daily life. And Niamh supposed you would have to build some kind of wall between the two, if only to protect yourself.

He examined her paperwork closely and nodded. 'Mmmm, yes,' he said in English. 'You have been expected.' He led them through a showroom of headstones and wreaths, of plastic flowers and urns, to an office in the back. He had yet more paperwork. This time for her to sign. She barely paused to glance at it all before committing her signature and date to the foot of the final page. Whatever it meant was of no consequence to her.

An assistant came in with a small box of polished wood and set it on the director's desk. It was about two feet long, twelve inches wide, and perhaps twelve deep. Niamh looked at it, perplexed, then at the funereal face of the director. He said, 'In cases like yours, we usually use this kind of box. It is favoured by parents who wish to bury a stillborn child. What remained of your husband after the explosion has been vacuum-packed in heat-sealed plastic pouches. The box itself is sealed and leakproof.' He lifted it to place inside a brown cardboard box, which his assistant closed and bound with plastic shipping straps.

Niamh's mouth was dry, unable to form words, even had she been able to compose them. She stared at the box on the table in front of her. This was the reality. All that was left of Ruairidh after the explosion. She'd had no idea what to expect, but it had not been this.

The funeral director slipped the paperwork into a clear plastic pouch which he taped to the outside of the box. 'Everything you will need for customs and airline security,' he said. His tone was flat, his face expressionless. And Niamh wanted to shout at him. To scream at him, 'This is my husband we're talking about! My Ruairidh. A living, loving sentient human being.' But all that would come were the tears that filled her eyes, and she wondered when they would ever stop.

She felt Donald take her hand and give it the gentlest squeeze.

The box sat between them in the back seat of the taxi, like the ghost of her dead husband. The remains of the biggest part of her life lay inside it, all that there was to take home with her to put in the ground. Donald stared silently from the window, and it was impossible to know what he was thinking, or feeling. Niamh turned her head to gaze sightlessly out of the other side of the car as the city spooled past in a grey blur.

All she wanted to do was curl up and die.

CHAPTER THIRTEEN

The sense of returning home had never been so bittersweet. As the 58-seater Saab 2000 banked beneath the cloud that lay low across the island, Niamh saw the old peat cuttings that scarred the moor, and the settlements that clung to the north side of Broad Bay – Tong and Back. Then as it banked again, the view south across the causeway at Sandwick to the Beasts of Holm. After twenty-four sleepless hours since collecting the box from the undertaker at Père Lachaise, the relief at being back was very nearly overwhelming. But only a part of her had returned from Paris, and she knew she would never feel complete again.

Donald had accompanied her on the journey, but apart from transactional exchanges had kept his own counsel. He sat beside her now in morose silence, his big hands folded together in his lap. She glanced at him and wondered what he was thinking. What he really felt. If he blamed her. As she was sure his parents would. And yet, since his arrival in Paris, he had offered her nothing but comfort. In his own quiet way. Someone less like Ruairidh would be hard to imagine, but she had been grateful for his company.

The airport was less busy on a Sunday. Not too long ago there had been no Sunday flights. Or ferries. She would have had to wait to bring Ruairidh home on the Monday morning, along with the Sunday papers.

The familiar blast of soft Hebridean air greeted her as she stepped down on to the runway, the smell of the sea never too far away. A glance across the airfield revealed a windsock at full stretch, inflated by the strong breeze that blew straight in off the moor from the west. Beyond reflections on tall windows that overlooked the apron, she saw pale anxious faces peering out from inside the terminal.

In the arrivals hall, curious eyes watched from a respectful distance as Niamh's mother held her in a tearful embrace. There would not be, she knew, a single soul on the island who was not aware of what had happened in Paris. She knew, too, that her mother's tears were for her, and not for Ruairidh. Oddly, her own eyes remained stubbornly dry.

Donald and her father shook hands awkwardly. Then as Niamh and her mother drew apart Donald said, 'Do you need a hand with . . .' His voice tailed off, and he found himself unable to finish the sentence.

Niamh shook her head vigorously. 'No, it's okay, Donald. Thank you so much for everything. I don't know how I'd have got through this without you.' He blushed with embarrassment and shuffled uneasily. 'I'll come and see your folks tomorrow to discuss . . .' It was Niamh's turn to find it hard to finish. She searched for a concluding word. 'Everything.'

He nodded, leaning past them to retrieve his overnight bag from the carousel. 'Mrs Murray. Mr Murray.' He presented them an uncomfortable smile, then headed off towards the exit where a friend was waiting to take him to Balanish.

Niamh's mother said, 'What's happened about the ...' Another sentence that was less than easy to finish. She composed herself. 'About Ruairidh.'

Right on cue the brown cardboard box with its shipping straps slipped through the plastic flaps from the loading bay beyond, and Mrs Murray followed her daughter's eyes. Her gasp was involuntary, and her hand flew to her mouth. Whatever she felt about Ruairidh, nothing had prepared her for the sight of that box. And Niamh remembered the first time that Ruairidh had come into her life.

CHAPTER FOURTEEN

I was just seven years old when I had my first encounter with death, and Ruairidh Macfarlane saved my life.

I was born three years before Margaret Thatcher became prime minister, and most of my growing up was done during the Eighties when she ruled our country with an iron fist in a velvet glove. I didn't know much about politics then. I was too young. But I learned to associate the name of Thatcher with economic depression and unemployment, growing up as I did in a community where barely a single soul had voted for her and unemployment was rife.

The population of Balanish was, and is, only a few hundred. When I was still a child most of our neighbours were crofters. They kept sheep on land divided into narrow strips, and grew mostly potatoes and root vegetables. There were a few fishermen, but even then there was no serious fishing being done from the west coast. A few folk worked in the mill at Carloway, and others had jobs with the council, like my dad, and travelled to and from Stornoway on a daily basis. Others were unemployed, and only the money from the buroo and subsistence crofting kept them going until better times.

I had, when I look back on it now, the best childhood I could have hoped for. Idyllic in many ways. I had two older brothers, Anndra and Uilleam. Anndra was the middle child. And maybe because the first child gets all the attention, and the girl gets all the adoration, he developed a mischievous streak. He knew I hated spiders, and I would find them everywhere. In my school bag, in my pockets, even in my bed. It gave him endless amusement.

But he and Uilleam were also ultra-protective. The merest hint of a threat to me, no matter who from, and they would rally round to stand resolute in my defence. Family came first. Tormenting Niamh second.

Sometimes, to escape their mischief, I would hide in the peat stack. My father was meticulous in the building of our stack. Long and beautifully rounded, a perfect herringbone construction to maximise drainage. But once it was built, it was the boys who were sent out to bring in the peats for the fire. And when I became old enough the peat-fetching was delegated to me. At an early age, I learned how to hollow out one end of it, hiding the peats I removed in the old blackhouse, and making myself a wee den inside that I could conceal by stuffing peats in the hole to block it. It was my secret place, though it had always disappeared by the end of the winter.

We had perfect freedom in those days to wander wherever the mood took us. As long as we were home in time for meals.

Looking back, it seems the world was a safer place then. I used to cycle three miles or more to the next village along the coast to play with Seonag. I went part of the way on the main road, and then over a rough dirt track that wound its way around the hills beyond the Doune Braes Hotel. And I went in all weathers.

It's a funny thing. Most folk on the mainland are obsessed by the weather. Because they get a fair amount of the good stuff, they don't take it well when it turns bad. On the island, the weather's almost always bad, and changes so fast that you don't really notice it. It just is.

I met Seonag on our first day at primary school and we sort of clicked. Her folks had a croft that ran right down to the shore, with a stunning view across East Loch Roag to Great Bernera. Her father owned a mobile shop, and he used to travel up and down all the villages on the west coast selling processed meats and root vegetables, fruit in season, and tinned goods and bread and sweeties for the kids. He also did some weaving, and we used to hear his old Hattersley clacking away in the shed at the top of the croft.

When Seonag came to our place we played in a small stone outbuilding, or *bothag* as we called it in Gaelic. *Houses* was the name of the game we indulged in there, furnishing it like a big doll's house that we could crawl in and out of, dragging our dollies with us, teaching them how to sit up straight and eat nicely.

It was where my father kept his tools, and we had to drag them all out to make space for our domestic fantasy. He would get mad at us and tell us to go amuse ourselves elsewhere. Which is when we'd head off to play down by the shore. I couldn't count the hours we spent down there trying to catch crabs in the pools left by the outgoing tide, or just sitting on the rocks with the stink of the kelp in our nostrils, watching the boats coming in and out of the harbour across the bay.

There was an old walled cemetery on the shore, by the foot of our croft, that hadn't been used for a hundred years or more. But it always reduced us to silence when we would pass by it, knowing that the spirits of the dead were kept somewhere inside it, behind its moss-smothered walls. I remember Seonag saying to me once in a hushed voice, 'Will they bury us in there when it's our turn to die?' I particularly remember that phrase – *our turn to die*. Somehow I'd never thought of it like that before, and maybe it was the first time I had ever fully understood that one day I, too, would die.

'Don't be silly,' I told her, a little shocked and trying to recover myself. 'They don't bury folk in there any more.' I remembered my grampa telling me that it was an accidental cemetery. In the old days they took the bodies by boat across the water to a burial ground on Little Bernera. But when the weather was too bad, they buried them right there, a stone's throw from the slipway.

'Where will we be buried, then?'

'Dalmore,' I said.

'On the beach?' Seonag was amazed.

'Don't be daft! There's a cemetery on the machair above the

beach. That's where everyone goes now.' Years later I always thought of Dalmore as being the valley of death. It was a place that took on a significance in my life that I could never have guessed at then.

Sundays were my least favourite day of the week. None of us was allowed out to play. I had friends whose parents made them sit in and read the bible all day, and although my folks were never that religious, we still got dragged off to midday service at the Free Church of Scotland. It sat right next door to the Church of Scotland. I never knew the difference then, and still don't today. Except that they present a shining example of how folk can never agree on anything. Even God.

You might think that with two churches Balanish was a big place. It wasn't. You could walk from one end of it to the other in a few minutes. Although folk who lived a mile or two out along the road in either direction would tell you that they were *balaniseachs* too. There was a primary school with two teachers, and when you completed your seventh year you went to Shawbost for the first two years of secondary. Then on to Stornoway. Either the Nicolson or Lews Castle. Right next door stood a community hall that was opened by Donnie 'Dotaman' Macleod, who was a kind of Gaelic TV celebrity and singer. Runrig, the Celtic rock band, played there once. I can remember sitting in class hearing them practise on the Friday afternoon before the concert that night.

There wasn't much to do in the evenings. The older kids ran a youth club in the hall, and there were usually discos on the Friday night, but me and Seonag were too young for that then. Too young, too, for the pleasures of cigarettes and alcohol enjoyed by village teenagers on wet, windy, winter nights huddled under the bridge, or in the bus shelter, smoking and drinking vodka straight from the bottle. We were dead jealous, and wishing away our lives till we were old enough to join them. Such were the heights of our childhood ambitions.

My favourite person when I was seven was my grampa. He was my dad's dad, but I never knew my dad's mother. She died before I was born. Grampa lived with us in the croft house. Or should I say, we lived with him. It was his house. His croft. Anndra and Uilleam shared a bed, and I slept on the settee in the front room. Grampa had his own room at the back. He had something about him, that old man. He knew stuff. About the world. And about people. He'd spent years at sea and was hard as nails. Even in his seventies. No man in his right mind would pick a fight with him, and yet I never heard him utter a word in anger, or say a bad thing about anyone.

I spent many a long hour sitting with him when he was weaving in the old blackhouse. I'd watch his hands, clasped together in front of him as if in prayer, as he worked the treadles with his feet. Big-knuckled hands spattered brown with age, and veins that stood out on them like ropes. And he would tell me tales of places I had never heard of, with exotic and sometimes daft-sounding names. Hong Kong. Shanghai. Abidjan. Dakar. 'Never judge a man,' he used to say to me, 'by the thickness of his wallet, but by the stoutness of his heart.' I had no idea what he meant then. But I do now.

My mother doted on that man. More than her own father, and maybe even her own husband. I look back sometimes now and wonder, had she known Grampa as a young man would she rather have married him than my dad?

When family came to stay, which they did quite often in the summer, they would sleep in an old caravan that we kept at the side of the house, lashed down to stop it from blowing away in the south-westerlies.

It was by the side of the caravan that Anndra found Grampa lying on the path one day. The old man had just returned from his daily walk through the village, and his cloth bunnet and his walking stick were lying on the slabs beside him.

Anndra came running into the house. 'Something's wrong with Grampa!' We were just gathering to sit down to dinner and so we all ran out on to the path. Immediately he saw his father, my dad turned and pushed me away. 'Get back in the house, lassie.' But it was too late. I'd already caught sight of him. Lying in a strangely unnatural position on the path. It was the first time I had seen a dead person, and although I'm sure he was still warm, his blue eyes were wide and staring at the sky, and it was clear that life had left him. It was his body alright, but it wasn't my grampa lying there. He was already somewhere else.

The coffin sat in the front porch for two days, and a procession of villagers came to see him lying in it and pay their last respects. Then the minister came and held a brief service in the back room, before the men closed up the coffin and carried it out to the waiting hearse. The days were long gone when they would have carried the coffin down to the slipway at the foot of our croft to sail him across to the island. And Dalmore was much too far to walk. So a hearse it was. But it was only the men who got into their cars to follow it.

'Are we not going, too?' I asked my mother.

'Women don't go to the grave,' she said simply.

'Why?'

'They just don't.' And to my knowledge, she never once went to visit him.

She left me, then, sitting in the front room, gazing out across the bay. It had been a miserable morning, the shadow of death reflected in the clouds that obscured the sun. Suddenly there was a break in the sky out over the bay, and sunlight fell in rings of silver on to the dull pewter of the sea, and with the rain that fell a rainbow arced itself perfectly across the harbour. To this day I like to think that was Grampa saying goodbye.

Even then it struck me as strange that I had not spilled a tear over the passing of the old man. Perhaps I didn't really understand the finality of death, or maybe it was just some kind of self-protection mechanism kicking in. But that was when I heard a soft sobbing coming from the back of the house, and I tiptoed out of the front room and down the hall. My mother was standing in the open door of my grampa's room, and beyond her I could see his bunnet and his stick laid out on the bed. It was the first time I had ever seen her cry. It wouldn't be the last.

That night I slept in his bed for the first time. His room was now mine. When I look back I think about how it might have spooked me to sleep where a dead man had lain. But I derived an odd comfort from it, and somehow felt that he was still and always there, looking out for me.

In my fancy, I might have imagined that it was Grampa doing just that when I nearly drowned a few months later. But, actually, it was Ruairidh who saved me.

It was the end of August, and nearly the whole village was up on the Pentland Road to bring home the peats that had been left to dry out there over the summer.

It is usual for the peats to be cut in the month of May, which is traditionally one of the driest of the year. Although in the Hebrides *dry* is a relative term. The peat is cut into slabs from a long bank of it, using a special spade or *tairsgear*, and tossed over on to the bog to dry. Every family has its own peat bank, established sometimes over generations. The deeper it is, and the blacker the peat you cut from the bottom of it, the hotter it burns. It costs nothing, except the blood, sweat and tears you spill to dig it out. This was how islanders had heated their homes for centuries, though these days it is more likely to be oil-fired central heating.

Some weeks after the first cutting you would go back to lift the peats, which had dried on the top side, and build them into tiny stacks. Two or three on the sides and one on the top, to let the air around them. Then before the end of the summer you would harvest the hard dry peats to take them home and build your big stack for the winter.

It had been a wet summer that year, though up on the moor the wind always does a good job of drying the peat. Finally, the clouds had blown off to the east, and there was a break in the weather. It was still and warm. A fine window for fetching the peats. We had one lorry in the village, a sort of communal vehicle that everyone shared, and this was its busiest time of year. Back and forth between Balanish and the peat banks up on the Pentland Road.

The Pentland is a single-track road that follows the contours of the moor all the way across from Stornoway to Carloway. At one point it divides, and a spur of it winds down the hill to Breasclete. It was originally intended as the route of a railway line that was never built, and it got its name from Lord Pentland, the Secretary of State for Scotland, who secured the funding for it. But it's not a road you would want to take if you were ever in a hurry to get anywhere.

I had rarely witnessed a sky so clear. You could see all the way down to the mountains of Harris in the south, cutting sharp purple contours against the blue. And to the west the Atlantic shimmered off into some impossibly distant horizon, beyond which lay Canada and America many thousands of miles away. But with the wind dropping, the midges were out in force, and so everyone was working hard and fast to get away from the wee biting beasts as fast as they could.

Seonag and I were still too young to be involved in the heavy work, and so we were running around like mad things making a nuisance of ourselves.

The Macfarlane peat bank was on the other side of the road, and Ruairidh's whole family was out carrying the peats to stack them at the roadside until they could load them on to the lorry when it was their turn. Ruairidh was a couple of years older than me, and although he was in my class – primary one to five – I had barely been aware of his existence. His big brother, Donald, had already gone to Shawbost. And the family lived at the north end of the village, so there wasn't much contact with us southerners.

It was our turn for the lorry, and Uilleam and Anndra were helping Mum and Dad pile on the peats while Seonag and I went running across the moor, jumping in puddles and getting ourselves soaked in spite of our wellies.

We had gone some way from the road when I spotted a makeshift path of old wooden pallets that someone had laid in the long distant past to access a particularly rich bank of peat. The bog was eternally sodden here, and if you weren't careful your wellies would get stuck and sucked into it and you'd lose them.

If I hadn't been so intoxicated by the childish pursuit of puddle jumping, it might have occurred to me that there was danger in leaping from pallet to pallet, feeling the rotten wood crack and break beneath my feet. But I was so intent on reaching the puddle at the end of it that I never stopped to think.

Seonag was infinitely more cautious. She had stopped and was shouting at me to come back. Which only spurred me on. My cotton summer dress was already soaked and spattered with slurry, and I was aware of my blonde curls streaming out behind me as I ran. Two, three more pallets and I could take off and leap feet-first into that puddle, which was sure to make the biggest splash. Bigger than any splash Seonag had made. I could see the blue of the sky reflected in its mirrored surface. And the anticipation of shattering its stillness, like breaking glass, was almost breathtaking.

I can still remember the thrill I felt as I launched myself off that final, disintegrating pallet, and then the shock of the cold as I dropped into the water like a stone, submerged right up to my neck. This was no puddle. It was a deep, water-filled trench, and immediately I could feel the mud beneath it claiming me.

You never think you will die, especially when you are young, but with a sudden clarity I realized that's exactly what was going to happen. It was all I could do to tip back my head and keep the water from going into my mouth.

I heard Seonag screaming, and then the voices of men shouting. I strained to turn my head and look back along the path of rotting pallets as my father and brothers tried to follow in my footsteps. But they were so much heavier than I was. The pallets would not support their weight. All around me the bog was impassable. Waterlogged after months of rain. It would have dragged a man down and drawn him under before he even realized there was no way back.

My father was up to his waist already and stuck fast. There was panic everywhere, more folk running from the adjoining peat banks. Someone threw a rope to my father and they managed to pull him out. But it was not long enough to reach me.

That was when I saw Ruairidh for the first time, standing silhouetted against the sky on an old abandoned peat bank. He was closer to me there than my father had managed, but still not close enough to reach me with the rope. He turned and ran off, and I looked up at the sky then, feeling the irresistible force of the bog, and knew that I was going under, and that no one would reach me before I drowned. I saw my grampa's eyes, wide and lifeless, and wondered what it felt like to be dead.

And then Ruairidh was back. He had Donald with him, and between them they were hefting three stout planks that they must have fetched from the back of the lorry. The rest of the men and several of the women appeared behind them. I could see my mother's eyes filled with fear, and the grim expression on my father's face as Ruairidh laid the first of the planks across the bog. I knew it would spread his weight, and that there was no one lighter who could do it except, perhaps, for Seonag. But she would have been hopeless.

After he had crawled about halfway along that first plank, Ruairidh turned to get the next one from Donald and manoeuvre it ahead of himself to extend the bridge. And then another to slide even further ahead as he inched forward on his hands and knees.

By the time he reached the end of the third plank he was within touching distance, lying flat on his belly. If he had slipped off, or if the plank had overturned, he'd have been sucked down into the bog himself. I felt his outstretched hands reach me below the water, slipping beneath my arms to stop me from going under. And I turned to look into his eyes. Deep blue Celtic eyes beneath a mop of black, curling hair. Eyes filled with concern. But if he was afraid, it was not evident. And for the first time I thought that maybe I wouldn't die after all.

Someone had found another rope, tying the two together to make it long enough to reach me. I saw my father throw the end of it out towards Ruairidh. It landed on the water beside me. Ruairidh let go with one hand and stretched out to get it, very nearly tipping himself off the plank in the process. I watched the concentration on his face, and the relief as his fingers closed around it and he was able to feed it below the water, beneath my arms and across my chest to tie in a knot at my back.

Then he let me go. I didn't want him to leave me as he worked his way back along the bridge of planks. But I felt the tension in the rope and knew that I would not go under now.

Slowly – it seemed interminable at the time – they pulled me from the water. The mud and peat beneath releasing me with great reluctance, but retaining my wellies for eternity. I clung to the rope with desperate muddy fingers as they hauled me finally to safety.

I suppose I had been expecting angry words of admonition. Adults grabbing me by the arm to shake me and tell me how bloody stupid I had been. But all I felt were arms of love and gratitude around me. Kisses planted on my wet, mud-streaked face as I wept inconsolably, soaked through now and shivering, even though there was still warmth in the sunshine. My over-whelming emotion was one of humiliation. That I had been so foolish, and had to be rescued by some boy! I knew how I must look, too. Slathered in glaur, my hair a tangle of peat and mud and bog water. And I glanced around to search out what I was sure would be the smug face of my rescuer. But among all the adults crowding around me Ruairidh was nowhere to be seen, and I found myself deeply disappointed.

'Come on, young lady,' my mother said, hoisting me up into her arms. 'It's home for you and into the bath.'

I sat up in the front of the lorry, shivering and sobbing with embarrassment, my mother on one side of me, the driver on the other. Back at the house I was stripped of my clothes and plunged into a hot bath, which stopped my shivering but failed to dissipate my shame.

Later, freshly dressed, my hair still wet and hanging in ropes, I stood at the front gate watching for the return of the lorry from the Pentland Moor. When finally it came, I saw Ruairidh and Donald sitting up in the back with the peats. As it passed our house I caught Ruairidh's eye. He seemed oddly embarrassed. I waved and mouthed *thank you*, before it disappeared around the curve of the road, heading north towards the Macfarlane croft.

School began again the following week for the autumn term, and that was the first time I had seen Ruairidh since he saved my life up at the peats. He was in primary five, and I was in three, so we were still in the same class. He sat at the foot of the row next to mine and I could barely concentrate on the lessons for watching him.

In the playground, too, I was distracted from the girls' games. Skipping and peever. Hardly able to tear my eyes away from the boys kicking their daft football around the playground.

Seonag was annoyed with me. Unaccountably angry. And it was a while before I realized she was jealous. 'Boys are so silly,' she said dismissively. 'Big and clumsy and stupid.'

As for Ruairidh, it was as if the incident on the Pentland Road had never happened. I never once caught him even glancing in my direction. And I began to think that perhaps he hated me.

It was another three years before I had the chance to pay him back for saving my life, even if it was in just a very small way.

He had paid me not the least attention in all that time, moving the following year into the class above mine, and the year after that to Shawbost. I caught the occasional glimpse of him getting on to the minibus that took the Balanish kids to secondary school, and from time to time at village functions, though I was still too young to go to the dances. When he had crawled out across those planks to rescue me from the bog up on the moor, he'd been quite a slight boy. Now he'd sprouted, and was taller than Anndra, who was a big lad himself.

He'd have been twelve years old by that time, and conscious then of how he looked. Clothes, it seemed, were important to him, and he always had a certain style about him. Narrow jeans, and designer T-shirts and short jackets that sat well on his square shoulders. His hair was cut short at the sides, but left long at the back in a mullet – as well as on top, where it piled up in waves and curls. I'm sure he was using some kind of gel to keep it all in place. I didn't know a single girl at school who didn't think he was gorgeous. Except, of course, for Seonag, who had retained her jealous contempt for him all this time.

As for me, I hated how I looked. I had freckles, and hair that I spent hours trying to straighten. It's funny how people with straight hair always want curls, and those with curly hair want it straight. I was never satisfied. I hadn't started my periods yet, and still had a boyish figure, and not even the beginnings of breasts. Unlike Seonag, who had already begun to develop hips and boobs, and looked years older than me. She had the most stunning red hair with a porcelain complexion, and was morphing into the kind of beauty that was starting to turn heads in the playground.

So if I was going to attract Ruairidh's attention at all, I was going to have to find other ways of doing it.

It was approaching Halloween. Kids on the mainland,

on October 31st, would dress up as pirates and fairies and Obi-Wan Kenobi and go out guising. But Lewis boys were up to something quite different. While the girls would gather in community and village halls, dancing and playing music and dooking for apples, the boys were out stealing gates.

I have no idea how it all started, but it was and is an island tradition. The boys would go out in gangs on Halloween to steal and hide as many croft gates as they could. The object of the exercise, it appeared, was to amuse the boys and annoy the owners. And if sheep got out, so much the better.

Of course, the boys got hell each year from their fathers. Fathers who had done the selfsame thing when they were young. And it would always be the same victims, too. Those crofters who reacted the most, shouting and chasing the boys. That, apparently, made it all much more fun.

There was one eccentric old *bodach* in Balanish who never failed to rise to the bait, and he had became the focus of attention every Halloween. His was the prize gate. His name was spelled E-a-c-h-a-n. But you have to know how that is pronounced in Gaelic to understand his nickname. The *ea* is pronounced *ya*, so the name is pronounced *yachan*. And everyone knew him as Yankee Eachan.

In the late Forties, after the war, Yankee Eachan had gone off to America in search of work. He left the island speaking only Gaelic, and when he returned a few years later, having picked up only a few words of English, he pronounced them with a broad American accent. Hence the nickname.

Now in his late sixties, he had a short temper and a foul mouth, despite being a respected elder of the church. Each year, as soon as he realized what was happening, he would be at his front door, spittle gathering about his lips as he shouted, 'Gorram sumbitch!' Followed by the Gaelic, '*Fhalbh a thigh an Diabhaill!*' Which translated literally as 'Go to the Devil's house!' Or in the vernacular as 'Go to hell!' And it never failed to amuse the boys, invariably producing the biggest laugh of the night. All the more because Yankee Eachan never seemed to have any recollection of the exact same thing happening the year before. He always gave chase, and on those rare occasions when he actually caught one of the boys he would give him a good smack round the side of the head for his trouble.

Both Anndra and Uilleam were now old enough to join the other village boys on the annual gate-stealing escapade, and that year I begged them to take me along because I knew that Ruairidh would be among them.

But they were scornful. Girls didn't go stealing gates. That was boys' work. Why didn't I go to the Halloween party in the community hall with the rest of the lassies? But I was determined not to. And if I couldn't actually tag along with the boys, then I was going to find myself a good vantage point and watch it all from a discreet distance.

The land rose quite steeply behind the church, before levelling out across the moor, and so I climbed up on to the hill that Halloween in order to see what was going on, and maybe catch a glimpse of Ruairidh.

It was a fine dry night, with a stiff breeze blowing in off the loch, and I sat cross-legged up there on my own with the wind tugging at my hair and my anorak, and watched as the drama of the evening unfolded below.

The boys divided themselves into two groups. One was to provide a distraction, while the other moved in to steal the gates. The distraction usually comprised a banger stuffed into the lock of a croft-house door. Once lit, the distraction team retreated to watch from a position of safety as the banger exploded and the startled crofter appeared in his doorway. The boys would then run off, encouraging the crofter to give chase. Which is when the second team would move in to lift the croft gate from its hinges and smuggle it away to hide someplace where it wouldn't immediately be found.

Stupid! But that's how it was.

The boys would usually manage to steal anything up to a dozen gates before darkness brought an end to the game. That night, watching from the hill behind the church, I saw them take five gates before they reached Yankee Eachan's place.

Ruairidh was with the gate stealers, about six or seven of them, and I saw them crouching behind the remains of an old blackhouse as the distraction team moved towards Yankee Eachan's front door. Most of them huddled by the fence as one brave soul crept up on the house to plant and light a banger at the front door. It went off with a crack that resonated around the hills, even before the boy who had lit the fuse was able to rejoin the others.

The door flew open almost at once, and Yankee Eachan stood there, a thick leather belt with a heavy buckle dangling from his hand. This year he was ready for them.

'Gorram sumbitch!' he roared into the night. He was a big man. Built, as they say, like a brick shit house after years of manual labour. There was no doubting that if he caught you he would do you some damage. He dragged his old tweed bunnet over his bald head, and charged down the steps towards the boys by the fence. Their initial laughter dissolved quickly into alarm, and they hared off around the side of his house. The old man chased after them, swinging the belt around his head.

When they had disappeared from view, I saw the stealers slip out from the cover of the ruined blackhouse and run across the field to lift Yankee Eachan's gate from its hinges. It was a galvanized tube gate, filled in with wire, so there wasn't much weight in it. But no sooner had they removed it from its gate post, than Yankee Eachan reappeared from behind the house. He had only pretended to give chase to the distractors, waiting instead until the gate thieves showed themselves. Now he came charging towards them, cursing and swearing in Gaelic, still swinging his belt through the air.

I stood up, startled, thinking he was going to catch them.

There was blind panic among the boys. A bunch of them detached from the others and took off across the croft, heading down towards the shore. There were only two boys left with the gate. Ruairidh, and a lad with acne that everyone called

Spotty. Carrying it between them, they starting running along the road towards the Free Church.

But even as they reached it I saw Ruairidh stumble and fall. He had gone over on his ankle. And although he was up again in a flash, I could see that he was limping heavily.

They ran around the side of the church, out of sight of their pursuer, stopping only briefly to heft the gate up on to the roof of a workers' Portakabin where construction was under way on a new toilet block for the church. And then they split up. Spotty sprinted away past the lights of the community hall, where the girls were still inside playing music and fantasizing about boys, while Ruairidh limped around the back of the Church of Scotland next door and headed off down a path that would take him past my house.

I could see he was in distress, almost dragging his twisted ankle behind him. His stertorous breathing seemed to fill the night air. I saw Yankee Eachan come around the church, and knew he could see Spotty disappearing beyond the curve of the road. There was no chance that he would ever catch him.

Then he came round the back and saw Ruairidh hirpling away down the path. It was no stretch of the imagination to think that the old man might catch him quite easily. But he hesitated, looking around for a moment, and I knew that he was wondering where the gate had gone. But it was quite safely out of sight on top of the Portakabin. So he started after Ruairidh with another mouthful of profanity.

That's when I had an idea, and went hurtling down the

hillside, arms windmilling to stop me from falling. Coming from the hill I could cut across the curve of the path and get to my house before either of them.

I reached the gate just as Ruairidh was approaching, and I waved to him from behind the caravan, calling his name as loudly as I dared without alerting my folks inside the house. He seemed startled to see me, and stopped dead, glancing back to see Yankee Eachan approaching as fast as a man in his late sixties could. 'Come on!' I urged him, and signalled him to follow me around the back of the house. I was at the peat stack before he turned the corner, pulling out peats as fast as I could to open up the entrance to my secret place. 'Get in!'

He looked at me as if I was mad. 'In where?'

'The peat stack. There's a wee den inside.'

The sound of old Yankee Eachan approaching on the path made his mind up for him, and he clambered quickly inside, squeezing himself into a space that I had made only for myself. It was a tight fit, and he couldn't move once he was in. I quickly piled the peats I had pulled out back into the hole and sealed it up. And just for good measure swung an old gate lying at an angle against the gable of the house, to lean up against the end of the stack. I even had time to dwell, if only for a moment, on the irony of it.

Yankee Eachan came puffing around the corner and stopped in his tracks when he saw me there. 'Where'd that boy go!' he shouted.

'What boy?' I said.

'Don't you play the innocent with me, young lady. I saw him come around the back of your house.'

'The light's not so good, Mr Macrae,' I told him. 'Your eyes must have deceived you.' I'd read that in a book at school – about eyes deceiving you – and it seemed like the perfect use of it.

But it only seemed to infuriate him. He looked at me as if I were the devil incarnate. 'Don't mess with me, you wee bugger. You think I came up the Mississippi in a bubble? Where'd he go?'

The back door of our house flew open, and a slab of yellow light fell out across the back garden, the shadow of my father standing right in the middle of it.

'What's going on here?' he bellowed.

'Your wee girl's hiding a boy who stole my gate,' Yankee Eachan said indignantly.

'What boy?'

'I've no idea what his name is.'

My father gasped his irritation. 'No I mean, where is he, this boy? Where's the gate he took? And where would my wee lassie be hiding them?'

Yankee Eachan was at a loss. He looked around. It was evident that there was no boy and no gate, except for the one leaning against the peat stack. My father looked at the belt dangling from the old man's hand.

'And what were you going to do with that, might I ask?'

'Give the bugger a good leathering.'

'Watch your language in front of the lassie. And you a church elder, too.' He snatched the belt from Eachan's hand and examined it. 'You'd do some damage with this. For heaven's sake, man, it's just a bit of fun. It happens every year. You know that!'

'Aye, and I'll be out half the night gathering my bloody sheep.' He snatched his belt back. 'Gorram sumbitch!' And he stomped off.

When he had gone my father turned and gave me a dangerous look. 'Where is he?' he said.

'Who?'

'Don't play the innocent with me, young lady!' The same expression that Yankee Eachan had used. I put on my most earnest face.

'Honest, Dad, I've no idea. I'm just back from a walk up on the hill.'

'I thought you were going to the Halloween party.'

'Nah . . .' I scuffed my toe on the path. 'Couldn't be bothered this year.'

He held the door wide. 'Time you were in anyway. It's getting dark.'

I had no choice but to go inside. My father hesitated for a few moments on the step, casting an eagle eye all around the garden in the twilight, before banging the door shut.

I spent a restless and frustrating evening then, trying to think of excuses why I should go out into the back garden. But I couldn't think of any that wouldn't arouse suspicion. We had plenty of peats in for the night, so that wasn't an option.

Ruairidh was jammed tight into the peat stack, and wouldn't be able to get out without my help, and I couldn't stop thinking of him stuck in there, and hating me for abandoning him. What if he needed the toilet? It didn't bear thinking about.

Eventually my folks packed me off to bed, and I lay wide awake in the dark, fully dressed beneath the covers. I heard Anndra and Uilleam coming back, and could hear my father cross-examining them about who it was who had stolen Yankee Eachan's gate. But they were no clypes, my brothers, and so no one ever knew that it was Ruairidh.

Eventually, my brothers went to bed. And I lay for what seemed like a further eternity before I heard my parents' bedroom door shutting. I forced myself to wait a good fifteen or twenty minutes beyond that before I eased open my bedroom window and dropped down into the back garden.

There was a good moon out, so I had plenty of light to see by as I carefully swung the gate off the stack and peeled away the peats one by one. I felt the heat of Ruairidh's body in the air that greeted me as I opened up the hole to the hiding place inside.

'What the fuck?' I heard him whisper. 'Where the hell have you been?'

'I had to wait till everyone was in bed,' I whispered back at him. Surely he would understand?

He scrambled out into the dark, stretching painfully stiff muscles that had all but gone into cramp. I saw the dark patch around the crotch of his jeans and realized he had wet himself.

He turned and glared at me, humiliation writ large all over his face. 'Find someone else to rescue next time,' he hissed. And I thought what an ungrateful pig he was.

I had ruined any chance I might have had with him. But right then I didn't care if I never saw him again for the rest of my life.

It didn't take long for word to spread around the village that Yankee Eachan had lost his gate and couldn't find it anywhere. Over the next few days he was to be seen tramping around the village, and from croft to croft, searching for it. Stories of how he had pursued the boys with a belt and buckle, intent on doing them harm, meant that no one had much sympathy for him. As my dad had said, it was just a bit of fun after all.

The story reached its conclusion on the sabbath.

Yankee Eachan always sat up in the balcony during services at the Free Church, despite his position as an elder. It was a tradition. Or, at least, his tradition. Perhaps he felt closer to God up there. Nobody knew. But on his way down the stairs at the end of the service, he passed a window that looked out on to the building work for the new toilet block, and the roof of the workmen's Portakabin. And there, plain as day, lay his gate. He stopped on the stairs and glared at it through the window. His voice reverberated all around the church. 'Gorram sumbitch!'

CHAPTER FIFTEEN

Her father fetched a trolley and lifted the two suitcases Niamh had brought back with her on to it. And then, with evident reluctance, as if it might somehow be contaminated, retrieved the plain cardboard box with the shipping straps from the carousel and placed it on top of them.

As they stepped from the terminal building, the wind blew Niamh's hair into her eyes. She swept it back with both hands to scan the car park. It was less than a week since they had flown out, and yet she had no recollection of where Ruairidh had left the Jeep.

Then she spotted it. He had parked the 4×4 two rows back. As they reached the vehicle, sunlight chased the shadow of a broken cloud across the tarmac and then vanished again in a moment. It felt strange to be opening up the SUV without him. Her father lifted everything from the trolley into the boot, and Niamh slipped into the driver's seat. She had to slide it forward to reach the pedals, and bring the back more upright. A change of the settings Ruairidh had needed for his longer legs. She adjusted the mirror. And every little thing she changed felt like losing one more piece of him.

Her parents stood by the open door and her mother said, 'You'll just follow us back to Balanish, then? Or would you like me to come with you?'

Niamh shook her head. 'I'm going home, Mum.'

Her mother looked surprised. 'Balanish *is* your home.'

'No. Taigh 'an Fiosaich is my home. The house Ruairidh and I built.'

Her mother drew in her chin, disapproval colouring her face. 'I still don't understand why he made you build a house way out there on the edge of the earth.'

'Maybe it was to get away from you.' The words were out of Niamh's mouth before she could stop herself, and she immediately regretted them. She added quickly, 'When it feels like the whole world is against you – *my* family, *his* family – you retreat into each other. We found peace at Taigh 'an Fiosaich. All our memories are there. And that's all I have left of him.'

The drive up the west coast to Ness in the north was a painful one. It was a journey she and Ruairidh had made together countless times since building their house out on the remote headland of Cellar Head, beyond the old ruined settlement of Bilascleiter.

The success of Ranish had put money in their hands for the first time, and they had decided to build their home in one of the remotest corners of the island. There had been more than a little truth in the words Niamh had spoken in haste to her mother. *Maybe it was to get away from you.* In fact it had been to get away from everyone. From the claustrophobic family atmosphere of the Macfarlane croft where the house they had restored in the early years of their marriage was now the headquarters of the company. To avoid the disapproval of Niamh's parents. And the gossip, sometimes malicious, that so characterized the community of Balanish. And although never acknowledged, it was also an attempt to escape the event that had driven so sharp a wedge between their two families. An event they had not once discussed in all their years together.

A hardcore track, pitted and scarred by time and weather, had already led south across the moor, along the east coast to the gathering of shielings at Cuishader. They had repaired and extended it, providing access to the headland for the building of the house.

So what if it was a fifty-minute commute south to Balanish? Folk on the mainland would think nothing of that. And while they would sit in lines of traffic, breathing in the pollution that belched from countless exhausts, Niamh and Ruairidh would see the sun rising pale in the east, or setting blood-red in the west. In all the summer daylight hours, when the sun barely ever set, the vistas offered by the drive up and down the west coast were incomparable. The mountains of Uig and Harris as they headed south. The Northern Lights as they returned late to Ness. The spring and summer flowers that turned the winter-dead moor into a sea of shimmering colour. Sunshine and rain spawning rainbows in profusion. On some days, it seemed, there was one around every curve of the road. Even in winter, under angry skies, Atlantic gales battered the cliffs which had stood resolute against the forces of the ocean since the beginning of time. Spume rising hundreds of feet into the air, white against leaden cloud. Before dispersing in a moment to salt the machair and saturate the bog.

Today there was very little sun to light Niamh's heart on this drive north. The equinoctial gales were late this year and the sky lay low on the island, grey and featureless. In this light, every village on the road seemed drab and depressing. Harled houses huddled together in treeless clusters, exposed to the full force of the weather. A profusion of Protestant churches feeding the faith of a hardy people who had put down their roots in this desolate place thousands of years before. And although it was always the desire of the young to leave, to get away, it seemed programmed somehow into their DNA that in time they would come back. If not them, then their children, or their children's children. In truth, there was no escaping the island. It was in your blood.

At Cross, in the shadow of the church that dominated the skyline, Niamh turned on to the road to Skigersta, cutting off the northern tip of the island and heading east. From Skigersta the track south bumped and rolled its way across several miles of peat-scarred bog to the retreat she had built with her dead husband.

There was a spattering of rain as she drove down the slope

past the old tin huts and caravans at Cuishader where crofters used to bring their beasts to graze during the summer months, allowing crops to grow on the crofts back home. Someone had even brought an old bus out here as shelter against the elements. *Maclennan Coaches* was barely visible now in red lettering along one side of it, almost obliterated by the weather. One wheel, still visible, lay at an odd angle. Beyond the shielings, to the east, a deep cleft in the cliffs cut right down to the shore, where a small sandy cove was hidden from view.

Niamh was forced to slow down to traverse the concrete slab laid over the stream that ran down from the Galson moor. In heavy rain the bridge would be submerged by this tiny waterway in spate, and crossing it could be treacherous.

On the other side the track rose steeply again, until Niamh had a clear, unobstructed view south across the moor towards the great fingers of gneiss that reached out into the Minch, as if holding on to it for dear life.

Her Jeep lurched and rattled over the rutted hardcore, swinging around the ancient village of Bilascleiter. All that remained of it now were the footings of a dozen old blackhouses, and a solitary shieling of green-painted corrugated iron with a rust-red and silver tin roof.

Now she could see, sitting out on the promontory ahead, the ruins of the house built there more than a century before by a man from Ness, John Nicolson – or Iain Fiosaich in Gaelic. Known simply as Taigh 'an Fiosaich, the house of Nicolson, only the gable ends still stood. The broken-down remnants of side walls revealed empty spaces where windows had once looked out over the edge of the cliffs. Two hundred feet of granite and gneiss that gave on to one of the most spectacular views anywhere on the island.

It was the remote beauty of this place that had tempted Niamh and Ruairidh to make their home here. They had built a state-of-the-art house on the near promontory, looking across towards Taigh 'an Fiosaich. Beyond it stood the ruined church where Nicolson had once preached his own brand of baptist theology to the crofters who came out here for the summer.

The house that she and Ruairidh built had been designed to withstand the gales that blew in off the Minch or down from the Arctic. Stone and brick, thickly insulated to retain the warmth from a geothermal ground source heat pump sunk deep into the nearby bog. Windows were triple-glazed, cutting down on noise as well as keeping in heat. The whole house was finished to a high anti-corrosion spec, to counteract the constant assault of the sea that would rise on stormy days in salt-filled spray from the waves that broke over the rocks below.

There were freshwater springs all around, and so supplying water to the house had not been a problem. Electricity had presented a greater challenge. They had been forced to pay for the laying of a cable from Skigersta, providing a power supply that proved unreliable in stormy weather. It had been Ruairidh's idea to install their own wind turbines as a backup. There were two of them at the far side of the house. They were supposed to kick in when the mains power failed, but it rarely worked out like that. The power supply was, at best, erratic. Television, internet and mobile-phone signals were provided by satellite, a huge dish firmly bolted to a concrete platform behind the house.

Beyond that was Ruairidh's workshop, where he had installed his own Hattersley loom, spending hours in there, weaving, thinking, singing along to the music he loved to listen to as he worked.

Both buildings were single-storey, presenting a low profile and minimum resistance to the incoming weather.

Niamh drew her Jeep into the gravelled parking area at the front of the house. The main door was set into the south curve of the building, facing away from the prevailing weather, although out here the weather could come from anywhere at any time. She took her suitcase out of the back, and looked for a long time at Ruairidh's case, and the brown cardboard box, before deciding that she would bring them in later. After closing the tailgate she carried her case to the front door. She paused for a moment before pushing down the handle and swinging the door into the house, knowing how painful it was going to be to walk in here without him. Of course, the door was not locked, just as they had left it. Just as they always left it. Most people on the island never thought to lock their doors. And out here there was even less reason to turn the key in the lock. Niamh smiled as she remembered Ruairidh telling her about an uncle who had sold his house after twenty-five years.

When the new owners asked for the keys he realized he didn't have any. He had never once locked the door in all that time.

She closed the door behind her, shutting out the sound of the wind. In here a thick silence permeated the house, a silence only invaded from the outside by the worst of storms. Light fell into a wide hallway from Velux windows set into the angle of the roof. Bedrooms to left and right were served by en suite bathrooms. At the far end, the hall opened out into the centrepiece of the house – a semicircular open-plan room built around a curvature of enormous windows that looked out over the cliffs to the ocean. The architect had been concerned by the size of the windows that Niamh and Ruairidh demanded. In the end he had come up with a design that divided the view into five still-life paintings which together framed the panorama. Except that these paintings were never still. They spooled an ever-changing movie of seascape illuminated by sunlight or moonlight, dramatized by a sky that sometimes raged, sometimes smiled, and often glowered. On clear days you could see the mountains of the mainland, so close you could almost touch them. Three layers of reinforced glass protected the interior from whatever the outside world might throw at it physically, but let in light and sea and sky to fill the eyes.

On one side, a long breakfast bar divided the living and dining areas from the kitchen. On the other, a settee and armchairs gathered themselves around two of the five windows, as if around giant TV screens. The dining table itself was set into a sunken area of floor, with a view straight out over the sea through two windows that rose from floor to ceiling.

To the side of the kitchen a passage led off to Niamh's office. Her private and personal workspace, from which she conjured orders for Ranish from around the world, an arc of cluttered desk space with its own view south-east across the Minch.

Niamh took the suitcase into their bedroom and heaved it on to the bed. She would open it later. For now she looked around the plain white walls that they had hung with the paintings and framed photographs they had chosen together on jaunts around Lewis and Harris, chasing down tiny galleries at the end of impossibly narrow single-track roads.

She walked out into the big room and stood gazing for several long moments at the view that she and Ruairidh had so often shared, marvelling at the changing light and mood of the world beyond. His reading glasses sat on the coffee table where he'd left them. A scarf lay draped over one of the armchairs. Slippers were pushed beneath his seat at the dining table. He was everywhere in here. Even the familiar scent of his aftershave lingered faintly in the still air.

There was an ache in Niamh's throat, her eyes dry and stinging. She went to the fridge and brought out a bottle of Olivier Leflaive burgundy, Les Sétilles, brought back from a visit to Puligny-Montrachet during a holiday the previous year, when they had met Olivier himself. The eighteenth generation of his family to make wine. They had savoured each of the bottles, and this was the last, destined to be drunk only by

Niamh. But not now, she decided. She did not want to filter her memories through alcohol, and she poured herself, instead, a large tumbler of sparkling water.

It misted the glass as she poured, then she closed her eyes as she sipped it and remembered the touch of Ruairidh's lips on hers. The thrill of that first time; the last time lost in a cloud of mourning and shattered memories. She had read in books, and heard people speak of breaking hearts. She'd always thought it a facile metaphor. Only now did she fully under-stand how it felt. As if a piece of her heart had been broken off. And even if she could find it knew she could never put it back. She recalled the awful image of Jackie Kennedy clawing her way across the rear of the car that fateful day in Dallas, trying to catch the pieces of her husband's brain detached by Oswald's bullet. As all the king's horses and all the king's men had found out, there were some things you could never put together again.

It was late afternoon and the wind had dropped when Niamh crossed the gravel to Ruairidh's loom shed. The cloud had thinned and was starting to break up, sending short and long shards of sunlight darting across the moor, lingering sometimes in pools and purple patches where the heather was still in bloom. The Minch seemed at peace with itself, eddying in a series of white rings around hidden rocks just below the cliffs.

Ruairidh had contrived his own view, looking south along the line of the coast, each successive promontory edged in the white foam that traced every contour. Two large windows facing his loom, so that he could sit and watch the sea in all its sulks and piques, its dark green anger and rolling liquid silver.

He had wanted to recreate the sense of a real loom shed, leaving the roof space open and divided by wooden beams. Buoys and green fishing net and loops of yarn hung from nails driven into the wood. There was a well-worn workbench set against the wall behind him, strewn with all manner of needles and cutting tools. The older pattern codes pinned to the wall above it had faded in the sunlight.

The computer where he worked on new designs, exchanging ideas with his mother, sat on a work station in the corner. From here, too, he managed the twenty or more weavers they now had working for them. A battery backup kept it running even during power cuts. A screensaver that bled shots of the island one into the other was still animating his screen.

Sunshine angling in the windows from the south-west fell on his scarred old acoustic guitar hanging on the wall. She had not heard him play it for such a long time, but still remembered with nostalgia those early days when he would serenade her on the beach, sparks rising into the night from the dying embers of a driftwood fire.

She could hardly bear to be here, his presence powerful and compelling. And she thought it extraordinary how people left traces, both physical and spiritual, so long after they had gone. She half-expected him to come through the door at any moment, full of excitement about a new pattern, or wanting her to listen to the latest download of a favourite musician. Ed Sheeran. John Mayer. Eric Clapton.

She crossed the room, squeezing past the loom where an unfinished length of cloth stretched across hundreds of threads, only waiting for the weaver to return to his pedals and send the shuttle carrying weft threads back and forth to finish the job. She switched on his sound system. And the shed was suddenly filled with the strains of a song that brought instant tears to her eyes. Strings holding a long, single note, then the repeated haunting refrain of piano and harp, before the pure falsetto voice of the singer raised goosebumps on her back and arms.

It was a song by a band called Sleeping at Last that they had listened to again and again. She recalled the night, not that long ago, when they had sat in the dark through in the well of the sitting room, watching a lightning storm perform for them out over the Minch. 'I'll Keep You Safe' played at full volume, an accompaniment to the storm, and he had put his arm around her shoulder, drawing her close and whispering, 'Whatever happens, my lovely girl, I'll always be there for you. I'll keep you safe, no matter what.'

Tears burned her cheeks. And she shouted at the empty loom seat, 'You lied to me, Ruairidh. You lied! How can you keep me safe now?' She switched it off, mid-refrain, and the silence that followed was almost startling.

She had no idea what to do. Now or ever. No idea how to survive in this world without him. She ran a finger across the strings on his guitar, but they sounded discordant, out of tune.

For the longest time she stood then, gazing from the window, before turning finally to sit down at his computer. She brushed the trackpad with her fingertips and banished the screensaver. His finder screen was a mess of icons. A reflection of the man. Somehow always able to contrive order from chaos. A red dot alerted her to the presence of fifty-six unread emails in his mailer. She opened it up to run an eye, almost unseeing, over a long list of emails from weavers and suppliers, a handful of spam circulars.

Then, from somewhere, came the memory of Ruairidh receiving an email on the RER as they travelled in a crowded coach from PV to Paris the day he died. Something in his face had made her ask him about it when finally they had reached their stop. He had dismissed it as 'nothing'. And now she looked through his in-box. Mail was synchronized between his phone, iPad and computer. So it was bound to be here. She scrolled back to the previous Thursday. Was it really only three days? And there it was. An email received while they were still on the train. And her blood turned cold, as if someone had just injected ice into her veins. It was from *well wisher*, and titled simply, *Goodbye*. The message beneath it read, *See you in hell*.

She had left the door to the shed lying open, and was startled now to hear the crunch of tyres on gravel outside. She was still in shock over those words that someone had sent to Ruairidh just hours before he was killed. *See you in hell*. From *well wisher*. The same person who had warned Niamh that he was having an affair with Irina. The meaning, it seemed to her, was clear. Whoever had sent the mail knew he was going to die. *Well wisher* was his killer.

Her heart was pushing up into her throat, and she heard the blood pulsing in her ears like a speeded-up soundtrack of the sea.

'Hello?' A woman's voice.

Niamh crossed quickly to the open door and saw a familiar red SUV parked next to the Jeep. Seonag had the door of the house open and was leaning in.

'Niamh, are you there?'

'Over here,' Niamh called and Seonag turned, momentarily startled. Then she almost ran across the chippings to throw her arms around her oldest friend, face wet with tears before she even reached her. Niamh responded to the soft comfort and warmth of her friend's embrace, dropping her head to Seonag's shoulder to let her own tears flow. And they stood like that for a very long time, Seonag's fingers spread across the back of Niamh's head and neck, like a mother holding her child.

When finally they broke apart, Seonag's face was shining wet. Forty years old and the years had been kind to her. She had never fully lost the weight put on during two pregnancies, and in a strange way it stood her in good stead now. Her face was full and soft and unlined, fresh and pretty as it had always been. Her hair was still as vibrantly red as in childhood, green eyes filled now with sadness and sympathy.

She shook her head. 'There are no words, Niamh. I'm not

even going to try. I just couldn't bear the thought of you up here all on your own. I've brought wine and food. I'm going to cook for you, even if you don't feel like eating. And we're going to get a little drunk. And . . .' She hesitated. 'And if you can bear to talk, I'm here to listen.'

Niamh shut the door of Ruairidh's shed behind her, and Seonag took her hand to lead her across the courtyard to the house. Inside, Seonag spotted the unopened bottle of wine on the breakfast bar. She forced a smile. 'You must have known I was coming.'

Niamh said, 'I thought I might get drunk on my own. But I've been avoiding that temptation. When I stop feeling the pain then I'll know I've really lost him.' She took out a corkscrew. 'But feel free.' She opened the bottle and poured a glass for Seonag, refilling her own with water. They slipped on to high stools at the breakfast bar and avoided a touching of glasses, which would have seemed inappropriate. And Niamh watched Seonag sip the wine that she and Ruairidh had always meant to share, realizing then that she could never have drunk it on her own anyway. 'I suppose everyone knows what happened?'

Seonag nodded. 'It's been all over the papers, and the TV news. Folk have been talking about almost nothing else. You know how it is on the island.'

Niamh pressed her lips together in grim resignation.

'When will you get the body back for burial?'

'I brought him back with me.' Niamh pushed her top teeth

down on to her lower lip to stop from crying again. 'What's left of him. He's in the back of the Jeep.'

'Oh, my God!' Seonag reached out and squeezed her hand. 'I don't know, I just thought . . . given that it was murder, they would have held on to the body.'

Niamh shrugged. 'They carried out some kind of post-mortem. Presumably they took the samples they needed. Tissue. Blood.' She paused a moment to collect herself. It was not easy to talk about such things as if they were the subject of everyday conversation. 'But I'm glad they let him go so quickly. I can't even start the process of closure or recovery until I've buried him.' And despite her best efforts the tears came again. She looked at her friend through the blur that filled her eyes. 'But to be honest, Seonag, I'm . . .' She searched for the right word. 'Broken. I'm not sure I can ever get past this.'

Seonag squeezed her hand again. 'You will, Niamh. You were always the strong one.'

'I don't feel very strong.'

'But you are. Remember that time we were all driving back from a dance at Bragar and we hit a rabbit on the road. Stupid bloody thing just froze in the headlights. And you were the one that insisted we stop the car and make sure it was dead. And then when it wasn't, and everyone was turning away, even the boys, you were the one to break its neck and put it out of its misery. There was no one else in the car that night who had the guts to do that.'

'I wish I had the guts to put myself out of my own misery.'

'Oh, Niamh, don't talk like that, for Heaven's sake.' Seonag gazed at her with earnest concern. 'We'll all get through this. Together.'

And Niamh wondered who *all* these people were who had to get through it. Right now it felt like she was the only one suffering. But then she knew his parents, too, would be devastated by the loss of their son. And how thick Seonag was with Ruairidh's mother.

Seonag took a mouthful of wine and slipped off the stool. 'Right, now I'm going to make dinner. Lasagne.' She smiled. 'Well, I'm cheating a little. I made it earlier. All I have to do is heat it up in the oven. But I'll make a salad to go with it.' She nodded towards the door. 'I'll just get the stuff in from the car.'

When Seonag had gone, Niamh wondered if she really wanted her here at all. She had intended to spend this last night alone with Ruairidh. But maybe that would just have been mawkish, indulgent, wallowing in self-pity. Although she knew from bitter experience there were times when you simply had to let grief run its course.

Seonag prepared dinner and served up piping-hot lasagne with fresh salad smothered in a honey and mustard dressing. They sat at the table in the well of the room, looking out at the sea below, and Seonag polished off the better part of a bottle of Chianti as they ate their pasta. It wouldn't start to get dark for an hour or two yet. As autumn progressed towards winter, and the sun began to slip below the equator, the days would quickly shorten, and the long dark nights that lay ahead filled Niamh with dread.

Miraculously the sky had cleared now. All that low-lying cloud dispersed by the wind and blown off to the mainland. The mountains of Sutherland were clearly visible, purple rising to pink in the reflected light of the sunset far to the west.

When they had eaten, Niamh and Seonag donned wellies and warm jackets, and went walking out from the house, around a gully that fell away steeply to a tiny rocky inlet two hundred feet below. Beyond it lay the headland where John Nicolson's house stood in silhouette against the sky.

'They say it's haunted,' Niamh said.

'Who by?'

'A young girl called Annie Campbell. She fell to her death from the cliffs while collecting grass for her cow. The best grass was closest to the edge, and apparently she thought it was too dangerous for the cow.'

'Have you ever seen her?'

Niamh laughed, and realized it was the first time she had done so since Ruairidh's death. Her smile faded quickly. 'No,' she said. 'I've never believed in that kind of thing. It seems a young man also fell from the cliffs while collecting eggs.' She pointed. 'There's a gravestone over there, near the remains of that old blackhouse beyond Taigh 'an Fiosaich. But it's unmarked.'

Seonag said, 'Remember that time when we were kids? And we stole all the eggs from Mrs Macdonald's henhouse?

Meaning to give them back, of course. But only after the old *cailleach* had found the henhouse empty. And then you slipped and dropped the basket and broke every single egg.'

Niamh laughed in spite of herself. 'We got into so much trouble.'

Seonag slipped her arm through Niamh's, and they walked in silence for some minutes along the cliff edge. Gannets and shags wheeled and swooped about their heads, cawing and shrieking in the soft evening air. Others were settling themselves for the night in nests they had contrived on impossible crags and ledges above the sheerest of drops. Far off to the west, the sky glowed gold along the horizon, rising through pink and purple to the darkest blue. There was every likelihood that the aurora borealis would put on a show tonight. Niamh breathed deeply and closed her eyes. She loved this place. But she didn't know if she could stay here without Ruairidh.

She opened her eyes to find Seonag looking at her. Seonag said, 'I've got an overnight bag in the car. Martin is happy to look after the kids. I thought you could do with the company.'

Niamh gazed out across the Minch and wondered if, beyond her need for sympathy and comfort, Seonag was really who she wanted to be with tonight.

CHAPTER SIXTEEN

Seonag and I had been inseparable as kids, but something changed between us the minute I'd shown an interest in Ruairidh. And it was a while before I figured out that she was after him herself.

It wasn't obvious at first. I'd thought that maybe she was just jealous, afraid of losing me to some boy. After all, at that age girls and boys kept themselves pretty much to themselves. The hormones hadn't started playing havoc with our emotions just yet.

But now that we were into our teens things were a little different. Ruairidh was fifteen and had already gone to the Nicolson where, by all accounts, he was the school heart-throb. I was frustrated to be stuck, still, at Shawbost.

Gone was his mullet, replaced by a Rick Astley haircut, short back and sides with a thick quiff on top. He was still tall, but had filled out by now, and was playing for the school rugby team. He had acquired a leather bomber jacket from the army surplus store in Stornoway, which he wore to death, along with drainpipe jeans with the knees out. He was the epitome of cool.

I had sprouted, too, and was taller than Seonag, and very proud of my budding breasts. My figure was still a bit too skinny and boyish for my liking, but there was a sense now of womanhood just around the corner. Clothes hung well on me, and I had let my blonde curls grow long, tying them back at times in a ponytail that hung halfway down my back, at other times leaving them to cascade freely over my shoulders.

Seonag, to my annoyance, grew even more beautiful as we passed into our teens. She had one of those classic hourglass figures, with boobs that drew every boy's eye, and a face that might easily have launched a thousand ships. Only on Lewis, they would have been fishing boats or trawlers, and the fishermen would have been interested in more than her face. She still looked much older than me, and although I was more confident within myself these days, in her company I definitely felt like the frumpy friend.

Her plan to take Ruairidh away from me – although it has to be said that he was a long way from ever being mine – began with a process of running him down. Trying to diminish him in my eyes with a litany of half-truths and downright lies. Had I heard about him getting drunk in Stornoway and being driven home by the police in disgrace? Did I know that he was going out with the captain of the hockey team, and had allegedly been caught having sex with her in the locker room? And one time, when he showed up at the youth club with a split lip and two black eyes, she told me confidentially that he'd been in some kind of a fight at school. I later learned that he had acquired his injuries playing rugby against a team from Inverness. Which taught me to take everything Seonag told me about him with a pinch of salt.

The community hall at Balanish was where the battle lines were first clearly drawn and the initial skirmish took place.

The hall, as we grew older, had become the centre of our limited lives. It was where we spent our Saturday nights, at a youth club run by some of the older village kids. When I say youth club, there was nothing formal or organized about it. It was usually one of my brothers who got the keys and opened up the hall for two or three hours on the Saturday evening. The boys played five-a-side football in the main hall, while the girls crowded into a room at the back, listening to music and gabbing about inconsequential things. Like clothes. And boys. And, more recently, make-up. We were always home by around eleven, and certainly before midnight. The sabbath, which began on the stroke of twelve, was inviolate. And any kind of activity beyond then, youthful or otherwise, was strictly forbidden.

Which was why the discos were always held on the Friday. In fact, they didn't usually start before midnight, after the older ones had got back from a night out in Stornoway.

It was a funny thing, I'd noticed, that the closer a village was to Stornoway, the more worldly the kids seemed. As if proximity to the 'big city' somehow bred sophistication. Way down in Balanish, we were like country yokels. And, then, when we were old enough to go to Stornoway with our friends on a Friday or Saturday night, we felt positively cosmopolitan, even if all we did was hang about the Narrows in the rain and drink beer.

I was still just thirteen when my parents first allowed me to go to the Friday night discos, and only then because Uilleam and Anndra were going. Anndra, by now, was the DJ. And he was good at it. He was a handsome boy with a shock of sandy curls, and an easy way with him. His *craic* always got folk laughing. Girls like boys who make them laugh, so he was popular with the opposite sex.

Any time I went, Seonag would go, too. She always stayed over at our house and shared my bed. The first few times we went, there was no sign of Ruairidh, and I began to think that he regarded the local disco as beneath him. I'd heard he went to Stornoway most Fridays with a group of older boys from Shawbost who had a car.

Then one night in November there he was. He and a group of boys I didn't know. Disco night usually wound up at around 3 a.m., and Ruairidh and his pals didn't arrive until after 1.30. You sensed a frisson of excitement among the girls when they came in. But the boys were playing it very cool, standing along the back wall, smoking and drinking beer from cans.

Anndra had recently acquired coloured lights that flashed in time with the music. And so blue, red and white light flashed intermittent accompaniment to the thump, thump of every track. Seonag and I had spent most of the night dancing with each other, handbags at our feet, in the absence of invitations from any of the boys. Now, along with all the other girls in the hall, we were anxious to be noticed by the newcomers.

For the first time, it seemed to me, in all the years since he had rescued me from the bog, Ruairidh Macfarlane finally caught my eye. I looked away immediately, both embarrassed and anxious not to seem too keen. When I stole another glance I found his eyes still turned in my direction. To my astonishment he smiled, and I think my heart rate went off the scale. I snuck a quick look at Seonag and almost recoiled from the animosity in her glare. She had noticed Ruairidh and me making eye contact, and her nose was well and truly out of joint.

I turned to look at Ruairidh again and very nearly fainted when I saw him pushing his way through the dancers in my direction. I'm sure I blushed bright red when he said, 'Hi, Niamh, haven't seen you for ages. Want to dance?' And I was grateful to Anndra and his coloured lights for hiding my embarrassment.

I tried to sound as if I was doing him a favour. 'Sure.' And made certain there was as little eye contact as possible during the dance itself. I was aware of him staring at me, and felt myself blush again each time I flicked a glance in his direction. I remember that the song Anndra played for that dance was Michael Jackson's 'Dirty Diana', and I focused all my attention on singing along to it, in the certain knowledge that Ruairidh wouldn't be able to hear me. Just see my lips moving. I didn't have much of a voice.

When it ended, I gave him a smile, almost relieved that it

was over. He nodded and drifted off into the haze of cigarette smoke caught in the lights. I turned to find Seonag still giving me the evil eye. We resumed our dancing around the handbags for the next couple of songs. I recall Maxi Priest's version of an old Cat Stevens song, 'Wild World'. And Deacon Blue's 'Real Gone Kid', with everyone pointing in the air and singing along with the 'ooh-ooh' chorus. Strange how such things stay in the memory. But really I was just treading water till Anndra played the smoochy song at the end, and hoping that Ruairidh would ask me to dance for that one. I would have the chance at last to put my arms around him and feel his body next to mine.

Seonag had disappeared off to the loo when Anndra announced the final song of the night. It was the Phil Collins hit, 'A Groovy Kind of Love', from the film *Buster*, and I just about melted at the thought of closing my eyes and surrendering myself to Ruairidh's arms. I tried to catch sight of him, to meet his eye and convey somehow that I was ready for this. But to my dismay it was one of his friends that I saw approaching through the crowd. Not an ugly boy, but he had acne spots around his mouth, and greasy-looking hair, and he wasn't Ruairidh.

He smiled awkwardly. 'Dance?'

I had one frantic last look around for Ruairidh, but there was no sign of him, and I submitted to the inevitable. I shrugged as indifferently as I could. 'Okay.' And to his disappointment immediately adopted the waltz position, keeping my body as far away from his as I could.

It wasn't until well into the song that I saw Seonag in Ruairidh's arms, resting her head against his shoulder, for all the world as if they had been going out with one another for weeks. They swayed together in slow unison, and neither of them glanced once in my direction.

I felt sick, and angry, and humiliated, and I have no idea how I managed to keep dancing until the end of the song. The lights came up, and amid a sprinkling of applause, those couples who had formed a union for the night headed quickly to the door, recovering coats and hats and scarves on the way out. I looked around for Seonag, but there was no sign of her. Her handbag had gone. No sign of Ruairidh either. His friend stood uncomfortably in front of me for a moment or two, as if he thought I might take his arm and head out with him. I threw him the most fleeting of smiles. 'Thank you.' Then retrieved my handbag and hurried for the door.

Kids in gangs and couples and singles streamed down the hill towards the war monument, warmth and smoke rising from them like steam in the cold November air. It was a clear night, I remember, the blackest of skies studded with stars. There was, for once, no wind, and frost lay thick on the tarmac, glistening on every blade of grass.

I stood at the top of the hill, wrapping my coat around me for warmth, and scanned the bodies making their way carefully down the slope, everyone holding on to everyone else for fear of slipping on the frost. And there they were. Ruairidh and Seonag. Hand in hand, nearly at the bridge by now. Even from this distance I could hear them laughing, imagining that it was me they were laughing at. Or about. I cursed myself for being so damned cool during that first dance, and turned to head off in the other direction towards home. Only to find Uilleam walking gingerly by my side.

'Where's Seonag?' he said.

'In hell I hope,' I growled at him. And in spite of the frost and the risk of slipping, I ran the rest of the way home, tears turning icy to burn my face as they tracked their way down my cheeks.

My folks were long in their beds by the time I got back, so at least I didn't have to face them. I slammed my bedroom door and undressed quickly, slipping beneath the cold covers to curl up foetally on my side, sobbing my anger and hurt into the pillow.

Of course, I couldn't sleep. Not before Seonag returned, and even then it was hours before I finally drifted off. I heard her coming in, softly shutting the door behind her. The rustle of clothes as she undressed before climbing into bed. I kept my back turned, fighting the urge either to cry or to punch her. Hopefully she thought I was asleep.

To my acute irritation I heard her breathing grow shallow, and then the soft purr of sleep as she drifted off long before I did.

When we got up in the morning not a word was said about the night before, and we never once discussed it in the weeks and months that followed. Though as far as I was aware nothing, in the end, ever came of it.

It was five years later that Seonag and I next came into conflict over Ruairidh. By then we had already started growing apart and had barely seen each other during our first year away from the island, studying at different colleges on the mainland. As it turned out, for me at least, this time provided the straw that well and truly broke the camel's back.

Both of us were lucky enough to secure summer jobs at Linshader Fishing Lodge at the mouth of the river Grimersta on the south-west coast of Lewis. The lodge was just a few miles south of Balanish, but they were live-in jobs because of the unsocial hours we were forced to keep. Having won prizes in home economics in fourth and fifth years at the Nicolson, I was allocated the position of cook's assistant. Seonag was put on the housekeeping rota, which was kept on its toes by a lady from nearby Linshader village who used to leave Pan Drops, a classic Free Church white mint sweetie, in hidden places around the lodge so she could check that the girls were cleaning everywhere.

I was lucky, working in the kitchen, that I could just wear jeans and T-shirts and an apron. The housemaids had to wear kilts and black blouses. Seonag hated it. We shared a room, but during the day had very little contact because of our very different duties.

The lodge was a grand old place dating back to Victorian

times and built in the early 1870s. It sat right down on the shore of Loch Roag, at the mouth of the river, a long two-storey white building. The hill that rose behind it was covered in Scots pines planted in the nineteenth century by the island's then owner, James Matheson, who'd made his fortune selling opium to the Chinese. What today we would probably call drug-running, but back then appeared to be the respectable pursuit of lords, admirals and prime ministers.

It had recently been extended at the north end, and against the south gable stood a long green-roofed shed that housed the ghillies and the watchers.

It had an atmosphere all of its own, that place. Sometimes mired in the mist that would drift in off the water on a still morning, or lost in the smirr that dropped down from the moor. I came into the loch once on a boat just as the sun was coming up, and mist like smoke rose up all around the lodge in the early-morning light, moving wraithlike among the trees. The water itself was alive with salmon breaking the still surface as they headed in from the sea on their journey upriver, and otters played around the stone slipway. It was magical.

Nothing magical about the hours I kept, though. Up at the crack of dawn, first to serve tea to the guests in their beds, then a cooked breakfast in the dining room before they headed off with packed lunches prepared by me and the cook to spend the day fishing somewhere up on the water system. The lodge accommodated sixteen guests, very often members of the syndicate that owned it, or their friends. Wealthy folk. Judges and newspaper editors, successful businessmen and Tory peers. Folk the like of which I had never come across before, but all of whom, nearly without exception, treated me with the greatest generosity and kindness.

I have very fond memories of the summer I spent at that lodge. I got my education there, too. I had known nothing of writing rooms and wine cellars. And although it seems hard to believe now, I had never even tasted wine. I remember one morning doing a nosey and wandering into what they called the writing room, thinking that all the guests were out fishing. To my surprise, there was an elderly gentleman sitting at the roll-top bureau scribbling in a large notebook. I apologized immediately and began to back out. But he insisted I stay, poured me a coffee from the pot, and asked me all about myself. At first I was shy, but he put me so much at my ease that before long we were sharing laughs and inconsequential secrets. At some point the housekeeper had come in to take away dirty cups, and afterwards she cornered me in the kitchen and said, 'Do you know who you were talking to in there?'

'Well, no,' I said. And in truth I had never even thought to ask his name, although he seemed to know mine.

'That was the poet laureate,' she said in hushed tones. I later looked him up in an encyclopaedia to discover that he had been recommended for the job by the Prime Minister, and appointed by the Queen. These were circles I was not used to moving in at Balanish.

The girls all went to bed for a few hours in the afternoon,

before getting up again to prepare afternoon tea when the ghillies brought the guests back from the fishing at five. And then we served dinner at seven-thirty following three loud strokes on the gong.

We were six girls in all, and the housekeeper, of course. Including the gamekeeper, there were four ghillies and four watchers. The watchers mostly slept during the day, and were out at night and the early morning keeping an eye open for poachers. When Seonag and I arrived there were only three ghillies. The fourth was yet to arrive. An experienced lad, they said, who had been coming for several years now.

He turned out to be Ruairidh Macfarlane.

I had only been there a few days when I discovered a lodge tradition. It was my birthday, and I suppose it was probably Seonag who told everyone, but that evening before dinner, the boys all came looking for me.

The cook knew what was coming, and there was a grin all over her face when the ghillies and watchers came trooping into the kitchen. 'Come on then, Niamh,' the gamekeeper said to me. He was an older man, a face like leather after years at sea. They called him Staines after a character in a TV series called *Captain Pugwash* that was years before my time.

'Come on where?' I said.

'It's bath time.' One of the boys grinned at me, and the others had trouble stifling their laughter. I was not getting a good feeling about this.

I tutted and shook my head. 'I'm busy.'

'Told you she might take a bit of persuasion,' the game-keeper said. 'Right, then, boys.' And to my absolute indignation they marched right in and swept me off my feet.

Big strong boys' hands all over me hoisting me into the air and carrying me shouting and kicking all the way down the hall and out of the front door. The other girls were gathered there, and some of the guests, all smiling in anticipation.

'Put me down,' I screamed, trying to wriggle free of their grasp. But it was hopeless. And they marched me over the gravel to the slipway and down to the water's edge. I realized suddenly what was coming and struggled even harder to free myself. To no avail. They swung me once, twice, three times through the air, before launching me out over the water.

I landed with a smack on its still surface, and the cold nearly took my breath away as I went under. It wasn't deep here, so I was able to scramble quickly to my feet, rising up out of the water like Aphrodite to stand waist-deep, drenched, my hair hanging in a sodden web all over my face. Everyone began singing 'Happy Birthday'.

It was only as I scrambled up out of the water, to a chorus of laughter and cheers, that I saw Ruairidh standing there for the first time. Grinning. My white T-shirt was virtually see-through when wet. Fortunately I was wearing a bra. But I felt as if I was standing in my underwear, exposed and humiliated.

I ran off into the house, gales of laughter following in my wake.

*

I didn't see much of him over the next few days as I settled into the routine of the lodge. They were long, hard days, but sleeping in the afternoon meant that we were all wide awake once dinner had been served, the tables cleared and the dishes done.

The weather was pretty lousy that first week, wet and blustery, which none of the fishermen seemed to mind. But it meant we were stuck in the lodge at night, either the girls in their tiny lounge off the kitchen, or all of us together in the boys' green shed, talking, smoking, listening to music. Ruairidh had been assigned to train up the new watchers, so he wasn't often there.

Then suddenly, the following week, summer arrived, and as soon as we were able to escape our duties in the lodge, we would all troop down to a tiny beach hidden beyond the headland, where we were out of sight and hearing of the guests.

We lit fires from driftwood to keep the midges at bay, and sat around in the flickering glow of the flames, talking and laughing, drinking beer and vodka, and sometimes one of the boys would produce a chunk of cannabis resin that we would break up and 'cook' in silver paper to smoke with tobacco in rolled-up joints.

It was about halfway through that week that Ruairidh first showed up with his guitar. He was finished training the new boys, and he sat cross-legged with his back to the dunes serenading us with ballads and rock classics, and pop songs that everyone knew and sang along to.

I remember those nights as being special. I didn't participate much in the singing, or the *craic*, but sat there with the fire in my eyes watching Ruairidh as he played and sang, and I think perhaps that's when I realized that I was in love with him. Not some childhood infatuation, or passing fancy, or even gratitude for the moment when he had saved my life all those years before. But with an ache somewhere very deep inside me, and a longing that I could barely contain.

Seonag, by contrast, was the life and soul of the party. Every fancy-dress night and silly escapade was her idea. She joked and flirted with the boys and was the envy of all the other girls. I watched how she eyed up Ruairidh in a sleekit sort of way, green watchful eyes peering out from behind her fringe. But whatever had happened between them that night after the disco, he showed no interest in her whatsoever. Neither, it has to be said, did he demonstrate the least interest in me.

Until the night that Seonag retired early to her bed, suffering from a streaming summer cold. There were only a handful of us down at the beach that evening. Ruairidh and his guitar, another of the ghillies with one of the housemaids who had become an item, and the cook.

I sat with my back to the sea, listening between songs to the sound of its breathing. I remember someone once telling me that the sound of the sea was like the sound we hear pre-birth, of our mother's blood passing through us. And that's why we are always drawn to the ocean. Like a return to the womb.

I didn't even notice the ghillie and his girl drifting off along the shore until the cook stood up and said, 'Time for bed. An early rise in the morning.' As if it wasn't always. And suddenly it was just me and Ruairidh sitting round the fire, looking at each other across the embers. He must have been twenty then. A young man. He had broadened out, and not having shaved for several days had the beginnings of a beard adding definition to a fine-featured face.

He smiled, patting the sand on his right, and said, 'Come and sit beside me.'

My heart was very nearly in my mouth as I shuffled around the dying fire and squatted cross-legged in the sand beside him. I think it was the first time in our lives that we had ever been alone together.

He had the most enigmatic smile on his face as he turned to look in my eyes. 'Fancy a smoke?'

'Sure.'

He laid the guitar aside and delved into a pocket, producing a small silver tin box containing several roll-ups. But they were no ordinary roll-ups. He lifted one out and grinned. 'Here's one I made earlier.'

I laughed. We had both watched *Blue Peter* as kids. Though I doubt if any of the presenters had made anything quite like these earlier. At least, not on screen. He lit it and took a long pull, drawing smoke deep into his lungs and holding it there for several moments before exhaling suddenly and handing me the roll-up. I saw the embers of the fire reflected in blue eyes that seemed so dark on this light night. I drew long and deep before handing it back.

There was the faintest of breezes blowing in with the tide. An almost full moon gave inner light to the slow swell of dark green ocean as it broke white along the sand. I could feel the warmth of his body next to mine, and we sat there without a word, caressed by the half-dark, and smoking his joint until it was done. He threw the dout on the fire. It flared briefly in a fleeting, flickering flame, then vanished. Ruairidh reached then for his guitar and played me the most beautiful song I think I had ever heard. I found out only much later that it was an old Beatles song, 'Here, There and Everywhere'.

He sang it slow and soft, a voice like velvet, eyes sometimes closed, sometimes gazing dreamily out across the water. When he finished he turned to look at me for the first time. Our faces were very close, and he leaned over on one elbow to kiss me. Had we not been smoking earlier, I might have rushed it, or pulled back too soon. As it was I just closed my eyes and lost myself in it. In the softness of his lips, the warmth of his tongue, the not unpleasant jag of his whiskers. I tasted smoke on his breath, and the sweetness of alcohol. It all seemed like the most natural thing in the world. As if everything in my life up until then had only ever been to prepare me for this moment.

When finally we drew back I saw that his pupils were dilated. He said, 'I've wanted to do that ever since I saw you nearly drown up on the Pentland Moor.'

I gazed at him in disbelief. 'Liar.'

'It's true. I'd never even noticed you at school before then. I don't know why. I remember lying along the plank and looking into your eyes. Feeling your total dependence on me in that moment. And it was the first time I'd ever felt the desire to kiss a girl.'

I felt indignation rising in my breast. 'Well, I'd never have guessed it from the way you totally ignored me afterwards.'

He shrugged and turned his eyes away towards the incoming swell. 'That's difficult to explain. I suppose I was a bit ashamed of the things I'd felt. Embarrassed. None of the other boys seemed remotely interested in girls. I didn't want to be any different.'

'And at the disco that time?'

He turned, frowning. 'What time?'

'You don't even remember, do you? About five years ago. We danced, and I was waiting for you to ask me for the last dance of the night. But you asked Seonag instead, and you both went off together at the end.' I had carried the hurt and humiliation of it somewhere deep inside for all these years.

His eyes opened wide in amazement. 'It was you that didn't want to dance with me.'

'Rubbish!'

'That's what Seonag said. That you fancied my friend Derek, and were hoping he'd ask you for the last dance. So he did.'

I felt my jaw slacken.

'And I asked Seonag instead. Then afterwards, when we'd left together, she didn't really want to know. We hung about, talking, down at the bus shelter until I was freezing my bollocks off. Then it was a quick peck on the cheek and she was off.' He pursed his lips in regret. 'I thought you hated me.'

I felt the deepest, trembling sigh suck itself from my chest and closed my eyes. 'That little bitch!' Then I looked at him very earnestly. 'I told her nothing of the kind. It was you I wanted to dance with.'

He started to laugh, then, and let his head fall back, directing his mirth at the vast firmament overhead. 'Jesus. To think of all the wasted years!' He stood up suddenly and held out his hand to pull me to my feet. 'Are you tired?'

'Never been more awake in my life.'

He grinned that infectious grin of his. 'Want to go out in a boat?'

'I'd love to.'

'Better get some decent footwear, then, and a jacket in case it gets cold. I'll meet you with the Land Rover at the back of the green shed.'

Seonag was deep asleep, snoring like an old man, when I snuck into our room to fetch my Hunter's green wellies and my parka. Ruairidh was waiting with the Land Rover, and didn't seem concerned about waking anyone as he started up the motor and drove us off towards the gatehouse and the single track that led to the main road. We turned south-west, then, on the B8011 until we passed the Bernera turn-off on our right, then swung left on to a track that only a 4×4 could handle, heading due south along the west shore of Loch Ruadh Gheure. Moonlight reflecting on still, black water followed our lurching progress up the water system. Ruairidh laughed. 'You know what this loch is called?'

'Ruadh Gheure,' I said.

'No, it's Loch One. There are four lochs on the system, and they're all called by their number. Every landmark on all the streams and lochs has its own English name. Daft things like Fish Bay, and Pyramid, and Alligator and Auburn Point. All because the English can't pronounce the Gaelic.' He laughed again. 'Mind you, most Scots couldn't pronounce the Gaelic either.'

It didn't take us long to reach the end of the road, and the boathouse at the top of Loch Two. There, Ruairidh dragged a 15-foot wooden boat down a short slipway into the water and we both clambered in. He yanked twice on the starter cable of a Tohatsu outboard and the engine exploded noisily into life, the sound of it echoing away across the hills that grew out of the twilight.

I cringed at the noise. 'Won't someone hear us?'

'Who? There's no one out here, except for maybe a couple of poachers, and you can bet your life the watchers are fast asleep in the bothy at Macleay's Stream.'

The initial roar of the motor settled down into a more gentle purr as Ruairidh guided us south along the loch, shattered moonlight dispersing in the luminescent wash we left in our wake. 'Is it bad, the poaching?' I had heard stories.

He nodded grimly. 'At times, yes. Used to be that no one really minded the locals taking one for the pot, but it's gone way beyond that now. Some of the poaching on the water up here is almost industrial. They're casting nets across the waterways, catching dozens, if not hundreds of salmon. They have taxis waiting for them at road-ends, and the boots get packed with fish on ice and driven off to Stornoway. From there, who knows where it goes. But there's a big international market for fresh-caught wild salmon.' He looked as if he might be about to spit his disgust out on to the water, then changed his mind. 'Trouble is, at this rate there'll not be any salmon left for anyone. The estate's not far from all-out war with the locals.'

'But the estate's taking the fish, too. And charging big money for it. What gives them the right to fish the waters when the locals don't?' I felt a certain indignation rising in my chest. I knew that my own father was not beyond a bit of poaching himself.

'Aye, but the estate manages the water system, Niamh. They have a hatchery down on Loch Roag, and a policy now of returning caught fish to the water. The emphasis is more and more on conservation these days.'

We motored the rest of the way in silence, then, and I watched in wonder as the landscape changed all around us, growing more rugged and mountainous. There was daylight still in the sky, with the moon washing its light across the land, scree slopes and rocky shorelines traced in silver. At this time of year it would never get fully dark, and I remembered being in Ness one June at a family wedding when I saw the sun rise in the east barely moments after it had set in the west.

Macleay's Stream was a short stretch of managed white water between Loch Two and Loch Three. There was no sign of life in the bothy, a stone-built dwelling with a tin roof that sat in the cradle of the mountains rising steeply now out of the valley. Ruairidh said, 'Either they are sleeping or out patrolling. Whichever it is, we don't want to disturb them.'

We berthed the boat at the mouth of the stream and followed a track on foot that led us along the path of Macleay's to the foot of Loch Three, where we clambered into another boat and headed deeper into the wilderness. Past landmarks to which Ruairidh attached names like McKillop's Point and Braithwait's Cairn.

We changed boats again at Skunk Point, and motored south in splendid isolation, beyond Summer House and Cheese Rock, into some of the most inaccessible wilderness in the whole of Scotland. The air was cooler now, and I was starting to feel the chill. So I sat at the back of the boat, leaning in to Ruairidh, who had one hand on the tiller and the other around my shoulder.

I realized how completely I had surrendered everything to him. Out here I was so far beyond my comfort zone, or ken, that all I could do was put my trust in him. And to me he seemed strong and knowledgeable and wholly at ease in his environment. So surrender felt good. I knew he would keep me safe, as all these years later he promised me he would.

He pointed towards the dark shape of an island looming ahead in the water. 'That's Macphail's Island. There's a lunch

hut there. We'll stop for a bit, and light a fire if you're cold.'
We could see the mountains of North Harris cutting jagged
lines against the sky in the distance. Tomnaval. The Clisham.
Ruairidh said, 'There are two rivers that run into the head of
Loch Four here, both from Loch Langabhat. One day I'll take
you up there. It must be the most beautiful spot on earth,
Niamh. You can see pairs of golden eagles circling way up
above the mountain tops, and red deer that come right down
to the water's edge. And if you ever want to feel like there's
no other human being on this earth, then that's the place you
need to go.'

I wasn't sure why I would ever want to feel so alone, but
I would happily have gone there with Ruairidh any time he
wanted.

The lunch hut was half wood, half stone, with a sloping
leaded roof. It sat on a rocky outcrop, with steps cut into the
rock leading up from a tiny jetty where Ruairidh tied up our
boat. With so much moonlight reflecting off water, and so
much daylight still in the sky, it felt more like day than night.

Ruairidh pushed open a wooden door with a leaping salmon
painted beneath a small square of window. The hut smelled
damp and fusty, intended only as a shelter for fishermen
to eat their packed lunches while out fishing the system.
Ruairidh said, 'Sometimes a watcher will overnight here.' And
he stooped to open up a cupboard and take out a couple of
rolled-up sleeping bags. 'We'll take these to keep us warm.'

We trekked across the tiny island then, to a sheltered inlet with a pocket-handkerchief patch of fine shingle, and he laid out the sleeping bags before gathering wood to light a fire.

'Back in a few minutes,' he said. And I saw him in silhouette returning to the hut, before emerging with a rod and a bag and vanishing across the island.

I sat for what felt like a very long time, watching fish out on the loch jumping clear of the water to catch insects, leaving rings that circled endlessly outward, cutting and cross-cutting each other until they broke upon the shore. If there were midges around, then the heat and flames of the fire kept them away. The air felt soft to me, and I took off my parka and kicked off my wellies. I had the strangest feeling in my belly, and a kaleidoscope of butterflies animating it. I pulled my knees up to my chest and wrapped my arms around my shins, rocking slightly back and forth. There was the strongest sense permeating every part of me that my life was about to change for ever. And I was, at the same time, both scared of it, and desperate to embrace it.

Ruairidh returned with a live trout. He killed it with a sharp blow to the head then crouched to gut it on a rock. From his sack he took a roll of tinfoil, a lemon and two portions of wrapped butter. He parcelled the trout up in the tinfoil with a slice of lemon and a portion of butter, and wedged it carefully among the embers of the fire. He sat down beside me. 'A few minutes. I hope you're hungry.'

'Starving.' And I was.

He reached for his sack and pulled out a bottle of white wine and two plastic cups. 'Not as chilled as it might be, but it'll do.' He took out a corkscrew and opened the bottle.

'You've certainly come equipped,' I said. 'Do you do this often?'

He grinned. 'First time. But I have been planning it.'

'Oh have you?'

He shrugged. 'Well, one should always be prepared.'

I smiled. 'Oh, should one?'

'I *was* a Boy Scout.'

'That would explain it, then.' I tilted my head towards him. 'I suppose your pal and his girlfriend, and the cook, were all well primed to leave us on our own at the fire.'

He just smiled.

When he gauged that the fish was ready, he scooped it out of the ashes with a couple of sticks and opened up the tinfoil between us. The smell that rose up with the steam was delicious. He unfolded a knife from his pocket and carefully separated the fillet from the bone, before lifting up the tail and delicately removing the whole spine and head. 'Just fingers, I'm afraid.' He glanced up at me. 'Is that okay?'

'I never use anything else.' He laughed, and I discovered that I liked to make him laugh. He poured us each a glass of wine. We chinked plastic and I took a mouthful of soft, fruity Chardonnay that tasted like the best thing that had ever passed my lips. Until we turned our attention to the trout. There was not the slightest smell of fish rising from the firm, succulent flesh, slick with butter and lemon juice. It was, quite simply, the best fish I had ever tasted. If I could recreate that moment, I would relive it a thousand times.

When we had finished it we washed our hands in the loch, freshening our mouths with more wine, and settling in close together on the outspread sleeping bags.

'Did it live up to expectations?' I said.

He looked at me, surprised. 'What?'

'That first kiss you'd been dreaming about all those years.'

He was very serious. 'More than.'

'I don't suppose you'd like to try it again? Just to make sure.'

He ran the backs of his fingers down my cheek, and then his thumb gently across my lips. I kissed it, before he leaned in to find my lips with his. Soft and warm, the taste of Chardonnay still on his tongue. The butterflies in my tummy went into hyperdrive as I felt his hands on my shoulders, gently laying me down on the softness of the sleeping bags. There was no invitation required. Neither did he seek or need permission.

Within minutes we were naked under the moon, making love for the very first time, and I knew that what I had taken for love on the beach at Linshader Lodge had not deceived me.

It was my first time, and although I wasn't going to tell him that, I think he'd probably worked it out. They say the first time can be the worst time. For me it was amazing, and only ever got better. I never, from that moment, wanted anyone else in my life.

When we were finished and lying breathless on our backs gazing up at the faintest of stars in a sky that was as dark as it would get, he turned his head to gaze at me with an intensity that was almost frightening. Then he said, 'Well, I'm glad to see that the hunter–gatherer approach still works.'

And I clattered him as he burst out laughing.

We got back just as the day was beginning at the lodge. The cook was already in the kitchen, and I hurried up to my room to change. Seonag was awake, but still lying in bed without any intention of getting out of it that day. Her eyes and nose were still streaming, and her voice had almost gone. It was obvious that my bed had not been slept in.

'Been out all night, then,' she said. A statement, not a question.

I wasn't feeling particularly well disposed to her after Ruairidh's revelations about what she had said to him at the disco. 'None of your business,' I said curtly, and I saw her face flush with anger, and maybe hurt.

'Finally got it together, then, you two?'

I slipped into clean underwear and pulled on fresh jeans and a T-shirt. I could shower later. 'No thanks to you.'

She had gathered her composure again, and drew it around her like the sheets on the bed. 'I wonder what your folks are going to say when they find out that you're going out with Ruairidh Macfarlane.'

I turned to glare at her angrily. If she was trying to puncture my happiness, she was succeeding. But I didn't want to let it show. 'I don't care what they say. I know they've always blamed Ruairidh for what happened, but they're wrong.' And I stomped out of the room. We never spoke about it again. But Seonag was in a huff with me, and I couldn't be doing with it. Within a week I had swapped rooms with another of the girls who seemed happy to share with Seonag, and I barely spoke to her for the rest of the summer.

Seonag aside, the next few weeks passed in a dream. I couldn't wait to finish work each night to spend the rest of it with Ruairidh. Sometimes we sat down at the beach with the others, weather permitting, singing around the fire. Some nights we wandered off along the shore. We found a tiny island that was only accessible at low tide. There were the remains of an old blackhouse on it and we would light a fire among the ruins and Ruairidh would sing and play just for me. We had our own name for it, *Eilean Teine*, or Fire Island. More than once we were caught out by the incoming tide, having to pull up our breeks to wade back across to the mainland.

When the weather was fine we made the return trek up to Macphail's Island and the tiny shingle cove where we'd first made love. There we explored each other's bodies and lives and got to know each other as well as two young people could. For the longest time, Ruairidh told me, he had been planning a career as a gamekeeper, working at Linshader Lodge every summer, with the intention of taking a gamekeeping and wildlife management course at an early incarnation of the University of the Highlands. Then, at the last minute, his brother Donald had persuaded him to follow in his footsteps, taking a business studies course at Aberdeen University, with the prospect of a job afterwards in the oil industry. I got the strong impression, even then, that it was a decision he regretted. We take these decisions that will forever change the course of our lives at an age when we are least qualified to make them. Ruairidh was born for a life out here in the wilderness, but it was destined never to be.

I told him all about my ambitions to work in the clothing industry. But also of my unhappiness, even after just a few days, with my choice of textile college at Galashiels, in the Scottish Borders. Too far from home without friends. Forced to remain in the student halls of residence while the girls from Glasgow or Edinburgh went home at weekends. I was dreading going back for another year.

For both of us the summer at Linshader was an escape from all that. An idyll that we could never have imagined in the months preceding it. But happiness so intense can't last. And it was mid-August when an incident on the water system changed everything.

It was one of those perfect summer nights. The world had turned a little by now, and it was getting darker earlier. Though there was still light in the sky, the stars stood out like crystal studs. The Milky Way was like breath misting on glass. A gibbous moon shed its colourless light across the hills, and almost everyone was gathered around the fire on the beach.

Our sing-song was interrupted by Staines, the gamekeeper, and one of the watchers, a sixteen-year-old lad called Calum.

Calum had spotted a party of poachers out on the top loch, not far from Macphail's Island, in the basin where the Langavat River ran into the loch, opposite a rock called Gibraltar.

'If we're quick we'll catch them,' Staines said breathlessly. 'They're laying nets. I want all the ghillies with me. The rest of the watchers are waiting for us up there.'

To my disappointment, Ruairidh was on his feet in an instant and heading off with the rest of the boys. They were quickly swallowed up by the night. I had grown so used to spending my nights with him and sleeping all afternoon that I was at a complete loss. The prospect of passing the rest of the evening round the fire with the girls was less than appealing, particularly in the company of Seonag, whom I had been assiduously avoiding. So I got up and said, 'Might as well have an early night, then.' I didn't wait to see if anyone else was going to join me, hurrying off back up the path to the lodge.

My body clock was not accustomed to my being in bed this early, and I lay awake in the dark for what seemed like hours. I was aware of my roommate coming to bed around midnight, but didn't let on I was awake. Within minutes I heard her slow, steady breathing as she slipped off to sleep long before me.

I had a tortured night, tossing and turning, drifting in and out of dreams until the alarm went at six.

I saw Ruairidh briefly after breakfast, when we were handing out the packed lunches to the guests. He looked grey and tired and just shook his head when I raised an eyebrow in query. I was anxious to hear what had happened.

There were rumours among the girls, of course, during the day. About some kind of violent confrontation and arrests by the police. But it wasn't until that night that I got the full story. As soon as we could, Ruairidh and I slipped off along the shore and made the slippery crossing over seaweed and stones to Eilean Teine. The night was still warm, but midges swarming around the old ruin forced us to light a fire. By its flame I watched Ruairidh's face as he recounted what had happened the previous night.

'It was a bunch of teenagers,' he said. 'A couple of lads from Balanish and, we think, three from Bragar. But we only caught the one.' He shook his head. 'They hadn't a clue what they were doing. I think one of them had been out with some real poachers and thought he knew how it was done.' He blew air in frustration through pursed lips. 'Their net was full of holes for a start, and they had no real idea how or where to lay it. Just lads out for a bit of a lark, really.'

'What happened?'

'They didn't even know we were there until we jumped them. There was a bit of a rammy in the dark, and four of them went haring away across the hills. I caught the other one. I always wondered if my rugby days would serve any purpose in real life.' He smiled ruefully. 'I brought him down with a beauty of a tackle, shoulder in behind the knees. He fell like a sack of tatties. It wasn't until we got him to his feet that I realized who he was.' He dragged his eyes away from the flames where they had been replaying the events of the night before and looked at me. 'You know him, too. He'd have been in your year. Iain Maciver. Lives just down the road from me.'

I nodded. I knew exactly who he meant. A thickset boy, dark hair cut in the classic Lewis fringe, dividing his forehead laterally in half. Not the best-looking lad, but bright. My age. Just eighteen. I'd heard he'd got himself into Glasgow University, studying Gaelic. He was known universally as *Peanut*, because of his predilection for the Reese's Peanut Cups they sold at Woolies in Stornoway. Which were the probable cause of the spots that had gathered themselves around his nose and mouth and forehead during his early teens, leaving him now with badly pockmarked skin.

Ruairidh returned his eyes to the flames. 'So Staines insists on calling the police. Peanut's begging him not to. It'll mean a criminal record, something that could affect him for the rest of his life. I pulled Staines to one side and said we could just give him a bollocking. Put the fear of God into him. He'd never do it again. But Staines didn't want to know. He had a real ugly look on his face and he said to me, "These fuckers need taught a lesson!" And that was it. We took the boy back down to the road and the cops were waiting for us.'

'That's pretty shitty,' I said.

He nodded. 'It was. And I'm sure Peanut blames me. I was the one that brought him down.' He shook his head then, frustration and anger etched all over his face. 'And the worst of it is, I've been hearing all day how Staines himself is in with the real poachers. A lucrative wee sideline. Just rumours, mind. But it would explain why he was so keen to warn off anyone else.'

'Jesus! Do you think that's true?'

'I don't know.' He breathed his helplessness at the night. 'But what I do know is that the boy's been charged. He'll appear at the Sheriff Court in Stornoway, and I'll probably be called to give evidence. It'll bring shame on his family. *My* neighbours. And could well ruin his chances of getting a job in the future. Employers don't like kids with criminal records.'

The whole incident cast a gloom over the lodge in the days that followed. Ruairidh was more subdued than I'd known him all summer, and I saw him on several occasions being short with Staines. Had he been able to verify the rumours I believe he might well have been tempted to put his fist in the man's face. Then one evening he said to me, 'Let's go up to Macphail's Island.' We hadn't been for some time, and I think it was Ruairidh's way of trying to break out of his depression.

It was not the best of weather. There was low cloud, and a light smirr blowing down off the hills. We had to wear our waterproofs for the trip up the water system, and it was hard to see with rapidly fading light and no moon.

It was too wet to sit out once we got to Macphail's, and so we huddled together in the lunch hut, drinking wine and saying very little. A comfortable, comforting silence. A shared sadness that needed no words. Just understanding. We smoked a couple of joints, held hands and kissed, but sex was never on the agenda for either of us. And it was not long after midnight when we set off in the boat again to head back to the lodge.

Ruairidh had to navigate us into the slipway at Skunk Point by the light of a torch. We had just clambered out of the boat and were pulling it out of the water when half a dozen shadows detached themselves from the darkness. A group of youths who had been waiting for us in the still of the night. I was knocked backwards into shallow water and screamed as the group of young men surrounded Ruairidh. I scrambled to my feet and saw him fighting like fury, but he was hopelessly outnumbered. They dragged him down to the ground, and boots went pounding into his stomach and chest and back as he curled up to try and protect himself. I screamed again, wading out of the water and throwing myself at his attackers. Punching, kicking, until an elbow in my face brought light flashing in my eyes and knocked me back off my feet.

I grabbed on to the side of the boat and saw that Ruairidh's torch was still lying inside it. I reached in to snatch it and fumble with the switch. Suddenly I was directing the glare of its light on to Ruairidh's assailants, and they stepped back, arms half-raised to shadow their eyes. I recognized almost every one of them. Boys I had been at school with. Including Peanut. They seemed startled, and frozen in the cold light of my recognition. But Peanut stepped boldly forward. 'Since when did you become a traitor to your class, Niamh Murray? Siding with the fucking toffs.'

I felt anger spiking up my back. 'Maybe about the same time you became a fucking thief, Iain Maciver.' I looked around the faces. 'Don't think I don't know who you are. Every last one of you!' My voice was shrill, and I could hear it echoing back off the hills.

Peanut said, 'You breathe a fucking word of this to anyone . . .'

'And you'll what?' I screamed back at him. 'Make things worse than they already are? You stupid bloody boys.'

They almost seemed chastened, shrinking back from my anger. Except for Peanut himself. He turned to look at Ruairidh still curled up on the ground, and sank his boot in one last time. 'That's for ruining my life, you bastard!' he shouted, leaning right over him and spitting on his prone form. He nodded to the others and as they turned away they were absorbed by the night just as quickly as they had appeared.

By the time Ruairidh got to his feet I could see blood on his face, and vomit on the ground where he had lain. He brushed aside my helping hand and marched off into the dark, following the well-worn track along the banks of the stream that led down to Loch Three. I struggled to keep up, and couldn't get a word out of him all the way back to the lodge.

Ruairidh wasn't the same after that. He spent the remainder of our stay at Linshader Lodge, it seemed, trying to avoid me. I never knew whether it was the humiliation of taking a beating in front of me, or being branded a turncoat for siding with the toffs. Or maybe guilt at the part he had played in ruining Peanut's future. Whatever was ailing him, he had no intention of sharing it with me. I almost started to believe that he blamed me for everything that had happened.

The change in his mood and demeanour was marked. He would turn up sometimes at the bonfire on the beach without his guitar, the worse for drink. He was smoking a lot of dope, and went off quite often at night with the watchers. I think he spent most of the remaining weeks of the summer sleeping up at the bothy at Macleay's Stream. We never passed another night together.

Of course, Seonag could barely conceal her glee. She would make a point of sitting talking to him those evenings he turned up on the beach, glancing in my direction to make sure I was watching. And I remember her once coming into the kitchen to inform me that, anyway, I was better off without him. It was with clear satisfaction that she said, 'My folks tell me that the Macfarlanes are outcasts in Balanish these days. No one'll talk to them because of Ruairidh getting Peanut arrested.'

I turned and almost spat in her face. 'It wasn't Ruairidh that got him arrested. It was that bastard Staines. And everyone knows he's in with the poachers.'

Seonag's eyes narrowed and she lowered her voice. 'You'd better watch yourself young lady. You could get into big trouble if people hear you talking like that.'

'Oh, yes? And you'd be the one to tell them, I suppose.' I

had long suspected that someone had tipped off Peanut and the Balanish boys that Ruairidh and I were up at Macphail's Island that night. And I wouldn't have put it past Seonag being the one to do it.

She put on her hurt face and her little girl's voice. 'We used to be friends,' she said. 'I don't know what's happened to you.'

Me? I wanted to shout at her. *Me? You're the one that's changed!* But I said nothing as she turned and retreated into the lodge like some wounded animal.

It was about a week before the end of our stay at Linshader that my mother took ill. A recurrence of shingles, that awful rash with its accompanying nerve pain and headaches. The doctor put her on antivirals and she retired to her bed. I had to excuse myself from duties at the lodge and return home for a couple of days to cook for my father and Uilleam, who was still at home then, and do their laundries. It never ceases to amaze me how hopeless men are at looking after themselves.

As it happened, I was able to get everything done during that first day. It was perfect drying weather, and I had all the laundry washed, dried and folded away in cupboards and drawers by teatime. The rest of the time I spent cooking. Meals that could be reheated and served at any hour that suited them. I had intended to stay overnight, but as it turned out there was no need. Uilleam drove me back to the lodge and I arrived shortly after ten.

It wasn't the warmest of nights. I sensed a change in the

weather. Those seemingly endless summer days of warm sunshine and gentle breezes were already beginning to feel like
a distant memory. The summer never seems to last, and the
older you get the shorter it becomes, like the days themselves.
While the winter stretches endlessly ahead towards some
far-off and uncertain spring. The change comes in a moment
and you detect it immediately. Like the first faint stab of pain
in the sinus that presages the onset of a cold.

I dumped my stuff in my room. There was no one at the
lodge, except for the guests, and I headed off along the path
to the beach. I met the cook and several of the others on
their way back. My roommate was among them. She said,
'I wouldn't bother, Niamh. Everyone's packing it in for the
night. Too cold.'

'Is Ruairidh still down there?' I was anxious to see him. We
had so little time left together before heading off again on our
very separate ways, and I was desperate to try to put things
right between us.

She seemed evasive. 'I'm not sure.' Then, 'Listen, we've got
some beer and vodka. We're planning a wee ceilidh in the
boys' hut.'

But I wasn't interested. 'Thanks. I'll catch you later.' I was so
intent on finding Ruairidh that I missed her warning.

I hurried on down to the beach, and as I rounded the dunes
I saw them sitting side by side in the light of the dying fire.
Ruairidh and Seonag, huddled together as if for warmth. The
wind was sending smoke and sparks off into the night, and

fanning the embers to cast their light on the pair. There was no one else there. They didn't see me coming as I walked with heavy legs through the sand towards them, stopping then in my tracks as Seonag turned her head towards him and they kissed.

My gasp was involuntary. Forced from me, as with a fist in the gut, and they broke apart, startled. I saw regret in Ruairidh's eyes immediately. Something verging on panic. Seonag just looked at me with her penetrating green eyes, glazed slightly from too much alcohol, but shining with something that looked very much like triumph.

There were no words to express my sense of betrayal. I turned and ran back up the path, the way I had come. And almost immediately felt, more than heard, the pounding of Ruairidh's footsteps in my wake. He caught up with me shortly before the lodge. His hand on my arm pulling me to a halt, half-turning me towards him.

'Don't!' I shouted at him. 'Don't dare tell me it's not what it seemed.'

'It's not.'

I turned my head away in disgust.

'I missed you.'

My head snapped back around, eyes blazing with anger and hurt. 'Is that right? Well, you've got a really interesting way of showing it.'

'I was drunk. Depressed, and . . .'

'And Seonag was just there.'

I could see the shame in his eyes. He shrugged. 'Yes.' And

even he realized how lame that sounded. 'It was stupid, I know. I don't even care about Seonag. I never have.'

'And you clearly don't give a damn about me. You've been avoiding me for weeks. And now this.' I paused, uncertain if I had ever felt this much pain before. Then remembered. Only once. 'We're through, Ruairidh Macfarlane. Finished. It's over.'

And I turned and fled in tears back to the lodge. In my room I lay on my bed and wept until my tears ran dry, leaving me with nothing but a sore throat and red and swollen eyes. Eventually, I sat up, swinging my legs over the edge of the bed and burying my face in my hands. My summer idyll had turned into a nightmare, and all I wanted was to get away.

The door opened and light from the hallway fell in a slab across the floor. Seonag stepped into the light, a silhouette in the doorway. I couldn't see her face as she said, 'Don't go reading too much into what you saw down there, Niamh.'

I found my voice with difficulty. 'And what should I read into it?'

'I don't care about Ruairidh.'

'Funny, he said the same thing about you.' Which seemed to take the wind out of her sails. But not for long.

'Just goes to show, then, doesn't it? You can't trust him.'

During the few days that remained I avoided contact with them both. The whole atmosphere in the lodge had changed. I'm sure even the guests must have sensed the difference. It felt as if every one of us had overstayed our welcome. The summer was finished and all we wanted now was to get back to our real lives. And when I returned to the mainland to start the autumn term of my second year at Galashiels, I was hugely depressed and determined to put Ruairidh and Seonag as far behind me as possible.

CHAPTER SEVENTEEN

Darkness had fallen by the time Niamh and Seonag got back to the house. The sky to the north was alive and flickering with colour. The aurora borealis had begun its spectacular celestial light show. Red, pink and purple grew out of the arc of green light that spanned the horizon, swirling and rising into the black of the sky, reflecting below on the darkness of the ocean. It all seemed to derive from tiny explosions of light moving back and forth just beyond the horizon. Niamh had seen it many times, but it was never the same twice and she never tired of it.

She and Seonag stretched out on the settee, and watched the show, framed as it was by the giant windows that looked out on the Minch.

For a while neither of them spoke. Niamh and Ruairidh had lain here watching their own personal display of the northern lights together on so many occasions, that somehow it didn't seem right for them to carry on without him. Just one more reminder that he was gone.

Finally, Seonag said, 'This is something I should have said years ago . . .'

Niamh turned her head towards her in the dark, seeing all the colours of the aurora borealis reflected on the pale ivory of her face.

'I'm sorry.'

'For what?' Niamh said, although she knew.

'For being such a shit all those years ago.' She looked at Niamh and shrugged. 'I can't even explain it to you now, any more than I could have at the time. Hormones, I suppose. That's my only excuse.' She took a sip of wine. 'Anyway, you should know that it's something I've always regretted. You do and say things at that age, and when you look back you just cringe with embarrassment.' A pause. 'I'm sorry, Niamh. I'm only glad it all turned out for the best, in spite of me.' And during a lull in the lights a shadow crossed her face. 'Until this.' She paused. 'I'm so, so sorry.'

Niamh nodded. What could she say? She had put it behind her a long time ago. And if she couldn't exactly forgive her friend, she no longer blamed her.

Seonag said, 'What are you going to do about Ranish Tweed?'

Present reality came flooding back, like water filling an empty pool. 'I've no idea. To be honest, I've not even thought about it. And I'm not sure I care.' She paused for reflection. 'Ranish was all about me and Ruairidh. A kind of physical manifestation of what it was we had between us. Of what was special about us. I don't know that I have any desire to carry it on without him.'

Seonag stared into her glass. 'It would be a shame to let it go, then. Like letting go of Ruairidh, too.'

And Niamh saw the truth in that. Ranish was the biggest piece of him that she had left. And yet part of her wondered if it wouldn't simply be a constant and painful reminder of what she had lost.

'I've enjoyed working for Ranish,' Seonag said. 'With both of you. And watching it grow. We're still getting more orders than we can fulfil. It has a long-term future ahead of it.'

Niamh wondered if Seonag saw herself as being a part of that future. She remembered how reluctant she had been to take Seonag on in the first place, and how she had been over-ruled by Ruairidh's mother. But in the end Seonag had proved to be the rock on which the company had built its expansion. She had a sound business head, persuading them of the need to computerize to manage growth. Now, perhaps, she wasn't just a part of the company's future. She *was* its future.

Niamh said, 'I'll think about it all after the funeral.'

It was late now, and Niamh could hardly keep her eyes open. The aurora borealis was still doing its thing all along the horizon to the north, but by now they had both stopped seeing it. The extraordinary had become animated wallpaper, and they stood to head along the hall to the bedrooms.

Seonag gave her friend a long, lingering hug, before kissing her softly on the forehead. 'See you in the morning,' she whispered, and slipped into her room, closing the door gently behind her.

Niamh stood for several long moments in the dark, tinnitus ringing in her ears like a distant echo of the bomb that had taken Ruairidh. The blast, and the screams, and the flash of light which had very nearly blinded her, replayed itself in her memory, and she wondered why she was so reluctant to go into the bedroom she had shared with him. After all, hadn't she taken comfort from sleeping in her grandfather's bed after he had died?

She forced herself into the room, standing with her back to the door after she closed it, staring at the unmade bed in the darkness. She switched on a light and pushed her suitcase off the end of it and on to the floor, before heading for the bathroom, discarding her clothes as she went.

In the shower she stood naked beneath the flow of hot water, hoping that somehow it might wash away the pain. Of course, it didn't. When finally she emerged, skin pink and stinging, and dried herself on a big soft white towel, she padded through to the bedroom and collapsed into the bed. The impression of his head was still pressed into his pillow, and she rolled over to lie on it, trying to recapture the sense of him, his scent, his body shape in the bed. But all she found was emptiness.

She reached over to turn out the light and was asleep almost before she had extinguished it.

She had no idea what time it was when she awoke. The bedside clock was flashing from some power blip that must have happened while she and Ruairidh were away. But she knew that something had wakened her. A sound, perhaps. Or a vibration. Something she had felt more than heard.

She sat bolt upright, sleep banished in a moment. And listened. Intently. There it was again. A sound, or a sensation, like a door closing, as if someone out there were moving around the house. But softly, secretly.

Niamh slipped from the bed, pulling on a black silk dressing gown embroidered with dragons and tying it tightly around herself. She eased open the bedroom door and saw moonlight falling in through the Velux windows in the roof, casting its silver light into the living room. She glanced at Seonag's door. It was firmly shut. She listened for a moment outside it, but could hear nothing from within. She drifted quickly down the hall, then, and into the living space illuminated by those vast windows that gave on to the Minch. Out on the water she saw burnished moonlight reflected on its surface, like silver poured from the moon.

She went into her office. By the light of the screensaver that animated her computer screen, she cast eyes over the litter of papers strewn across her desktop. Had something been moved? Or was that just her imagination. She couldn't remember exactly how she had left things.

Then the faintest dull thud came again from somewhere towards the front of the house. She ran back through the living room and into the hall. Nothing. Seonag's door was still shut.

Niamh returned cautiously to her bedroom, turning on all the lights to be certain that there was no one there. The bathroom, too, was empty. She hurried back to the bedroom and lowered the blinds she normally left raised, and turned the snib on the bedroom door to lock herself in.

When the lights were out she slipped back into bed. But it felt cold now, and sleep a long way away. She lay for the longest time, staring at the ceiling, listening intently. But she heard no other sound than the faintest howl of the wind as it rose from the west, and sometime not long before dawn she slipped away into a troubled unconsciousness.

It was the smell of food cooking that awoke her next. Still she had no idea of the time, but it was daylight now and she padded out in her dressing gown to the kitchen where she found Seonag frying up the bacon and eggs she had brought with her the night before.

She was fully dressed and made up, and glanced towards Niamh as she came in. 'Thought you might like some breakfast before I head off.'

Niamh's head was still thick with sleep, and she was confused. 'Where are you going? What time is it?'

'It's after nine, Niamh, and I'm already late. Monday morning. I've got to go and open up the office.'

Niamh slumped into one of the breakfast stools and dropped her head into her hands, wiping her eyes and trying to clear her thoughts. She looked up. 'Were you up and about during the night?'

Seonag shook her head. 'No, I was out like a light. Wouldn't have wakened up either if I hadn't set my alarm.' She paused. 'Why?'

But Niamh just shrugged. 'Nothing. Thought I heard someone, that's all.'

Seonag slipped a plate on to the breakfast bar in front of her. Two eggs, yolks winking at her and turning her stomach. Several rashers of overcooked bacon. She would wait until Seonag had gone before sliding them into the bin. 'There's coffee made,' Seonag said, and she lifted her overnight bag off the counter top. 'Is there anything you'd like me to tell Ruairidh's folks?'

Niamh shook her head. 'No. As soon as I feel fit to face the world I'll drive down and see them myself. Donald will have told them to expect me this morning.'

Seonag nodded, stooped to give Niamh a quick kiss on the cheek. 'Maybe see you later, then.' But she didn't leave, and Niamh looked up to find her standing there watching her, eyebrows drawn together in concern. 'Are you going to be alright?'

Niamh said, 'I'll be fine.'

'Well, if you need me. Any time, day or night. Call.' She implored Niamh with her eyes. 'Please.'

Niamh nodded acknowledgment.

After Seonag had gone she let her head drop and pictured the scene that lay ahead when she went to see Ruairidh's parents. And she wondered how she would ever muster the courage to face them.

CHAPTER EIGHTEEN

It was one of those sticky sultry Paris days that seemed always to announce the imminent arrival of autumn. Low cloud bubbled across the sky and everyone carried an umbrella. If it felt like it was going to rain, then it probably would.

Braque was slick already with perspiration. She wore a T-shirt out over her jeans, black so that the dark patches under her arms would not show. Her hair was sticking to her forehead, and she brushed it back and out of her eyes as she hurried up the stairs to the offices of the *brigade criminelle*, known more popularly as *La Crim'*.

Capitaine Georges Faubert was in a foul mood. He was always in a foul mood. Ever since he had been banned from smoking in his own office. He resented the three or four cigarette breaks he allowed himself daily, standing outside in the rear courtyard in all weathers with other ranks. The camaraderie of the smoker had passed him by. It would have reduced him in importance somehow, and so he always stood aloof and alone.

Braque smelled fresh smoke on his breath when she entered

his office, so perhaps, she hoped, he might not be too ill-disposed towards her tardy arrival. She was wrong.

He had some kind of psoriasis on his scalp and forehead, and when he scratched it to relieve the itching, which he did often and vigorously, he shed a snowstorm of skin on to his desk. It seemed that he was particularly troubled by it this morning, and so on a scale of one to ten his bad temper ranked around eight.

'You're late, Braque!'

'Yes, boss.' She really didn't want to go into explanations, but mere acknowledgment seemed insufficient. 'My friend who normally takes the girls to school called off at the last minute, and I had to take them myself. The thing is . . .'

He cut her off. 'No one's interested in the details of your domestic dramas, Lieutenant. The only thing that matters here is whether or not you're up to the job. And there are several voices of concern being raised on that count.'

Braque felt her face redden.

'If you'd got here when you were supposed to, then you wouldn't have put yourself under pressure to get out to the airport on time.' He rubbed his face with the flats of his hands, and more skin flaked off to join the drifts of it on his desk. His eyes were red-rimmed and crusted with conjunctivitis when he turned them back on her.

Braque was at a loss. 'Where am I going?'

'A flight to London, with onward connections to Glasgow and then Stornoway. You know where that is?'

'Vaguely.'

'Well, you'd better get yourself some clarity. Stornoway is the main town on the Isle of Lewis, where the Macfarlane woman comes from. In fact, the only town.'

'Yes, I knew that, sir. Just not where it is, exactly.'

Faubert shook the skin off a map lying on his desk, unfolding it to turn towards her. He stabbed a nicotine-stained finger at a long archipelago off the north-west coast of the British Isles. 'Some God-forsaken place on the edge of the bloody world.'

'And I would be going there why?'

He looked at her with irritation. 'Why there, or why you?'

'Well . . . both.'

'It's your case, Braque. And you've made bugger-all progress on it. It's reasonable to expect that Macfarlane will bury her husband's remains within the next day or two. There will, no doubt, be a very public funeral. Always are on occasions like these. It's also reasonable to assume that whoever killed the man knew him. So there's every chance he'll be at the funeral.'

'What about Irina?'

'What about her?'

'Who'll be keeping an eye on her funeral?'

'Lieutenant Cabrel.'

Braque said. 'I wouldn't have thought it very likely that Georgy Vetrov would turn up at either.'

'Well, no.' Faubert stood up. 'Particularly since you seem to have lost him.'

Braque bristled at the implication that she was somehow responsible for mislaying their prime suspect.

'If he *has* made it back to Russia, then the likelihood is that we'll never see him again.' He paused. 'But here's the thing . . .' He picked up a manila folder and held it out to her. 'Forensic examination of Vetrov's computer.' She opened it as he spoke. 'Deleted emails recovered from the hard drive.'

She ran her eye down the list, then stopped suddenly. Three from the bottom was an email from '*well wisher*'. It was titled '*Something you should know*'. Almost the same email that was sent to Niamh Macfarlane. '*Irina is having an affair with a Scottish textile supplier called Ruairidh Macfarlane. Why don't you ask her about it?*'

She looked up to find Faubert watching her intently. 'Someone sent this email, Braque, intent on mischief, or malice, or both. Now perhaps it did provoke Vetrov into planting that car bomb and killing them both. But we have absolutely no proof of that. All we know is that he has vanished. He didn't send this email to himself. Nor, it would be safe to assume, the one to Madame Macfarlane. So there is someone else out there who can most definitely help us with our enquiries.' He opened another folder and lifted out an electronic airline ticket, before dropping it on the desk in front of her. 'Which is why I want you to be at the funeral.'

Clarity dawned suddenly on Braque. 'That's why the remains were released so early.'

'The only reason. We had to rush through bone and tissue

matching. Damage was so extreme that DNA comparison wasn't always possible. If we'd waited, the whole thing would have gone cold. Sometimes, a simple blood test was good enough to tell us which parts were male, which parts female. The rest, the slush, whatever, got washed down the pathologist's drain, disposed of along with the bits that couldn't be matched.'

'Jesus, boss!' Braque was shocked.

Faubert waved her shock aside with a dismissive hand. 'This is a very high-profile case, Lieutenant. People upstairs want a high-profile resolution. And fast.' He drew a deep breath, as if inhaling smoke, and looked at her critically. 'And why you?' He shook his head. 'I'm asking myself the same question. But you are the only detective in the department with the level of English required for an assignment like this. So you get to go to sunny Stornoway.'

He rounded his desk, feeling in his jacket pocket for his cigarette packet. Evidently dealing with Braque had brought on nicotine cravings.

'We've already been in touch with Police Scotland. They've been briefed, and a local officer on the island will be allocated to look after you. Find out everything you can about the couple. Friends, relationships. Enemies.'

'She'll recognize me.'

'Well why shouldn't she? You're not going there undercover. You'll need to talk to her, too.' He brushed a hand across each shoulder and clouds of fine skin filled the air. Then he looked at his watch. 'You'd better hurry. You've got less than three hours to get yourself out to Charles de Gaulle.'

Braque watched her fingers shaking as they punched out Madeleine's number on her phone. The chatter of keyboards and voices filled the detectives' office, along with the aroma of freshly brewed coffee. Braque's panic shut it all out.

Madeleine's voice sounded feeble. '*Oui, allô*? The reason she had been unable to pick up the twins that morning was what she claimed to be the onset of *la grippe*, although Braque was sure it was more likely to be a simple cold than the flu. Madeleine had a habit of dramatizing things.

'Maddie, I've got a bit of an emergency. They're sending me to Scotland for a few days and I need someone to take the girls.'

'I'm fine. Thanks for asking.' Madeleine's tone suggested that she wasn't being entirely flippant.

'Oh, I'm sorry, my poor darling. How are you?'

'Terrible, now that you ask.'

Even before she pressed the question, Braque knew what the answer would be. 'I don't suppose . . .'

'Sylvie, it's out of the question. I can't even take care of Patsy, never mind the twins. Yves is having to pick her up from school. It's going to be a few days before I'm up and about again.'

Braque exhausted all other possibilities before resorting, finally, to calling her ex. It simply wasn't an option going back to Faubert to tell him she couldn't go to Scotland because she was unable to find a babysitter.

Gilles answered the phone with a sigh, caller ID betraying her identity in advance. 'What is it now, Sylvie?'

'Gilles, I need a huge favour.'

'You always do.'

She ignored his tone. 'I'm being sent abroad on a case. Just for a few days. But I can't get anyone to take the girls.'

There was a long silence.

'Gilles?'

'You know, we should never have had children. You're not fit to be a mother.'

'*We*, Gilles. That's the salient word here. *We* had children. It's a shared responsibility.'

'Except that you have custody and I only get to see them when it suits you.'

'I have to work!'

'Bloody hell, so do I! The difference is that I've got a partner, speaking of *shared* responsibility. You don't. And you can't cope, can you? It's not even about money. It's the job, the hours you work. The same things that made you a bad partner making you a bad mother.'

'I love my girls. And they love me.'

'They do. But they never get to see you. You're never there. You're always letting them down.'

'That's not fair.'

'Not fair on them, no. Listen, girl, you were the one that fought for custody. You were the one that didn't want them spending time with Lise. Scared that she was going to steal

them away from you. Well, if you can't live up to your obliga-
tions as a mother, then we really are going to have to revisit
the whole question of custody.'

Braque contained her emotions with difficulty. 'Are you
going to take them or not?'

'Of course I'll bloody take them! But when you get back,
Sylvie, we're going to have to talk. This cannot go on. The
girls need a mother, not a babysitter. A home, not a crêche.'

CHAPTER NINETEEN

Balanish sat at the mouth of the river, overlooking the sea loch, and with easy passage from the harbour out to the ocean. Hills rose on three sides and it nestled in the valley where it was protected from the worst of the weather that the Atlantic could muster.

The Macfarlane croft was accessed from the turn-off just before the bridge, and sat halfway up the hill. It fell away on a long, gentle slope to the shore. Ruairidh's father still kept a handful of sheep, but they had long ago stopped growing anything other than a few potatoes on a patch they cultivated at the side of the house.

The old croft house, now providing offices for Ranish Tweed, had been built next to the ruins of the original blackhouse halfway down the hill at the end of a steep pitted track. The new house sat just below the road at the top of the hill, commanding spectacular views over the loch, as well as the village below.

Niamh pulled her Jeep in alongside the Macfarlanes' Audi A3. It was not a vehicle that could ever have negotiated the track across the moor to Taigh 'an Fiosaich. But beyond the initial tour of the house that Ruairidh had given them when he drove them out himself in the Jeep, the Macfarlanes had never been to visit.

As she walked around the granite-chipped walls of the house, Niamh felt the full fresh blast of a stiffening wind and noticed that Seonag's red SUV was not outside the office further down the hill. She knocked on the back door and opened it into the kitchen.

Donald was sitting at the kitchen table eating toast and watching the news on a small TV set placed on top of the fridge. He seemed startled by her arrival, and then embarrassed.

'Hi,' he said, turning off the television and getting hurriedly to his feet. 'Mum, Dad,' he called through the open door into the hall, 'that's Niamh.' Then he shuffled awkwardly. 'Everything okay?'

Niamh shrugged. 'As okay as anything can be in the circumstances.'

Mr Macfarlane came in first, wiping shaving foam from his neck with a towel that he then hung over the back of a chair. He looked gaunt, dark semicircles below his eyes. 'Aw, Niamh,' he said, and gave her the warmest of hugs. 'I'm so sorry, my love. It's the most awful thing to have happened. Donna's been inconsolable.'

Donna appeared at the door. Niamh had never been able to bring herself to call her mother-in-law anything other than Mrs Macfarlane. She might have been inconsolable, but she stood now with a face like gneiss. Whatever grieving was going on inside was not visible on the exterior. She said, 'Seonag told us you were coming.' A pause. 'It might have been nice if you had told us yourself.'

Niamh stiffened. 'I didn't want to disturb you on the sabbath. But I did tell Donald that I would be here today.' She glanced at Donald and he blushed to the roots of his ginger hair. Niamh had little doubt that he had told them just that. But Mrs Macfarlane revelled in being contrary. Niamh said, 'I didn't see Seonag's car down by the office.'

'She's been and gone,' Mr Macfarlane said. 'Off to collect some finished cloth from the mill at Shawbost.'

Niamh nodded. 'We need to talk about funeral arrangements.' It sounded so blunt and businesslike, but she had no idea how else to say it.

'You can leave that to us,' Mrs Macfarlane said. 'I think it's down to the family to organize the funeral.'

Niamh felt anger colour her grief. But she retained control. 'As his wife, and next of kin, I am his family.' She saw Mrs Macfarlane bristle. 'But I do think we ought to agree on the details together.' The last thing she wanted was to fall out with Ruairidh's parents.

'Aye.' Mr Macfarlane nodded his approval, but his wife was not to be so easily mollified.

'Was he really having an affair with some Russian fashion designer?' she demanded, as if it might all somehow be Niamh's fault.

'I have no idea. It's what they're saying.'

A puff of contempt blew from between puckered lips. 'I think if my husband was having an affair with a Russian fashion designer I would have known about it.'

Niamh glanced at an awkward Mr Macfarlane, who didn't know where to look. Niamh wanted to say, *If your husband was having an affair with anyone, Mrs Macfarlane, who could blame him?* But she bit back the retort. Instead she said, 'Whether or not Ruairidh was having an affair is not something I'm going to discuss with you, or anyone else.'

'What about Ranish, then?' she said coldly.

'What about it?'

'We need to discuss the future of the company.'

And finally Niamh lost patience. 'For God's sake! I'm here to talk about burying your son. Not some business venture. Frankly, right now I don't give a damn about the future of Ranish. I don't know how it even finds a place in your thoughts.'

For the first time, Mrs Macfarlane appeared chastened and at a loss for words.

Mr Macfarlane said, 'Donald tells us you've brought the body back with you.'

'Yes.'

'Where's it being kept?'

'It's in the boot of the car, Mr Macfarlane.' And she saw the shock on both their faces, glancing then at Donald, who blushed again. She realized there were things he had clearly felt unable to tell them. She said quickly, 'I phoned the funeral director in Stornoway first thing this morning to make an appointment. We should probably all go together.'

The cardboard box with its plastic shipping straps sat on the table in front of them. No one knew quite what to say. The awful realization that this was all that was left of her son had reduced Donna Macfarlane to tearful silence.

The funeral director, Alasdair Macrae, stood with his back to the window, looking at it thoughtfully. Here was a man who had seen and dealt with all manner of death, all degrees of grief. A dapper, soft-spoken man with sympathetic blue eyes and the smudge of a sandy moustache on his upper lip. Coffins in racks rose from floor to ceiling against one wall. And through the window behind him Niamh saw a line of refuse bins pushed against the wall. One blue, two black with coloured lids. For recycling the refuse. Just as here, on the inside, they recycled death.

Mr Macrae had already removed and examined the shipping papers, and now he took a knife to cut the strapping and lift the coffin for still-borns from inside its box. He picked it up, almost as if weighing it, and said, 'Come through to the back.'

Niamh and Donald and his parents trooped along a corridor with a shiny linoleum floor into a workshop at the rear of the building. A large clear plastic fanlight let daylight through into the workshop where they had once made the coffins on site. Old workbenches were pushed against painted breeze-block walls, and two coffins stood, lengthwise, on trestles in the middle of the floor. The funeral director removed the lid from one to reveal that beneath its veneer the coffin was constructed of biodegradable MDF.

'I'll line the interior as I normally would,' he said, 'and place pillows at the head of it. We have to do things properly.' He laid the box of Ruairidh's remains in the middle of the coffin and looked around for a couple of cardboard boxes to brace it at either end. 'I'll construct something like this to hold it in place, so it doesn't slide about when it's being carried by the bearers. I'll make it look nice, of course. Even if nobody sees it.'

Niamh put her hand to her mouth and bit down hard along the length of her forefinger. This was almost too much to bear. The dreadful banality that came in the aftermath of death. Everything practical for the dispatch of the body following the departure of life. And yet it all had to be gone through, step by painful step. The road to closure. The consignment of a lover to eternity.

Outside the rain had begun to fall, swept in across the Barvas Moor from the west coast. Stornoway was a dull town in the rain. Figures huddled in coats and hats, bent over against the wind. Umbrellas were rare, and never lasted more than a few minutes. They could hear the plaintive cries of seagulls circling the inner harbour below.

It was possible to pass the funeral parlour in this residential back street without noticing. The only indication being discreet gold lettering painted on a small square of window. A*MACRAE FUNERAL DIRECTORS. Barely two doors along stood the Body & Sole beauty parlour. Opposite, the Associated Presbyterian Church. This was a street, it seemed, that catered for all aspects of life and death.

The funeral was set for Wednesday at the cemetery at Dalmore Beach, the irony of which was not lost on any of them. Two more days, and all that was left of Ruairidh would be dispatched to the earth for good.

Inside, Mrs Macfarlane had said, 'The coffin should be available at the house for mourners to pay their last respects.' And Mr Macrae had promised to deliver it to the croft at Balanish by that evening.

Now, as they stood outside in the rain, she said, 'I'll arrange things with the minister.' And although Niamh had wanted to keep control of the process, she was almost relieved to pass on the baton. It had been a long and painful journey, and she was not at all sure she had the strength to see it through to the end.

By late afternoon the wind had blown the rain away, and gathered in strength. From the clifftops at Cellar Head, Niamh felt buffeted by it. Far out across the Minch she saw the rain still falling, like a mist obliterating the swell of the sea and the mainland beyond. The ocean thrashed white against black rocks two hundred feet below, and she wondered how it might feel simply to step off into the void, spreading her arms like a bird and falling to oblivion. No more pain, no more grief, no more missing Ruairidh, or contemplating the life that lay ahead without him. But she did not have the courage for that.

Half a mile further along the coast, she could see the house they had made together standing proud and defiant on the promontory, and beyond it the ruined house and church built by Iain Fiosaich. A hundred years from now, she wondered, what would remain of *their* home? Would it vanish without trace like Ruairidh and Niamh themselves? Would anyone remember them, as folk today still remembered Iain Fiosaich and his wealthy wife from New York?

In the gully below, on a rocky shelf cut by nature into the face of the cliff, Fiosaich had built his first home, balanced somewhere between life and death, a precarious if spectacular place to live. But he had abandoned it soon enough, and when Ruairidh and Niamh arrived to build their own home, all that remained of it were the scattered stones of the walls and foundations. Over time, and on countless sabbaths beyond the disapproving glare of the Church, they had built a tiny stone bothy in its place, a refuge for the walkers and hikers who made the pilgrimage out to see the house that Fiosaich had built.

From where she stood Niamh could just see it, with its roof of stone slabs in overlapping layers set upon the wooden structure below, walls of stone hewn from the cliffs, like camouflage, making it difficult to spot if you didn't know it was there.

It was here that she and Ruairidh had opened the urn containing Róisín's ashes, to let the wind take them where it would. Nearly eight years ago now.

When she had fallen pregnant, Ranish was in its first flush of success, and her initial thoughts had turned to abortion. How, she had wondered, could a baby possibly fit into the lives they were making for themselves? Working ten or twelve hours a day. Frequent trips abroad or to the mainland. Ruairidh would have carried on as before. Seonag, and no doubt Ruairidh's mother, would have taken greater control of the company. Leaving Niamh with a primary role as mother and babysitter, and a back seat in the forward progress of Ranish Tweed.

Ruairidh had been opposed to the very idea of termination. Not for any religious or philosophical reasons, but because he wanted a child. And when his mother got wind of Niamh's thinking she had accused her of trying to murder her grandchild.

It had been a fraught time, filled with argument and aggravation. Ironically it was Seonag who had finally settled Niamh's mind on the matter. A throwaway conversation, even before she knew that Niamh was pregnant. Already with two children of her own, Seonag had said simply that they were the greatest gift that God had given her. It had crossed her mind, she said, when first pregnant, that she was too young for children and that abortion would have allowed for future planning. Niamh remembered how her childhood friend had gazed off into the middle distance, and with a slight shake of her head said, 'I'm so glad I didn't do that. Knowing what I know now, I don't think I could ever have forgiven myself.'

Niamh knew she could never have lived with that kind of

regret, and so she took the bold decision to let her pregnancy run its course, determined that their baby would have to fit in with *their* lives, rather than the other way around.

She had relaxed into her decision, then, and begun to relish the prospect of becoming a mother. A scan had revealed that their child was a girl, and she and Ruairidh had chosen the Irish Gaelic name of Róisín for their daughter.

But then two months before the baby was due, Niamh had begun to bleed. Unaccountably. She'd been rushed to hospital in Stornoway, then airlifted to Inverness, where the baby was stillborn. As if it had not been devastating enough to lose their child, the doctors told Niamh that due to internal damage she was unlikely to have more children.

Ruairidh had been stoic and supportive, despite his disappointment. But his mother, though never saying it in so many words, had implied that somehow it was Niamh herself who had contrived the miscarriage. That dark cloud of suspicion and mistrust had cast a shadow on their relationship ever since.

Róisín had been cremated in Inverness. A ceremony attended by just Niamh and Ruairidh. They had returned to release her ashes here on the cliffs, as if releasing her spirit to rest with her parents in this place for eternity.

Niamh had regretted it immediately. With Róisín's ashes dispersed instantly by the wind, it was as if she had lost her all over again. Vanished without trace. And in all the years since, she had lamented not burying her child. A grave to visit, a place for flowers. A piece of this earth forever Róisín's.

Niamh sat on a cluster of stones and gazed at the rock face below. A complex pattern of molten rock which had cooled in layers to form these cliffs untold millions of years before. If only she could be absorbed by them, subsumed to become a part of the whole. Instead of remaining this wretched speck in the universe, this tiny repository of grief and sorrow, so filled with regret at the loss of her man, and her child.

Never in her life had she felt so small and alone.

CHAPTER TWENTY

The flight north from Glasgow was a bumpy one, in and out of cloud with only occasional glimpses of the ground below. Lochs and green valleys, and now mountain ranges that seemed unnaturally close.

Braque had read that the ferry crossing from Ullapool to Stornoway took three hours on a good day, but the flight across the Minch took only a matter of minutes. It was difficult to tell when the plane was over water, because it was the same colour as the cloud. Dull, grey, featureless.

Only now, as she saw fingers of white-ringed black rock reach out into pewtery water, did the island announce itself to her, appearing slowly out of the haze like some lost, mythical land.

As the plane dipped beneath the cloud, she saw peat-scarred purple bog stretching off into a misted distance, tiny clusters of houses clinging to the very edges of the island itself. And her heart sank at the prospect of the days that lay ahead of her, alone in this strange and foreign place.

Detective Sergeant George Gunn was waiting for her by

the luggage carousel. She knew at once who he was. He looked like a policeman. Big feet in shiny black leather shoes, sharply pressed dark grey trousers, a quilted black anorak, and a face shaven to within an inch of its life. Pink and shiny and crowned by oiled black hair that divided his forehead in a widow's peak.

It seemed he knew her, too. Perhaps police officers everywhere recognized fellow travellers of the same species. He stepped forward to shake her hand as she put out her own, and said hesitantly, '*Bonjour madame*. Detective Sergeant George Gunn. *Je suis enchanté. C'est quelle, votre valise?*' He blushed and smiled and said, 'School French.'

Braque forced a smile in return. 'Perhaps we should stick to English.'

His smile vanished immediately. 'Of course. Your French is much better than mine.'

'I should hope so.'

He laughed awkwardly. 'Oh. Haha. Sorry, I meant . . .'

'It's alright,' she said, lifting a small suitcase from the conveyer belt. 'And I can manage my bag myself, thank you.'

'Of course.'

At the car-rental desk he said, 'You really didn't need to hire a car. I could have driven you wherever you wanted to go.'

She signed the rental and insurance documents. 'I prefer to have my own wheels.'

He nodded and watched as she presented her French driver's licence, wondering if Britain's exit from the European Union would make this process more complex in the future. He said, 'How did you recognize me?'

'The same way you recognized me.'

He frowned. 'They sent you my photograph?'

She turned, surprised. 'No. They sent you mine?'

'Some kind of faxed personnel document. Not a very good likeness.' He thought about it for a moment. 'So how . . . ?' But he decided to let it drop.

The wind that battered them as they stepped outside had an icy edge to it, feeling to Braque more like winter than autumn. She decided that she was distinctly underdressed in her short denim jacket and T-shirt.

'I'm in the black Ford,' he said. 'If you want to just follow me into town . . .'

The drive into Stornoway depressed Braque further. Featureless harled houses lining the road, long grasses bowed by a biting wind that swept across the moor. An old, yellow-painted mill looked like it might have been abandoned. A grey concrete municipal edifice just beyond the roundabout embodied the blighted architectural style of the depressed decade that was the nineteen seventies.

At the top of the hill they turned right into a long, wide street, affluent villas set back from the road and brooding darkly behind mature trees still in autumn leaf. Then into Church Street, descending past Indian and Thai restaurants, and the Kingdom Hall of Jehovah's Witnesses, to a white-painted police station on their right. At the foot of the hill, pleasure and fishing boats rose and fell on the leaden swell of the inner harbour, seagulls circling like shreds of white paper thrown to the winds.

Braque followed Gunn into a tight square parking area, and then into the police station via the back door. Past the charge bar where a big red-faced uniformed sergeant nodded at them. Off to their right a row of police cells flanked a short corridor. Gunn followed her eye and laughed. 'Not much use for those, except for drying out drunks on a Friday and Saturday night.'

Upstairs he led her into his office and closed the door. From the window she could see a charity shop on the corner opposite. He waved her into a chair and slumped into his own, which he pulled out from a desk pushed against the wall. He tried a smile, perhaps hoping that it might draw something reciprocal. 'Not quite Paris,' he said.

Braque nodded. It was not quite like anything she had ever seen.

'So . . .' He rested his palms on his thighs. 'Niamh Macfarlane.'

'Yes.'

'I did a little checking. It seems she arrived back yesterday afternoon with what's left of Ruairidh. They were at the undertaker's this morning. The funeral will be on Wednesday.'

Braque cocked an eyebrow in surprise. 'How did you find all that out so quickly?'

He chuckled. 'Ma'am, there's not much happens here that I don't know about within the hour. It's both a good and a bad thing, but everyone knows everyone else's business. And if they don't, someone else will tell them soon enough. Hard to keep a secret on this island.'

'So you would know if anyone here bore Ruairidh Macfarlane a grudge of some kind?'

'Well, I don't know the Macfarlanes personally. Just by repu-tation. Though I did meet him once about twenty years ago, when he caught some lad poaching on the Linshader Estate.'

'What happened?'

'Ruairidh was working as a ghillie at the lodge for the summer, taking guests out fishing. He and the gamekeeper broke up a gang of poachers and caught one of them. Handed him over to us. Ruairidh and the boy were neighbours, from the same village.'

'Was he charged?'

'Aye, and fined. Nothing more. But it was a stain on his repu-tation. A criminal record. And I believe he's not done too well for himself since.' He smiled. 'Though I doubt if that would have been motivation enough for blowing Ruairidh to bits in a car in Paris twenty some years later.'

Braque said, 'I've seen people moved to murder by less.'

'Aye, well, Ma'am, folk here tend to work out their differ-ences without killing one another.'

'You have a low murder rate in the islands, then?'

Gunn pulled in his chin and sucked air through his teeth. 'Maybe about one every hundred years or so.'

Braque looked at him with astonishment. 'If you exclude

terrorism, there are around seven hundred murders a year in France.'

Gunn nodded. 'Must keep you quite busy, then.'

Braque wondered if he was joking, and decided that he was, despite his straight face. 'So what else can you tell me about the Macfarlanes?'

'Well, I can tell you that there's no love lost between his family and hers. There was a . . .' He paused to search for the right word. 'An incident. A tragedy, you might say. Must be a quarter of a century ago now. I wasn't even on the island at the time. But I doubt if there's a single soul in Lewis and Harris that doesn't know the story.'

Braque's interest was piqued. 'So tell me.'

Gunn stood up. 'Time enough for that tomorrow. I'll take you there. It'll make more sense to you if you can visualize where it happened.' Then he said, 'But I'm at your disposal. If there's anywhere you'd like me to take you, just ask.'

Braque got stiffly to her feet. The trauma of leaving the girls, followed by the long journey from Paris to the Outer Hebrides, had taken its toll. 'I should call on Madame Macfarlane, make it known to her that I'm here.'

'You're not undercover, then?' He seemed disappointed.

'No, Detective Sergeant, I'm not.'

'Well, you'll not make it out there in that car you've hired. You'd rip the arse out of her – excuse my French. I'll get us a four by four.' He rubbed his hands together. 'Better get you to your hotel.'

Braque followed Gunn's black Ford through the town. Along Bayhead and past the inner harbour where trawlers sat high above the quay riding the tide. Shops and houses were painted blue, or yellow, or pink, sometimes harled, and sometimes just drab, rain-streaked stone. Two- and three-storey buildings clustered together along the spit of land that separated the inner and outer harbours, and it was opposite these that they parked, along the side of the quay.

Gunn led her up a short slope to the door of the Crown Hotel, self-conscious about letting her carry her own bag, and she checked in at reception. Gunn said, 'There's a lounge bar on the first floor. They do good grub. And the restaurant's got a nice view over the harbour. The pedestrian street out there runs right through the town. You can get fish and chips there. They call it the Narrows. It's where the kids all hang out on Friday and Saturday nights. There's not much else to do if you don't have any money, or you're too young for the pubs. It can be a bit noisy.' He glanced at her key. 'But it's only Monday, and I think your room looks over the harbour anyway.'

They stood awkwardly for a moment, and she said, 'Do you want to join me for a drink in the bar?' She registered his embarrassment again, and wondered if he saw her as attractive. She didn't feel attractive. No make-up, hair drawn back severely in a ponytail. And why would she care? He was at least ten years her senior, carrying more weight than was good for him, and judging by the ring on his finger, a married man.

He looked at his watch self-consciously. 'I can't really stay, Ma'am.'

'It's Sylvie.'

He nodded and confirmed his marital status. 'My wife will have my tea waiting for me.'

She had an image of his wife at home with a cup of tea, piping hot and ready for him coming through the door.

He must have seen her confusion. 'My dinner,' he clarified. And suddenly it occurred to him to ask her if she would like to eat with them. 'I'm sure whatever we're having would stretch to three . . .'

She smiled wearily. 'Thank you, but no thank you.' She had no desire to pass an awkward evening with this prosaic island policeman and his wife. 'I should probably get an early night.'

He seemed relieved. 'Righty-ho, then. I'll drop by to pick you up in the morning. About eight?'

She nodded. 'Thank you. *Bonne soirée*, Detective Sergeant.'

'You, too, Ma'am.'

When he was gone she carried her case up to her room with leaden legs and a heavy heart. The room was clean and tidy and modern, with a view across the harbour which, on a good day, might be stunning. But now, with the wind ridging the water and rain marbling the window pane, was just depressing. On the far side of the harbour a castle of some kind stood sentinel on the hill. Grey and red sandstone with crenellated towers. It seemed oddly out of place in this weather-lashed fishing port on the very edge of Europe. And she wondered what sort of people lived here, and what kind of lives they led.

She sat on the end of the bed feeling sorry for herself and took out her mobile phone to call Gilles and speak to the twins. But there was no reply, and she hung up feeling emptier and lonelier than she could ever have imagined.

CHAPTER TWENTY-ONE

It was only as she approached the house that Niamh noticed Seonag's red SUV parked next to the Jeep. She hadn't seen it arrive, and her heart sank. She really had wanted this time to herself. To mourn, to grieve, to deal with her demons on her own.

When she stepped into the house she could smell cooking. She kicked off her wellies and hung up her parka and padded through to the living room. Seonag was busy at the stove, steam rising from a large pan of boiling water filled with spaghetti. A meat sauce bubbled in another. Discarded food wrappings and the remains of ingredients lay scattered across the worktop. A bottle of Amarone stood open on the counter next to a couple of glasses, one of which contained a good two inches of ruby-red wine and displayed Seonag's lipstick all around the rim. Seonag looked entirely at home, as if it were she who lived here and not Niamh.

She turned, smiling, as she heard Niamh come in. 'Hello *a ghràidh*. Hope you don't mind pasta two days running. But bolognese is a wee bit different from lasagne. And I brought some more Italian wine to go with it.'

Niamh supposed she meant well and forced a smile. 'Great. But I'll stick with the fizzy water, if you don't mind.' She took a fresh bottle from the fridge and poured some into the empty glass. 'I've got to get an email out to my list before I eat. Just to let everyone know when and where the funeral's going to be.'

'No problem. The pasta's got a way to go yet. I'll just keep the sauce warm.'

Niamh took her glass with her through to the office and shut the door behind her. She slumped into her chair and took a sip of water, gazing out across the Minch in the dying light. She had sent an email to her list as soon as she got back from Stornoway, and was annoyed at having to lie to steal a moment to herself in her own house.

She let her head fall back and closed her eyes. So many things to think about, so many things to do. And she had no will to think or do any of them. She had an overwhelming urge to sleep, but knew that if she went to bed she would probably just lie awake.

She resented Seonag's uninvited presence, and yet there was a comfort in the sounds of domesticity coming from the kitchen. Of life in this house that had been deprived of it. How could she ever live here on her own? The only point of it had been to be with Ruairidh.

She had finished her water before she knew it, bubbles fizzing around her lips, and realized she would have to go back through. Seonag had the table set and was transferring spaghetti with pasta tongs from the pan into deep plates. 'Perfect timing,' she said. And began spooning minced beef and tomato sauce over the pasta before grating big flakes of parmesan over the top of it. She carried the plates to the table and they both sat on the round, facing the view. Just as Niamh and Ruairidh had always done. Seonag refilled her glass. 'So how did you get on with the Macfarlanes?'

Niamh flicked her a glance and was sure she already knew, but told her anyway.

Seonag listened in grave silence then said, 'I suppose it's best that the coffin is on display at the croft rather than up here. Folk would never make it out on that road.' She canted her head in the direction of the track that snaked its way across the moor from Ness.

Niamh nodded. 'No.'

'What were you doing up on the cliffs? I saw you in the distance when I arrived.'

Niamh shrugged and spooned pasta into her mouth. It tasted good and she realized just how hungry she was. 'Walking, thinking, remembering. It was out there above the bothy that we released Roísín's ashes.'

Seonag said, 'I've never been out to the bothy. What possessed you to build it in the first place?'

Niamh washed down her bolognese with a mouthful of clear sparkling water. 'Years ago Ruairidh took me out on to the cliffs at Mangersta. You know how exposed it is down there. Those amazing sheer rock faces, stacked up in layers, as if they were God's archives, a geological history of the Hebrides.

Seams of rock like the rings of a tree, but taking you right back to the very beginnings of time.'

'Hard to believe, but I've never been as far south as Mangersta. Uig Beach is about my limit.' Seonag sipped her wine.

'Really?' Niamh was surprised. 'I must take you some time. There are rock stacks in the ocean all around the cliffs. The sea just breaks white all along that stretch of coast. Anyway, there's a bothy there, built just below the lip of one of the cliffs about thirty years ago by a couple living in the area. It was their daughter that died in Afghanistan, remember? She was an aid worker kidnapped by the Taliban, and then killed during an attempt by American marines to rescue her.'

'Linda Norgrove,' Seonag said. I remember the funeral. The procession was miles long.'

'Well, it was her folks who built the bothy. No idea why, but Ruairidh knew about it. He'd been out there a few times and wanted to show me it.' She smiled, remembering the trek across the cliffs, almost getting lost before finding it, suddenly, tucked away on a hidden shelf below a tumble of broken rock. 'It sits perched up there, almost invisible, built right into the wall of the cliff. There's a couple of windows, with the most amazing views, and skylights. In clear weather you can see all the way out to the Flannan Isles, and St Kilda. We got there at sunset, and honest to God, Seonag, I'm not sure I've ever seen anything so beautiful. Like looking out from the roof of the world. We set a fire and made love, and spent the night.' A tear came with the memory and rolled slowly down her cheek. She wiped it away and forced a laugh. 'It wasn't the most comfortable place I've ever been made love to, or slept in. But it was magical.'

Seonag gazed at her in the semi-darkness, then rose to lean into the centre of the table and light candles. As she settled in her seat again she said, 'So that's what inspired the building of the bothy here?'

Niamh nodded. 'It's not as good as the one the Norgroves built, but we sort of borrowed their design, and the stone was all there from Iain Fiosaich's first house. We made a half-decent job of it, I think, and in the beginning we used to go there quite a lot.'

'Does anyone ever make use of it?'

'The occasional hiker, I think. And some people seem to seek it out, just for the novelty value. To be honest I haven't actually been in it for ages. A year or two, maybe. Ruairidh kept an eye on it and took care of any maintenance that was required.' And almost as she said it, Niamh realized that he would never be out there again, and that in all likelihood it would fall into desuetude, a ruin, like the life she saw stretching ahead of her.

Seonag finished the Amarone and opened another bottle. Niamh watched, concerned. She tried to make a joke of it and told Seonag she was drinking too much. But Seonag was dismissive and refilled her glass, slurring her words slightly for the first time.

They talked about childhood, recalling the days when they had played 'house' in the shed in Niamh's back garden and caught crabs on the shore, and cycled miles on disused single-track roads without ever seeing another soul. Pre-adolescent days when they had still been the best of friends, before hormones and adulthood had complicated simple lives.

Niamh got to her feet, finally, if only to stop Seonag from finishing another bottle. 'I've got to go to bed, Seonag. And you've drunk far too much to drive.'

Seonag smiled. 'It's okay. I told Martin I might not be back tonight anyway.'

She remained sitting at the table as Niamh made her way towards the hall and her bedroom door, calling back over her shoulder as she went, 'Don't worry about the dishes. I'll do all that in the morning.'

'*Oidhche mhath*,' she heard Seonag whisper as she shut the door.

For the second night she felt lost in this big, sprawling bed that she had once shared with Ruairidh. It seemed so empty without him. She remembered how he had insisted that they buy the biggest and the best, and she still cringed when she thought about the cost of it. But he had said, 'We spend a third of our lives in bed, why would we skimp on it?' And she couldn't argue with that.

She turned over on to her side, facing away from where he had once lain, turning out the light and curling up in the foetal position, the duvet pulled tightly around her. Fatigue overwhelmed her after days of sleep deprivation. And she drifted off into the deepest of sleeps from almost the moment she closed her eyes.

She had no idea how long she slept before a strange awareness brought her drifting slowly back to the surface. Of warmth and human comfort, a body spooned into hers, just like Ruairidh after they had made love. For the longest time, floating still in that netherworld between sleep and consciousness, she believed that he was there in bed with her. Although some part of her knew that it was impossible, she didn't want to let go of the illusion. That somehow he was still alive, his body moulded into all her curves and hollows. The comfort and happiness that accompanied it was almost too much to bear. If waking up would dispel the fantasy, then she never wanted to wake up again. Ever.

But, still, consciousness forced itself upon her, and as she rose up from the euphoric mists of delusion, she turned over to realize, with a sudden, waking clarity, that there really was someone there in the bed beside her.

She sat upright, heart hammering, reaching for the bedside light. And was shocked to see Seonag lying naked where Ruairidh had once slept. 'For God's sake, what are you doing?' Her voice sounded shrill, even to herself, and resounded around the room.

Seonag didn't move. She reached for Niamh's hand. 'Don't be angry with me.' But Niamh pulled her hand away.

'Seonag . . .' Niamh was at a loss.

Seonag said, 'I only wanted to comfort you. I know what you're going through. How lonely and lost you must be.'

'You have no idea how I'm feeling.' Anger replaced alarm.

Seonag sat up now, drawing the quilt self-consciously around. She reached for Niamh's hand again, found it and held it tightly. 'Niamh, there's never been anyone else. You know that.'

'Jesus, Seonag, I thought you'd got over all this.' She shook her head. 'That it was just some kind of teenage crush.' She forced her hand free of Seonag's. 'For heaven's sake, you're happily married. You've got two kids!'

Seonag sucked in her top lip, as if trying to hold back tears. 'Marriage has never made me happy. It was only ever what was expected. I love my kids. But God forbid that I should also be in love with another woman.'

All the tension drained out of Niamh now, and she let her head drop. She felt Seonag's pain, but knew there was nothing she could do to end it. And when next she looked at her saw the tears that Seonag had been unable to contain, running in big slow drops down her cheeks. She said, 'I can't help you, Seonag. I'm not ever going to be the person you want me to be. Not in that way.' She reached out to brush away the tears from her friend's face. 'You should go. You really should.' And when she didn't move, 'Please.'

The first sobs tore themselves from Seonag's chest, and she slipped from the bed and ran naked from the room. The door slammed shut behind her, and Niamh closed her eyes in despair.

CHAPTER TWENTY-TWO

It was with dread that I returned to Galashiels in the September following my summer at Linshader Lodge. A long demoralizing journey. Three-and-a-half hours across the Minch on the *Suilven*, from Stornoway to Ullapool. Then bus to Inverness, and on to Edinburgh. I recall what seemed like hours of waiting, stamping my feet in the cold of the old bus station at the St James Centre, waiting for the bus to the Borders.

My first year at the Scottish College of Textiles had been profoundly lonely. My room in the halls of residence, at Netherdale on the outskirts of the town, was little better than a cell: painted brick walls, a single bed, a wardrobe, a desk, and a view on to the back of the halls. The merest glimpse of grass and the road beyond, where the bus would drop me on my return from trips home. I felt like I had stepped on to the set of *Prisoner: Cell Block H.*

Some of the girls had arrived with duvet covers and towels, stereo systems and posters, transforming their rooms into little dens. I came down from the islands with nothing more than a suitcase. My room was as cold and impersonal when I left it as when I arrived.

I had *cianalas*, what we Gaels call homesickness, within the first five minutes, and it never left me the whole year. I remember queuing up on bitter cold nights for my turn on the shared payphone to call my folks, with the hope of catching maybe a breath of the sea somewhere in the background. It all seems extraordinary to me now. In these days of iPhones and every other kind of smartphone, keeping in touch with friends and family could hardly be easier. Back then, I might as well have been on the moon.

The girls on my floor shared a toilet and shower at the end of the hall, as well as a communal sitting room with a single TV set and fights every night over which channel we would watch.

The halls of residence were catered, which meant that we had to queue (again) with a tray in the canteen, and carry our food to shared melamine tables. *Cell Block H* (again). I was utterly miserable.

Gala, as everyone called it, was a friendly enough place, but on the downward slide after years of decline in the textile industry. It had once been a prosperous little mill town. But most of the mills were gone, and it felt seedy now, grey and depressed.

The college itself had retained its reputation, and most of the designers, salespeople and mill managers in the Scottish textile industry went there. It was the career I wanted, but as I returned for that second year, I was not at all sure that I could stay the course.

It was doubly depressing going back to Gala after events at Linshader. I was still hurting, and haunted by the memories of the halcyon summer I had passed in the weeks before the poaching incident on Loch Four.

I had, however, brought numerous personal items to dress up my cell for this second year, and was in the process of pinning posters of Runrig and Deacon Blue to the wall when there was a knock on the open door. I turned to see Seonag standing grinning in the doorway. I've often heard the phrase *You could knock me down with a feather*. But if anyone had so much as breathed on me in that moment I'd have fallen over.

'Surprise,' she said. And if she saw my dismay she gave no outward sign of it.

'What are you doing here?'

'Switched courses. Joined the second year at Gala. The Dough School in Glasgow was a drag. And, anyway, I didn't really make any friends there.' She jerked her thumb over her shoulder. 'I've got the room right opposite.'

In other circumstances I might have been glad of the company, but right now Seonag was just about the last person in the world I wanted to see.

'Oh,' I said, without the least enthusiasm.

She retained her cheerful façade. 'So we'll have lots of time to spend together. I know how fed up you were here last year.' She sauntered into the room, folding her arms and casting eyes over Donnie Munro and Ricky Ross. 'Cool posters.' And without taking her eyes off them, 'I don't suppose you've heard anything from Ruairidh.'

'No.'

'Good riddance, eh?' She turned towards me. 'So are there any decent pubs in Galashiels?'

I don't know how much she was aware of it, but I spent the next few weeks doing my best to avoid her. I took up running so that I had an excuse to get out on my own. Or I would simply tell her that I was studying and couldn't be disturbed, shutting myself away in my cell. Of course, I couldn't avoid her in class, or in the canteen, when she would invariably come and sit beside me. In a crowd, when a bunch of us would go to the student union, I would involve myself in conversation with one of the other girls as a discouragement to Seonag, and happily chat to any of the young rugby players who would come into the bar after matches at weekends.

Seonag was, as usual, Miss Personality superplus. The best-looking girl on the course. There were very few boys at the college, but I noticed how their eyes always seemed drawn in her direction. And the Gala boys would fall over themselves to buy her drinks in the pub, in return for which she seemed happy to flirt outrageously.

More than all that, I noticed how popular she was with the other girls. There would always be gatherings of them congregating around her in the common room, laughing and whispering. Or walking together across campus in giggling groups. Squeezing into a booth at the pub. A sisterhood from which I felt excluded. It seemed then that she was the one avoiding me, rather than the other way around.

We were two months into the term before I got my first real insight into something I had never even suspected. And when I look back on it now, I realize how naive and innocent I must have been.

At the weekends, when a lot of the girls went home, those of us left would often go to a pub called The Salmon. There was a rumoured connection between the owner and Linshader Lodge, where it was said he had once worked as a ghillie. Whether or not that was true I couldn't say, since I never met the man. But it was a comforting sort of link with the island.

It was one of those bright, cold November Saturdays, with a haze of frost on the grass and a mist on the hills. A group of us had gone to the pub after lunch and sat there drinking all afternoon. There was an international rugby match on the telly. Scotland versus someone or other. I didn't know, or care. I had never been turned on by rugby, but wouldn't have dared give voice to my indifference here, of all places. It would have been like denouncing God from the pulpit of the Free Church.

I remember that Seonag had been there when we arrived, but she was gone by the time we left. I hadn't noticed her leaving. I had been feeling sorry for myself, with the prospect of another month before the Christmas break and the chance, finally, to go home. As a result of which I had drunk more than was good for me and was almost overcome by melancholy. The prospect of another Saturday night sitting reading alone in my cell was very nearly unbearable, and I decided that maybe it was time I gave Seonag another chance. In truth, although I was the one who had started out avoiding her, it was me who was now feeling excluded. Time to address all those things that had come between us. The misunderstandings and petty jealousies.

So it was with an alcohol-fuelled courage and determination that I climbed the stairs to the girls' floor and walked along the hall to Seonag's door. I hesitated, resolution deserting me only for a moment, before I knocked once and walked in.

At first, I didn't really understand what I was seeing. And the moment passed so quickly I couldn't be sure in the immediate aftermath that my eyes had not deceived me. An English girl called Jane, who had also been with us earlier in the pub, was lying naked on Seonag's bed, dark hair splashed across the pillow. Seonag, too, was naked, lying on her belly between the other girl's legs, Jane's fists tightly clasped around bunches of Seonag's burnished red hair. Milky white bodies impossibly conjoined.

They broke apart immediately, startled by my sudden appearance, and sat up, grasping at sheets to cover their nakedness. I was so taken aback I had no idea what to say. I felt the colour rising on my cheeks, and stammered something stupid like 'Sorry. Didn't mean to interrupt.' And closed the door quickly as I stepped back into the corridor.

I stood breathing hard for a moment, trying to process what I had just seen. Then hurried back along the hall to the common room, and slipped inside, shutting the door behind me. The other girls had not yet returned, and I stood there trembling and dreading the thought of having to face Seonag alone. How naive had I been never even to suspect? And, yet, nothing in my God-fearing sheltered island upbringing had prepared me for such a moment. I had no idea how to deal with it. It seems ridiculous to me now, in the wake of all the years of experience I have clocked up since. But I was shaken to my core.

I heard a door opening and then closing further down the hall. A knock. And then silence. Before soft footsteps came hurrying along the linoleum. I stepped away from the door as it opened, and Seonag stood there with her dressing gown wrapped around her. Bare feet, tousled hair, bright spots of red high on her porcelain cheeks. She pushed the door shut behind her and her green eyes sought mine, imploring, filled with fear and longing. I found it impossible to maintain eye contact and looked away towards the floor. She reached out to grab both of my arms. 'You really didn't know?'

I forced myself to look at her. 'No.'

She sighed heavily and seemed distraught. 'My poor, inno-cent Niamh.'

'It's disgusting!'

She let me go and stepped back, almost recoiling, as if from a slap. 'No, it's not! It's the most natural thing in the world if that's how you feel.' I could see the emotion bubbling up inside her. 'All those times cuddling together in the *bothag* with the dollies, playing mums and dads. All those nights in the same bed, sharing the heat of our bodies, arms around each other for comfort.'

'Like sisters!' I was horrified that she could ever have seen it as anything else. 'I never thought . . .'

'I've had a crush on you, Niamh, ever since we were little. Just wanted to be with you. You and nobody else. I looked up to you. I *loved* you.' She sighed. 'As far back as I can remember, I was hoping that one day you would feel this way, too.'

'Well, I don't.'

It was as if she didn't hear me. She stepped towards me again and took both of my hands. I was too distracted to resist. 'It wasn't until we were teenagers that I realized why. What it was I wanted from you. That no boy could give me. I can't tell you how disappointed I was by your infatuation with Ruairidh. How much it hurt me.' She turned her head back towards the door. 'There've been other girls like Jane. But that was just physical. Satisfying a need. I don't care about her. Or any of the others. Only you, Niamh. Just you.'

It took a moment for me to realize as she drew closer that she meant to kiss me. I jerked away, pulling my hands free. 'Don't!' I was seething with anger and confusion. And uncertainty. I know now that our sexuality is just an extension of ourselves. We don't choose to be, we just are. Somewhere deep inside, a part of me wanted to take her in my arms and tell her everything was going to be okay. She was my best friend. We had shared the better part of our lives together. But it was never going to be okay the way she wanted.

I saw her tears through mine before I brushed past her, out into the hall, and ran all the way along to my room. I closed the door behind me and locked it, before throwing myself on the bed and crying into my pillow, stifling my sobs in case anyone would hear me. I felt . . . and I can't think of any other way to describe it . . . bereaved. I had just lost the part of me that was Seonag. A part of me that, clearly, I had never really understood. But loved all the same. I couldn't see, then, how I would ever get over it.

In the weeks that followed I felt trapped in a nightmare. My unhappiness in Gala compounded now by the fractious end of my relationship with Seonag. Who was still just across the hall, who still attended the same lectures, who was still Miss Personality superplus in a crowd at the union. But behind the face that she wore for the world I could see her pain. The tears of the clown behind the mask. We avoided each other like the plague.

Then, mid-December, entirely out of the blue, I received a letter from Ruairidh. He had put his name and a return address on the back of the envelope. Some student accommodation in Aberdeen. It was a Saturday morning, and I sat in my cell and tore it open with trembling fingers. Inside was a printed card. An invitation to the student Christmas dance at Aberdeen

University. Clipped to it was a return air ticket from Edinburgh to Aberdeen in my name. Not a cheap purchase for someone on a student grant. I turned over the card, and saw that he had handwritten on the back of it, *Saving the last dance for you.* Beneath it a phone number.

It took me all of half a second to decide that I was going. I ran along the corridor to the pay phones and dialled the number on the back of the card. The phone rang several times at the other end before someone picked it up, and a woman's voice said, 'Yes?' It seemed very abrupt and I was momentarily taken aback.

'Can I speak to Ruairidh Macfarlane, please.' I heard the receiver being set down and then the same voice calling off into the distance.

'Ruairidh . . . Phone!'

'Coming,' even more distantly, then hurried feet on stairs. When he picked up the phone and said, 'Hello?' I very nearly hung up. I'm not sure why. Except that I knew this was very possibly a watershed in my life. One of those crossroads you arrive at without any certainty of which road you are going to follow, always with the possibility in your mind that you could just turn around and walk back to the safety of everything you have known up until then.

I said, 'It's Niamh.' I could almost hear him hold his breath at the other end.

'Hi.'

'Hi.' I closed my eyes and took the plunge. 'I got your letter.'

'Yes?'

'I'll be on the flight.'

A long silence, then, 'I'll meet you at the airport.'

'Okay . . . See you then, then.'

'Yes.'

A hesitation. What else to say? Nothing. 'Bye.'

'Bye.'

I hung up and stood breathing rapidly. The butterflies were back. And the palpitations. All the things I had felt during those weeks at Linshader when Ruairidh and I were together. I hurried back along the hall to my room and stood by the window, gazing out at the distant bus stop where I would board the bus to Edinburgh to catch my flight to Aberdeen in just ten days' time. I would rearrange my transport home for Christmas from there. Bus from Aberdeen to Inverness. Then Inverness to Ullapool. And the *Suilven* back across the Minch. I had not felt this good in months. Which is when I realized that I had left the letter with the ticket and invitation on the table beside the phones. I turned to go back and get them but was stopped in my tracks by a knock at the door.

It swung open and Seonag stood there, with the letter and ticket and invitation in her hand. She held them out and said, 'You left these by the phone.'

I stepped forward to take them. 'Thanks.'

She shrugged, and the sadness in her face in that moment very nearly broke my heart. She said, with a tiny smile, 'Guess I lose.'

*

As it happened, I never did go home for Christmas that year. Ruairidh met me off the plane at Aberdeen, and he saved not only the last dance for me, but every other dance that night. We went back to his digs and made love in his room, trying hard not to make a noise and disturb the other students, or his landlady. We spent half the night cooried up together beneath the duvet, stifling laughter and whispering conversations. I told him, as if he hadn't heard it before, how unhappy I was at Galashiels. And he was shocked to hear about Seonag's unexpected arrival, and how that had only compounded my misery. I didn't tell him then, or ever, about what had actually transpired between us, only that the dissolution of our friendship seemed final, and that I didn't see any way I could go back to Gala.

He said, 'You know, I've heard that the RGU Dough School at Kepplestone runs a really good course in home economics.' He shrugged as if it were just a casual or throwaway thought when he added, 'If you could get in there for the second term, then we could be in Aberdeen together.' He grinned. 'And miles away from Seonag.'

I phoned and went to Kepplestone for an interview the next day. It was my good fortune that someone else was dropping out, and they were happy for me to step in and fill her place. And so Ruairidh and I stayed in Aberdeen all across the festive season. I remember it as probably the happiest Christmas of my life.

When term resumed I took up my new place at the Aberdeen

Dough School and completed my degree over the next year and a half.

After graduating I surprised even myself by returning to Gala to do a Master's in Clothing Management. Just six months at the college, and then six months on release at Mackays in Paisley, my first real job in a fashion buying office, while I researched and wrote my dissertation on the Harris Tweed industry and its marketing.

By the time I got back to Gala Seonag was long gone. She had abandoned her flirtation with the textile and clothing industry, and left to take a course in business and computer studies at Manchester, which I discovered later just happened to be Jane's home town.

CHAPTER TWENTY-THREE

Braque sat at a table in the window, looking out over the inner harbour. Most of the fishing boats appeared to have gone, leaving only the pleasure boats and a few rusting hulks lined up along the quayside and the pontoons. The sky was broken, white clouds scudding across areas of blue, as if competing with each other to hide the sun, chasing their own shadows across the water.

She had not slept well, and was worried because she had still been unable to raise her ex on the phone. He had changed his mobile number after the split and all she had was his home number. Someone should have been there, even if it was only Lise. But, then, she probably wouldn't have wanted to lift the phone when she saw who was calling. All the same, Gilles should have responded by now. She had left several messages. All she could think was that he had taken the girls somewhere for a treat. Maybe stayed over-night. But there was school this morning . . . She breathed in deeply and pressed her palms flat on the pristine white linen tablecloth. She did not want to let any other thoughts in. As Gilles had always been in the habit of telling her, she had a vivid imagination.

'Bonjour, Ma'am. Penny for them.'

She turned to find George Gunn standing by her table. 'I'm sorry?'

'Penny for your thoughts. It's an English idiom,' he said, before realizing she might not understand what an idiom was. 'A saying. It just means I was wondering what you were thinking.'

She forced a smile. 'Dark thoughts.' And waved to the chair opposite. 'Join me?'

Gunn grinned. 'Don't mind if I do, Ma'am.'

'Sylvie,' she corrected him again.

'Yes, Ma'am,' he said, and it was clear he had no intention of ever calling her by her name.

An elderly waitress in a black skirt and blouse and white apron asked if he would like toast.

'Yes, please.' He rubbed his hands together. 'And a coffee.'

They indulged in polite conversation about how well each had slept. She lied, and wondered if he had, too. Then they talked about the weather, and he elevated what she had taken to be an unpromising start to the day, to being 'grand'. His toast arrived and she watched as he spread it with slabs of quickly melting butter, before slathering it with thick-cut marmalade, and wolfing it down between large gulps of coffee sweetened with two spoons of sugar.

She smiled and said, 'Does your wife not feed you?'

The toast paused halfway between his plate and his mouth and he glanced at her over it, suddenly self-conscious. 'Actually,' he said, 'she doesn't.'

She cocked an eyebrow, surprised. 'And why is that?'

He laid the toast down again, reluctantly. 'The doctor gave her a strict diet for me. I'm not long returned to work after a heart attack a few months back. Damn near killed me, too. I've lost quite a bit of weight.'

Braque glanced at the white cotton of his shirt stretched taut across his belly. Not quite enough, she thought.

'And I've been working out at the gym.'

'You shouldn't be eating that toast, and all that butter, then.'

He looked at it, shamefaced, on his plate. 'No. I shouldn't.' A pause. 'Shouldn't be drinking coffee either.' He looked at his watch and stood up suddenly. 'We should go.'

Braque rose from the table and wiped a napkin across her lips. 'Where are you taking me?'

'You said you wanted to talk to Niamh Macfarlane. So that'll be our first port of call. I managed to secure a four-wheel-drive vehicle.'

For someone who had grown up in Paris, a city of stone and trees and traffic, the west coast of the Isle of Lewis was a shock to Braque's system. Miles of barren peat bog as far as the eye could see. Occasional villages strung out along a ribbon of road laid precariously across the undulating contours of the land. Not a tree in sight. Flowers and bushes planted by optimistic *Leòdhasachs* in barren gardens, stunted by the wind and salt that arrived with the relentless onslaught of the Atlantic Ocean. A coastline at once beautiful and dangerous. Towering cliffs and rocky outcrops punctuated by unexpected scraps of beach with the purest gold or silver sand.

It was both breathtaking and bleak, and Braque wondered how people survived in this place without the shops and restaurants she took for granted, the sun-dappled apartments that looked out on leafy boulevards, the cinemas and theatres, the roar of traffic replaced here by the howling of the wind.

Gunn swerved to avoid a handful of sheep that had wandered on to the road. They seemed entirely unconcerned by the vehicle that had so nearly ploughed into them. 'It's worse when the wind drops and the midges come out,' he said.

'Midges?'

'Aye, wee flies. They breed in all that water out there on the moor, and emerge in bloody black clouds when it's dull and windless. People think it's just them the wee bastards go after. But it's sheep, too. When the poor beasts start congregating on the road, you know the midges are out in force on the moor.'

Braque nodded. But in spite of Gunn's colourful description had no clear idea of exactly what a midge was.

She sat in the passenger seat and watched the villages spool past, each one indistinguishable from the next. 'There are a lot of churches,' she said. She had counted five so far, and not seen a single soul. She found herself speculating about where it was that all the people came from to fill so many churches.

'Aye,' Gunn said. 'Folk here have divided God up into different pieces and shared Him around.'

Braque glanced at him across the car and wondered if he were making some kind of joke. If he was, she didn't get it, and he wasn't smiling.

Several times spits of rain had caused automatic wipers to smear them across the windscreen then stop. Gunn said, 'It's always trying to rain here. And usually succeeds.'

But today it didn't, and by the time the silhouette of the Cross Free Church stood stark on the horizon, sunshine washed itself across the land in waves, like pure gold water. And everything caught, however fleetingly, in its light came suddenly to life.

Gunn turned on to the Skigersta road, and by the time they reached the east coast at Skigersta itself, the sky had cleared and the Minch sparkled all the way across to the mainland. The road came to an end, and Gunn slipped the vehicle into four-wheel drive as they began their potholed journey south across the moor to Taigh 'an Fiosaich. On either side of the track, peat banks curved away across the moor, scraps of water catching sunlight, the peat itself blacker, somehow, in comparison.

'They actually live out here?' Braque was incredulous.

'Oh, a good bit further on yet,' Gunn said. 'They built their house at a place known as Taigh 'an Fiosaich. Nicholson's house. Named after the man who built it. Iain Nicholson, from Ness. He went to New York sometime around the end of the nineteenth century and found himself a wealthy woman to marry. Brought her back here and built a house and church out on the cliffs. No doubt with her money. Apparently all the sand for the cement was taken there by boat and carried up the cliffs a pailful at a time. The cement itself was brought out on the backs of men from Ness.'

Braque had trouble imagining it. 'Who else lives there?'

'No one, except for the Macfarlanes.' He corrected himself. 'Or, rather, just her now.'

Braque fell silent then, until she saw the profiles of the ruined house and church standing out against the dazzle of sunlight on the water beyond. To the left of them, no more than two hundred metres away, stood the Macfarlane house, shining white and incongruous in the sunshine. The blades of two wind turbines turned at speed in the stiffening breeze. There was something inestimably sad about the young couple who had built their perfect home out here on the edge of the cliffs, on the very edge of Europe, meeting tragedy and death on the streets of Paris. A shattering of dreams in a far-off land. Even to Braque, or perhaps especially to the policewoman, her home city seemed very distant now.

As what passed for a road swept around the ruined settlement of Bilascleiter towards the house, they saw two vehicles parked outside it. A white Jeep Cherokee and a Red Mitsubishi SUV. 'Looks like she has visitors,' Gunn said. He drew their 4×4 into one side as the door of the house opened, and a woman with the whitest skin Braque had ever seen stepped out on to the gravel. She carried a holdall in one hand, her flame-red hair whipped immediately back from her face by the wind, and Braque that saw in spite of her advancing years this was still a very beautiful woman.

She barely glanced in their direction before throwing her bag on to the passenger seat and slipping behind the wheel. She started the engine almost before her door was closed, then backed out at speed, sending chippings flying up behind her, before turning sharply and accelerating off into the distance.

Braque said, 'I thought that islanders were renowned for their friendliness. Who was that?'

Gunn watched thoughtfully in the rearview mirror as the red Mitsubishi vanished over the near horizon. 'That was Seonag Morrison,' he said. 'I don't know her personally, but I do know that she works for Ranish Tweed. I think she might be an office manager, something like that.'

'A good-looking woman.'

'Oh, aye, a real beauty.'

CHAPTER TWENTY-FOUR

It was the sound of the house door slamming shut, more than the roar of Seonag's engine as she turned the key in the ignition, that woke Niamh.

She felt terrible. Long after Seonag had fled her room the previous night, Niamh had lain awake wrestling with past and present demons. To be confronted again by what she had taken for some distant and long-forgotten adolescent infatuation had further unbalanced her already fragile equilibrium. It seemed extraordinary to her that Seonag could have kept that torch burning all these years in some dark and hidden place, undiminished by time, or marriage, or children.

Sleep, too, had seemed a distant and evasive memory, until sometime after first light, when she had slipped away into the most shallow and dream-filled unconsciousness.

Now she sat up startled, the recollection of waking all those hours ago to find a naked Seonag in her bed flooding back with painful clarity. She slipped quickly from the bed and hurried to the window, parting the blinds with her fingers to see Seonag's red SUV disappearing beyond the ruins of Bilascleiter. And be startled by the presence of another vehicle, two figures clearly visible beyond the reflections on the windscreen.

She let the blinds fall shut and grabbed her dressing gown to wrap and tie around her, pushing her feet into slippers and sweeping the hair from her face with both hands. She was in no way ready to receive visitors. But a firm knock on the door, and the knowledge that her Jeep parked outside betrayed her presence, meant that she had little choice.

In the hall she blinked away the sleep from her eyes and opened the door to let in a gust of cold, salty air. She was shocked to see Lieutenant Braque standing there, dark hair pulled back from a tired and lined face, ponytail flying out like a flag behind her. A portly middle-aged man with a widow's peak stood beside her, and although Niamh didn't know him, she recognized him as a police officer from Stornoway. Her first thought was that there had been some unexpected development.

'What's happened?' she said.

'Nothing more than any of us knew when you left Paris, Madame Macfarlane,' Braque said.

Niamh shook her head in confusion and disappointment. 'What are you doing here, then?'

Gunn held out his hand. 'Mrs Macfarlane, my name is George Gunn. I'm a detective sergeant with the Stornoway police. Lieutenant Braque has been sent to monitor Ruairidh's funeral, just in case whoever planted that bomb decides to show up there.'

Niamh frowned. 'I thought Irina Vetrov's husband, Georgy, was your prime suspect.'

Braque shrugged non-committally. 'That is one line of enquiry. Unfortunately we have been unable to trace him, to rule him in or out. And if it was not him, then it may be that the killer is known to you.'

Gunn shuffled awkwardly and cleared his throat. 'May we come in, Mrs Macfarlane?'

Braque and Gunn settled themselves on stools at the breakfast bar while Niamh popped pods into the coffee maker.

'Is coffee alright?'

Braque glanced at Gunn. 'I think Detective Sergeant Gunn may prefer tea.' He looked as if he might protest, before meeting her eye and then nodding reluctant acquiescence.

'No problem,' Niamh said. She put the kettle on and noticed that it was stone cold. Seonag had made herself neither tea nor coffee. Nor had she eaten, and Niamh wondered how much, if at all, she had slept. Perhaps, like Niamh, she had been unable to sleep until late, then drifted off and slept longer than she meant to. She had certainly left in a hurry.

Braque said, 'Don't you feel very isolated away out here?'

'Not at all,' Niamh said. 'We're barely twenty minutes from Ness.' She glanced at Braque. 'I've heard people say you can feel lonely in a crowd.'

Braque avoided her gaze, almost as if the widow might see the loneliness of the spurned woman in her eyes. Mother of two children with whom she hardly ever spent time. Lonely and alone in a city of ten million people.

'We built this place to be on our own. It's where we felt most at home. Most ourselves. I never thought I would want to be anywhere else in the world. Until now.'

Gunn said, 'You wouldn't think of selling up, surely?'

'I don't know what I'm going to do, Mr . . . Gunn, is it?'

'Aye.'

'I hadn't planned on being here on my own.' She poured two coffees and a tea, and they sipped in silence for a few moments as Gunn and Braque took in the view from the windows. The sunlight playing on broken water was dazzling, and they could see the silhouettes of seabirds circling and diving, only to emerge moments later with writhing fish in their beaks.

Braque turned towards Niamh. 'So . . . have you had any further thoughts about what happened in Paris?'

'I've thought about almost nothing else,' Niamh said, her voice flat, her face without expression, anxious to hide the emotion that too often had reduced her to unexpected tears.

'Nothing fresh has occurred to you?'

Niamh shook her head. 'No, nothing.' Before the memory returned of her first moments back at the house. 'Except . . .'

'Except what?' Gunn said.

And Niamh wondered how she could have forgotten. But Seonag had arrived just moments later, and life, or was it death, had taken over everything since.

'The email,' she said.

*

Ruairidh's weaving shed was filled with reflected light from the Minch. Niamh had not been here again since her return on Sunday evening, and she found it just as painful now as it had been then. The essence of him lived on here. In the half-finished weave, the bolts of cloth, the skeins of wool, his guitar, his computer, all his handwritten scribbled notes on the workbench and the wall. His accumulated dreams and hopes. All of which had outlived him.

'I'm amazed you get internet this far out,' Braque said.

'We get it by satellite.' Niamh crossed towards Ruairidh's computer.

'Lots of folk in the islands opt for internet by satellite,' Gunn said. 'It's faster and more reliable. But it's expensive. And if the weather's bad . . .' He chuckled. 'Which it usually is, then you lose the satellite signal.'

'So you didn't know about the email when you were in Paris?' Braque said.

'No.' Niamh dismissed the screensaver and opened Ruairidh's mailer. 'Ruairidh didn't tell me about it. It wasn't until I looked at his computer when I got home on Sunday that I saw it.' She pulled it up on screen and both Braque and Gunn shaded their eyes against the light from the window to read it.

'From *well wisher*,' Braque said.

Gunn read out loud, '*See you in hell.*'

'And you say he received this while you were on the RER coming into Paris? About two hours before the car bomb went off?'

'From the time on the email, and the time I remember him receiving one on the train, I would say yes.'

'Why didn't he tell you about it?'

Niamh shook her head. 'You're really asking me that?'

Braque shrugged and took out her mobile phone. 'Can you forward it to me?'

'Sure. Give me an address.'

Braque wrote it down and Niamh forwarded the email. Braque said, 'I'll also need the access code for your wifi. I have no phone signal here. I would like to pass this on to our computer expert in Paris.'

As Braque was tapping in the code, the telephone rang on Ruairidh's work desk. Niamh answered it quickly. 'Hello?'

It was her mother. 'Oh. So you *are* there?' Her voice laden with sarcasm. 'Nice of you to come and see us. I hear you visited the Macfarlanes yesterday.'

Niamh glanced self-consciously at the two police officers and turned away towards the window, where she could see the reflection of someone who looked only vaguely like herself. 'Ruairidh is their son, Mum. We had to make the funeral arrangements.'

'And it never occurred to you to drop in?'

'We went straight to the funeral director in Stornoway.' She tried to lower her tone, but it still came out full of anger. 'For God's sake, do you have to be so selfish?'

There was a long silence at the other end when she could hear her mother draw a slow breath. 'Your brother is on the ferry.'

'Uilleam?'

'Do you have another?'

Niamh closed her eyes, fighting to keep control.

Then her mother said, 'Can you pick him up at Stornoway and bring him down to Balanish?'

Niamh clenched her jaw. 'Yes. What time?'

'The ferry gets in at one.'

'I'll be there.'

There was another long silence before her mother said, 'He's coming for you, you know. Not for Ruairidh.'

'I never imagined for a minute he was.' Niamh hung up and took a moment to collect herself before turning back to her guests. 'Sorry,' she said, barely in control. 'I need to get showered and dressed. I have to go and pick my brother up off the ferry.'

'Of course,' Gunn said, and he took Braque's elbow to steer her towards the door. 'Don't you worry, Mrs Macfarlane, we'll see ourselves out, no bother.'

CHAPTER TWENTY-FIVE

Gunn pulled in on a hardcore passing place on the edge of the old Bilascleiter settlement and he and Braque got out to feel the wind filling their mouths and tugging at their clothes and hair. They had a good view from here back towards the Macfarlane house, and the ruins beyond it. A green corrugated tin hut stood resolute against the gales that swept across the moor in all seasons. A blackened wooden door was bolted, but peering through net curtains, Gunn could see into a gloomy interior where an old settee was pushed up against the back wall.

A stainless-steel sink lay in what remained of an old black-house in front of it, abandoned to its fate, bog moss and grasses slowly claiming it. The footings of perhaps a dozen more old stone dwellings were still visible here, climbing the slope to the top of the hill.

'What was this place?' Braque asked.

Gunn shrugged. 'A settlement of some sort. More than just shielings, I think.' It didn't occur to him to explain what a shieling was, and she didn't ask.

She was just baffled that anyone would ever have chosen to settle here. 'Looks like they didn't stay long.'

'Oh, they might have been here a century or more, I have no idea,' Gunn said. 'They're hardy souls that hail from these parts.'

Braque didn't doubt it.

Gunn removed a walking stick from the back seat of the 4×4 and used it for support as he walked up to the top of the hill. Braque picked her way carefully after him. While he was wearing a pair of stout wellies, she had only leather boots with Cuban block heels. And by the time she reached him she could feel peaty bog water seeping through to her feet. It was with dismay she accepted that the boots were probably ruined.

As she scrambled up the last few feet to stand beside him, she saw the coastline zigzagging off to the south, each succesive headland reaching further out, it seemed, into the Minch. Gunn said, 'I put out a few feelers when they told me you were coming. I got some feedback first thing this morning.' He turned to look at her, and she saw his oiled black hair whipped up by the wind to stand on end. 'You've heard of Lee Blunt?'

'The fashion designer?'

'The very one. A few years back he was using Ranish Tweed in his collections, and making a name for it all over the world. Then he had a very public fallout with Ruairidh. Fisticuffs, I believe, in a pub in London, though there were no charges ever brought.' He paused. 'Turns out he was here on the island just a few weeks back. Flew in on a private chartered jet.' He took out a black notebook and flicked through it. 'Tuesday the fifth of September to be exact. Stayed a couple of days, and hired a car to take him to the mill at Shawbost.' He turned to look at her. 'What do you know about Harris Tweed?'

She shrugged and admitted, 'Not much.'

'It has to be hand-woven by weavers in their own homes. The big mills spin the wool and supply the weavers with both the orders and the wool. When the weaving's done, the cloth goes back to the mill to be finished. They repair any flaws then wash and dry it. They even shave it to make it nice and smooth. With very few exceptions the weavers work to order for the mills.'

'So if you were going to place an order you would go to one of the mills?'

'Indeed.'

'But Ranish isn't Harris Tweed.'

'No. Because they use different types of fibres that don't conform to the requirements that are defined for Harris Tweed by Act of Parliament. They have their own designs and patterns, take their own orders, and only use the mills for the finishing process.'

'So what was Blunt doing at the mill?'

'I've no idea. But here's the interesting thing. Air traffic at the airport tell me that he's due in again this afternoon. Another private charter. Him and a few others coming for the funeral, apparently.'

'Why would he be coming for the funeral if he had fallen out with Ruairidh?'

'A very good question, Ma'am. And that's something you might want to ask him.'

The sound of a vehicle starting up carried to them on the wind and they looked down to see Niamh backing her Jeep away from the house, turning and then heading along the track towards them. As it passed their 4×4 at the foot of the hill, they saw Niamh glancing up towards them. A pale face behind reflections on the driver's window. She must have wondered what they were doing there, standing among the ruins.

When the Jeep had gone, Gunn said, 'In the meantime, maybe we should make a wee visit to the mill to find out just what Mr Blunt was doing there.'

The mill at Shawbost stood on the far side of a small stretch of slate-grey water just north of the village, a collection of blue and white sheds and a tall white chimney that reached up to prick the pewter of the sky. Beyond it, the brown and purple shimmer of autumn moorland undulated away into a changeable morning, off towards an ocean that broke along a shoreline somewhere unseen.

It was in the dyeing shed that they found the brand director of Harris Tweed Hebrides.

Two young men in dark blue overalls were hoisting steaming batches of freshly dyed wool from vast stainless-steel vats. Virgin Scottish Cheviot wool sat around in half-ton bales waiting to be transformed from peat-stained white to primary red or blue or yellow. From adjoining sheds came the deafening clatter of the machinery that dried, blended and spun the dyed wool into the yarn that would eventually go out to weavers in their sheds all over the island.

Margaret Ann Macleod was an attractive woman in her late thirties or early forties. She was tall and slim, and wore a long Harris Tweed jacket over jeans and boots. Straight red hair, cut in a fringe that fell into green eyes, tumbled over square shoulders. 'I'm afraid I wouldn't be at liberty to tell you,' she said, when Gunn asked her about Lee Blunt's visit earlier in the month.

They followed her through to the drying room, where the noise level grew louder and Gunn had to raise his voice. 'This is a murder inquiry, Ms Macleod. You can either tell us here or at the police station.'

Which stopped her in her tracks. She turned her gaze in his direction and he felt momentarily discomfited. 'We take customer confidentiality very seriously,' she said.

'I'm sure you do.'

Margaret Ann glanced at Braque and then back again. 'He was choosing patterns to place an order. In fact, he was back again last week to finalize it.'

'An order with Ranish?'

'No, Detective Sergeant, with Harris Tweed Hebrides.'

Braque said, 'But it was with Ranish that he had a relationship in the past.'

'Yes it was.'

Gunn scratched his smoothly shaven chin thoughtfully. 'So he's switching from Ranish Tweed to Harris Tweed.'

'So it would seem.'

'That's going to be a bit of a public slap in the face for Ranish, isn't it?'

The merest smile played around Margaret Ann's lips. 'You might say that, Detective Sergeant, I couldn't possibly comment.'

Outside, the wind had stiffened further, shredding the sky, allowing sunlight to sprinkle itself in fast-moving patches across the land. While further out at sea, bruised black rain clouds gathered ominously along the horizon. Braque and Gunn stood by their 4×4 and she said, 'Interesting timing. Choosing Harris Tweed over Ranish just weeks before Ruairidh's death. And then coming to the funeral. Sounds like he is celebrating the death rather than mourning it.'

Gunn nodded. 'Come to gloat rather than grieve.'

She looked thoughtful. 'So where to now?'

'Dalmore,' Gunn said. 'The beach and the cemetery. That's where they will bury Ruairidh tomorrow.'

The single-track road that led down to the beach descended gently between the hills. Off to their left, sheep that thought Gunn and Braque might be bringing them feed came running down a rough track towards the road. They stopped abruptly in disappointment as the 4×4 carried on by.

The blades of a couple of small wind turbines turned in the wind up on the hillside, and they passed a croft house and outbuildings on their right before descending steeply to the metalled area of car park. Straight ahead the cemetery rose in a gradual slope across the machair to where wooden piles had been driven deep into the sand, delineating the line between cemetery and beach. The erosive nature of the weather, and the sea, had been in danger of eating into the soft sandy soil of the cemetery to spill bones and headstones on to the giant pebbles below.

A sandy track beside a waterway led along the side of the cemetery to the beach itself, and on the far side, set proud on an elevation, stood a newer patch of burial ground where residents commanded an even better view of the beach.

Braque's heart sank when Gunn retrieved his walking stick from the back seat. Her feet had only just dried out. But the ground he led them on to, beyond the tarmac, was firm and dry and took them on a relatively easy climb towards the top of the cliffs at the north end of the beach.

'Is it not dangerous for you to be exerting yourself like this?' she called after him, hoping that he might go slower.

'Not at all,' he called over his shoulder, oblivious to the unsuitability of her footwear. 'The doctor says the more exercise the better.'

When finally they reached the end of their climb, the most spectacular vista opened up below them. A crescent of pale gold arcing away to the south, tide receding in white foam across smooth shiny sand to the sparkling turquoise of water that turned a deep marine as the sand shelved steeply away beneath it.

Accumulated all along the foot of the wooden piles at the innermost curve of the beach were marvellously marbled pebbles the size of dinosaur eggs, rock squeezed into layers during the first days of creation, then worn smooth and rounded by aeons. To be washed up here on this far-flung European outpost, well beyond the reach of what had once been the Roman Empire.

Immediately below them, the ocean foamed fiercely around jagged black rock stacks that rose sheer out of the water and stood stubborn against the relentless power of the Atlantic. The sun flitted intermittently across the sands, and there was not another soul in sight. The rain clouds they had seen in Shawbost were, thus far, biding their time out at sea.

Gunn pointed to the far headland. 'Just a year or so ago, an oil rig being towed around the Hebrides broke free and washed up at the other end of the beach there. Because of the bad weather it stayed put for quite a while before they managed to tow it away. Brought as many tourists to see it as the beach itself. A huge bloody thing it was.' And then self-consciously, 'Begging your pardon Ma'am.'

But Braque had not noticed his lapse of language, and wouldn't have cared if she had. She was gazing in wonder at the view that filled her eyes. 'I cannot imagine,' she said, 'a more beautiful place to spend eternity.'

'Personally, Ma'am, I'd rather see it from the perspective of the living than the dead.'

She turned a smile on him. 'But we are all going to die sometime, Detective Sergeant.'

'That we are, Ma'am. But some are taken before their time.'

'Like Ruairidh.'

'Aye. And others.' His own gaze turned reflective as he panned it across the beach and cemetery below. 'The brother that Niamh Macfarlane has gone to meet off the ferry. Uilleam . . .' He drew a deep breath. 'There was no love lost between him and Ruairidh Macfarlane.'

Braque frowned. 'Love lost?'

He smiled. 'Sorry. They didn't like one another very much. And that would be an understatement.' He snorted. 'Not that there was much contact between them. Not for a long time, anyway. Uilleam's been away from the island for years. Based in Dundee, on the east coast of Scotland. A software developer, I'm told, for one of the big online games companies.'

She frowned again. 'I'm not sure I understand.'

'Computer games. You know, things like *Grand Theft Auto* and *World of Warcraft*. Stuff like that. I'm no expert myself.' He turned to look at her. 'I wouldn't even know what they called *Grand Theft Auto* in France.'

She shrugged and smiled. '*Grand Theft Auto*, I believe.'

He grinned. 'Oh, well, that's original, then.' The grin faded. 'The thing is, Ma'am, I heard this morning that Uilleam was on the island himself earlier this month. It never came to my attention officially at the time, but I understand that he and Ruairidh had a confrontation in McNeill's bar in Stornoway. A chance meeting apparently, that ended in fists and flying beer glasses. No complaints made, and no arrests, but I gather that Uilleam took a bit of a beating. Ruairidh was a big lad. But it was Uilleam that picked the fight.'

'Why would he do that?'

'Well, like I said, Ma'am, there was no love lost.' He turned his eyes back towards the beach. 'And the seeds of it were sown right here on these sands. Something that happened twenty-five years ago now. And there's probably not anyone on the island who doesn't know the story.'

Braque looked at him, intrigued. 'Tell me.'

CHAPTER TWENTY-SIX

Niamh had arrived in Stornoway far too early for the ferry, and spent her time wandering aimlessly around the town, remembering places she had been with Ruairidh, things they had done together. A drunken meal at Digby Chick that had left neither of them in a fit state to drive home. The night subsequently spent at the Royal, making love noisily and keeping the people in the next room awake until they banged on the wall. The day that Ruairidh dropped his iPhone into the inner harbour, trying to photograph curious seals which had swum right up to the pontoons. A first night spent in a room at the luxuriously refurbished Lews Castle that sat up on the hill overlooking the town and harbour below. A new perspective on a familiar place.

The times they had attended HebCelt, drifting from tent to tent in the castle grounds, listening to some of the best Celtic music to be heard anywhere. Or Rock Night in the theatre at the An Lanntair arts centre, a tribute by local musicians to a long line of rock classics.

Moments spent together. Lost now for ever. For while they

remained still strong in her recollection, what were memories if not to be shared?

Finally, it was at An Lanntair that she ended up, nursing a coffee at a table with a view over the outer harbour where she could see the ferry as it rounded the point and ploughed its passage across the bay to the pier. The angled silver roof of the terminal building caught moments of fleeting sunshine and more resembled a flying saucer than a ferry terminal.

She could see the Jeep from here, too, where she had left it in the car park, its white roof, like that of the terminal building, flashing intermittently in the sporadic sunlight.

As the time passed so her dread grew. She could not remember now the last time that she had seen Uilleam. Probably at some family funeral, or wedding, where they would not have spoken or even caught each other's eye. She would have loved him to be the happy-go-lucky protective big brother she remembered from childhood, awkward with girls, taking delight in tormenting his wee sister, along with Anndra. But those memories were tainted now by animus, and the innocents they had once been were long lost.

When the MV *Loch Seaforth* finally powered her way around the headland Niamh's heart pushed up into her throat. The *Loch Seaforth* was a big, luxurious ferry compared with her predecessors, the *Isle of Lewis* and the *Suilven*. It was the *Suilven* that had ferried Niamh back and forth to the mainland in her early student days, sailing right up until the mid-Nineties, when the boat was sold into service between the North and

South Islands of New Zealand, only to capsize and sink in Fiji twenty years later.

This new ferry seemed huge, with her three levels of passenger deck above a vast hull that carried the cars of the tourists and the trucks that supplied the islands with most of their provisions. Niamh waited until the very last minute, when she could see passengers streaming off the boat, before abandoning the remains of her coffee and crossing the road to the car park.

She was shocked by how much Uilleam had aged since the last time she had seen him. His once black hair brushed through with steel and thinning a little. He had developed the stoop that so many taller people adopt as they grow older, as if bowed by years of leaning down to hear the chatter of all those smaller people around them.

He was wheeling a suitcase and she stood waiting by the car as he approached her across the tarmac. To her astonishment, when he reached her, he released the suitcase and folded his arms around her, with all the protective big brother love she remembered from when they were children. She buried her face in his chest and wished away all the miserable years between then and now. Remembering how it had been, and what it was that had caused the rift.

CHAPTER TWENTY-SEVEN

I turned fifteen not long before it happened.

They say that your teens are a difficult time, and that your mid-teens are the worst. But for the most part I enjoyed my teenage years. That transition from childhood to womanhood was so full of discovery and pleasure that I revelled in it – apart from its one obvious downside. I embraced the changes that were moulding me, growing into the young woman I was to become. Secondary school gave way to further education and then to real life beyond. But right then, it was the Nicolson that was stretching my mind and my imagination. I was enjoying the challenge. The world seemed full of possibilities. The sun shone endlessly that summer, at least in my recollection, and the freedom I enjoyed in finding myself was simply delicious.

The cares of the world had not yet descended on my young shoulders, my independence unfettered by adult prohibition, and if I could have lived the rest of my life in that state of uncomplicated serenity I would have made that choice without a second thought. But as summer inevitably fades to autumn and then winter, such happiness could not be sustained, and

I could never have foreseen the tragedy that brought it to an end.

Every other summer my uncle Hector would arrive from his home in the south of England with his exotic English wife, Rita. At least, exotic is how she seemed to us. She spoke with a creamy posh accent, a large-bosomed, bountiful lady whose perfume smelled of flowers. She wore glamorous clothes that looked as if they were just off the peg, and extravagant hats that she always had trouble keeping on her head in the wind.

My uncle, who was my father's brother, was a doctor, and to us seemed fabulously wealthy. He and Rita lived in a big house in a picturesque village somewhere in the county of Hampshire. We had never been, mainly I think because my father could not afford the cost of travel for the whole family. But we had seen plenty of photographs, and to me it was like another world. A place you might read about in books.

Although my uncle was just an islander like us, he seemed different somehow. Better. He had ironed out his island accent, the *blas* he had acquired from speaking Gaelic as he grew up, and had made a success of his life in a bigger pond. It is a character trait of islanders to believe that they have to go away to better themselves, and perhaps the mainland offers more opportunity. But, in truth, I think that we are who we will be regardless of where we might end up. And most islanders, in the final event, come back. Or, at least, want to.

Visitors to our house slept in the caravan that we kept in the garden. But Uncle Hector and Aunt Rita always got my room. Not that they thought they were above sleeping in the caravan. It was my mother who thought that.

I was always delighted when they came to stay, because I was the one who got to be in the caravan. I loved it. My own little world, quite separate from the house and the rest of the family. As if I was all grown up and on holiday by myself.

It was usually August that they came to stay, when my uncle could get a locum to look after his surgery. They took three or four days to motor up, normally via Skye, taking the car ferry from Uig over to Tarbert in Harris, and driving up through Lochs. Uncle Hector liked his cars, and they always arrived in something big and shiny and expensive that made our wee Ford Fiesta seem dowdy and old. This particular year they turned up in a car the likes of which none of us had ever seen before. And not just us. It turned heads everywhere it went on the island, and I'm sure on the mainland, too.

It was what my uncle called a vintage car. A Humber Hawk. A big black sleek American-looking thing with a green-leather bench seat in the front and a column gear change. My uncle was so proud of it. 'They stopped making these in sixty-seven,' he told us, more than once. He frequently related the story of how Rita's father had bought one of the last models off the production line, about the same time The Beatles were releasing *Sgt. Pepper's*, but never registered it. He had kept it in his garage, wrapped almost literally in cotton wool. It was another thirteen years before he finally declared it to the authorities, registering it in 1980, and making it unique and very nearly priceless. He had gifted it to Hector and Rita as a wedding present.

The couple had treasured it ever since, keeping it mostly in the garage and taking it out on only rare occasions. It was the first time they had brought it up to the Hebrides.

Me and Anndra and Uilleam crowded into the back seat and rode like royalty around the island when my aunt and uncle took us shopping in Stornoway, or out for the day to Uig, or Luskentyre in Harris. It made you want to wave from the window, like the Queen, when people would turn their heads to watch us going by. Other motorists would slow almost to a stop in passing places so they could get a better look.

From time to time Anndra got to sit up front. He must have been nearly seventeen by then, and desperate to learn to drive. But lessons cost money, and it was likely he couldn't afford it until he was out working himself. Which would be some way off. Because he was anxious to go to university in Glasgow to study Gaelic.

One day, on the road down to Uig, Uncle Hector turned off on to a disused stretch of single-track and got out of the car. He waved Anndra into the driver's seat. 'On you go, son,' he said. 'Just a few hundred yards, mind. But it'll be enough to give you a feel for it.' And my uncle slipped into the passenger seat beside him and gave him instructions. It was quite a sacrifice for Uncle Hector to take a risk like that, and I can remember him wincing as Anndra crunched into first gear. But once my brother got her running, it was a smooth drive in a straight line, and he actually managed to get into top gear before finally running out of road and slowing to a stop. We all clapped, and Anndra glowed with pleasure. Uncle Hector said, 'One day maybe, Anndra, I'll leave her to you in my will.' Me and Uilleam were dead jealous.

That summer we had been enjoying one of the finest spells of weather that I could remember. The wind was soft from the south-west, bringing warm air with it, but for once no rain, and we had day after day of clear blue skies and baking hot sunshine. Even the midges got burned off in the heat, and we spent days on end on this beach or that, getting tans like none of us had ever had before.

The day it happened, Dad and Uncle Hector were going fishing together. I don't know where, and it probably wasn't legal. They weren't saying, and no one was asking. But they went off at first light with their sacks on their backs and their rods over the shoulders.

Aunt Rita had decided that we should go to Dalmore Beach for the day, and she and Mum spent half the morning preparing a sumptuous pack lunch that we could take with us. In the end, Mum decided that she would stay home and cook, and that we would have a big family dinner that night, since my aunt and uncle were scheduled to leave the next day.

We set off late in the morning, after Seonag's mum had dropped her off, and we all squeezed into the car. Me and Seonag in the back with Uilleam, and Anndra up front with Aunt Rita.

I'll never forget driving down that road to the beach. The colour of the sea simmering between headlands, the painfully clear blue of the sky. And the hills rising on either side of us burned brown by all the weeks of sunshine. I have never driven down that same road since with anything other than lead in my heart.

When we arrived at the metalled parking there were no other cars there, but I noticed half a dozen bikes leaning against the cemetery fence, and when we got out of the car the whoops and cries of their owners carried to us on the wind from the beach. Which was disappointing. Nine times out of ten we would have had the beach to ourselves.

Seonag and I ran on ahead, carrying fold-up canvas chairs and travelling rugs, and Aunt Rita followed with the boys, carrying two big hampers. A veritable feast!

When we got down to the beach, and picked our way over the stones to the sand, we saw that the bikers were in fact half a dozen lads from Balanish. And my heart skipped a beat when I saw that one of them was Ruairidh. They were playing football, stripped to the waist and wearing only shorts, kicking their ball about on the firm sand left by the receding tide. I heard Seonag beside me issuing a grunt of disapproval. 'Bloody typical,' she said. 'Why do boys have to go and ruin everything?'

The boys saw us arriving, and probably had very similar thoughts. But I noticed that Ruairidh had clocked who we were, and his eyes lingered just a little longer in our direction than the others'. This was after the incident at the village disco, and before Ruairidh and I finally connected during my first summer break at Linshader, so I was playing it cool and chose to ignore them entirely.

I heard Uilleam cursing in Gaelic as he and Anndra and Aunt Rita appeared on the beach behind us. Rita would have lived with Hector long enough to recognize a few Gaelic oaths, and she shushed Uilleam and suggested we set up camp on the far side of the beach, just about as far away as we could get from the noisy, football-playing youths.

She was wearing a beautiful blue print dress with flaring skirts that billowed in the wind as she strode off through the soft warm sand to pick a spot. Her wide-brimmed straw hat fibrillated in the breeze and stayed on her head thanks only to the ribbons tied in a bow beneath her chin.

Uilleam growled at the footballers as we passed them. He had never liked Ruairidh, and I had always thought that maybe he was jealous that it was Ruairidh who'd had the initiative and courage to rescue me from the bog, when Uilleam was the older boy, and my brother to boot. As if Ruairidh had somehow done it just to show him up. By now Uilleam was already away from the island at university, and was only home for a couple of weeks following a summer job working at a hotel in Pitlochry.

He and Anndra hammered stakes into the sand to stretch out a windbreak while Aunt Rita spread the travelling rugs and arranged the hampers and chairs. Seonag and I stripped off to the bathing costumes beneath our clothes and went splashing and shrieking into the water. Despite the heat of the summer, the sea was still ice-cold and a shock to the system.

'Don't go in too far,' Aunt Rita called after us. 'You know how deep it gets.'

I knew only too well from past experience. When the tide goes out it leaves a stretch of gently sloping wet sand, before suddenly shelving steeply away into deeper, darker water. You could tell from the way the waves broke as they came in and were quickly sucked out again by a powerful undertow. Sometimes you saw surfers out in the bay, but they would be strong swimmers, often with life vests. The waves weren't big enough today to attract the surfers, but forceful enough to knock you over and drag you back out if you weren't careful and strayed too far in.

It's true there was a time when most islanders couldn't swim. In fact, fear of the water was almost instilled into us. If you had a healthy fear of it and couldn't swim, then you wouldn't be tempted to go into the sea. But a drowning tragedy at Uig had persuaded my parents that we should learn. Anndra and I were sent off to Stornoway for lessons, but Uilleam refused to go. I think his fear of the water was already too deeply ingrained.

Anndra came and joined us splashing about in the sea for a while before Aunt Rita called us back to eat, and we all sat around the travelling rugs, Uilleam still fully dressed, and tucked into the grub that was laid out on plates. There was cheese and pickle, and bread and cold meats. Egg sandwiches, cucumber sandwiches. Flasks of tea and coffee, and bottles of lemonade in a cold bag.

The ball came out of the blue, from somewhere on the other side of the windbreak. It landed smack in the middle of our lunch, upsetting plates of food and tipping over an open flask to spill still piping hot coffee all over the rug.

Seonag and I screamed, startled, and Uilleam roared with anger, jumping immediately to his feet to hurl Gaelic abuse over the windbreak at the culprits. Aunt Rita remained remarkably unperturbed. 'Alright, keep calm, it's not the end of the world,' she said. Nothing if not practical, she handed the ball to Anndra and began rearranging the plates and food, taking napkins from the hamper to mop up the spillage.

But Uilleam was not so easily mollified. He snatched the ball from Anndra as Ruairidh came running up, panting, from beyond the windbreak. He regarded the chaos of food and plates with dismay. 'I'm so sorry,' he said. 'The wind caught the ball, and . . .'

'You fucking idiot!' Uilleam shouted at him.

'Uilleam, please, it was an accident,' Aunt Rita said, retaining her accustomed calm. But Uilleam wasn't about to let it go, and he knew that Rita wouldn't understand him if he stuck to Gaelic.

'You stupid fucking boys just don't care, do you?' He stabbed a finger into Ruairidh's chest. 'And you, you wee fucker, you've been nothing but trouble your whole life.'

'Oh don't be such an arse,' I told my big brother, but he wasn't listening.

Ruairidh was bristling with anger. He had apologized for what was obviously an accident, but he wasn't about to stand down when it came to taking abuse from Uilleam. He looked at my aunt. 'I'm sorry, Mrs Murray. It was an accident. Is there any chance we could get our ball back?' His friends were gathered watching from a discreet distance.

'No fucking way,' Uilleam shouted in his face, and I saw Ruairidh clench his teeth, and his fists.

'Aw grow up, Uilleam,' Anndra said. 'Give them their ball.' He and Ruairidh were around the same age and had long been friends.

'I'll give them their fucking ball,' Uilleam hissed, and he stuck it firmly under his arm and went marching off towards the water.

Aunt Rita called after him, 'Uilleam, don't be silly. Let it pass now.' She had no idea just how strong the language was, but the tone of it was a powerful clue. Me and Seonag and Anndra jumped to our feet and went chasing after him. Ruairidh stood seething for a moment, before turning and running past us to try to wrestle the ball away from Uilleam. But Uilleam put a hand in his face, for all the world as if fending off a tackle on the rugby field, and ran on right up to the water's edge. There he released the ball from his hands and kicked it with all his might. Caught by the wind, it went sailing over the incoming waves to land with a splash in the bay, a good thirty yards out.

I remember groaning at the stupidity of it. 'Uilleam. Jesus, what an idiot!'

One of the other boys detached himself from the group and came running up to the rest of us. 'That's my ball!'

Uilleam turned on him, and I remember thinking he was old enough to know better than this. 'Go and get it, then.'

'I can't swim!'

'Awww, that's a shame. Looks like the game's a bogey.' This in English. Pure Glasgow slang that he must have picked up at university.

I glanced towards the ball. It was riding the incoming swell, and seemed to be drifting even further out, drawn by the currents.

Aunt Rita joined us at the water's edge, then, hands on hips. 'Well, that's just the stupidest thing I've ever seen.' She turned to the group of village boys. 'Whose ball is it?'

The boy put his hand up.

'I'll buy you another one,' Aunt Rita said.

Uilleam snorted his disapproval. 'It's not that far out. Any decent swimmer could go and get it.'

'Aye, like you?' Ruairidh said. He knew perfectly well that Uilleam couldn't swim.

Uilleam bridled. 'Why don't you go and get it, then, big-mouth? You won the swimming championship at the Nicolson, didn't you? Or maybe you're a chicken.'

Ruairidh glared at him, and I saw his eyes flicker just for a fraction of a second in my direction, before he turned and without another word went plunging out into the water.

'For God's sake, lad, what are you doing?' Aunt Rita shouted after him, and was almost drowned out by a chorus of voices imploring Ruairidh not to do it.

'Stop it!' I screamed after him. 'Stop it!'

But by now he was already out of his depth and wind-milling his arms in strong steady strokes to break through the incoming swell and set a course for the ever-diminishing ball.

We all watched, then, in silence, barely daring to breathe, as he got further and further away. It took an interminable time for him, finally, to reach the ball. I don't think any of us had realized just how far out it really was.

Even from where we stood on the edge of the water we could hear him fighting for breath. Big, deep, barking gasps. Having reached the ball, he clung on to it now to keep himself afloat as he tried to control his breathing, but we could see that all the time the current was drawing them both further out.

Real fear stalked among us then, and I could see from his face that even Uilleam was starting to panic.

For two or maybe three very long minutes Ruairidh clutched the ball to his chest, floating on his back as he slowly regained his breath. Then, without letting it go, he started kicking with his legs and setting a course back towards the beach. But even as we watched, he seemed to make no progress at all. The pull of the current was stronger than the kick of his legs. If anything, it seemed to me, the swell was growing, the waves breaking a good twenty yards out where the seabed fell away and the undertow dragged everything down.

Ruairidh's friends were screaming encouragement at him,

but not one of them could swim, or at least weren't admitting to it.

'You idiot! You stupid idiot!' Aunt Rita shouted at Uilleam. I had never seen her so angry. She hoisted up her skirts and went wading off into the water, waist-deep, as if by somehow getting closer to him she could reel him in. But she must have realized the futility of it and stopped, her dress floating on the surface of the sea, and spreading out all around her like ink from a squid.

Suddenly, Anndra went sprinting past me, legs pumping as he pulled them up out of the water to plunge forward, and then launch himself past Aunt Rita and into the sea. Everyone, almost in unison, called him back. But Anndra had made up his mind and nothing was going to change it. He was a strong boy, my brother, with muscular shoulders and a ripped chest and stomach. A good swimmer, too, and the courage of a lion.

Our protests tailed off as we watched him power his way through the incoming waves, fear nearly choking us. For a moment he vanished, and no one dared breathe until we saw him again breaking the surface of the water beyond the swell. Long, elegant strokes of his arms took him quickly out towards Ruairidh, and he reached him much more quickly, it seemed, than it had taken Ruairidh to get out there himself.

Now we could hear him gasping for breath, too, and both boys clung to the ball, dipping beneath the surface then emerging again with water streaming down their faces. Anndra was shouting something to Ruairidh, but it was impossible to make out what. Then, of a sudden, they both struck out for home. Ruairidh was still on his back, one arm crooked around the ball for buoyancy, the other arcing through the water as he kicked frantically with his feet. Anndra remained on his belly, his left arm making arcs through the water in sync with Ruairidh's, the other hooked around the arm that held the ball.

With both sets of legs kicking against the current, it was with relief that I saw they were actually making progress towards the shore. Until they arrived at that point where the incoming swell reached its peak and broke in furious white foaming spume. Both boys vanished from view, and with a shock, like a punch to my chest, I saw the ball shoot up into the air and go skidding back across the surface of the water in the bay.

Still no sign of either Ruairidh or Anndra.

And now it was Aunt Rita who went plunging off into the ocean, still fully dressed, her hat whipped from her head to bob momentarily on the crest of a wave before being washed, spinning, back up on to the sand.

I remember feeling immersed in the strangest silence. Even though the sound of the sea breaking all around us and the howl of the wind was very nearly deafening. It was as if time had stood still, or at least slowed to the merest crawl. Almost exactly as I would experience so many years later in the Place de la République.

Aunt Rita had vanished now into white water, and I saw only a flailing arm, before she re-emerged, pulling one of the boys behind her, fighting to keep her head above water as she sought to find some kind of foothold below it. And then, when she touched down, emerging head and shoulders from the water, dragging Ruairidh in her wake. I heard him coughing and choking, gasping desperately for a breath that wouldn't carry more water into his lungs. He was alive, and I almost collapsed with relief.

All of the boys went wading then into the water to grab him from my aunt and pull him up on to the beach where he lay retching and vomiting seawater. But there was no sign of Anndra.

In the moment before she turned to go back for him, I saw the fear in Aunt Rita's eyes, but also the courage that it took to risk your life for a loved one. Or maybe it takes no courage at all when you love a person. You just do what your heart demands, even though your head is calling you a fool.

By this time I was in tears, howling uncontrollably as Seonag stood staring out to sea, her face whiter than I have ever seen it. Uilleam was rooted to the spot, his feet sunk in the soft wet sand, rabbit eyes scanning the waves as panic filled and emptied his chest in a series of rapid shallow breaths.

Aunt Rita had vanished again from sight, and the horrible thought began to worm its way into my brain that neither she nor Anndra would ever be seen again. Not alive, anyway.

And then there she was, on her back, arms around Anndra's chest, kicking for shore, before turning to push her legs down in search of traction, finding it and pulling Anndra behind her.

This time we all ran into the water to help her. Everyone except Uilleam, whose abject fear of the stuff wouldn't permit him to set so much as one foot in it. Anndra was a dead weight. Unlike Ruairidh before him, there was no coughing or gasping for breath.

Panic propelled us up on to the firm sand left by the receding tide, and Anndra lay on his back, head tipped towards the water. His eyes were wide open, just like Grampa's that time by the caravan. Except that water foamed backwards out of his mouth, washing over his open eyes as if trying to flush all the life out of them. But with a terrible constriction of my chest I knew that he was already gone.

Aunt Rita, though, hadn't given up hope just yet. Her sodden dress clung to every contour of her body, and I could see her underwear beneath it. Her usually coiffured hair hung down in rat's tails over her face as she knelt down by the prone form of my brother and began pumping at his chest with both hands. Gouts of water spurted from his mouth, before she leaned over him to pinch his nostrils and breathe into his mouth. Then more pumping. I remembered that Rita had been a nurse before she married my uncle, which was how they had met, and I willed her to breathe life back into Anndra.

She carried on long beyond the point where all of us knew there was no longer any hope. A desperate reluctance to accept that he was dead. Maybe because she was the only adult there, she felt in some way responsible for what had happened.

Ruairidh, meantime, had struggled to his knees, still

retching, tears streaming from his eyes, watching with horror as Rita pumped and pumped with despairing hands on Anndra's chest.

I understood even then that Ruairidh was going to get the blame. The fact that it was Uilleam who had kicked the ball into the water and goaded Ruairidh into going after it would get lost in the telling. All that anyone was going to remember was Ruairidh's stupidity in going into the sea to get it, causing Anndra to risk and lose his life in the process of trying to rescue him.

I glanced up at Uilleam. He was gazing in disbelief on his younger brother lying dead in the sand, and whatever guilt he was busy tucking away somewhere deep inside him, I knew he would never admit it to the world. His eyes flickered towards Ruairidh, and I saw hatred there. He sensed my eyes on him, and when he turned to look at me, I knew in that moment that I had lost not one brother, but two.

Of course, there were no mobile phones in those days. No one to call for help, and no help to be given anyway. And so the boys carried Anndra up past the cemetery, where just a few days later we would put him in the ground. When I looked back I could still see the football being washed remorselessly out to sea. I was sobbing uncontrollably, Seonag with an arm around my shoulders, Aunt Rita following behind us, stooped with grief and crying silent tears. When we got to the car park, the boys laid Anndra out on the back seat of the Humber Hawk, while Seonag and I squeezed into the front with my aunt.

There was no room in the car for Uilleam and he returned to the village with the other boys, one of them giving him a backie. But not before, I heard later, he had taken out his wrath on Ruairidh. Punching him into the long beach grass and kicking him until the others pulled him off. From all accounts Ruairidh didn't lift a finger to defend himself, and in all the years that followed, not a word ever passed between him and me on the events of that day.

I can't even begin to describe how awful things were in our house over the next few days. I don't think I have ever witnessed grief like it. Or anger. As I suspected, no blame was ever apportioned to Uilleam. Teflon Uilleam. All the shit stuck to Ruairidh.

Anndra's coffin was laid out in the front porch, just as our grandfather's had been before him. Everyone in the village, and from a good way beyond, came to pay their respects. But when the Macfarlanes turned up, my mother wouldn't even let them past the gate. She must have had her hate radar set, because somehow she sensed them coming before any of the rest of us.

The first I knew about it was when I heard her screaming at them in Gaelic from the doorstep. They and their son would never be welcome in our house again. Not that they had ever been regular visitors anyway. She hoped that their God would forgive them, because she never would. That, in spite of the fact that while she blamed their son for the death of hers, it was Ruairidh who had saved my life all these years before.

Which is when I first began to suspect that maybe my mother valued Anndra's life above mine. The preference for a son over a daughter.

The funeral was held on the Saturday. A long procession that followed the hearse down that single-track road to Dalmore Beach and the cemetery that overlooked it. Still the good weather had not broken, and the sea in its innocent blue lay calm and still in the bay, breaking in only the gentlest of waves upon the sand.

Things had changed somewhat since my grandfather's funeral and the women came right down now to the car park, but remained on that side of the fence as the men carried Anndra across the machair, between the headstones of all the dead who had gone before him, to a freshly dug grave in a plot that commanded a view of the very spot in the bay where he had drowned.

I stood by my mother's side, Seonag holding my hand tightly, and let silent tears roll down my face as we said goodbye. Goodbye to the brother who had taunted and tormented me all through my childhood. What I wouldn't have given in that moment to find one of his spiders in my pocket, and hear him stifling laughter from some hidden place as I screamed in panic.

Which was when I noticed the lone figure silhouetted on the clifftops away to our right. Ruairidh, too, had come to pay his last respects. I'm sure he was riddled with all the guilt that everyone felt was justified. For he certainly knew that but for Anndra it would have been his funeral here today. And I couldn't help feeling sorry for him, blamed and excluded, a pariah among his peers.

At the far end of the cemetery the minister had delivered his final words, and the mourners were picking up spades to shovel the sandy soil over the coffin and fill the grave. The headstone was not raised for another six months, and although I am not sure if my mother ever visited his grave, I went to see Anndra often over the years, just to sit with him and pray that he would forgive me for marrying the man who everyone blamed for his death.

Uncle Hector and Aunt Rita made their delayed departure on the Monday morning. A solemn affair, in which there were few words spoken and more tears spilled. Just before they left I noticed my aunt covering the back seat of the Humber with a tartan travelling rug. The leather had been ruined by the salt water from Anndra's body, which had left its pale imprint in the green. A permanent reminder of the tragedy of that summer's day on Dalmore Beach.

They never came to stay with us again, and I heard much later that my uncle had put his beloved car up for sale as soon as they got home.

CHAPTER TWENTY-EIGHT

Niamh and Uilleam drove in silence along Bayhead, past the inner harbour, slowing over the speed bump and then accelerating up towards the roundabout. Trees in the golf course to their left were already taking on their autumn colours.

The rain clouds that Braque and Gunn had seen earlier gathering out at sea off the west coast were now sweeping their way across the island, rain falling in dark, fast-moving patches that Niamh could see in the distance across the Barvas Moor. For the moment it was just spitting at their windscreen.

'Nothing changes, does it?' Uilleam said.

'That's what I love about this place,' Niamh told him. 'The world changes around us like a silent movie on speed, but the islands never do. They're the one constant in my life.' She glanced at him across the Jeep. 'Must be a while since you were last here.'

She thought he looked fleetingly uncomfortable, but she had to turn away to focus on the road. 'I was back seeing the folks earlier this month.'

'Really? She turned her head again in surprise. 'They never mentioned it.'

'Probably thought you wouldn't be interested.' He could never resist the barb.

She said, 'Maybe they know me too well.' And she could tell from the colour that rose on his cheeks that her reciprocal retort had not missed its mark. Then immediately she regretted it. He was her brother, for God's sake! Why did it always have to be like this?

They drove on into the rain as it swept west across the moor, past the shieling with the green roof that sat away off to their right. Then up over the rise, and a misted view through the cloud and rain to the distant ocean washing up at Rubh' a' Bhiogair beyond Barvas itself.

As they turned off towards Bru, Uilleam said, 'I'm only here for you, you know.'

'Mum told me.' Niamh paused. 'I'm to be grateful, I suppose?'

He bristled. 'I'm not going to the funeral.'

'Then you're not here for me. If you were, you would.'

'Mum and Dad aren't going either.'

She turned her head towards him sharply. 'Really? They told you that?'

He nodded.

'Well, it's more than they've told me.'

'You can't be surprised.'

'Surprised isn't the word I would use, Uilleam. Hurt, maybe. Betrayed.' She tried to control her voice. 'I'm their daughter. Your sister. I just lost the man I loved and you're all still so eaten up by your misplaced hatred of him that you won't even stand by my side when we put him in the ground.'

'He killed our brother.' His voice was screwed tight by sanctimonious certainty.

'No!' Niamh almost shouted. 'You killed Anndra. You!'

'For God's sake, Niamh!'

'Oh, don't give me all that self-righteous innocence!' She almost spat it in his face, then had to swerve to stay on the road. 'You know it was your fault. It's the elephant that's always been in the room. The thing that none of us ever wanted to say out loud, because who could deal with the thought that it was your stupidity that caused the death of your own brother.'

'That's not true,' he barked back at her.

'Yes it is. Yes. It. Is. If you hadn't gone and kicked that ball into the sea like some spoilt thirteen-year-old adolescent, then challenged Ruairidh to go get it, none of it would have happened. None of it. "Any decent swimmer could go and get it." Remember that? You can't tell me that you haven't spent every minute of every day since regretting it. Somewhere deep inside you that you won't admit. Because I wouldn't believe you. Ruairidh was just the scapegoat for your guilt. Someone else to blame. Mum and Dad did it, too. I mean, how in God's name could they ever have dealt with the thought that one of their own children was responsible for the death of another? Much easier to turn grief into hatred and direct it all at Ruairidh.'

There. She had said it, and it could never be taken back. All the things she had kept pent up inside her for all these years. Perhaps it had always been understood. Felt. Perceived. But it had never been given voice. And now that it was out, it didn't make her feel any better, as she had always thought it might. The overwhelming feeling was one of emptiness. She had drained the boil, but the pain remained.

There was no comeback from Uilleam. No denial, no justification, not even an expression of the hurt he must have felt. Just silence. A silence that stretched out like the road ahead of them.

A road that took them past Arnol, with its ruined blackhouse village. Past Bragar, the jaws of an eighty-foot whale mounted in an arch above a gate. Past the mill and the school at Shawbost. Past the turn-off to Dalmore Beach where the innocence of childhood had come to an end, and the deceptions, jealousies and hatreds of adulthood had taken root.

Not a word passed between them during all that long drive down the west coast. Nothing more to be said.

As they turned down towards the bridge at Balanish the Free Church tower rose high above the village rooftops, and all the memories of what had been a happy childhood up until that fateful day on Dalmore Beach came flooding back. Niamh felt silent tears rolling down her cheeks.

Past the war monument, where Anndra and Uilleam had once tied her to the railings and left her there until their father passed in the car on his way home from work. Past the road that led down to the pier, from which the three of them had often set out in the family dinghy to catch fish, or simply lie bobbing and basking in the sun of a warm summer's day. Past the community hall where Niamh had first danced with Ruairidh. Past the croft where a tup had broken free of the sheep fank and knocked Anndra over, breaking his arm, as he tried to herd it back in.

All those memories, both sweet and sour, invested in one place and time. A place which had once been home and felt alien now, unwelcoming.

Niamh drew the Jeep to a halt at the road end above the Murray croft and Uilleam got out to retrieve his case from the back. He hesitated before walking down to the house. 'Are you coming in?'

Niamh shook her head. 'No,' she said, in what was little more than a whisper. She wound up the window and turned the car in the road, before heading back the way they had come, without so much as a glance in the rearview mirror.

It was a long, lonely drive north to Ness in the rain. A road with many faces revealed in different weathers and seasons. This face set now in stone, gloomy and hard, its lack of light reflected in the darkness of Niamh's heart.

She drove fast, breaking the speed limit through all the deserted villages that streamed past her window. Shadar, Borve, Mealabost. Galson. She saw not one single person, and passed only a handful of other vehicles on the road. The landmark that was the Free Church at Cross emerged, wraithlike, from the rain and mist, and she swung off on to the Skigersta

Road. Past the Cross Stores where Ruairidh used to buy their *marag dhubh*. The best black pudding on Lewis, he used to say, an assertion frequently disputed over a dram at MacNeill's in Stornoway, where Charley Barley was the preferred maker of the famous blood sausage.

Her blackest moment came after crossing the northern tip of the island to Skigersta and turning south on the track to Taigh 'an Fiosaich. The rain blew almost horizontally across the moor and the road ahead became as fogged and obscure as her own future. A future that, suddenly, she could no longer face. A future that seemed pointless without the man she loved. A future estranged from her own family, at odds with her oldest friend. A future that, simply, did not seem worth living. She had never felt as low in her whole life.

Then something strangely magical happened. Those rain-clouds driven in from the west by strong autumn winds began to lift and break, and the sunshine that slanted low across the land from behind them formed a rainbow almost directly ahead of her, straddling the road. An archway to a future perhaps less bleak than her heart in its darkness had foreseen. The tiniest chink of light bringing hope to the blackest of places. And quite unaccountably, she felt her spirits lift.

Her Jeep bumped and lurched its way past the shielings at Cuishader, up and over the hill to the long vista that would lead her down eventually to the safety of what, for all its emptiness, was still her home. And as she rounded the bend at Bilascleiter, she was startled to see a vehicle parked at the back of the house. The curve of its roof caught and flashed in the sunlight that crept all across the land now in the wake of the rain.

As she got closer she saw that it was a big Mitsubishi four-wheel-drive Shogun, and a figure in a long black coat and homburg hat stood leaning against the driver's door smoking a large cigar. He pushed himself away from the vehicle, turning as he heard her Jeep approach. A small man, dwarfed by the size of the Shogun he was driving. Niamh's humour improved immediately as she saw who it was.

She had barely pulled on the handbrake before she jumped out of the car and threw her arms around him. He laughed and clutched his hat to stop her from knocking it off, then held her close as she laid her head on his shoulder. When, finally, she stood back to look at him, his hand shot to his hat again, this time to stop it from blowing away. His smile faded, then, and she saw sadness in his dark eyes.

'I'm so sorry, Niamh. So, so sorry. I arranged flights as soon as I got your email.' He looked around with mock despair. 'Not the easiest place in the world to get to from New York.'

Jacob Steiner was probably in his late sixties or early seventies by now, although he looked no older to Niamh than when she had first met him the better part of ten years before. And she had thought him old then.

He had a long, lugubrious face, with a large, bulbous nose veined from too much good living. The remains of his hair beneath the hat were shorn to a silver stubble. A goatee grew

336

in salt-and-pepper profusion, providing definition to a collapsed jawline. Born of Jewish Holocaust survivors who had found their way to America after the Second World War, his corpulence bore testimony to their success in the aftermath of horror. He was one of the nicest and most genuine people Niamh had ever met.

'I can't tell you how grateful I am that you came,' she said.

He took her hand with one of his and raised his other to his mouth to take a pull on his cigar. Smoke whipped away in the wind. 'Young lady,' he said, 'there ain't nothing in this world that could have kept me away.' Then he turned a wry smile on the track that wound down to the house from the ruins of Bilascleiter. 'Except maybe this goddamned road. If you could call it that.' Another puff of his cigar. 'You know, I had a rental car all lined up at the airport till I asked them directions to this place. Goddamn! The young guy nearly snatches the keys out of my hand. "Sorry sir," he says. "Can't let you take that car up there, you'd rip the underside out of her."' To Niamh's amusement, he managed a passable Stornoway accent. 'They drove me into Stornoway to another rental place which gave me this.' He jerked his thumb towards the Shogun. 'Couldn't understand why I would need a brute like that till I actually got here. Damn, Niamh! What possessed you and Ruairidh to build a home away out here in this godforsaken place?'

'I'll show you,' she said. And still holding his hand she led him into the house. He tossed his cigar into the wind as he passed through the open door.

'Jees,' he said. 'If I'd known it wasn't locked I'd have been inside like a shot, instead of hanging about out there in the cold. Did you forget?'

Niamh laughed, and realized how good it felt to be doing just that. Only half an hour ago she couldn't have imagined ever laughing again. 'No. No one locks their doors here.'

'You're kidding?'

She shook her head. 'No need.'

'Hell, I gotta come and live here. In New York City you need deadlocks and bolts and chains, state-of-the-art security systems and God knows what else. Every other schmuck wants to break into your house and steal what you got.'

He stopped and whistled softly as they stepped into the living area, eyes scanning the panorama from the windows. 'Take it back. I see exactly what possessed you to come and live out here. If only I could take a view like that back to Manhattan.' Then he turned to hold her other hand. There could have been little more comfort than the refuge she saw in the soft sympathy of his dark eyes. 'How you doing, honey?'

She dipped her head a little. 'Not great, Mr Steiner.'

'Jake,' he corrected her. She pulled a face and he laughed. 'I know, I know. Must be a generational thing.' His smile faded again. 'Helluva thing, Niamh. Helluva thing.'

She nodded and chewed her lower lip.

'At least you have friends to rally round. Lee tells me he saw you in Paris, just after it.'

She was surprised. 'You've been speaking to Lee?'

'Bumped into him at the airport. His private charter landed just after my scheduled flight. You know, anyone who's anyone in the world of fashion was on Lee's plane. Some big-name models. It's gonna be quite a send-off. Lot of folks thought a lot of Ruairidh.' But not her own family, Niamh thought. Steiner said, 'The Press are arriving in force, too, from what I could see.' And Niamh felt a wave of despair wash over her. What she had hoped might be a quiet, sombre farewell seemed to be turning into a two-ring circus.

'You'll have a drink,' she said, dropping his hands and crossing to the kitchen.

'I will,' he said. 'Scotch on the rocks. Splash of soda if you've got it.'

As Niamh prepared his drink, he took off his coat and hat, and slipped on to a stool at the breakfast bar. 'I'm staying at a hotel in town. The Cabarfeidh. Any good?'

She shrugged. 'As good as you'll get in Stornoway, I guess. You should have tried Lews Castle. They do rooms and suites there now. Very luxurious.'

He smiled sadly. 'Next time. Other circumstances.' She had prepared two drinks the same, except that only one had whisky. She pushed it across the counter to him. They chinked glasses. 'To Ruairidh,' he said. 'One of the good guys.'

Niamh couldn't bring herself to speak.

'And speaking of castles, Lee tells me his party has taken a whole castle to themselves on the Isle of Harris.' He raised his hands in confusion. 'Which I'm told is the same goddamned island as the Isle of Lewis. Who knew?'

'What castle?'

'Oh some unpronounceable place. Avan . . . Avin . . . something.'

'Amhuinnsuidhe?'

'Yep. What you said.'

She nodded thoughtfully as he sipped on his whisky soda.

'You know,' he said, almost lowering his voice, 'Ruairidh should never have mentioned the Tony Capaldi shooting in that interview he did for the *New York Times*.'

Niamh raised her eyebrows in surprise. The paper had carried the interview earlier that summer in an article on the success of Ranish Tweed. They had described it as *a cloth derived from a weaver's hut on a remote Scottish island, rising to become one of the world's most sought-after fashion fabrics*. Ruairidh's story of the shooting in New York had been a throwaway line in passing. 'What do you mean? Why not?'

'Jees, Niamh. You don't fuck about with these people. I gotta tell you, I've been keeping my own head pretty low ever since it came out.'

CHAPTER TWENTY-NINE

It was the first time either of us had been in New York. At the time it felt like the most extraordinary adventure. And of course it was.

It came in the aftermath of that first Lee Blunt collection which rocketed the name of Ranish Tweed to international stardom. It was a name on the lips of fashionistas everywhere, and we were having to pick and choose which orders to accept, because it would have been impossible to fulfil them all.

It was dizzying. There we were, tucked away in an old croft house on the Isle of Lewis, with half a dozen weavers in tin sheds churning out cloth to our own designs, and people in America and Japan, Australia and Europe were clamouring for the stuff.

Ranish had become famous overnight. Magazines like *Vogue* and *Elle* and *Cosmopolitan* were featuring clothes in our tweed. Models we had only read about or seen on TV, or on the covers of *Harper's Bazaar* and *Vanity Fair*, were wearing it on the cat-walks of Paris and Milan and New York. Kate Moss, Naomi Campbell, Linda Evangelista.

And to us it all seemed that it was happening to other people somewhere else. Until we got the call from an assistant to the buyer in the tailoring department of Gold's of 5th Avenue. This was one of the most prestigious tailors in the world. They dressed presidents and movie stars, pop idols and royalty.

The way it worked was clients would get measured up by Gold's in New York, choose their material and style of suit, then the cloth would be sent off to Yves Saint Laurent, or Armani, or whoever, to have it cut. The suits might cross the Atlantic umpteen times during the course of several fittings, and then the finishing would be done by Gold's themselves. Their customers paid thousands, sometimes tens of thousands.

And Gold's wanted to introduce an exclusive line of Ranish Tweed as an option to offer clients. Designer suits in the hottest new tweed on the market. They wanted to fly us to New York, the assistant told us. They wanted us to bring samples and designs, and meet with the head of the tailoring department, Jacob Steiner, to discuss exactly what was going to suit Gold's needs. They would, she said, reserve us first-class seats on Virgin Atlantic and put us up at the Waldorf Astoria.

I can remember dancing around the room after taking that call, and having trouble finding my breath to tell Ruairidh. The *Waldorf Astoria*! I had only ever seen or heard about the legendary New York hotel in the movies. And someone was going to pay for us to stay there! And flying first class to New York? Something you could only dream about. Who could afford that? Certainly not us. It seemed no time at all since we had taken the bus down to Lee's show at London Fashion Week and stayed in the cheapest hotel we could find.

How could this be happening to me and Ruairidh?

But it was, and it did. We arrived in New York on a steamy hot summer's day in July to be met at the airport by Mr Steiner himself. Immaculately suited, wearing the whitest shirt I had ever seen, and the most delicious plum-red tie, he was the personification of charm. Not a greasy or sleazy or manufactured kind of charm, but a real charisma that genuinely reflected the man himself.

I suppose he must have been in his early sixties at that time. He reeked of expensive aftershave and Cuban cigars (I only found out later they were Cuban when he confessed to having his own illicit supply line from the Caribbean island in contravention of the US ban).

'Guys,' he said, and shook both our hands warmly, 'I cannot tell you what a great pleasure it is to meet you at last. I was blown away by Ranish Tweed the first time I saw it. But when I felt it, actually ran it through my fingers . . .' He seemed to run out of words to express his feelings. 'I can only say there have been very few times in my life that I have genuinely felt I was touching the future. That's how it was for me when I first handled Ranish Tweed.'

An assistant collected our luggage from the carousel, and Mr Steiner led us out to a waiting stretch limo. He slid into the back and sat opposite us.

'I want us to have a relationship that is going to make our

suits in Ranish Tweed the most expensive and exclusive in the world. Which means we gotta be friends. We need to understand each other, to have a feeling for what each of us is about. That's why you're here. I want to get to know you guys, and for you to know what it is that makes me tick.' He opened a small refrigerator and tossed ice cubes into three glasses, before filling them with whisky and topping them off with a splash of soda. 'Glenturret,' he said, handing us our glasses. 'Oldest distillery in Scotland, I'm told. So it should be good.' He raised his glass. 'To Ranish.'

We echoed his toast and sipped from our foaming glasses. I had never tasted whisky and soda before, and was surprised at how good it was. It was to be the first of many.

'Sit back and enjoy, *meine Kinder*. First we get to know each other. Then we do business.'

The Waldorf Astoria exceeded all my expectations. The white stone building in Park Avenue seemed to drip gold, a constant procession of limousines and taxis drawing up beneath its extravagant canopy, an enormous Stars and Stripes furling and unfurling in the slow-motion movement of hot air. After the cool brisk summer winds of Lewis, New York City seemed burdened by the weight of its own heat and humidity.

We hurried from the air-conditioned bubble of our stretch limo, through the hot, wet, slap-in-the-face air on the sidewalk, and into the almost chilly atmosphere of the hotel itself. Up steps and into a vast marbled area of lobby and lounge. Our room was huge, but to my mind gently disappointing. It had all the trappings of grandeur. Heavily embroidered curtains, a gold-braided bedspread, antique furniture. And yet there was something tired about it all, careworn. Rotting wooden window frames, tashed wallpaper and worn carpets. But nothing could take the gloss off our excitement.

We were in our room only for as long as it took to deposit our luggage and slip the bellboy an extravagant tip, and then it was off again in the limo to Central Park, where Mr Steiner had arranged a horse-and-carriage tour.

'You wanna get to know me?' he said. 'First you gotta get to know my city.'

For the second time in my life I felt like royalty. This time in the kind of open horse-drawn carriage I had seen convey the Queen and visiting heads of government along the Mall on State occasions. Steel-rimmed wagon wheels clattered over the metalled surface of roads that wound through this extraordinary rectangle of greenery in the heart of urban Manhattan. There was something timeless in the clip-clop of our horse's hooves, and startling in the red-trimmed livery set against the shining chestnut of its flanks.

Mr Steiner told our driver that his spiel was not needed, and he gave us his own running commentary as we rounded the Pond and passed the Wollman Rink, which in winter, he said, would be alive with skaters in scarves and hats, wrapped against a cold which was unimaginable in this heat. Past the carousel and the children's zoo. Skirting the literary walk, the sun slanting off all the angles of Shakespeare's bronze. The Angel of the Waters Fountain, Cherry Hill and then, most poignantly, Strawberry Fields. This quiet area of the park dedicated to the memory of John Lennon, fresh flowers laid with love on the black and white circle of stone marquetry with the legend, *Imagine*, at its heart.

Only two-and-a-half miles long and half a mile wide, wherever you were in the park you could almost always see the skyscrapers pressing in all around its perimeter. And now, here we were, right opposite the distinctive Dakota Building where Lennon had been shot by a deranged fan. I was, I think, only four years old when it happened, but my dad had been a big Beatles fan, and we had watched all the VHS videos of The Beatles' movies. *A Hard Day's Night*, *Help!*, *Yellow Submarine*. I knew every song, and had treasured the twinkling-eyed John Lennon like some kind of big brother. I cried when I heard he was dead.

Mr Steiner took us then to Gold's on Fifth Avenue, in Midtown. I'd had no real sense of what exactly to expect of Gold's, and found all my preconceptions swept away by the discovery that it was actually a luxury department store. Its various departments occupied seven floors, with galleries that ran around a central well at the heart of the building.

The tailoring department was on the fifth floor, and staff had been expecting us. They lined up inside the door to shake our hands, each one meeting our eyes with such warmth that I have rarely been made to feel so welcome. Mr Steiner took us on a whistle-stop tour of the facilities. 'We'll come back tomorrow for the real work,' he said. 'But right now we gotta hurry. I've got us tickets to a dance musical at the Marquis Theatre on Broadway.'

Neither Ruairidh nor I were affected by the heat or the jet lag. Such was the adrenalin rush of our first day in New York, that we could have stayed up all night. And now we were going to a show on Broadway! I felt like I had just stepped into my own private movie.

The show was called *Come Fly Away*, an exuberant production starring people I had never heard of. Keith Roberts, John Selya, Ashley Tuttle. The story followed four couples as they searched for love. Amazingly, it was built around a selection of Frank Sinatra songs featuring his actual voice backed live by an orchestra of eighteen instrumentalists. Mr Steiner had reserved us the best seats in the house. Neither of us was a big Sinatra fan, nor particularly interested in dance, and we would never have bought tickets for a show like this, but I was totally spellbound by the spectacle. And when I glanced at Ruairidh I saw that he was, too.

Afterwards, Mr Steiner took us backstage to introduce us to the perspiring performers, radiant and animated, breathless among the flowers that bedecked their dressing rooms after another successful show. They all seemed to know him, and greeted us as if we, too, were stars.

As first days in New York go, this one must have been up there among the best. And it wasn't finished yet.

After the show it was on to dinner. Torrisi's was a little Italian restaurant in Mulberry Street at the top of Little Italy. As we got out of the limo Mr Steiner said, 'This city is full of great and expensive restaurants. But Torrisi's? For good Italian-American food you can't beat it. Hard to believe, but it's a sandwich shop during the day. They do great chicken parm, or turkey hero, and they got some cool beers. Then at night, it transforms itself into this classy little restaurant. Twenty seats. Fixed price. Impossible to reserve a table. You just gotta turn up and hope.' He grinned. 'Except that I reserved us a table.'

Inside, booths and tables were set around a red-painted brick wall, with more plain wooden tables and tubular chairs pushed into the centre of the floor. A black-and-white portrait of a young Billy Joel clutching a pair of boxing gloves jostled for wall space with shelves laden with cans of peeled tomatoes and bottles of Manhattan Special espresso soda.

We had just squeezed into our seats beneath Billy Joel, when a voice called a loud greeting from across the room. 'Hey Jake!' Mr Steiner turned and looked towards a booth at the far side. Four men wearing expensive haircuts above tanned faces and designer suits that folded neatly over Gucci shoes sat around a table eating pasta and drinking champagne. Amazingly, even though it was dark by now, two of them wore sunglasses and looked like extras from *The Godfather*.

Mr Steiner excused himself and stood up to hurry over and shake their hands. He almost bowed as the one to whom all the others deferred stood up to shake his hand and slap his shoulder. He was an older man, dyed hair receding, belly expanding into his waistcoat. But no shades. After a few words, Mr Steiner turned and waved us over. It was only as we got nearer that I saw that all their suits were cut from one of the darker and more conservative weaves of Ranish Tweed. Mr Steiner said, 'Mr Capaldi, meet Niamh and Ruairidh. These are the good folks that made the cloth you're wearing. In fact, as I understand it, Ruairidh himself might well have woven the very stuff you got on your back.'

Capaldi shook our hands vigorously. 'Well that just doubles the pleasure in meeting you,' he said. He felt the cloth at the cuff of his jacket between thumb and forefinger. 'This is just the most amazing material I've ever worn. Like silk with balls. It's got class. When we was ordering our suits, Jake here suggested we try it. And hey . . .' He spread his arms wide. 'Look at me now. Best-dressed man in New York City. This calls for more champagne.' He waved a hand in the air, and somehow, as if by magic, fresh chairs appeared and we found ourselves wedged in around their table.

Glasses foamed, and we drank toasts. To Ranish. To Scotland. To Jake Steiner. 'One day I gotta get to Scotland,' Capaldi said. 'But I hear the weather ain't so good.'

I said, 'Well, if you ever got too hot, which is most unlikely, you could always cool yourself down with some Capaldi's ice cream.'

There was a strange and immediate silence around the table. Mr Steiner looked uncomfortable, and Ruairidh jumped in quickly to explain. 'You've heard of the Scottish actor Peter Capaldi?'

'Sure,' Capaldi said uncertainly.

'Well his grandfather came from Italy. Bought a ticket to New York but somehow ended up in Glasgow, where he set up an ice-cream company.'

I held my breath, feeling that in some way I had managed to put my foot in it. Then to my relief Capaldi burst out laughing. 'Made a big mistake then, didn't he? Should have come to New York as he planned. Then maybe he woulda ended up wearing a jacket like this instead of peddling the cold stuff like some back-street nobody.' And he tugged at his lapel.

'There's a big Italian community in Scotland,' I said, but it was clear that Capaldi had already lost interest.

'Is that so?'

Mr Steiner got to his feet, all smiles. 'Well, we should leave you good folk to it.' And he shook Capaldi's hand. 'It was a pleasure to see you again, Tony, as always.'

We thanked him for the champagne and retreated with Mr Steiner to our table, where a waiter immediately delivered warm mozzarella on garlic toast, sprinkled with salt and drizzled with olive oil beneath a garnish of sun-dried tomato. Mr Steiner ordered red wine, and when the waiter had gone he leaned confidentially into the table, lowering his voice. 'You know who that is?' he said, tipping his head discreetly in the direction of the Capaldi table. That's Antonio Capaldi. Otherwise known as Tony C. Just about the most notorious mafia crime boss in New York City.' He pulled a little smile. 'We make suits for all sorts at Gold's.'

'He seemed nice,' I said.

'Yeah.' Mr Steiner raised one eyebrow. 'Nice.'

We had only just finished our pasta dish when a rammy at the door drew our eyes from our plates. Two men who had just been told that the restaurant was full pushed the maître d' aside and split up as they weaved among the tables towards Capaldi's booth. I suddenly realized what it was about them that seemed so out of place. They were wearing coats. In this heat.

The men at Capaldi's table started to get up as they arrived. But as if by magic, handguns, barrels extended by silencers, appeared from beneath the coats. A flurry of strangely muted shots left all four men at Capaldi's table blood-spattered and dead. Their assassins turned and walked out of the door as if nothing had happened.

Chaos broke out as soon as the shots were fired, tables overturned, diners diving for cover on the floor. Screams filled the air, even as the killers disappeared out into the night.

Me and Ruairidh and Mr Steiner were left stunned in our booth, food half-eaten on the table. One glass of red wine overturned and dripping on to the floor like blood.

At first I could barely process what it was I had just witnessed. Like a scene from a movie. Lurid and unreal. As if I half expected the director to call, 'Cut, let's go again,' with everyone dusting themselves down and retaking their places.

But as the truth of it dawned on me, I began to understand that had these assassins arrived just ten minutes earlier, we would have been sitting at that table with Capaldi and his associates, and would almost certainly have been shot too, lying dead on the floor or spreadeagled across the table.

Screams still filled the restaurant, and somewhere far off in the night I could hear a police siren. I glanced at Mr Steiner. His face was pale but his eyes were shining. 'You realize,' he said in a small voice, 'that the biggest mafia boss in New York has just been shot dead wearing Ranish Tweed.' He pushed his eyebrows up to wrinkle his forehead. 'That's a rare distinction.'

CHAPTER THIRTY

Niamh and Steiner lounged in soft chairs looking out at the Minch, sunlight playing in burned-out patches on the water, dazzling briefly before vanishing to appear somewhere else, like spotlights shining through breaks in the cloud. Successive headlands to the south faded in silhouette into the mist of rain and late afternoon sun.

Steiner was on to his second whisky soda, and Niamh was troubled. She said, 'You don't really think that the mafia would have killed Ruairidh in revenge for telling that story in a newspaper?'

Steiner shrugged and sipped thoughtfully on his whisky. 'The truth of it is, the thing that happened with Capaldi and his guys . . . it was just one of life's little brain-fuckers. Comes out of the blue, and you can't quite believe what it is you've just witnessed. I mean, hell, it happened so fast I never even had time to shit myself.' He grinned, then the smile slowly faded. 'But damnit, Niamh, it's the kind of story you tell in smoke-filled rooms with old friends or trusted customers when you've had a drink or three. It just ain't something you

353

brag about in the national media. Know what I mean? Even though it was a long time ago. Jees, someone out there might just have thought that Ruairidh was trying to profit from it. And you don't tell tales about the mafia for commercial gain. These guys have got long memories and hold grudges for even longer.'

It was something that would never have occurred to Niamh. And it was disconcerting. 'That would seem like a lot of trouble to go to for very little.'

'What you and I think of as very little, Niamh, ain't always seen that way by others. And it's classic mob MO. Bombs and cars.' He finished his drink and stood up. 'But who the hell knows? If it was them ain't nobody ever gonna tell.'

He crossed to lay his glass on the breakfast bar and collect his coat and hat.

'I better go. Get myself checked in.'

Niamh crossed the room to help him on with his coat and give him a hug. 'Take care on the road. I know you're not used to driving on the left.'

He shook his head. 'Gotta think it through at every junction. Crazy thing you Brits do, driving on the wrong side of the road.' He kissed her cheek. 'I'll see you tomorrow, at the funeral. I guess someone at the hotel can point me in the right direction.'

She nodded and stood by the open door to watch him turn the Shogun and lurch off up the track towards Bilascleiter. This brief moment of animation and unexpected laughter, memories shared with an old friend, had passed too quickly and left her feeling bereft and lonely again. In her heart she didn't really believe that the mafia had anything to do with Ruairidh's death. That was just Jacob Steiner being dramatic. After all, why would the mob have sent her and Ruairidh emails? What did they know of, or care about, Irina Vetrov?

She looked at her waterproof jacket hanging on the rack by the door, mud-caked wellies on the floor beneath it, and decided she would rather walk out along the cliffs in the hope of a good strong wind to blow away her mood, than sit festering in an empty house.

CHAPTER THIRTY-ONE

Braque came down the carpeted staircase from her room and found Gunn sitting at the bar in the lounge where she had left him. He was nursing the same pint, and she thought that probably alcohol was another item on the banned list that the doctor had given to his wife.

'Sorry about that,' she said. Condensation from her glass of Chardonnay lay in a pool around the bottom of it, and the wine had lost its chill.

Gunn glanced at her and said, 'What's wrong?'

She darted a quick look in his direction. She was, it seemed, an open book to everyone but herself. 'It's that obvious?'

'I've been interviewing folk for nearly thirty years, Ma'am. I think I know when something's amiss.'

She shrugged helplessly. Confiding in others was a habit she had lost in these last years. But maybe it would be easier with a stranger, and certainly after a glass or two of wine. 'Do you have children, Monsieur Gunn?' And she immediately saw disappointment in the set of his mouth.

'Afraid not, Ma'am. Something we were never blessed with.'

She shrugged, toying with her fingers on the bar in front of her. 'They can be a blessing. And a curse.' She glanced across at him. 'No doubt your wife would have stayed at home and looked after them.'

'Probably.'

'But, you see, I couldn't stay home. I had a job. And not the kind of nine-to-five job my husband had. It was a job that could call on me at any time, keep me out half the night, make me give up my days off. And Gilles was the one who ended up looking after the girls.' She paused to clarify. 'Twins.'

'Gilles? That's your husband?'

'Was,' she corrected him. 'We split up a couple of years ago. He found someone else. After we broke up, he claims. But I figure it started long before.' She glanced at him again and saw his discomfort. This was personal, not professional. But it felt good just to talk. She drained her glass and waved at the barman to refill it. 'I got custody, but the truth is that they spend more time with him than me. I just can't seem to be a mother and a police officer at the same time. And do you know what day care costs?'

Gunn didn't.

'Much more than I can afford. So Gilles takes them. All the time. And now he wants to revisit the custody agreement.'

'Would that not be for the best?'

She gazed gloomily into her glass. 'For the girls, maybe. Not for me. I can't bear the thought of my babies looking on someone else as *maman*. Which is what would happen.' She took several swallows of wine. 'I'm just off the phone to Gilles. Been trying to get him for two days. It turns out that Claire is not well.'

'That's one of the twins?'

She nodded. 'She's got a fever of some kind, and he's had to call the doctor.' She turned imploring eyes on Gunn. 'I should be there.'

'Aye, Ma'am, you probably should.'

'But I'm here.'

'Aye, Ma'am, you are.' Gunn pursed his lips and drew a long slow breath through his nostrils. 'But you know, sometimes you just have to make choices. It wouldn't make any difference to Ruairidh Macfarlane if you were to go home now. He'll still be dead. And as for whoever killed him, they'll just put someone else on that.'

'Yes, and I'd probably lose my job.'

Gunn shrugged. 'Choices again, Ma'am.' And she heard the echo of Madeleine's voice in his. He sipped on his beer, but he was still less than halfway through it. 'When I had my heart attack in March, there was a time I thought I wouldn't see the year out. There's nothing quite like death, or the threat of it, to bring home to you just how precious and precarious life really is. It made me think about what was most important to me, about where my priorities should lie. With my wife or my job.' He scratched his head. 'I know it's different for me. Being a policeman in Stornoway is quite another thing from being a policeman in Paris. And I was lucky, I was able to keep both.

But, believe you me, if I'd had to choose between this –' he took out his warrant card and slapped it on the bar – 'and my good lady . . . being any kind of a policeman would have come a very distant second. Because in the end, people matter more than jobs. Your heart is more important than your pay packet.'

Braque looked at him with something like envy. How wonderful, she thought, to have such a clear vision of life. To cut through all the fog and obfuscation to make unequivocal choices. Maybe only proximity to death can force such focus. She said, 'I'll go home after the funeral. Day after tomorrow.'

He nodded. 'I think that's a good idea, Ma'am.'

When he was gone, she was tempted to order yet another glass of wine, but in the end decided against it and climbed wearily back to her room. She stood for a long time at the window gazing out over the inner harbour, seeing how the early-evening sunshine cast long shadows on the water. Gilles was right. She *was* a bad mother. *And* wife. There had only ever been one real focus in her life, and that had been her job. Other people sacrificed personal ambition for family. Not Braque. She had always put herself first. And now, as she found her life slipping away only too quickly and easily towards single middle age, here she stood, lonely and alone, in some strange hotel room far from home with no one to turn to but an island policeman she had just met. And herself. They both had damaged hearts. And she came up wanting.

The trill of her mobile phone drilled into her consciousness, dispelling introspection, and she fumbled in her bag to find it.

'Lieutenant, it's Marc Bouquand.'

It took Braque a moment to place him, before remembering that he was the ANSSI computer expert on attachment to her department. He had briefed her on the Dark Web, and found deleted emails on Georgy Vetrov's hard disk.

'I got that email you forwarded to me. From *well wisher* to Ruairidh Macfarlane. Interesting, when you start looking at the e-trail all these phoney IP addresses leave in the ether.'

'It helped?'

'Oh yes. With three different paths to follow you start to come up with points of correlation, which in the end lead you to the source.'

Braque felt her heart skip a beat. 'You mean you know who sent them?'

'Not who sent them, no. But it would seem you are in the best place to find that out. I know where they were sent from.'

'The Isle of Lewis?'

'More specifically, Lieutenant, from two different computers in the public library in the town of Stornoway. Two from one, one from the other.'

Braque felt her jaw go slack. She had walked past the library during a stroll through town the previous night. It was just around the corner in a rust-painted building next to the Argos store. 'I'll get back to you,' she said quickly and hung up. She slipped her phone into her pocket and ran down the stairs, out into Castle Street and down to the harbour, hoping that she might catch Gunn before he drove off. But he was long gone.

She dialled his number and hurried back into the hotel. It was still ringing as she climbed the steps, then switched to voice mail when she went into the bar. 'The emails were sent from the public library right here in Stornoway, Monsieur Gunn,' she whispered into the phone. 'Call me back.' She hung up and found the barman looking at her curiously. 'Do you know what time the library closes?'

The barman checked his watch. 'You've missed it, I'm afraid,' he said. 'It closes at five on a Tuesday.'

CHAPTER THIRTY-TWO

The light summer nights lingered for a while in autumn. Or *fall* as the Americans would call it. A nice way, Niamh thought, to describe a season when leaves turn the colour of gold and fall from the trees. But not a word that anyone on these islands would ever think to use. There were no trees outside of Stornoway, and no leaves to fall.

As she stood on the clifftops and gazed across the moor, nothing grew more than a few inches for as far as the eye could see. Grasses burned and bowed by the wind. A wind that somehow characterized everything about this place. Blowing weather in, then ushering it away. In from the sea, out to the sea. The only constant in an ever-changing skyscape.

Niamh drew her parka around her, protection from the chill blowing now from the north. There was a change in the air. She could feel it. Something different, almost indefinable. Summer was finally gone and autumn, ephemeral and capricious, had turned its face towards winter. There was a quality, too, about the light, that was different. It slanted across the land, clear-eyed and cold, and even where the sun set in the west it lacked strength, an insipid yellow against the washed-out blue of the sky.

She had walked some way from the house, and stood now where the cliffs crumbled and fell away through a jumble of rock spoil to a tiny beach far below. Mostly shingle. But hidden from view, just to the right of it, a small patch of fine silver sand hugged the foot of the cliffs. Ringed by black rock, it remained, in clement weather, impervious to the incoming tide, a tiny oasis of calm, where she and Ruairidh had some-times made love on warm summer evenings in the early days of their marriage. Today, with the heavy swell coming in off the Minch, it would become, at high tide, a foaming treacherous pool of turbulent white seawater dashed against the cliff face. But the tide was still a good way out, and she decided to climb down and revisit precious memories before they vanished for ever.

She jumped from a ring of crumbling peat on to a gentle slope descending to the shelf where she and Ruairidh had built their bothy from the stones of John Nicholson's first house. It always, somehow, came as a surprise to her. Stone the same colour as the cliff, heaped around the face of it in a low round building that seemed almost subsumed by it. Perfectly cam-ouflaged. She knew, from walkers who had come knocking at their door, just how difficult it was to find if you did not know exactly where it was.

A wall curved around one side of it, protecting and leading to a stout wooden door jammed shut by a boulder. She pushed the stone aside with her foot and unlatched the door to step inside.

She was struck at once by the warmth of the air, and the smell of peat smoke. There were two windows in the curve of the outside walls, and two triangular skylights in the roof, and so there was plenty of light to see by. She stooped and stepped down into the circular floor area, where a stout central wooden beam held up the roof.

A wooden bench sat below the far window, and to her left a wooden platform at waist height served as a table, or a bed for anyone with a sleeping bag who wished to stay overnight.

In the opposite corner they had built a tiny fireplace against the wall, with tin cowling to prevent smoke from seeping into the room. Niamh knelt now by the fireplace and felt the warmth that resided still among the ashes. She turned to look across the interior of the bothy. Beneath the bed lay a plastic bag that Ruairidh usually kept full of dried peat slabs. It lay on its side, most of the peat gone. All that remained of it, black crumbs and dust, strewn across the flagstones.

It was an inescapable conclusion. Someone had been here. Very recently. Maybe even earlier today. And perhaps for a day or two before that. Ruairidh's peat was almost exhausted.

Niamh stood up and looked around for other clues. But there was nothing alien to be seen. No litter or belongings left behind. No cigarette ends. Had it not been for the burning of the peat, you would never have known that the bothy had been occupied.

She felt the first stirrings of disquiet, remembering the

footfalls behind her in that dark Paris street. Then waking in the night to the sounds of what she thought was someone moving around the house. She had seen nobody since returning to Taigh 'an Fiosaich. Not a soul, except for the visitors who had arrived by car. And yet it was perfectly possible that some late-season walker had sought refuge here for a night or two without her being aware of it. That, after all, was its purpose. And she could not see the bothy from the house.

For some time, then, she sat on the bench by the window and marvelled at how effective this little stone hut really was at shutting out the weather and the sound of it. Perched here, beneath the lip of the cliff, its tiny windows looking out on to the mercurial Minch, a miniature protective bubble to keep you safe. *I'll keep you safe*, Ruairidh had told her. But he hadn't. Unlike the bothy they had built. That was still there, and probably would be long after she too was gone.

She got stiffly to her feet and made her way back outside, to be met by a blast of cold air, and the roar of the sea breaking over rocks far below. She fought to shut and latch the door, then push the boulder back against it, before setting off on the narrow path that led along the broken exterior of the cliff face before turning down in a steeply zigzagging natural stairway to the hidden beach at the foot of it.

The sand was wet and firm, and strewn with shells. The force of the sea against the cliff behind it had hollowed out a space that might one day, eons from now, become a cave. Niamh kicked off her wellies and rolled her jeans up to the knee, to walk barefoot across the sand, feeling it fill all the spaces between her toes. And then clamber carefully over slabs of gneiss worn smooth by time and water. She found a favourite perch and sat there, dangling her feet in the crystal-clear water of a rock pool. It was icy cold, and she could only hold her feet in it for a short time before pain forced her to withdraw. Still, it felt good. Cleansing, somehow.

The sea broke against shell-crusted outcrops of rock just feet away, to send rivulets of foaming salt water among all the crevices. She felt the spray of it on her face in the wind.

It was hard to believe now that she and Ruairidh could ever have made love here. And yet on a fine summer's day this little hidden beach would bask for hours in sunshine, and in the evening, sheltered from the westerlies by the cliffs, the sand would still be warm, and the water almost tempting. But within half an hour, she knew, the tide being swept in by a heavy swell from the Minch would break across these rocks and swamp the beach.

She sat for as long as she dared, holding on to every elusive memory, with the very real fear that they might all soon be swept away by time and false recollection, and lost in the incoming tide of an uncertain future.

By the time the first waves were breaking over her feet, the light was starting to fade, and would quickly be gone. She had left it too late to climb back to the top in daylight, and it was panic that propelled her across the beach to retrieve her wellies, and clamber upwards over the rocks.

Twilight was the worst of all lights. Car headlamps seemed to make little impression in it, and the human eye coped almost better with illuminated darkness. She was only halfway up when she found herself having to peer carefully through the gloom to find her next footing. She fumbled in a pocket for her phone. She had a torch app that would light her way. But the beam of light it cast was not much better than the little natural light that remained, and she picked her way carefully along the ledge that overhung the beach and the rocks now thirty or forty feet below.

The wind had increased in strength, and whistled around her as she eased her way towards the scree slope that would allow her to scramble upwards to the safety of the bothy and the cliff tops beyond. She felt it tugging at her jacket, and then a noise immediately above caused her to look up, startled. The shadow of a figure silhouetted against the sky seemed to extend a helping hand. She reached up and felt the hand make contact with hers, before it grabbed her collar and pushed her violently away from the cliff face.

It was with a dreadful sense of disbelief that she found herself falling, all sense of orientation lost, her phone and the light it cast whipped away in the wind. And realization dawned that she was going to die. Her shoulder struck some protruding rock where a tiny patch of grass grew and seabirds nested. The pain of it jarred through her body, and she felt herself propelled out into the void, dropping helplessly into the breaking spray of incoming water.

She closed her eyes tight shut and braced herself for impact. She surely would die quickly on the rocks. But it was water she struck, hard and cold, expelling all breath from her body as it sucked her down and pulled her out into the Minch.

It felt as if her whole being were in the grip of a giant hand that she was powerless to fight against, dragging her under, spinning and twisting her amidst a turmoil of conflicting currents. All she could think was, 'Don't breathe! Don't even try to draw breath. Or it will be your last.' Lungs filled with water, darkness drowning consciousness. Life slipping hopelessly through fingers incapable of retaining their hold on it.

She opened her eyes and sought the light. Only to find darkness. She had no idea which way to the surface. Except that her wellies had filled with water and were pulling her down. Bubbles of spent air escaping her lips and nostrils were going up. She fought to divest herself of her wellies, and the leaden weight of her sodden parka, and kicked hard with her feet, thanking God now for the swimming lessons her parents had forced her to attend in Stornoway.

Suddenly, unexpectedly, she broke the surface and saw light in the sky above her. For the first time she understood the absolute dread that Anndra must have felt as he was sucked under for the last time and gave up the unequal fight to stop water rushing into his lungs. She sucked air into her own lungs now, desperate for oxygen, before a wave broke over her and she found herself thrown towards the rocks.

The cliffs rose up black and formidable, tilting overhead,

and she braced herself for impact on all those jagged outcrops and their razor-sharp crusting of shells.

But the expected pain of impact never came. Instead she felt something soft and warm. Another body in the water. Hands grasping her and suddenly, unexpectedly, lifting her up over the rocks.

The next impact was hard, but giving, and she found herself sprawling on the little patch of silver sand, her footsteps still visible and filling with water. Only there was another set of footprints now. Bigger. The treads of stout walking boots pressed into the softness. Coughing the water from her lungs, half choking, and shivering with the cold, she had only the vaguest impression of her rescuer leaning over her, before a heavy warm jacket seemed somehow to wrap itself around her, and the shadow of whoever had pulled her from the water was gone.

Niamh managed to haul herself to her knees and looked up. But caught only the fleeting glimpse of movement above her on the rocks. Whoever it was had vanished, leaving her their jacket. But she was still barefoot, and knew that somehow she had to get back to the house before hypothermia took her.

The climb back up the cliff without footwear was treacherous, and she was thankful for all the years of running barefoot along the shore as a child. Still, she moved carefully. Some of these rocks were sharp-edged and could slice open the tender soles of her feet with a single slip. Obversely and unexpectedly, bare feet and flexible toes gave her a better grip.

She was more sure-footed. And it was, finally, with great relief that she pulled herself up on to the soft bog grass along the top of the cliff.

She lay on her back breathing hard for several minutes, her rescuer's thermal jacket wrapped around her. Her feet ached, from the cold and the pain of the climb, and above her she saw twilight wash itself darker across the sky, the first stars twinkling faintly beyond fast-moving broken cloud.

Eventually she summoned the strength to pull herself back to her feet and went hobbling off across the moor towards the house, where lights on a timer lit up its interior against the night. All the way, peaty black mud oozed between her toes, and she fought to understand what had just happened.

Someone had climbed down to push her off the cliff. Someone intent on killing her. Only the fortuitous collision with a grassy outcrop had sent her spinning beyond the reach of the rocks below, and certain death. But, then, the sea too had been set to claim her, to drag her down and drown her, or smash her against the rocks. Before strong hands had plucked her free of it and dumped her unceremoniously on the beach. Leaving no trace, except for footprints in the sand, and this weatherproof jacket that she wrapped tightly around her now.

Once inside the house, she slammed the door shut and leaned back against it, fumbling with the latch to do what she never did, and lock it. The warm air in the hall made her realize just how cold she was. Her first instinct was to go and stand below a hot shower to raise her core temperature. But first she went through all the pockets of this jacket she had been gifted. They were empty, and the jacket itself seemed new, barely worn.

She hung it up where she normally hung her parka and ran through the bedroom to the bathroom, wriggling out of her sodden jeans and T-shirt, discarding her underwear, to stand finally beneath the spray of hot water in the shower. Eyes closed. Breathing slowly and deeply. Still shivering, but more from shock than cold. She opened her eyes and turned her head to look at the bruising that already blackened her shoulder. The skin was grazed and broken, but not bleeding. Her parka had protected her from worse injury. She revolved her arm on the axis of her shoulder, and although it was painful she was pretty sure it was not broken.

The full realization of just how lucky she had been broke over her like the water from the shower, and her legs very nearly buckled beneath her.

She staggered from below its powerful spray to wrap a thick towelling robe around her and return to the bedroom, where she sat on the edge of the bed and examined her feet, each in turn. They were bruised and grazed, and she rubbed antiseptic cream into the broken skin before wrapping several of her toes in fine bandaging. She would live.

A tiny burst of ironic laughter escaped her lips. *Aye, you'll live*, her mother used to say to her when she cut a knee or skinned an elbow. Right now she was only alive because someone's attempt to kill her had failed. Because someone else had pulled her from the Minch and saved her from drowning, or worse.

Why had one not seen the other? Or were they both one and the same person? If so, why try to kill her with one hand, and then save her with the other? None of it made sense.

She lay back on the bed, trembling now from neither shock nor cold. But from fear. And she wondered if she would sleep a wink tonight.

CHAPTER THIRTY-THREE

Although the library did not open until 10 a.m., Gunn had been briefed that staff would be there half an hour before. He and Braque were standing outside in Cromwell Street and saw that there were lights on beyond the windows. But the door was locked, and the *Closed* sign turned out.

Brown marble tiles lined the frontage beneath the painted stonework, and Braque noticed that there appeared to be letters missing above the windows. *EABHAR ANN* read the Gaelic in gold letters fixed to the wall on the left. *IBR RY* read the English to the right. Gunn banged on the door with the flat of his hand until a young lady with long brown hair came to peer through the glass. He pressed his warrant card up against the window and then waited patiently until the library assistant let them in.

'Morning, Ma'am,' he said. 'We need to speak to the librarian.'

The assistant led them through the empty library to the reception desk, which also welcomed visitors in Gaelic. *Failte*. And asked them to wait. There were three computers around the desk, and an array of printers and faxes behind it. They were in the heart of the children's section, bedecked with triangular red and white flags hanging from the ceiling. A row of five computer terminals sat on desks pushed up against the back wall. Braque and Gunn exchanged glances.

Within a minute, the librarian swept through a door at the back. An attractive lady in her middle years, dressed in a grey suit and black blouse, her hair cut short, the colour of brushed steel shot through with black. She spoke with an accent Gunn found hard to identify. German, or Eastern European, perhaps.

'How can I help you?'

Braque let Gunn do the talking.

'Ma'am, we're interested to identify a person or persons who may have used computers in this library to access the internet and send emails.'

The librarian smiled and raised her eyebrows. 'Detective, we have hundreds of people using our computers.'

'But you keep some kind of record of who they are?'

'Well, yes.'

'So if we provided you with IP addresses for the computers, and the date and times they were being used, you would be able to tell me who was using them?'

'Only if they were a member.'

Gunn frowned. 'Of?'

'The library of course.' It seemed perfectly obvious to the librarian. 'A member provides us with their library card, which has a bar code, and a record of use is entered into our system. Name, address, which computer, and when it was being used.'

'And if they are not a member?' Braque asked.

'Then they are categorized as a PC guest, and there would be no record of their identity.'

'Then let's hope they were a member,' Gunn said. He took a sheet of paper from an inside pocket and unfolded it on the desk in front of them. 'Here are the IP addresses of the two computers we're interested in. And the dates and times of use. Could you check that for us, please?'

'Of course.' She smiled and handed the sheet to her assistant, who was only too keen to sit down and tap at her keyboard to bring up the required information. It took her about thirty seconds.

She looked up and pulled a face of apology. 'Sorry,' she said. 'Guests on both occasions.'

Braque heard Gunn cursing under his breath. He turned towards the row of computers against the wall behind them. 'I take it these are the computers?'

'Not unless your user was a child,' the librarian said.

'I think definitely not,' Braque told her.

'Then it would be these computers over here.'

They followed her to the back of the library where there were fourteen numbered computer terminals lined up along desks among the Reference shelves. Walls were pinned with maps of Europe and leaflets about VAT moving online, and notices warning against eating or drinking or using mobile phones in the library.

'They are all linked to the main server in the Council offices,' the librarian said. 'And there are restrictions on use. Pages that cannot be accessed online. Pornography, for example.'

Braque said, 'Restrictions that could no doubt be worked around by someone with a little expertise in computers?'

The librarian shrugged defensively. 'I am no expert on that. You would need to talk to our IT people.'

Gunn said, 'Can you show me the two computer terminals that we are interested in?' The emails to Niamh and Georgy Vetrov had been sent from the same computer at the same time nearly three weeks ago. The email to Ruairidh had been sent from a different terminal less than seven days ago.

After a consultation with her assistant, the librarian identified terminals three and twelve. Braque scanned the ceilings and seemed disappointed. 'Are there no security cameras in the library?' she asked.

The librarian smiled. 'I'm afraid not, Security is not really an issue here.'

Again Braque exchanged a look with Gunn. It seemed that they were having no luck at all. Gunn scratched his head thoughtfully, disturbing his carefully gelled hair, and he cocked an eyebrow. 'A wee thought,' he said. Then turned to the librarian. 'Many thanks, Ma'am.' And he steered Braque back through the library towards the door. 'You realize,' he said, 'that there were at least three folk of interest to us who were on the island when those first emails were sent.'

Braque stopped. 'Who?'

'Lee Blunt. Niamh's brother, Uilleam. And Iain Maciver, the boy Ruairidh caught poaching all those years ago. He's still living here, at least.'

'And we know that Blunt was back on the island last week. What about William?'

Gunn shrugged. 'That, Ma'am, remains to be seen.' He stopped at the door. 'And it might just be possible for us to see exactly that.' He held the door open for her to step out into Cromwell Street and a breeze that was growing stiffer on this grey funeral morning. Lights burned in the Baltic Bookshop opposite. McNeill's pub next door was still locked up securely. Too early yet for Stornoway's drinkers to be out. 'There.' He pointed, and Braque followed his finger. Fixed to the wall, high up on the corner with Francis Street, hung a black globe in a bell-shaped hood. A CCTV multi-camera security orb that would provide a perfect view of anyone entering or leaving the library.

Braque understood the significance of it immediately. 'Where can we access the footage?'

'At the police station, Ma'am. It's all held on a hard disk, as far back, certainly, as we're going to need it.' He smiled. 'We do keep up with the latest technology, you know, even if we are just a wee island.'

'We can check it now, then?'

Gunn pulled back the sleeve of his anorak to look at his watch. 'Well, Ma'am, it'll take a wee while to set it up. And we don't want to be late for the funeral. And who knows who we're going to see there, that we might not otherwise recognize on the CCTV footage. Best we go to the funeral first, and check out the footage this afternoon.' He grinned. 'After all, it's not going anywhere.'

CHAPTER THIRTY-FOUR

Just as she had driven up the west coast yesterday afternoon in the rain, so Niamh drove down it again this morning in the rain. A light rain, finer than drizzle. A smirr. Almost a mist, blowing in off the sea.

In the middle of the night, after lying in the dark for so many sleepless hours, she had finally got up to wander through to the kitchen and make herself a cup of tea. Anything to calm her growing sense of paranoia. For the first time since she and Ruairidh had built their house out there on the cliffs, she felt unsafe in it. That, in spite of having locked every door and secured every window.

The tiniest sound, or creak, or muted gust of wind, caused a flutter in her chest. It had occurred to her sometime in the small hours that whoever had tried to kill her might be the same person who had killed Ruairidh. Though the why of it escaped her. Just trying to make some kind of sense of it all had given her a headache that the tea did nothing to alleviate.

Eventually she had gone back to bed to lie tortured and

afraid, stricken still with grief for the man she was going to lay in the ground in the morning.

Sometime, not long before the arrival of daylight, she drifted off into a shallow sleep that was interrupted immediately, it felt, by the alarm she had set the night before. Just that short period of sleep, while blessed in its fleeting relief, had left her feeling worse than if she had remained awake all night.

Now she found it hard to focus on the road. The smear of rain across her windscreen in poor light forced her to blink repeatedly to stay awake. Why, she wondered, could she not have felt this sleepy the night before?

Balanish was deserted as she drove through the empty main street. Away to her right, beyond the protective arm of the peninsula that sheltered the harbour, she saw the ocean rolling in, relentless white tops crashing all along the coast.

As she parked on the road above the house where she had grown up, and stepped out into the wind and rain, she felt like a ghost revisiting a past life. Wraithlike and insubstantial as she walked down the path, past the loom shed to the back door. She almost expected that her mother would not see her when she opened it.

'Since when does a daughter of mine have to knock on the door of her own house,' her mother reprimanded her. And Niamh was almost relieved that she was not invisible after all.

In spite of the oil-fired central heating, and the peat fire smouldering in the hearth, the atmosphere in the house was frigid. Uilleam sat by the window at the back of the sitting room and would not even meet her eye. Her father was installed in his habitual armchair by the fire, the morning paper folded across his thighs. He glanced at her over his reading glasses, and all that Niamh could see was his embarrassment.

'So . . .' her mother said. 'To what do we owe the honour?'

'You know it's Ruairidh's funeral today.' It wasn't a question.

'Of course.'

'Uilleam tells me you plan not to attend.'

Her mother glanced at her son, who turned his head to look out of the window. 'Did he?'

'Is that true?' Niamh turned towards her father. 'Dad?'

'Your father's not been feeling so good.'

Niamh wheeled angrily on her mother. 'Why don't you let him speak for himself, just once in his life?' Her mother recoiled, as if from a slap. And Niamh turned back to her father. 'Dad?'

He gave a feeble shrug of his shoulders. 'I don't see why we couldn't.'

'We're not going.' Her mother's voice was hard as steel.

Niamh turned to look at her again. Stared directly into her eyes until her mother was forced to avert them. She said very quietly, 'I'm not asking any of you to go for Ruairidh. I'm asking you to go for me.' She paused. 'And if you can't do that . . . If you can't do that, then I have no family.' She turned and pushed her way from the room, out through the kitchen and the back door, almost hyperventilating. To stand for a moment on the back step, gazing out across the garden where she had played as a child. At the *bothag* which she and Seonag had imagined so colourfully as a house, filling it with dollies and miniature plates and cups and saucers. At the old blackhouse where her grandfather once wove Harris Tweed.

And still the rain wept from a sky that leached all happiness from once precious memories.

There was a large gathering of cars outside the Macfarlane croft house. Too many for the metalled parking area, and they extended well down the hill on the single-track road that led to the bridge. More were arriving all the time. Niamh parked by the bridge itself and walked up the hill through the rain. She wore a black dress and shawl, and a pillbox hat and net that she had bought for a previous funeral. Her hair was pinned up beneath it, severe and uncompromising. She wore no make-up and her skin was ghostly pale, penumbrous shadows beneath sad hazel eyes.

Mourners arriving at the house appeared almost embarrassed to see her, nodding solemnly before quickly averting their eyes. People parted to let her through, as if somehow death had contaminated her.

The hearse was parked on the road, and the coffin prepared by Alasdair Macrae sat across several chairs in the porch at the front. Ruairidh's final view from the house in which he had grown up, blurred through windows distorted by rain.

Mrs Macfarlane led her through to the porch from the sitting room. 'We've had literally hundreds come to pay their respects,' she said. 'A constant stream of family and friends, and well-wishers from around the island.'

Well-wishers. What irony. How could Ruairidh's mother ever have known that this was the name adopted by her son's killer. *Well wisher*. Whatever else he had wished Ruairidh, it wasn't well.

'The minister'll be here soon. I wanted to have the service in the house, like they used to do it. As you know, Ruairidh was never much one for the church himself. So it seemed, you know, more appropriate.'

Niamh nodded. For once, Mrs Macfarlane had judged it right.

'I'll leave you with him for a few moments.' And she withdrew discreetly to leave Niamh with the coffin and the knowledge of what lay inside. There was no comfort in it. Nothing could take away the horror of the moment in the Place de la République when the explosion had knocked her from her feet. Or when the undertaker in Paris had placed the coffin for still-borns on his desk, and Niamh had visualized for the first time exactly what that explosion had done to the man she loved. What little of him it had left her.

A slow tear, like molten sadness, trickled its way down her pale cheek, and she turned, startled by the sudden realization that there was someone standing beside her.

Donald looked awkward. Embarrassed like all the others, but there was something else in his eyes that went beyond mourning or sympathy. He could not hold her gaze for long. 'What news?' he said.

Niamh frowned.

382

He clarified. 'Of the investigation.'

'Oh. That.' She succumbed to indifference. What did it matter now? 'None.'

He hesitated, then to her surprise wrapped protective fingers around her arm. 'You know . . . if they haven't caught anyone for it, it's just possible that you could be at risk, too.'

She turned her head up to look at him, crinkling her brows in surprise. 'Why do you say that?' It seemed an extraordinary coincidence, coming the morning after someone had tried to kill her.

He shrugged. 'Just worried about you.' His freckles were even more striking than usual against the whiteness of his skin, and she saw that his eyes were watery and bloodshot. Perhaps he had not been sleeping. 'What are your plans after the funeral?' he asked.

'I have no plans.'

He let go of her arm. 'You shouldn't be on your own, Niamh.' Then, as if he had spoken out of turn, added quickly, 'It's an emotional time.'

'Every minute since it happened has been an emotional time.'

He nodded, and she saw what seemed to her like a fleeting shadow of guilt cross his face. And, yet, what would Donald have to feel guilty about? Ruairidh was his wee brother, after all. Grief showed its face in many ways. She took and squeezed his hand, and succeeded only in increasing his discomfort.

*

It was impossible to say how many folk were crushed into the house for the brief service conducted by the minister. And there were many more outside, standing in the rain.

The minister himself was an elderly man. The wind had ruined the careful parting of what was left of wiry white hair, and then the rain had flattened it so that it stuck in fine wet curls to his forehead. He was tall and impossibly thin, and in spite of the strictness of the Free Church had always, to Niamh's mind, presented the human face of his dour religion.

In the silence that filled the house, pervading every corner of it, Niamh listened to the intonation of his voice rather than his words. It was hard to find the vocabulary truly to express your feelings. People and religions fell back on platitudes and favourite biblical readings. But the heart spoke through the voice, and Niamh just closed her eyes to listen. Here was the man who had thrown the first handful of sand over Anndra's coffin, read the same blessings, offered the same sympathies. Drawing no distinction between one and the other. Apportioning no blame. For he, at least, carried the certainty in his soul that only God knew the truth of what happened all those years ago, and that it was His justice that would prevail.

But his final words rang out loud and clear, bringing tears to almost every eye in the house. Song of Solomon 4:6. So often read aloud at funerals, written in obituaries, carved on headstones. *Gus am bris an latha agus an teich na sgàilean.* Until the day breaks and the shadows flee away.

*

PETER MAY

It was not until she got outside, drawing cold fresh air into her lungs, that it became apparent just how many people there were out here. Among the many she knew were others that she did not. Journalists, perhaps. A drone hovered high overhead and she realized that some TV news outlet, or freelancer, was filming the funeral for broadcast later in the day. She caught a glimpse of Lee Blunt, solemn and subdued, dressed all in black, and surrounded by so many of the famous faces of British fashion. Models and designers, photographers and fashion writers. Faces familiar around the world, turning up here for an island funeral, drawing stares of curiosity and wonder from awestruck locals. Such was the celebrity of Ranish Tweed, and Ruairidh's renown, that people like these would travel the world to say their farewells.

Jacob Steiner tipped his hat towards Niamh as six men, Donald among them, carried the coffin out to the hearse. When the rear door closed on it, Ruairidh's brother came to take her arm. 'You come in the car with me,' he said. 'We can pick yours up later.'

She saw that her parents and Uilleam were standing among the mourners watching her, maintaining a discreet distance. She wondered why they had come after all. Perhaps to stop the gossips from whispering among themselves how her own family had failed to turn out for Ruairidh's funeral. But she cut short the thought, even as it formed. And preferred, instead, to believe that for once maybe it was her father who had prevailed.

She sat in the front of the Audi with Donald. Ruairidh's parents sat in the back. And they drove in silence down the hill behind the hearse. When they turned at the bridge, Niamh saw Seonag and her husband, and their two children, getting into their SUV to join the procession. For the briefest of moments their eyes met, before Seonag turned away to say something to her husband. And Donald accelerated up the hill on the main road towards the turn-off to Dalmore Beach, little more than half a mile away.

The car park at the beach was inadequate to accommodate all the vehicles in the procession, and most of them were forced to park in a line all the way up the hill, perched precariously on the verge, leaving the road clear for mourners to walk down to the cemetery.

The undertakers unlocked the door of a small concrete hut by the gate to slide out the bier on which the coffin would be carried. As well as half a dozen or more shovels to be taken to the grave for use by the family to fill it in afterwards.

Niamh could see where the grave had been dug at the far end of the cemetery, almost overlooking the beach, and only a few feet from where her brother lay.

Flowers and wreaths were carried from cars and laid by the gate, too many for the undertakers to carry to the grave themselves. And Niamh decided to break with convention. She stooped to gather up as many of the flowers as she could, and started off on the long walk through the cemetery herself. A lone figure. The coffin had not even been taken yet from the hearse. Others, who had no idea of the conventions, followed suit. Catwalk models in hopelessly inappropriate footwear, picking their precarious way across the uneven sandy soil, bearing bouquets and wreaths, like some procession of funereal fashionistas at a dark autumn collection. The coffin and all the male mourners followed on behind. A funeral the like of which had never before been seen on the island.

When Niamh reached the grave and looked back, she saw that Seonag was among the carriers of flowers. But that her mother, and Mrs Macfarlane, and many of the older women remained behind. Whatever else they might disagree upon, they remained punctilious in their adherence to the old ways.

The wind whipped the rain in off the sea, umbrellas abandoned or blown inside out. The gathering in black around the grave seemed drawn together in a collective huddle against the elements. But it was so exposed here that there was no protection to be had, and even the pages of the minister's bible were stuck together by the wet, so that he had to peel them carefully apart to avoid tearing the delicate paper. And in an ultimate irony, his final words were lost in the roar of the sea and the howling of the wind, as if Nature herself were determined to have the last say.

When it was over, most of the mourners hurried off towards the shelter of their cars. Donald and several friends lifted the spades brought by the undertakers to start shovelling sand over the coffin, stooped by the weight of grief and sand and weather.

Niamh wandered away to the fence where a wooden bench provided a view across the beach. The crescent of sand was deserted, the sea thundering angrily over it in wave after wave of white breaking water. Off to her right she saw a lone figure standing watching from the far side of the cemetery. It took her a moment to realize that it was Iain Maciver. Peanut, as she had always known him. No longer the boy she remembered with his twisted, angry face as he sank his boot time and again into Ruairidh's prone form on the ground. A man now, old before his time. Almost completely bald, a dark beard greying in streaks of silver. Strangely, he too was dressed in black, though he had not stood among the mourners.

Satisfied that Niamh had seen him, he turned and walked away, strangely bowed, hands plunged deep into his pockets. And she wondered why he had come. Not to mourn, she was sure.

Beyond, on the headland, stood two more figures, watching proceedings below. Even as she spotted them, they turned and headed back down the slope towards the car park. Only then did she recognize who they were. Detective Sergeant Gunn, and Lieutenant Braque of the Paris Police Judiciaire. What, if anything, could they possibly have gleaned from this sombre gathering in the rain? Somehow, she felt, it was not here that Ruairidh's murder would be resolved.

A hand on her shoulder startled her, and she turned to find herself gazing into the rain-streaked face of Lee Blunt. She wondered if it was eyeliner he was wearing. Whatever it was had smudged all around his eyes in the rain, tears of black, creating the illusion of sunken sockets. The eyes at their centre had an oddly glazed quality, pupils dilated unnaturally, even in this light.

He slipped his arms around her and drew her tightly against him, turning her head to press it to his chest, and resting his chin lightly on top of it. 'You don't still think that Ruairidh was having an affair with Irina, do you?'

'I don't know that I ever did, Lee. In spite of evidence to the contrary. I'm even less inclined to believe it now. Back here with all my memories of him, and everything we shared.'

'You're quite right,' he said. 'I never believed it either. She was such a little nothing. Couldn't hold a candle to my Niamh.' He stepped back, still holding her by the shoulders. 'Jake tells me he called at the house yesterday.'

She nodded.

'So you know we've taken over Amhuinnsuidhe Castle for a couple of days? Me and everyone else on my plane.'

'Yes.'

'We're having a party tonight, Niamh. What do you Scots call it, a wake? A celebration of the life rather than a mourning of the death.' Apparently he had given up numbering himself among the *Scots*. 'I'd like you to come. We all would.'

Niamh shook her head. 'I couldn't, Lee. Honestly. I couldn't.'

'Of course you could. What else are you going to do? Go home alone and cry into your pillow? Too many tears already. You need to come and get drunk with us. Raise a glass or ten to Ruairidh and Ranish.'

'Lee . . .' she started to protest, but he placed a forefinger on her lips. 'Shhhh. I'm not taking no for an answer. You're coming with us girl. Today is the first day of the rest of your life.'

CHAPTER THIRTY-FIVE

Braque and Gunn drove in thoughtful silence from Dalmore back up the west coast to Barvas before turning off to head across the moor to Stornoway. There wasn't much to say. No one unexpected had turned up at the cemetery, except perhaps for Iain Peanut Maciver, and he certainly couldn't be arrested for attending a funeral.

They were both drenched. Although Gunn's anorak had protected him from the worst of the rain his trousers were clinging to his thighs. Braque's sodden jacket lay across the back seat, filling the car with the smell of wet denim. Her jeans and boots were almost black with the rain, and even her T-shirt was soaked down the front, half-revealing her bra, which Gunn tried not to look at. She had come hopelessly ill-prepared for the island weather.

He said, 'I checked with air traffic control. Lee Blunt's plane is due for take-off at midday tomorrow – if you want to talk to him before they fly out.'

She nodded, and he seemed uncertain whether that was an affirmative or otherwise.

'Have you booked a flight for yourself yet?'

'No. I'll do that when I get back to the hotel.' A depression had fallen over her. Deep and penetrating. Hurrying back to the car park with Gunn, she had examined each and every face as the mourners returned to their vehicles, wondering which, if any of them, was capable of the murder of Ruairidh Macfarlane. Earlier she had watched Niamh from a distance, felt her grief in the tension of her shoulders. Her sense of isolation and loneliness. Even among the crowd of mourners she stood out on her own. Only now, really for the first time, did Braque fully empathize with her, identifying in her the sense of loss that she felt buried somewhere inside herself.

As they had stood watching her carry flowers across the cemetery, ahead of the coffin and the male bearers, Gunn had remarked with barely concealed incredulity how much it went against every convention of island funerals. And Braque had thought it was exactly what she would have done.

Off to their left, a tiny dwelling with a green tin roof sat in a fold of the moor, and the road climbed towards a plateau that would carry them south-east, descending eventually into Stornoway itself. Gunn said, 'We can go straight to the police station and view that video, if you like.'

Braque held out her hands, palms up. 'Look at me, Detective Sergeant. I am soaking wet. I think I need to go to the hotel and change first.'

'No problem, Ma'am. I'll drop you off, then go to the police station and get it all set up. I'll give you, say, half an hour, then call back to pick you up.'

'Perfect.'

It was mid-afternoon by the time they drove down through Newmarket and Laxdale, past the hospital, and along Bayhead to the harbour. The rain had increased in its intensity, and the sky lay black and bruised all across the land behind them. The wind was up, tearing leaves prematurely from trees. The air seemed filled with them, like large golden snowflakes, as Gunn pulled over at the top of Castle Street. 'I'll see you shortly, Ma'am.' And he glanced up at the sky, pulling a face. It could hardly have been darker. 'Looks like we're in for a bad one.'

At reception the girl said to her, 'Your husband has phoned several times, Madam Braque.'

Braque was startled. It was rare for Gilles ever to phone her. Why hadn't he called her mobile? Then she remembered that she and Gunn had turned their mobile phones to airplane mode at the cemetery. She had forgotten to switch it back. On the stairs she fumbled with trembling fingers to restore it, and stood outside her door looking at the screen, waiting for the phone to find a signal. Immediately it did, it beeped and alerted her to the presence of messages. There were three.

She slipped into her room, shutting the door and leaning back against it to listen to the most recent.

'Sylvie, where the hell are you? Call me as soon as you get this.' She could hear the stress in Gilles's voice, and it sent her own heart-rate skyrocketing. She tapped the *Call Back* button and stood listening, aware of her own breath quivering in her chest. 'Jesus, Sylvie, I've been trying to get you for hours.' There was anger now in his voice.

'What's wrong?' She wasn't interested in explanations, or excuses. She heard him sigh.

'They think Claire has meningitis. She's been taken into hospital.'

Braque's hand flew to her chest. 'Oh, God! What are they saying?'

'I don't know, I'm waiting to hear.'

'Where are you?'

'In a waiting room outside the children's ward.'

'What about Jacqui?'

'She's here with me.'

'Is she alright?'

'Pretty upset. But seems okay otherwise.'

'Let me speak to her. Put her on FaceTime.'

She called up the app and the screen flickered momentarily before a tearful Jacqui appeared. '*Maman*, where are you?' Too distressed to play the *which twin am I* game.

'Baby, I'm coming home. I'll be there just as soon as I can.'

'Jacqui's sick, *maman*.'

'I know, darling. Are you okay?'

The little crumpled face nodded. 'Is Claire going to be alright?'

'She's going to be just fine, sweetheart. Dad'll take care of you till I get back.'

'When? When will you be back?'

'Just as soon as I can, darling, I promise.'

The image of the child swung away, and Gilles's face appeared on the screen. He looked tired as he raised his eyebrows. She heard the sarcasm in his voice. 'More promises?'

Braque clenched her teeth and tried to hang on to control. 'Soon as I get off the phone I'll book my flights. Should be home by tomorrow night. Keep me in the loop. Please. I want to know what's happening.'

He sighed and nodded. 'You should have been here, Sylvie.'

'I will be.'

And he hung up before she could say any more. Even goodbye to Jacqui. She slumped on to the edge of the bed and sat, head bowed, hands clasped around her phone between her thighs, consumed by guilt. Yes, she should have been there. So many times she should have been there. And so many times she wasn't. She remembered George Gunn's words. *Sometimes you just have to make choices.* Exactly what she hadn't done. If anything she had chosen the status quo, a means of avoiding making those impossible choices. Career or family. It had been clear to her very soon after the break-up of her marriage that she could not have both. And all she had done was put it off, and put it off. Until now it was too late. She should have been there. She should never have left her girls.

She spent the next hour on the phone and the internet, booking herself on the first flight from Stornoway to Glasgow in the morning. Then on to London, and from London to Paris.

Flight schedules too tight to offer smooth connections, leaving her with no option but to sit fretting in Glasgow and London waiting for onward flights. Two hours in the case of Glasgow, three in London. Arriving in Paris at rush hour. The *Périphérique* at a standstill if she took a taxi or a bus, the RER jam-packed beyond capacity.

Her stress levels by the time she concluded her bookings left her shaking. She wanted to call Gilles again. She wanted to hear the verdict on Claire's diagnosis, and the prognosis if the news was bad. But there was no point. He would call her if there were any developments.

She gazed now at the phone in her hand, and knew she had to make the call she had been putting off for so long. A call she should have made months, if not years ago. But even as she selected the number and touched *Call*, she realized she was going to fudge it. She asked switchboard to put her through to Capitaine Faubert's office.

'Faubert.'

She couldn't tell from that one word what kind of mood he was in. Whether he had just been for a cigarette or was suffering from nicotine withdrawal.

'Capitaine, it's Lieutenant Braque. I'm coming home.'

'I've been wondering why the hell you haven't called, Braque. What's happening?'

'Nothing's happening, Capitaine. The funeral's over. One of my twins has suspected meningitis and has been admitted to hospital. I've booked flights home tomorrow.'

'*Putain!*' she heard him mutter under his breath. But she knew, too, that he could hardly argue. 'I want your report on my desk first thing Friday morning.' Which would mean an all-nighter Thursday night.

'Yes, Capitaine.'

'And we'll talk then, Braque.'

'Yes, boss.' She understood perfectly well that 'talk' was code for 'lecture'. A lecture on her failure to prioritize, to make a decision one way or another. Mother or cop. And she would be faced, finally, with the choices that Gunn had spoken of.

Two simple words would put an end to it all. *I quit.* So easy to say, but how hard might it be to live with the consequences? Especially if it turned out that Jacqui was okay, or made a full recovery. In fifteen years, when the girls left home for university, or got married, or grabbed whatever other opportunities life might offer them in adulthood, what would become of Braque? Alone and unfulfilled. Left with a life on which the clock was counting down, a life filled only with regrets for all the might-have-beens. How would she feel then?

She stood up and realized she had not changed out of her wet clothes. They were now nearly dry. But she decided to change them anyway, divesting herself of damp jeans and T-shirt, and slipping into the shower to wash away the salt and sand carried on the wind at Dalmore. It wasn't until she was dressed, and drying her hair by the window, that she remembered the CCTV video footage waiting to be viewed at the police station. Gunn had said he would pick her up in half an hour, but that was hours ago.

She glanced from the window across the choppy waters of the inner harbour, boats rising and falling on a heavy swell, rolling in the wind that blew down the hill from the castle. Rain hammered against the window, and the sky was black as night. One of those equinoctial storms that the Atlantic threw at the island this time every year. Brutal and unforgiving. Shrugged off by islanders who were used to it by now. Had seen it all before. And tomorrow, in all likelihood, the sun would be out, shining on wet streets and houses, as if they had just been painted and everything was brand-new again.

Braque felt her jacket, which was draped over the back of a chair. Still damp. Her hair still wet from the shower. So what the hell? She decided just to make a dash for the police station. It wasn't that far.

In the event, it was much further than she remembered. Especially in the rain. And by the time she had run breathlessly up Church Street from the harbour, and ducked into the warmth and shelter of reception at the police station, she was soaked to the skin once again. She shook the rain from her jacket, to the amusement of the duty officer, and swept rat's tails of hair out of her face. 'Better indoors on a day like this, Ma'am,' he said.

She took out her ID to show him. 'Lieutenant Sylvie Braque of the Police Judiciaire in Paris. I've been working with Detective Sergeant Gunn.'

'Ah yes,' he said. 'George was trying to call you earlier.' And she remembered the phone in her room ringing twice while she was talking to someone on her mobile about booking flights. By the time she got off the phone she had forgotten. Gilles would have called her mobile. 'I believe he left a message.'

She took her phone from her pocket and saw that there was indeed a message. She replayed it and heard Gunn's voice. 'Sorry to mess you about Ma'am. I've been trying to reach you. I'm afraid I've been called away to an unexplained death down at Uig. More than likely a suicide, but it's a three-hour round trip, and I'll probably not have a signal for most of that time. I've left a terminal set up for you in the interview room. Any of the duty officers will show you how to use it. I'll see you when I get back.'

She looked up from her screen and the duty officer smiled. 'This way, Ma'am.'

He took her upstairs to an interview room at the back of the building. A computer with an external disk drive attached, a keyboard and a mouse sat on a plain white table with a single chair drawn up to it.

'It's quite simple, Ma'am.' And the duty officer showed her how to scroll back and forth through the CCTV video using the time-code as her guide. 'I'll leave you to it.'

For all her training, Braque had never been comfortable with computers. Her girls were more adept with a keyboard and a touch screen. It took her a while to master the scrolling process, and then she found herself absorbed by the images. The familiar frontage of the library, and Bayhead stretching away beyond it. People passing below, oblivious of the eye in the sky watching them from the corner. Stopping, chatting. In and out of shops. In and out of the library. The images were poor if the weather was bad, amazingly sharp in sunshine.

She went first to the earlier date, when the emails had been sent to Niamh and Georgy Vetrov. Then scrolled as quickly through the hours as she could until the time, mid-afternoon, when they had been fired off into the ether from computer terminal three in the library. User unknown. A guest. How far back, she wondered, should she go before the time of their sending? But it was possible the sender could have spent some time at the computer first. She could waste an hour or more if she wound back too far watching for someone going in. So she set the time code to the exact hour and minute, and started the video running at normal speed, banking on the sender leaving immediately after they had finished.

It was a bright, blustery day. She saw coats flapping in the wind. People hanging on to their hats. But bright sunlight slanted down across the street, and although shadows were deep, detail was sharp. Traffic in and out of the library was light. A clutch of giggling schoolgirls in uniform pushing inside. Two elderly ladies emerging with books under their arms, then standing talking for what seemed like an eternity. A young man stopping to exchange a few words with them before hurrying on. And then a familiar figure pushing between them to exit the library and turn right towards the harbour.

Braque nearly jumped out of her seat. She fumbled with clumsy fingers to stop the video. Then rewound it to the point of exit, and managed finally to slow it right down. She had only caught the merest glimpse of the face, but now she held it in a still shot, and had no doubt who it was.

She spooled backwards, then, at speed, knowing who she was looking for, watching carefully as Charlie Chaplin figures retraced their footsteps at a ridiculous tempo up and down the street. Then, suddenly, there it was again, and Braque slowed right down to get a much clearer shot of that familiar face as it came down the street. Past Argos and the Fast Food Chinese Takeaway, to turn into the library and disappear from view.

She sat back breathing hard, sweating now and uncomfortable in her wet clothes. This was not, she knew, proof of anything. That would only come if she could tie the same person to the same time and place for the sending of the second email. The one received by Ruairidh on the RER on the day of his murder. *See you in hell.*

She entered date and time into the computer, advancing the video nearly three weeks to the afternoon of the previous Thursday, and then scrolling through to the exact moment that the email had left computer terminal twelve inside the library. Hardly daring to breathe, she set the video running and watched as again people came and went up and down the street. In and out of the library and Argos next door, and the Baltic Bookshop opposite. The weather was less good, but it was at least dry.

And then there it was. The face she had seen before. She hit the pause key, then manipulating the arrow keys, managed to zoom in on it, frozen in time as the killer exited the library and turned towards the CCTV camera. Not a single doubt remained.

Braque shook her head in disbelief and sat back again in her chair. What to do? She took out her phone and called Gunn. But it went straight to voicemail and she hung up. He had warned her that he would likely be out of signal for some time. She thought quickly, her mind and her pulse racing, then called his number again. When the beep came to leave her message she said, 'Detective Gunn, I think I know who our killer is. I'm leaving first thing tomorrow, so I don't have much time. I'm going to drive up to the Macfarlane house to speak to Niamh tonight. Look at the video when you get back and tell me if I'm right. I've left a note of the time-code.'

She closed her eyes and tried to remember where she had parked her hire car. She had barely driven it since her arrival. And then she remembered leaving it next to Gunn's in the harbour car park the night she arrived. She would, she realized, have to drive it very gingerly on the road out to Taigh 'an Fiosaich, or she would rip the sump from its underside.

CHAPTER THIRTY-SIX

Amhuinnsuidhe Castle was to be found precisely in the middle of nowhere. Miles along a single-track road whose dips and curves and swerves and hollows made speed impossible. Past occasional croft houses clinging to hillsides in splendid isolation. An incongruously sited all-weather tennis court set just below the road, within sight of nothing at all. A tiny primary school perched on a bend of the road offering pupils an unrestricted view of island wilderness.

The castle itself came out of the blue. Through stone gates, and hidden beyond a bank of unlikely rhododendrons, it appeared around a bend in the road as if out of nowhere. Scottish baronial in style, with turrets and gables and steeply canted slate roofs, it looked out beyond a crenellated wall with black-painted cannons to the comparative shelter of a sea loch and an almost completely enclosed bay.

Through an archway beyond the castle, the road continued on for several miles to the tiny settlement of Hushinish, where it ended in drifts of silver sand and a handful of crofts. And, of course, the Atlantic ocean.

Lee Blunt and his party had taken it for two nights. Niamh, against her better judgement, drove down to Harris after spending a difficult afternoon at the Macfarlane croft. Family and neighbours had gathered there to eat the cold meats and sandwiches and cakes that Mrs Macfarlane had prepared. The men sipped at single malts with an unusual lack of relish, making them last until they could take their leave without presenting the appearance of undue haste. No one wanted to linger.

Niamh's own parents, and Uilleam, had disappeared immediately after the funeral. But Seonag was there with her family. She and Niamh did not speak, and barely exchanged glances. Donald sat her down in the porch, with condensation forming on all the windows, and tried to dissuade her from going to Harris for Lee Blunt's party. She should go home, he said, and lock herself in. Or better yet, stay overnight here. There was a spare bed, still, in the old croft down the hill that they used now as offices.

His odd insistence was making her increasingly uneasy, and she used the excuse of helping Mrs Macfarlane with the dishes as a means of escaping him.

Only after most of the visitors had gone, did she herself finally leave, the pale concern on Donald's face staying with her as she turned south on to the bridge at the foot of the hill, setting a course for Harris and Amhuinnsuidhe.

The drive, turning right at Tarsaval, past the old whaling station, was the stuff of nightmares. The storm had bled almost all light from the sky. Wind buffeted the high side of her Jeep, driving rain on to a windscreen that her wipers, even at double speed, had trouble clearing. She guessed, more than drove, the length of that road, and several times thought of turning back. Until suddenly, rounding the bend beyond the gateposts, the lights of the castle shone out in the darkness.

Niamh was not sure whether to feel relieved or depressed. A party was the last thing she felt like, and yet Lee had made it seem as if refusal would give offence. He and everyone else had, after all, flown up to the island at great expense to be there for Ruairidh's funeral. And where else was she going to go? Back to Taigh 'an Fiosaich, and the pain of all the memories that lay waiting for her there? Power to the house was always erratic, but in a storm like this she could expect to spend most of the night in darkness. And with the memory of the attempt to kill her the previous evening still in the forefront of her mind, a night spent in the dark, miles from the nearest neighbour, seemed less than appealing.

There were several cars drawn in on the gravel around the front of the castle, and as soon as she stepped from her Jeep she heard, above the wind, the sound of loud music pounding from somewhere deep inside the building. She heard, too, whoops and shrieks of laughter tumbling down the stairs as she went through the entrance lobby. Past furled flags leaning up against the wall, the Stars and Stripes, a Union Jack. A stag's head. A sculpture of dolphins leaping from water.

The polished wooden staircase curved around a half-landing, red flock wallpaper lurid in the light that spilled down from the first floor. The ground floor, by contrast, simmered in semi-darkness. The only light Niamh could see was along a corridor, beyond those rooms where fishermen gathered before and after sorties, and the boot room where they hung their wet waterproofs. She wondered where all the staff were. This was not the kind of clientele they would be used to.

As she climbed the stairs, she heard someone playing a piano. A mad, drunken ragtime, only faintly and incongruously discernible above the monotonously hypnotic voice of a rapper that rose above an endlessly repeating electronic refrain. Through an open doorway along a panelled hall she saw people with cues moving like shadows around a snooker table.

At the top of the stairs, beautiful people lay about on the sofas and armchairs of a TV room off to the right, the volume on a BBC-24 news bulletin turned up to an absurd level that almost hurt the ears. To the left an honour bar had been mercilessly assaulted. Bottles stood open next to a broken glass, spilled spirits stripping varnish from antique furniture. In a vast lounge, with two enormous fireplaces, a solitary figure played the grand piano. A beautifully tall, shaven-headed black model, chiffon gown barely concealing her bony ebony curves, emerged from the dining room. She had a bottle in one hand, and in the other a glass filled with some vividly coloured green drink. 'There you are, darling,' she said, as if they were old friends, and thrust the glass into Niamh's hand. 'Drink and be merry, for tomorrow we die.'

Niamh looked at the drink. There were slices of orange and

lime floating in it along with the ice. 'What is it?' She sniffed and took a sip. It was both sweet and sour.

'St Patrick's Day Punch.'

Niamh almost laughed. 'It's not St Patrick's Day.'

'No, darling it's the six-month anniversary.' And she threw her head back and laughed as if she had said something uproariously funny. 'You'll love it! Green apple pucker and lemon-lime soda. It's Lee's favourite. Ever since he discovered a little Irish somewhere in his ancestry.'

'I've got a long drive ahead of me. I shouldn't drink.'

The model laughed again. 'Darling, do you think I keep a figure like this by drinking alcohol? Lee's been looking for you everywhere.'

Niamh took a long pull at the glass and welcomed the chill sweetness of this unexpectedly non-alcoholic punch. It had an odd flavour.

The model put her arm around Niamh's shoulders, steering her into a sitting room at the front of the castle from which most of the noise was coming. The sound of music struck her like something physical. This was an elegant salon, hung with large oil paintings and a crystal chandelier. Bodies sprawled in various stages of undress across antique furniture, and Niamh felt as if she had wandered accidentally into the tableau of some Hieronymus Bosch representation of hell. The air was thick with smoke that hung in subdued lighting, acrid and heady.

Jacob Steiner emerged from the smoke, his habitual cigar in one hand, his favourite whisky soda in the other. From the flush of his cheeks, Niamh figured that it wasn't his first. 'Jees, honey,' he said. 'Where you been? Lee's been getting all agitated, thinking you stood him up.'

'I had to go back to Ruairidh's parents' house after the funeral. I came as soon as I could.'

'You got some catching up to do, then, girl,' he said. And as she took a sip of her drink he nudged it up with his own glass and she nearly choked on it. 'Another glass for our widow,' he shouted out. And she was shocked. Both to hear herself called a widow, when she had never even considered that that's what she was, and at Jacob Steiner's insensitivity in addressing her like that.

Someone took the empty glass from her hand and thrust another into it.

And then like a punch in the gut she heard the first familiar strains of the song that had meant so much to her and Ruairidh. That haunting, repeating piano refrain, a counter-melody played on the harp. And then the painfully sad falsetto of the singer who promised to keep her safe. Just like Ruairidh. How could anyone possibly know the significance of that song and those words? She realized, of course, that no one could. It was just one of life's sick little ironies, designed to turn the knife in an open wound. As if God was not yet finished with her and wanted to inflict yet more pain.

'There you are!'

She turned to find herself confronted by a wild-eyed Lee Blunt. Eyes glazed and dilated at the funeral were now filled with fire. He had to raise his voice and shout to be heard above all the promises of safety, oblivious to the tears that the music had brought to Niamh's eyes. She took a stiff pull at her drink. It seemed less sweet and more sour than the last one.

'Don't know what you ever saw in that fucker!' He had lowered his face so that his words were shouted directly into hers. She smelled something rank on his breath, recoiling from the smell of it, as well as from his words.

'What?'

'Leave it, Lee.' She heard Jacob Steiner's voice, only barely aware of him trying to pull Lee away. Blunt shrugged him off. They had been partying all afternoon and into the evening. Smoking, drinking, snorting, and God only knew what else. Niamh had seen him like this just once before, that afternoon in the pub in Shoreditch when he and Ruairidh had ended up on the floor, punching and kicking each other.

His face was inches from hers, and she seemed unable to back away as others crowded in around them, sensing conflict and drama above the blare of the music. 'I'm glad he's dead. Arrogant, shitty little fucker!'

Niamh stared at him in disbelief. 'And all that sympathy in Paris? If that's how you felt, what was all that about?'

'It was about revelling in your grief. Seeing your tears first hand. Laughing behind mine. You can't begin to know how much pleasure I took from your unhappiness, my little Niamh. Encouraging it. Stoking the fires of your loss so the embers would burn just a little hotter a little longer. Just so you'd know how it felt to have your life totally fucked up.'

'It was your fault for not paying us. Ruairidh never did you any harm that you didn't do to yourself,' she shouted at him.

'He lost me Givenchy!' He screamed it in her face. 'Givenchy! It should have been the pinnacle of my career. My life. And his little rant in the press took that away from me.'

Niamh's breathing was so rapid she was close to hyperventilating. 'You told me yourself that your own company would never have done so well if you'd gone to Givenchy.'

But he just shook his head vigorously. 'Not the same. Not the same at all. Nothing was ever the same again after that. Never.' And then a strange, sick smile spread across his face. 'And as for Ranish . . . All that shit I told you in Paris about doing another collection.' He pushed his face even closer. 'I lied. I've got a deal with a company to supply me with the real McCoy. *Real* Harris Tweed. Not that soft, phoney, silky shit that you and Ruairidh made.'

Anger and hurt fuelled the power that Niamh found in the backward swing of her hand, directed then with full force across Blunt's puce and contorted face. He staggered back with the weight of it, caught completely by surprise. He blinked in momentary disorientation, before hurling himself at her, spittle flying all around his mouth. Her glass was knocked from her hand, foaming green liquid spraying everywhere. And hands grabbed at Blunt from every side, restraining him from hitting her right back.

Steiner was there, somehow inveigling his way between them, but he seemed small and insignificant in the turbulence of this sea of anger. 'Stop it, stop it!' he was shouting.

Blunt shook himself free of restraining hands and stood panting and staring his hatred at Niamh. 'I'm glad he's dead! I'm fucking glad he's dead!' he shouted, and he strode from the room, crashing into the door jamb as he went. Several of his acolytes went chasing after him.

Steiner stood shaking his head in distress. 'I'm so sorry, honey.' And he turned to hurry out after the self-proclaimed king of British fashion.

Amidst all the angst and angry words the music had stopped. Nothing replaced it except for a silence that seemed even louder. People moved away from Niamh, like rings of water from the point where a stone has entered it. Her legs felt weak, and she clutched the arm of a settee to lower herself on to the edge of the seat, shaking like a leaf. It was several moments before the black girl sat beside her, placing an arm around her shoulder and another drink in her hand. 'Here, darling, take this. It'll make you feel better.' Niamh gazed into its green intensity before taking a long pull at the glass, to feel the ice-cold liquid salve the burning in her throat. 'Anyway, pay no attention to Lee. He's out of his head. You know what he's like.'

Niamh had no idea how much longer it was before a despondent Jacob Steiner came back into the room. 'He's gone off in one of the cars,' he said. 'Couldn't stop him. He's going to kill himself in that state.' And the storm outside bowed the rain-streaked windows all along the front face of the castle.

CHAPTER THIRTY-SEVEN

In the dark, Braque got hopelessly lost. She missed the turn-off to Skigersta at Cross, and carried on until the road descended gently into Port of Ness, with its row of bungalows and its white villa standing in solitary defiance on the clifftop overlooking the harbour. The storm drove the sea with relentless violence into an already shattered harbour wall, breaking fifty or sixty feet into the air, spray joining rain to lash the village. Somewhere away off to her left she saw the intermittent beam of a lighthouse rake the dark, but somehow instinct told her that was not the way.

She cursed herself for not paying more attention when Gunn had driven her up to Ness the day before. At the end of the road she turned her car and headed back the way she had come, making another wrong turn that took her this time to the settlement of Five Penny and closer, she saw, to the lighthouse. Following the road took her on what felt like a long loop, past some sort of social club where cars stood parked beneath sodium street lamps, and then a school, before rising again to what she was sure was the road she had left earlier.

Which way to turn? She went left, and then to her relief saw a sign to Skigersta. She turned right, up through Crobost, and headed south into darkness until she saw the tiny clutch of street lights around the settlement at Skigersta itself. From this point, she was fairly confident, she would soon find herself at the road end, and the beginning of the track that led out to Taigh 'an Fiosaich.

Out here, if anything, was even more exposed to the wind, and she felt waves of it battering her car. She clung, white-knuckled, to the steering wheel and leaned forward in her seat to peer through the rain that washed relentlessly across her windscreen, straining to see in the darkness that lay ahead. A darkness barely penetrated by her headlights.

It was almost with relief that she found herself on the pitted and potholed track that stretched away across the moor, her car lurching and pitching from one hole in the road to the next. She never got out of second gear the whole way, and spent much of it in first. She could have walked faster.

Finally she reached the shielings at Cuishader. Tin huts and caravans, that somehow miraculously survived everything this climate could throw at them. A red light flickered momentarily in her peripheral vision, and she thought for a moment her lights might have caught the rear reflectors of a vehicle tucked away behind the old rotting bus. She glanced towards it but saw nothing in the darkness, then forced her concentration back to the track, which dipped down across the concrete bridge at the foot of the hollow. The stream it spanned was in full spate, and for a moment Braque thought her car might get washed away. Then she was over it and climbing the other side, only to be hammered again by the full force of the gales that swept unrestrained across the moor from the west.

Gunn, she was sure, must be back in Stornoway by now. And he would have seen the video. She wondered if he might follow her up to Ness, and wished now that she had waited for him. Driving all the way out here in a storm to see Niamh Macfarlane seemed like the worst idea she had ever had. She checked her mobile phone. No signal. No point in turning back now. She was almost there.

She navigated the bend in the track at Bilascleiter and to her relief saw the lights of Niamh's house burning into the night, like tiny welcoming beacons of hope. She let her car trundle down the hill, then, to pull it into the gravel apron at the house. She sat for a moment, lights on, engine idling, and wondered where Niamh's Jeep was parked. There was no sign of it anywhere. So how could she be home if her car wasn't here? It was possible, she realized, that the lights could be on a timer, set to come on when it got dark. That would make sense if you were returning at night.

She was just about to switch off the ignition and get out of the car, when the house was plunged suddenly into darkness. She was startled. Had there been a power cut? Or had someone inside turned off the lights? Then they flickered, several times, and Braque saw the blades of the two wind turbines at the side of the house spinning manically in the wind. Backup power, perhaps, in the event of a mains failure. But if that was their purpose then they failed, for the house remained in darkness.

Braque decided to leave her engine running and the headlamps on. That would at least provide some light inside the house through the windows. She ducked out into the storm, fighting to close the door of her car against the power of the wind. Then dashed for the house. The door was unlocked. On the drive up yesterday, Gunn had taken great pride in telling her that islanders felt no need to lock their doors. Niamh, obviously, was no exception.

Braque pushed the door shut behind her and stood dripping in the hallway, amazed at how the insulation of the house immediately snuffed out the storm. It seemed now like a very distant threat. The house warm and dry inside, almost silent.

Light from the car outside permeated faintly through the back windows, casting deep shadows in their reflected illumination. She could only just see along the length of the hall to the large living–dining–kitchen area she knew lay beyond. The darkness there seemed impenetrable.

'Hello?' The sound of her voice calling into the dark was swallowed by the silence of the house. 'Is there anyone home?' She leaned to her right and opened the door into Niamh's bedroom. Yellow light from the window lay across an unmade bed. She turned back to the hall. 'Madame Macfarlane, are you there? I believe I know who killed your husband.'

Saying it out loud, even to no one, seemed to make it more

414

real. She really did know who had killed him. Or, at least, ordered his execution. Though she had no idea why.

'Madame Macfarlane?'

Still no response. Braque debated what to do. She could wait, but had no idea when, or if, Niamh would be home tonight. If she left, she might pass Gunn on the road without seeing him. And that would be stupid. Even if Niamh didn't show up, Gunn would. Almost certainly.

She moved forward carefully towards the living room at the end of the hall, fingertips on the wall so as not to lose her orientation. Her eyes were growing accustomed to the faintest of light provided from the outside by her headlamps. Furniture began to take shape around her. The breakfast bar off to her left.

Then suddenly a shadow rose up straight in front of her. A face, barely lit, but burning with some inner intensity. A face she had seen on CCTV video footage barely two hours ago. She had no time to react before she felt the blade punching into her abdomen. Ice-cold, razor-sharp. Once, twice. The third time it slid between her ribs and up into her heart. She dropped to her knees, clutching feebly at her wounds and feeling the blood running warm through her fingers. The life ebbing out of her.

She realized, with a sense of disbelief, that she was going to die. How was that possible? How could this have happened?

She would never catch those flights tomorrow, or tell Faubert what he could do with his job. She would never see her children again, nor they her. The choices she should have made long ago would never now be taken. And as darkness consumed her she knew, too, that there was nothing she could do to stop her killer from taking Niamh's life as well.

CHAPTER THIRTY-EIGHT

The fog was impenetrably deep. Niamh felt lost in it, wandering about with arms outstretched, hands like antennae feeling the way ahead. Somewhere in the far distance there was a light. So faint it was barely discernible in the mist. But sounds came to her now. Voices and music. Distant, too. Travelling the way that sound does across water.

And then she opened her eyes to a wave of nausea washing over her. It was all she could manage to keep down the contents of her stomach. She retched and gagged and rolled over to see that the light came from a landing beyond an open door. A cold yellow light that penetrated the darkness of the bedroom.

It was with a shock that Niamh realized suddenly that there were two other people on the bed with her. Two young men, barely more than boys, fast asleep and folded into each other's arms. Fully dressed. As was Niamh. To her relief.

She swung her legs over the edge of the bed and felt another wave of nausea, accompanied by a searing pain in her head. What in God's name had been in those drinks they gave her?

If not alcohol, something much worse. She sat for several minutes simply breathing, deeply, letting the pain and the nausea
pass. She looked around for a clock on a bedside table. But
there wasn't one. Then she focused on her watch and saw with
a shock that it was after midnight. She had been unconscious
for hours. A small sash window had been left open, and the
rain was driving in on to the carpet, soaking curtains that
billowed into the room.

Niamh found her handbag on the floor, and got unsteadily to
her feet to stagger to the open window and breathe in deeply,
feeling the rain cold and delicious in her face, before sliding
it shut. Neither man on the bed stirred.

There was still music pounding away somewhere downstairs
as she made her way out on to the landing and a staircase that
led down to the next floor.

The vast lounge with the grand piano stood empty but fully
lit. People lay around sleeping in the salon and in the TV room.
No one else in the house seemed to be awake, or troubled by
the music. Bottles lay about the floor, glasses leaving rings on
table tops and dressers. Cigarettes smouldering in makeshift
ashtrays. It was almost as if someone had pressed a pause
button and brought the world to a standstill. All except for
Niamh, who drifted through it like a shadow, slipping now
down the stairs to the entrance hall, where she stood for some
moments listening for signs of life. There were none.

She fell down the steps on to the gravel outside, and immediately emptied the contents of her stomach, almost fluorescent

green, on to the chippings. She crouched on her hands and knees in the rain, gulping in air. By the time she had forced herself back to her feet, her head felt less fogged, and her stomach less liable to further retching. She looked around and realized that she had no idea if Lee Blunt had ever returned. But the Range Rover he had been driving at the funeral was nowhere to be seen.

Niamh stumbled to her Jeep, and holding the door open against the wind managed to climb up into the driver's seat. She knew she shouldn't drive. That it was madness in this state. But all she wanted was to get away. To escape these people, and this nightmare.

She fumbled in her bag for her key and turned it in the ignition, revving hard before backing out across the gravel and turning on to the road that would take her back in the direction of the old whaling station, and the A859 heading north. To Ness. And home.

The storm had begun to abate a little as she nursed the Jeep through the rain-filled potholes that pitted the track south across the moor to Taigh 'an Fiosaich. It was some time after two, the night as black as sin beyond the tunnel cut through it by her headlights. She felt physically and mentally drained, as if someone had pummelled her with boxing gloves. Her fatigue was very nearly palpable, the longing she felt to fall back on her bed and close her eyes only marginally more powerful than the desire to pull over here and now and let herself fall asleep behind the wheel.

She was not surprised when she navigated past the rise at Bilascleiter to see that there were no lights on in the house. But startled by the presence of a car there, its headlamps reflecting light back from its walls. She pulled up beside it on the gravel apron. The rain had stopped now as she slipped from the Jeep, but the wind still hit her with a force that nearly knocked her from her feet. Holding on to her vehicle, hair whipping into her face, she made her way around it to look at the other car. A saloon car. Not many people would have risked a vehicle like that on the road out here. Its engine was running. And she saw a rental sticker on the rear windscreen. Lewis Car Rentals. She frowned. One of Lee Blunt's party? But how would any of them even know how to get out here? Where to come.

She felt a sudden foreboding. Someone had tried to kill her yesterday. And now there was someone in her house. In the dark. Someone unknown. For a long time she stood buffeted by the wind, trying to decide what to do. The safest option would be to climb back into her Jeep and drive away. But she had neither the strength nor the will. She was being over-dramatic, she decided. If someone had come to kill her, they would hardly leave their car parked outside, engine running, lights on to signal their presence.

She approached the door and opened it slowly, carefully, into the house. The darkness inside was penetrated only by the lights of the car outside. She eased the door shut behind her and reached for the shelf above the coat hooks, fumbling for the torch they always kept there for emergencies. Clumsy fingers knocked it off the shelf and it went clattering to the floor, rolling away into the hall.

Niamh cursed under her breath, forced to drop to her hands and knees to find it, reaching out to feel for it ahead of her. Whoever was in the house would know by now that she was back. Her fingers closed with relief around the curvature of the torch's long handle, and she stood up, feeling for the switch to turn it on.

Its light, cold and hard, was startling. And at almost the same time that she directed its beam along the hall and into the living room, she became aware of an alien odour in her house. Very background, but off-pitch and disquieting. Like rusted iron.

'Hello?' Her voice seemed tiny. She cleared her throat and called again. 'Hello? Who's there?'

The absence of any reply pushed her heart up into her throat, real fear quickly displacing disquiet. She swung the beam of her torch from left to right in the darkness ahead of her, seeing it reflected in the windows all along the far side of the living room. Now she moved forward very carefully, adrenalin heightening all her senses, but it wasn't until she reached the end of the hall that a shadow on the floor ahead drew her eye.

She directed the beam downwards and released the most feral howl she had ever heard pass her lips. It felt almost as if it had come from someone else. But as she took a step back, the full realization of what she was seeing only now dawning on her, it came again. Quite involuntarily.

Lying hunched on her side, in an extended pool of thick, black blood, lay a woman whose hair fanned out across the tiles. Her cheek was pressed to the floor, and in profile Niamh could see that both her mouth and her eyes were open wide. She recognized her immediately as Lieutenant Braque. The woman who had been there in the Place de la République moments after Ruairidh's car had been ripped apart in that explosion. Who had interviewed her afterwards in the company of the anti-terror officer. Who had come to her hotel to tell her she could take the remains of Ruairidh home. Polite, efficient, and lacking either warmth or empathy. And here she lay dead in Niamh's home, more than a thousand miles away from where it had all begun.

Disbelief fought with confusion and panic for space among the turbulent emotions that replaced almost everything else in her head. Her lungs barely responding to the need for oxygen.

She swung the beam of her torch wildly around her, but there was no one there, nothing but furniture and the shadows it cast in the living room and kitchen.

The faintest sound from behind made her turn. In time to see the dark shadow of a figure launch itself at her. She saw light glint momentarily on the blade of a kitchen knife as it arced towards her and she threw out a protective hand. She felt it slice into fingers and the fleshy muscle of her palm, sending blood spraying into her face. But it was enough to deflect the blade from her body. She swung her torch into darkness and felt it connect with solid bone and flesh. Heard a gasp of pain.

422

But the strength of the blow knocked the torch from her hand, and it went spinning off into the living room. She struck out again, blindly, this time with her fist, and felt the pain of connection. Enough to distract her attacker long enough to scramble away, out of the hall, into the living room, where she slipped on the pool of Braque's blood and fell heavily on to the tiles, knocking all the air from her body.

Her head hit the floor with a sickening thud, and she rolled herself over in time to see the dark form of her attacker falling on top of her, soft and heavy, a strangely familiar scent carried in the warmth and weight of this unexpectedly slight body.

Niamh looked up, her eye drawn first by the blade caught in the reflected light of the torch. It was raised at arm's length above her, and Niamh knew there was nothing she could do to stop it. Then her gaze jumped focus to the face of this person intent on killing her, and she gasped her astonishment and disbelief.

There was the oddest, twisted smile on Seonag's ivory-pale face. Her silky red hair hung in flames on either side of it, and her eyes burned with a madness Niamh had never before seen in them.

'Why?' It was the only word she could bring to her lips.

Seonag's voice was little more than a whisper as she gently shook her head. 'It started as a game. A fantasy. How hard could it be to access the Dark Web? Were there really people out there who would kill for money?' She almost laughed. 'It was so easy. And suddenly fantasy became reality.' The smile faded. 'I thought with him gone you would want me. Finally.' Her face crumpled as tears blurred her eyes. 'But if I can't have you, no one else will.'

Niamh braced herself for the certainty of death as Seonag's knife plunged into her heart. But something dark and heavy swung through the light of the torch and crashed into the side of Seonag's head, hitting her with such force that it knocked her sideways to slam into the wall and lie motionless on the floor. The sound of her knife skidding away across the tiles filled the room as Niamh looked up to see a man standing over her, a wheel brace dangling from his hand. Then, as he turned his head away from Seonag to look down at her, and she saw who it was, she thought that she must be dead after all. That Seonag's knife had penetrated her heart and taken her life before the blow from the wheel brace. But she was still breathing, and the pain from the deep cut in her hand was still excruciating. This was neither dream nor afterlife. This was real, even though she had absolutely no way of processing what she was seeing.

The man who had just saved her life, yet again, was Ruairidh Macfarlane.

CHAPTER THIRTY-NINE

Niamh sat on the floor, her back to the settee. Ruairidh had effected a makeshift bandage for her hand which had, at least, stopped the bleeding.

He sat beside her now in the slowly fading light of the torch. There was a good chance that the batteries would give out before power was restored.

Braque's blood had turned rust-brown, coagulating on the tiles, but still red where Niamh had lost her footing in it, smearing it all across the floor as she fell.

Seonag had not moved from where she lay heaped up against the wall. There was a small pool of blood around her head. Niamh found her eyes wandering across the floor towards her, feelings for the girl who had been her best friend all through childhood frozen now. Paralysed. Her way, perhaps, of coping with the unthinkable. 'Is she dead?' she asked Ruairidh.

He shook his head, indifferent to her fate. 'I don't know. I don't care.'

Niamh turned to look at him, still in shock, still struggling to come to terms with the impossible. 'Are you going to tell me now?'

He hung his head and shook it slowly from side to side. 'I was never having an affair with Irina, Niamh. I'd commissioned her to make a dress for you. For our tenth anniversary. Something special. Something unique. It was Seonag who got me your measurements. She was the only one who knew. It could only have been her that sent those emails.'

Niamh's face creased in confusion. 'What about the explosion? If it wasn't you in the car . . . Who?'

Ruairidh closed his eyes as he remembered. 'Georgy Vetrov. I'm assuming he got the same email you did. Thought me and Irina were lovers. We were sitting at the lights, and the door flew open and Georgy was pushing a gun into my face. Ordered me to get out of the car. When I did, he hit me with it. Hard. I went spinning off into the dark between those workmen's skips at the side of the road. I was just getting to my feet when the car pulled away from the lights and blew up. I was protected from the worst of the blast, but still knocked off my feet.' He turned with eyes appealing for forgiveness. 'All I could think was that I should have been in that car when it exploded. Me. That someone had just tried to kill me. And that but for Georgy I would be dead.'

He paused and drew his knees up to his chest, arms around his shins, lost in the moment.

'I did a stupid thing, Niamh. I suppose I just wasn't thinking straight. But I thought if someone wanted to kill me and they knew they'd failed, they were probably going to try again.' He screwed his eyes up tight. 'I should have turned myself over to the police straight away. But I didn't. I ran. Up a back street, then along behind the hotel to the far end of the square.'

In the quietest voice she said, 'Have you any idea what you put me through?'

He dropped his head in shame. 'I think I do. I've watched you almost every minute of every day since. I saw them taking you away from the square that night. And I suppose even then I could have owned up to the truth. But I didn't. And from that point on, it seemed there was just no way back.'

She gazed at the bandage on her hand. 'I'm trying to decide whether I still love you or hate you more than I've ever hated anyone in my life. Even Seonag.'

He was silent for a long time. Then he said, 'I followed you in a taxi to the police building on the Quai des Orfèvres, and sat in a café on the other side of the river for hours until you came out.' He glanced at her. 'With that guy. I had no idea who he was, but you seemed strangely close. And then you went for a drink together.' It had clearly been preying on his mind.

'Dimitri,' she said, all emotion spent now. She felt consumed by emptiness. 'Irina's brother.' She looked at Ruairidh. 'It was you that was following me when I left to go back to the hotel.'

He nodded. 'You've got to understand. Someone had just tried to kill me. I had no idea why. It was possible, perfectly possible, that they might try to kill you, too. I promised always to keep you safe, remember?'

She looked at him long and hard, unable to decide how she felt. Whether to be furious or forgiving. 'How could you follow me that whole time? In Paris. Back here to the island. You had no money, no passport.'

Guilt washed across his face. 'Don't be angry with him,' he said. 'I needed help. And he's my brother.'

'Donald?' Niamh was incredulous.

'I phoned him. I had some cash in my wallet and checked into a cheap hotel in Pigalle. I knew I couldn't use a credit card. I did have my passport, but I couldn't use that either. Donald was . . .' Ruairidh sighed deeply. 'If I think you're going to give me a hard time, Donald just about crucified me. He did everything in his power to make me change my mind, to go to the police, but I knew there was no way back. Not then. So I made him promise to look after you, keep you safe when I couldn't.'

'It was you who phoned me at the hotel that night?'

He nodded. 'I wanted so much for you to know the truth. And I just couldn't . . . couldn't find the voice to tell you.'

'And you took my iPad when I was out with Lee.'

'I still had my keycard in my pocket.'

'But why?'

'I needed that email. So Donald could get his IT people to try and trace the sender.'

'So how did you get home?'

'The night before you flew back to the UK Donald hired a car and drove me overnight to Calais. Smuggled me across the Channel in the boot of his car, then hired another for me on the other side. He made the return crossing on the next ferry and was back in Paris by morning. He must have been wrecked.'

Niamh recalled how strangely Donald had behaved. She had put it down to grief, and the Scottish male predilection for burying his feelings.

'I drove all the way home, but left the car parked beside a rental cottage at Skigersta and came out here on foot. I've been living in the bothy. Just watching. Waiting. Donald's guy traced the IP address of the emails to the library right here in Stornoway. But we had no way of confirming who'd sent them.'

Niamh shook her head in pure frustration, exasperation welling up inside her. 'Jesus, Ruairidh!' She gazed across the floor at the body of Sylvie Braque. 'That poor woman might still have been alive if you hadn't taken off on this crazy deception.'

'And you'd have been dead,' Ruairidh said. 'Seonag would have killed you. And I might not have been here to stop her. She tried to kill you on the cliffs. I couldn't see who it was. Just the shadow of someone climbing down to push you into the sea. And then I was too busy trying to pull you out of it.'

Niamh dropped her face into her hands and felt tears burning her eyes.

'Tonight, I waited and waited for you to come back from the funeral. I didn't see Seonag arriving. She must have left her car somewhere. Cuishader, maybe. And come the rest of the way on foot.' He nodded towards the prone form of Sylvie

Braque. 'But I saw her car arrive. She went in and didn't come back out. Then, when you arrived, I thought I should come and see what was going on.'

For the longest time, they sat without a word passing between them. An unspoken agreement that they should wait until the power returned, when they could call for help. Rather than head off into the night, and the storm, leaving Seonag here alone with Braque, alive or dead. The torchlight had faded now to a feeble yellow. Eventually Ruairidh picked it up and got stiffly to his feet. 'You want some water before the light goes?'

She nodded, and he headed towards the kitchen. She saw only the most fleeting shadow flit through her line of sight as Ruairidh rounded the breakfast bar, his back towards her. She screamed at the top of her voice. 'Ruairidh!'

He spun around as Seonag flew at him, knife in hand, and felt the blade sink into the soft flesh of his neck. He saw her face, distorted by madness, streaked with the blood that matted her hair all down the right side of her head. And he grabbed her knife hand, swinging it out and away from his body, forcing it down. It was her own momentum that propelled her on to it, and he felt the blade slice through soft tissue before hitting a rib that deflected it upwards and into her heart. She fell, a dead weight, at his feet.

Niamh was across the room in several strides, stepping over Seonag's body to retrieve the torch and shine it on Ruairidh's wound. She saw blood oozing through his fingers, where he pressed his hand against it.

'Don't know how bad it is,' he whispered. 'Guess she missed the artery.' He paused and managed a pale smile. 'I'm going to be in trouble, amn't I?'

And suddenly the lights came on. Blinding them. They stood blinking in surprise and shock, and Niamh realized in that moment, however much she had to forgive him, however insanely stupid he had been, she still loved him. Still loved that little boy who'd rescued her from the bog up on the Pentland Road all those years before.

CHAPTER FORTY

It would be some time, they were told, before they would be allowed to return to the house at Taigh 'an Fiosaich, but Niamh had the sense that no matter how it might clean up, the stain of blood and death would always haunt their home.

They signed into the Royal Hotel under the curious eye of the receptionist, who couldn't take her eyes off the bandaging on Ruairidh's neck. There couldn't be anyone in Stornoway who did not know by now what had happened out on the moor south of Skigersta in last night's storm. Or at least some version of it.

They had both spent most of the day being interrogated separately and giving statements at the police station in Church Street. Senior officers from the mainland were apparently on their way. Niamh and Ruairidh had been warned not to leave the island.

George Gunn, it seemed, had never made it back to Stornoway the previous evening, detained at Uig until late by a tragic accidental death on the cliffs at Mangersta, and staying there overnight. It was only on his return in the morning that he had picked up Braque's message and watched the video.

Lee Blunt's car had been found in a ditch near Hushinish, Blunt himself unconscious but alive.

Once in their room, they drew the curtains and sat in disconsolate silence. Who knew how long it might take to get over something like this, if ever. It was some time before Niamh finally got to her feet to search her bag for the slim parcel in its brown paper wrapping that she had intended to give to Ruairidh in Paris. She held it out to him and he looked up in surprise.

'What's this?'

'Maybe the only bright spot anywhere on our horizon,' she said.

He frowned, then took it and tore away the wrapping. He looked up in consternation. 'A compendium of Scots Gaelic Christian names and their history?' It was the tiniest booklet.

She said, 'I was afraid, after she pushed me into the sea, that I might lose it. But they scanned me at the hospital this afternoon while you were still with the police.'

His eyes opened wide. 'But I thought . . .'

She nodded. 'I know. Me, too.'

He stood up. 'You really are?'

'Yes.' And she felt his arms around her, pulling her close and holding her tight in a way she had thought he never would again. And it felt like life had given them a second chance.

ACKNOWLEDGMENTS

My grateful thanks for their help in my researches for this book to: Margaret Ann Macleod, Brand Development Director, Harris Tweed Hebrides, for her knowledge of weaving, and her insights into growing up on the Isle of Lewis in the Eighties and Nineties; Brian Wilson, Chairman, Harris Tweed Hebrides, for allowing me access to the mill; Mark Hogarth, Creative Director, Harris Tweed Hebrides, for his introduction to Première Vision in Paris; Iain Finlay Macleod, Breanish Tweed, for his insights into building a successful weaving enterprise; Annie Macdonald, Carloway Mill, for rescuing the mill and allowing me access to it; Simon Scott, Factor, Grimersta Lodge, and his team for taking me round the lodge and explaining the workings of the estate; Anna Murray and Donna Morrison, for their observations and anecdotes on island life; Derek Murray, for his tales of gate-stealing, and who took me out across the moor on a foul day to introduce me to the delights of Cuishader, Bilascleiter and Taigh 'an Fiosaich, which became such important locations in the book; the entire team at *Comunn Eachdraidh Nis* (Ness Historical

Society) for their help and friendship, and access to historical and geographical information about Ness; Alasdair Macrae, funeral director, Stornoway, for his invaluable insights into island funeral customs; Derek Macleod, weaver, Carloway, for taking the risk of letting me try out his loom; George Murray, retired police officer, for advice on island policing; Dr Steve Campman, Medical Examiner, San Diego, California, USA, for his advice on forensics and pathology; Tatiana Lebedev, Russian fashion designer, for allowing me access to her Paris workshop and boutique; and a special word for Professor Joe Cummins, emeritus in genetics at the University of Western Ontario, Canada, who provided scientific advice on many of my books over the last twenty years. It was Joe who inspired me to write *Coffin Road* in defence of the bees. Sadly Joe passed away last year. RIP.

Peter May
January 2018

Read on for an exclusive extract from
Peter May's forthcoming thriller

THE
MAN WITH
NO FACE

Published in riverrun hardback, ebook
and audio on 10 January 2019

CHAPTER ONE

Kale watched the train through the rain-spattered glass and thought, this time will be the last. But even as the thought formed in his mind it clotted and he knew he would kill again.

He twirled his cigarette nervously between nicotine-stained fingers and sipped the sour dregs of his coffee. The coffee machine on the counter hissed and issued steam, and with the rain beginning to fall outside the window was misting over. The first drops of condensation formed and ran clear lines through it.

An old man sat in the corner making his coffee last so he could remain in the warmth, and a hard-faced woman behind the counter sat smoking a cigarette and watching Kale. She had seen the likes of him before. A place like this was a constant stream of men and women who had seen better days. There was the familiar suit, perhaps expensive once, but now fraying at the cuffs, crumpled, baggy, shiny at the elbows and the seat of the pants. The old blue overcoat, rubbed and coffee-stained down the front, dandruff on the collar. The clothes hung loosely on his lean frame. She had seen worse, but maybe this one was just starting out.

He would be around thirty-nine or forty, hair thinning, greased back. A hollow face with high cheekbones; clear, pale, slightly yellow skin, remarkably unlined. It was his eyes that interested her, if it was possible to say that she was interested in anything. They were dark, deep-sunk eyes, set too close, and they burned with a bleak intensity that she had not seen before. There was something sullen in his face, but it was not the face of defeat as was the face of the old man in the corner – as were most of the faces that came in here to stare morosely into endless cups of coffee.

Kale caught her watching him and she looked quickly away, becoming aware for the first time that she was actually afraid of those eyes . . . almost intimidated by them. *You're letting your imagination run away with itself, Nance*, she told herself without conviction.

'Oi, you!' she shouted with a voice as hard as her face at the old man in the corner. A Cockney voice, a long way from home. 'You've 'ad yer coffee. Now clear aht!'

The old man looked up with resignation. He had learned to accept such things. You grew used to them, as you grew used to the constant gnawing pain of an ulcer. He pushed back his chair, rising slowly with what might have been an attempt at dignity, and shuffled past the counter and out into the wet. Nance had only done it to take her mind off Kale, but now she realized her folly. She had left herself alone with him. She stubbed out her half-smoked cigarette and lit another between thin, painted lips, crossed to the jukebox and punched two plays. The noise would make her feel more secure, and still she wished she could have called the old man back.

But she need not have worried, for Kale had barely noticed his going, and was only mildly irritated when the jukebox began belting out a scratchy hit record. And Nance was of no interest to him. He was thinking about his meeting with Swinton in a dingy London tearoom three days earlier.

Swinton was a small, fat, busy man. He had sat across a wooden table from Kale. One of those people who perspire constantly.

'It's a big one, Kale,' he had said with an air of confidentiality, leaning across the table and breathing garlic at the other man. 'Big money this time. You could retire. Where you been anyway? The boys was thinking you was maybe dead or something. The word's been out for over a week.'

Kale had felt uncomfortable there, surrounded by elderly ladies drinking tea from china cups. But Swinton had insisted they should not meet at the usual pub. 'How much and who's paying?'

Swinton's smile widened. 'Oh, come on, Willy boy. You know me. Even if I knew I wouldn't tell you who. But truth is, this time I don't even know myself.' He paused and sat back as a waitress scurried by with a pile of empty cups and saucers clinking on a tray, and then leaned forward again. 'It's not the usual form. You'll deal direct. I'll get my commission for finding you, but honest to God I don't know who's paying.'

'How much?'

'A hundred thousand smackers, Kale. A hundred thousand!

Jesus, I'd do it myself for a quarter of that, but I'm not in your class. No one's in your class, mate.'

Kale toyed with his cup, the undrunk tea cold now, milk solids forming a scum on the surface. He was not happy. If he had not needed the money . . .

'Tell me.'

Nance was relieved when Kale pulled up his collar and pushed back his chair. She watched him out the door then crossed to his table to collect the empty cup and found twenty pence under the saucer. Funny, she thought, how some of them never lose the habit. Maybe he wasn't as bad as he seemed.

Kale crossed the railway yard, asphalt crunching under his feet, the January rain stinging his face. The locomotive had shunted three coal trucks into a siding and was chugging back towards the depot. Ahead of him this small industrial township rose up the hillside, a jumble of blackened brick terraces. The tall chimneys of the mills belched smoke into a heavily laden sky away to his right, and he could hear children playing somewhere behind a wall that ran alongside the road down to the station. The cobbled street shone in the wet, reflecting the grim poverty of the place. On the station wall a fly-blown poster urged a vote for Labour, its red vivid against the grey, a smile on the candidate's face above the slogan – *FOR A BETTER BRITAIN*.

He crossed Church Street to the newsagent's on the corner and stood looking out across the town square with its black memorial statue, hands sunk deep in the pockets of his coat. For three days he had come to this spot every morning and every afternoon, checking all the routes that led to and from the square. He knew this town now as well as anyone could who had walked every street. Each road leading out of it was marked in red on the map in his pocket, each identifiable by some feature that could not be seen, but might be felt or heard. He had been relentless and thorough, and yet he was still far from satisfied. He shuffled uneasily and watched the traffic carefully. Three days, he told himself, was not enough. The clock on the church tower showed three but did not chime. The minutes ticked past slowly and the rain stopped, leaving only the chill wind to sweep across the square.

He saw the van come in from the north side and watched it as it drove past him, along the top end and back round again. This time it stopped, a white Ford Transit. Kale saw the fresh mud splashed along the side from the front wheels, and took a mental note of the registration, though he doubted if that would prove useful. Still, every scrap of information might help. A slight smile curled his lip. Others would not have gone to such lengths.

A short, thickset man stepped from the van, his crop of white, wiry hair catching in the wind above a brown leathery face. He wore a heavy tweed coat and was not what Kale had been expecting. His blue eyes incongruously honest.

'Kale?' he said. Kale nodded. 'Into the back of the van then, lad.' He rounded the van and opened the doors for Kale to climb in. 'Here, stick this over your head. And don't think you can whip it off when we get moving. I'll be watching you in the mirror.'

Kale pulled the black cotton hood over his head and squatted down on a rug on the floor as the driver shut the doors. There were dog hairs on the rug and there had been fresh mud on the man's brogues. Despite the good coat and shoes, his hands were those of a working man. Heavy, hard-skinned, calloused hands. His accent was northern, and he had a weathered outdoor air about him, uncomfortable in his expensive city gear. Kale adjusted his senses to the darkness, pressing his back up against the side of the van. He smelled dog and stale cigarette smoke.

They seemed to have been driving around the town for an eternity. Several times Kale had lost his bearings, but always he picked up their position again. The hoot of a train as it approached the station, the steep cobbled climb up Cotton Street, the quarter-hour chime of the church clock on the edge of the new housing estate – the only chiming clock in the town. They were leaving the town now, he was certain. The roundabout on the north side with roads leading north and west. The sound of a pneumatic drill, and a slight delay at temporary traffic lights erected for roadworks. They had taken the A road west. It was a road Kale had checked on his first day.

The driver stuck to the A road for what must have been nearly twenty minutes. That would take the time to around three forty. Kale would check the time when they stopped. Another seven or eight minutes perhaps, and then the van turned off the main road. Kale heard the click, click of the indicator before they slowed to take the corner, tight, the driver forced to crunch into first gear. It would be a narrow road, maybe a farm track. The van bounced and clattered over the uneven surface. Kale heard the splash of mud along the side. Then they stopped, and above the idling engine Kale could hear a man's voice and the sound of hooves, the lowing of cattle. He strained to catch more. The scraping of a wooden gate, again a man's voice calling, cattle retreating, and they were moving again, very slowly. Up a sharp incline and then suddenly down. A bridge? Over water? Yes, he could hear the water. The driver had rolled down the window. And now they were picking up speed, the surface a little better, the swish, swish, swish of fence posts or perhaps trees along the route. Slowing again, the clatter of a cattle grid, and then the crunch of gravel beneath the tyres. They stopped. The driver cut the ignition and climbed out.

'Just keep yer hood on, lad.' The back doors opened and Kale felt the working man's hands help him out. Even in his enclosed darkness he could sense the presence of trees and a building. Stone. Something big, impressive. Up steps and into a hall, a great sense of space around them. A flagstone floor, or tiles maybe. The man with the white hair and the big rough hands felt the tension in Kale's arm. 'Okay, lad. Take it easy.' Kale was surprised by the odd friendliness of the voice, its inappropriate innocence. This man could know nothing of what Kale was about. It's strange, he thought, how much a voice can tell you about a man when you cannot see his face. 'In 'ere.' The big hands guided him across the hall and through a doorway. 'You can take yer hood off when I've shut the door. There's a bell press below the light switch when you're ready to go.' The door closed, the key turned in the lock, and the sound of the man's heavy tread receded across the hall.

Kale removed the hood and screwed up his eyes against the sudden glare of electric light. It took nearly half a minute for his eyes to adjust fully. He checked his watch. It was just after four. Then he looked around. This was a small room. No windows, no fireplace, cream-painted walls, bare floorboards. A smell of dust and age. Perhaps a storeroom. But there were no clues, the room completely bare save for a wooden bench against the far wall. Kale's eyes fixed on the bench. Towards one end of it lay a briefcase, a heavy black phone placed beside it. He was startled by the sudden loud ring of the phone – a short, single ring. He crossed the room and lifted the receiver, checking the dial as he sat. It was not an outside line, but an internal phone with only an extension number. Four.

'Kale?' a voice rasped in his ear.

'Yes.'

'Good. Now understand this . . .' The voice seemed without particular accent, but it was an educated voice, mature. Even from the five words Kale had heard he detected a quality of confidence. A man used to speaking, a man used to having others listen. 'You and I are the only ones who will ever know the purpose of this meeting. You do not know who I am and so it shall remain. I know very little about you except for your reputation.' The voice paused. Kale let the silence drag out and became aware for the first time that he was cold in this empty room. Then the voice was there again, insistent, demanding his attention.

'In the briefcase you will find fifty thousand pounds in cash, the first half of your fee. On top of it you will find a folder containing two photographs marked A and B.'

Kale switched the phone to his other ear and opened the briefcase. The money was there beneath the folder in bundles of £100 notes, but he did not count them. He lifted the folder and opened it to take out the photographs and lay them side by side on the bench.

'Listen carefully to what I tell you because you will receive nothing in writing and you may not take the photographs with you. If you wish me to repeat anything, ask.'

'Hold on.' Kale took out a small, dog-eared notebook and a biro pen. 'Okay.'

'Photograph A is Robert Gryffe. He is a Minister of State at the Foreign Office.' Kale had recognized the face but been unable to place it. So, political assassination. It meant nothing to him. 'Gryffe has special responsibilities in acting for the Foreign Minister at the European Commission of the EEC in Brussels. He is there at least one week a month, during which he stays at a terraced house he owns in the Rue de Pavie, number twenty-four. Today is Thursday. On Sunday morning Gryffe has an appointment there to meet the man pictured in photograph B. That man's identity is of no importance to you, just so long as you remember the face. I want both men dead . . . without suspicion of murder. How you do that is your business.' The voice paused and Kale waited.

'You will then proceed to the Rue de Commerce, the top-floor flat in the apartment block at number thirty-three. It will be empty. There is always a key below the mat. Let yourself in and go straight to the main living room. On the fireplace wall hangs a painting by Brueghel, behind it a safe set in the wall. The combination is three, zero, five, nine, six, two. Inside you will find a black briefcase . . .'

'Burglary ain't my thing,' Kale interrupted, his voice flat and cold.

The other hesitated. 'The apartment has already been checked out by a professional. You will simply be required to collect the case and leave.' Again the hesitation, the reluctance to answer Kale's unasked question. Kale was only too aware of the power of his silence. 'The case cannot not be taken before the . . . before you have fulfilled your task at the Rue de Pavie.'

'Go on.'

'You will take it straight to the Gare du Midi and deposit it in box thirty-nine at the left-luggage lockers. The key is taped to the inside of the lid of the briefcase beside you. If you return to the station at midday on Monday you will find a further fifty thousand pounds in cash in the same locker – assuming, of course, that you have successfully fulfilled the contract. Do you have any questions?'

'No.'

'Good. Then I shall allow you five minutes to study the photographs. Should anything occur to you in that time, dial six. Ring the bell by the door when you are ready to leave and remember to replace your hood.'

A click and the line went dead. Kale replaced the receiver. He lit a cigarette and looked at the two photographs. Gryffe would be around forty. A smooth, prosperous face. The other man was, perhaps, a few years younger. A lean, bearded face below a crop of fair, or perhaps red, hair. Two anonymous faces. Two men whom Kale would kill. There would, he knew, be no satisfaction in it, but neither would there be conscience or remorse. For Kale was the complete killer: cold, efficient, deadly. A man who showed no mercy, a quality he reserved for no one, including himself.

He sat for a while drawing slowly on his cigarette, a small shabby figure in the nakedness of the room. He would find this place again. On the map, or physically if need be. It was invariably important to know who it was that employed you to kill. And this one had taken such elaborate precautions to conceal his identity. *You all think you are so clever*, Kale thought. *But in the end I have always got you, one way or the other.* He stood on the last inch of his cigarette and closed the briefcase, leaving the photographs on the bench. He lifted the cotton hood, and his money. Then crossed to the door and rang the bell.

CHAPTER TWO

It was raining. Not a particularly auspicious day. It had rained yesterday and it would probably rain tomorrow.

Bannerman remembered a cartoon he had seen once in an old *Punch* magazine. Two crocodiles basking in a jungle swamp, heads facing each other above the muddy waters. One of them was saying, 'You know, I keep thinking today is Thursday.' Bannerman smiled. It had amused him then, as it amused him now. What bloody difference did it make . . . today, tomorrow, yesterday, Thursday? It was ironic that later he would look back on this day as the day it all began. The day after which nothing would ever be quite the same again.

But at the moment, so far as Bannerman knew, it was just a day like any other. He gazed reflectively from the window a while longer, out across Princes Street, the gardens beyond, and the Castle brooding darkly atop the rain-blackened cliffs. Even when it rained Edinburgh was a beautiful city. Against all odds it had retained its essential character in the face of centuries of change. There was something almost medieval about it; in the crooked hidden alleyways, the cobbled closes, the tall leaning tenements. And, of course, the formidable shape of the Castle itself, stark and powerful against the skyline.

In the office the day had barely begun. Reporters sat around reading the morning papers, sipping black coffees and nursing hangovers.

'Morning, Neil.'

Bannerman turned from the window in time to see George Gorman drifting past. 'Morning,' he called after him, and watched the retreating figure as he headed for the news desk. Bannerman felt some sympathy for his news editor. Gorman was a dapper little man, good at his job without being inspired, nervous under pressure. A nice man, just waiting for the axe to fall.

It had already fallen on a number of his colleagues: John Thompson in features, Alex McGregor in sport. And there had been casualties in the reshuffle on the subs desk. It had been inevitable really, ever since it was announced that Wilson Tait was being brought up from London to fill the recently vacated editor's chair.

The *Edinburgh Post* had never been able to boast a particularly high circulation. For years it had lived off its reputation as a serious newspaper of quality and reliability. It was read by politicians, members of the legal and medical professions, teachers, academics. But their patronage alone was no longer enough to balance the books. Profit was more important than prestige. Hence the appointment of Tait, a hard newspaperman of the old school; a Fleet Street-toughened Scot returning to his old hunting grounds and bringing with him his personal hard core of hatchet men whom he was moving into key editorial positions. Blood was being spilled. And only the approaching general election – just three weeks away – had provided a stay of execution for Gorman. When it was over, he would receive a quick sideways promotion to make way for one of Tait's rising stars. And while Gorman was allowed to vegetate quietly in some out-of-the-way office with an ambiguous brief from the editor, the paper would move slowly but surely downmarket, where it would endeavour to pick up new readers, almost certainly alienating its existing readership in the process.

It was then, Bannerman thought, that he would have to consider his own future with the paper. Though that was already in doubt. He and Tait had clashed almost immediately over Bannerman's role with the *Post*. And there was no love lost between them.

The phone rang on Bannerman's desk. 'Bannerman.'

'Good morning, Neil. You're in early.'

Bannerman smiled. 'What is it, Alison?'

'The editor wants you.'

'You mean he's in early, too?'

'Ha, ha.'

'I'll be right there.'

Alison smiled up at him when he came into her office. 'Set your alarm an hour early by mistake?'

Bannerman grinned. She was a good-looking girl, easygoing but very efficient. 'Actually I came in early to ask you if you might be free tonight.'

'Oh, that's nice. I am actually. But you're not.'

Bannerman frowned. 'Oh? You know something I don't?'

'Only that you'll be too busy packing. I've just booked you on the first flight to Brussels in the morning.' She nodded towards the editor's door. 'Orders from His Imperial Highness.'

She watched him go through into Tait's office and wondered what it was that was so attractive about him.

Tait was hunched over his desk in shirtsleeves. He glanced up momentarily from his paperwork as Bannerman knocked and came in. 'Take a seat. I'll be with you in a moment.'

Bannerman sat down and watched the other man patiently. Tait liked to make you feel that he was seeing you on sufferance, that you were interrupting much more important matters. Bannerman was not impressed.

The editor was a small man and had the arrogance and puffed-up sense of self-importance of many small men. A compensation for lack of height. He was of indeterminate age and could have been anything between forty and sixty. His hair was steely grey, cut short above a squat, ugly face.

He gathered together several printed sheets and slipped them into a folder before looking up again. He surveyed his investigative reporter with caution. He disliked him, but was also intimidated by him. By his calm, powerful presence, his obvious self-confidence. Bannerman didn't jump, as the others did, on Tait's command. And that annoyed him.

'I'm sending you to Brussels for a few weeks,' he said.

'Oh?' Bannerman endeavoured to show no surprise.

'We need some good stuff on the EEC in the couple of weeks after the election. Corruption, fraud, political back-stabbing, that kind of thing. Particularly when Common Market issues have been given such high priority in the election speeches of the major parties.'

Bannerman gazed at him thoughtfully. 'Why so keen to get me out of the way?'

Tait leaned back in his seat and eyed Bannerman coldly. 'Because I need time to consider what I'm going to do with you. You're a troublesome bastard, Bannerman. A one-man band. I want to build a team here and there's no room for buskers.'

Bannerman pursed his lips thoughtfully and Tait watched him with apprehension. Bannerman wasn't tall, perhaps five feet nine or ten, but he was stocky, broad, and gave the impression of a bigger man. Tait knew from personnel records that he was thirty-five, but it would have been difficult to judge had he not known. He could have been younger, or older. Dark, wiry hair without a trace of grey fell carelessly across his forehead. He was not what Tait would have thought of as good-looking, but he had a certain presence, and there was something compelling in the gaze of his hard blue eyes.

Bannerman said, 'Maybe you would rather I got a job somewhere else, Mr Tait.' His voice was flat, toneless.

Tait grinned maliciously. 'Trouble is, Bannerman, you're too good just to ditch. Probably the best investigative journalist in Scotland right now, and very highly regarded south of the border. I'd like to keep you. But on my terms.'

'I'm flattered. Maybe I should be asking for a rise.'

Tait laughed. 'Cheeky bastard!'

Bannerman tilted his head. 'So long as we both know where we stand.' And he knew that he was going to have to think about his future sooner than expected.